PENGUIN BOOKS

TALES FROM THE KATHĀSARITSĀGARA

Although his dates have not been conclusively established, according to some historical records Somadeva was a Kashmiri Śaivite Brāhmin who lived in the eleventh century during the rule of King Anantadeva. Legend has it that he composed the *Kathāsaritsāgara* around AD 1070 for queen Sūryamatī (also known as Sūryavatī), wife of King Anantadeva. However, the stories in the *Kathāsaritsāgara* were in circulation long before Somadeva compiled them into this particular collection. The *Kathāsaritsāgara* is supposed to be part of a larger text, the *Bṛhatkathā*,composed by Guṇāḍhya who is generally reckoned to be a mythical figure.

*

Arshia Sattar has a Ph.D. from the Department of South Asian Languages and Civilizations from the University of Chicago. Her areas of interest are Indian epics, mythology, and the story traditions of the subcontinent. She also reviews books and writes on women's issues and contemporary culture for various newspapers and magazines.

Somadeva

Tales From The Kathāsaritsāgara

Translated from the Sanskrit with an Introduction by Arshia Sattar

Foreword by Wendy Doniger

PENGUIN BOOKS

Penguin Books India (P) Ltd., 210, Chiranjiv Tower, 43, Nehru Place, New Delhi 110 019, India
Penguin Books Ltd., 27 Wrights Lane, London W8 5TZ, UK
Penguin Books USA Inc., 375 Hudson Street, New York, NY 10014, USA
Penguin Books Australia Ltd., Ringwood, Victoria, Australia
Penguin Books Canada Ltd., 10 Alcorn Avenue, Suite 300, Toronto, Ontario M4V 3B2, Canada
Penguin Books (NZ) Ltd., 182-190 Wairau Road, Auckland 10, New Zealand

First published by Penguin Books India (P) Ltd. 1994

10 9 8 7 6 5 4 3 2 1

Typeset in Palatino by Digital Technologies and Printing Solutions, New Delhi

This book is for Wendy Doniger who taught me that life is less without stories and who gave me the courage to plunge into the Ocean.

Key to the Pronunciation of Sanskrit Words

ā	as in *a*fter
e	as in g*ay*
ī	as in cr*ee*p
ū	as in sch*oo*l
ai	as in h*i*gh
ṛ	as in cr*y*stal
kh	aspirated k sound
gh	aspirated g sound
c	as in *ch*ose
ch	aspirated ch sound
jh	aspirated j sound
ṭ	as in *t*ile
ṭh	aspirated t sound
ḍ	as in *d*oor
ḍh	aspirated d sound
t	as in steal*th*
ṭh	as in *th*ick
ḍ	as in *th*e
ḍh	aspirated th sound
ph	aspirated p sound
bh	aspirated b sound
ṇ	as in *ind*olent
n̄	as in goi*ng*
ñ	as in pu*n*ch
ṃ	as in *ins*tant
s	as in *s*ee
ś	as in *sh*ow
ṣ	as in cla*sh*

Contents

Translator's Note

The stories in this abridged collection have been chosen and put together such that they represent, to whatever extent possible, the whole of the Sanskrit *Kathāsaritsāgara*. While the text has been abridged, no individual story has been shortened except by a phrase or two. Where possible, whole cycles of stories (for example, *Kathāpīṭha*) have been translated so that the English reader has some sense of how the text works and holds together in Sanskrit. The story of the *vidyādhara* prince Naravāhanadatta that binds the *Kathāsaritsāgara* has been used in this translation as an outer frame to introduce stories as well as to indicate to readers where in Naravāhaṇadatta's adventures a particular story occurs or was told.

Individual stories have been selected more or less randomly though I have made an effort to represent as many of the eighteen books of the *Kathāsaritsāgara* as possible. Some of the stories are ones that I particularly like, others are so strange that they deserve to be brought to the attention of non-Sanskrit readers and still others are just plain funny. I have also tried to indicate through my selection the many kinds of tales that the *Kathāsaritsāgara* contains. There are histories and legends (like the Cāṇakya story and the story about the founding of the city of Pāṭaliputra); there are myths (like the Ahalyā and Indra story); there are para-epic tales (like the story in which Lohajaṅgha meets Vibhīṣaṇa who is now king of Laṇkā and the story in which Vālmīki creates Kuśa for Sītā); there are animal tales and folk-tales and riddles and gnomic stories. There are also stories about deceitful women who are punished and clever women who outwit men, stories about corrupt Brāhmins and pious ones, wicked mendicants and holy ascetics, evil non-human creatures as well as benign and friendly magical beings, wise ministers and foolish men. The *Kathāsaritsāgara*, 'The Ocean of Story', creates a universe of stories as well as encompasses a universe of being.

Readers will also notice that one of the stories has been repeated. The story of King Brahmadatta and the golden swans is told briefly within the story of the founding of Pāṭaliputra. The story is told in all its colourful detail of boons and curses in Book XVII, Padmāvatī. I have included both versions in this translation because the repetition of stories, once briefly and once at length, occurs fairly commonly in the *Kathāsaritsāgara*. The reason for including both versions in this translation is so that the English reader can get a feel for the structure of the Sanskrit text.

Many of the stories in this translation are well-known and readers may be surprised to find that some of their favourite stories form a part of the *Kathāsaritsāgara*. In the case of the best-known cycles of tales, like the *Pañcatantra* and Vikram and the vampire, I have included only selections. Since these tales have already appeared in complete English translations and are also familiar to readers from other languages and other sources, I felt that many of them could be left out of this collection without too much damage.

The Sanskrit text contains books and chapters that were the handiwork largely of nineteenth century colonial editors and translators. Each book of the eighteen that comprise the *Kathāsaritsāgara* has an independent name and opens with an invocation, either to Gaṇeśa or Śiva, which is usually followed by a verse dedicated to Kāma. I have translated the invocations for each book as they appear in the text, once again, to give the reader a sense of the original work. However, the chapters within the books are not quite as organized. Stories run over from one chapter into another and none of the stories have titles. I have titled each story separately and have tried to indicate the sub-stories that it contains. While this does have the effect of damming the flow of the rivers that all lead into the ocean, I believe that it will help the contemporary reader enjoy the book better.

The *Kathāsaritsāgara* is written in a curiously flat and largely unembellished Sanskrit. The usual rhetorical flourishes of the language are conspicuous by their absence. This, and the fact that the text has no religious or moral underpinnings, has led scholars to argue that the *Kathāsaritsāgara* is perhaps the sole example of 'pure narrative' in Sanskrit. I have tried to retain the simplicity of the original language in my translation. The fact that the Sanskrit in this text is free from its usual ornamentation makes it easier to render into a contemporary English idiom, one that particularly suits simple storytelling. Nonetheless, I have kept phrases like 'that excellent minister said' or 'that woman whose beauty rivalled that of the moon went out of the house' so that some taste of the original language flavours the translation into English.

I have retained coventional transliteration patterns for the Sanskrit words in the text. A key to Sanskrit pronunciation and transliteration is included. I have also chosen not to translate *ṛṣi*, *muni*, karma, *dharma*, *āśrama* and other similar words which have become a common part of our English vocabulary and are a standard feature of English renderings of English texts. Most English renderings of such words are inadequate and fail to convey the universe of meaning that these words encompass. For the reader unfamiliar with such terms, there is a brief glossary at the back of the book. I have also chosen to retain words like *rākṣasa*, *piśāca*, *gandharva*, *vetāla* and *yakṣa* within the stories because they denote non-human creatures. The appearance of a non-English word in an English translation will usually alert the reader to the fact that s/he is now about to encounter the magical, the mysterious, since so many of the stories in the *Kathāsaritsāgara* weave between the human and non-human worlds.

Thanks are due to my parents and to the friends who read early versions of the translations, gave me their comments and suggestions and bore with me while I somewhat obsessively inflicted my thoughts about the text on them. Grateful thanks to Wendy Doniger for agreeing to write the Foreword to this book, but much more than that, for leading me by the hand into a world of Sanskrit, introducing me to the wonder of stories and, most of all, for being a friend to cherish. Sanjay Iyer had to live with my outrageous demands on his computer, his time and his intelligence for the length of this project. Without his unique brand of encouragement as well as his insightful criticism, this translation would have suffered immeasurably. I cannot imagine working without him.

Arshia Sattar

Bangalore
May 1994

Introduction

The *Kathāsaritsāgara* tells 'tales of wondrous maidens and their fearless lovers, of kings and cities, of statecraft and intrigue, of magic and spells, of treachery and trickery, murder and war, tales of blood-sucking vampires, devils, goblins and ghouls, stories of animals in fact and fable, and stories, too, of beggars, ascetics, drunkards, gamblers, prostitutes and bawds.'[1] The 'Ocean of the Sea of Story' is a vast, rambling and thoroughly captivating treasure trove of tales. For their sheer widespread popular appeal, the stories in the *Kathāsaritsāgara* rank with the *Arabian Nights* and Grimms' fairy tales (both of which have likely borrowed from the *Kathāsaritsāgara*). However, despite the fact that the *Kathāsaritsāgara* shares a universe with other collections of popular tales in other cultures, within the context of classical Indian Sanskrit texts, it remains unusual, if not an outright aberration.

In many of its formal and structural features, the *Kathāsaritsāgara* conforms to Indian literary convention, with its framed narratives, its semi-divine author and its tales of the interaction between the gods, mythical creatures and human beings. But equally, it has its own niche. Like Viṣṇu Śarmā's *Pañcatantra*, a compendium of fables (in the Aesopian sense), where animals stand in for humans and each tale is a medium for teaching, the *Kathāsaritsāgara* has worldly concerns. But unlike the *Pañcatantra*, the tales in this text have little or no moral intent. There is no overarching unity of theme, religion or perspective. The *Kathāsaritsāgara* speaks of the world as a many-splendoured place, one in which humans and non-humans of various persuasions and motivations act and interact with varying degrees of success and failure. Generosity and pettiness, love and betrayal, sacrifice and selfishness are emotions displayed equally by Brāhmins and Śūdras, by kings and courtesans, for everyone in this text is concerned with only one thing—worldly pleasure and power.

Of the four *puruśārthas* (human goals) in the Hindu world, the *Kathāsaritsāgara* is animated by *artha*[2]. Scholars have often pointed out that the truly remarkable feature of the *Kathāsaritsāgara* in its Indian context is that it is very clearly not about *mokṣa,* or liberation from worldly ties. It is a collection of stories that celebrates earthly life with all its joys and sorrows, its triumphs and defeats, its petty ambitions and noble aspirations. The characters in almost all the stories seek power, money and success on earth.

The *Kathāsaritsāgara* is generally regarded as a Hindu text because it comes out of a Hindu milieu and because it is in Sanskrit, the classical language of Hinduism. But even a cursory glance at the stories that it contains will indicate to the perceptive reader that the collection is eclectic and profane, rather than religious. Religious mendicants and rogues, forest tribes and Brāhmins, Buddhists, *pāśupatas, vidyādharas and piśācas* are handled with the same ironic detachment. 'Caste destinies' in the *Kathāsaritsāgara's* ocean are most often not immutable; on the contrary, they are fluid. Nonetheless, the pervading ethos of the *Kathāsaritsāgara* is Hindu, one that is familiar to the general reader from other Indian texts and from Indian history.

The *Kathāsaritsāgara,* as we have it today, was put together by a Kashmiri Śaivite Brāhmin, Somadeva, around 1070 CE. This however, does not mean that Somadeva 'invented' the stories that comprise the *Kathāsaritsāgara,* for these tales had probably been in existence and in common currency for centuries already. The presence of Jātaka tales (Buddhist birth-stories, parables and fables) and stories from the *Pañcatantra,* as well as brief versions of Puranic myths and references to stories and incidents from the epics, indicate that Somadeva performed the function of a compiler, a re-teller of tales, rather than that of an 'author,' in the modern sense of the term.

Somadeva states in his epilogue that he composed the *Kathāsaritsāgara* for the queen Sūryavatī (sometimes also called Sūryamatī), wife of King Anantadeva of Kashmir. Kalhana's *Rājatarangiṇī* (1148 CE), a historical chronicle of the kings of Kashmir, states that Anantadeva's rule was a time of political turbulence and strife in the kingdom, with Anantadeva and his son Kalasa battling each other for the throne. Kalasa killed his father in 1081, and his mother, Sūryavatī, is said to have committed *sati* on the pyre of her husband. While she lived, the queen was known for building monasteries and temples and supporting Brāhmins. Somadeva hoped that his collection of stories 'would, even for a brief while, divert the queen's mind from its usual inclination towards worshipping Śiva and acquiring learning from the great books.'

It is the great god Śiva himself who sets up the pedestal (*Kathāpīṭha*) upon which Somadeva's dizzingly complex web of tales is built. The *Kathāsaritsāgara* opens with Pārvatī asking Śiva to tell her a story that she had never heard before. Śiva relates the adventures of the *vidyādharas* to Pārvatī because 'the gods were always too happy and mortals were always too miserable, whereas the adventures of semi-divine beings were always interesting.' As Śiva narrates the tales of seven *vidyādhara* princes, they are overheard by one of his attendants who repeats them to his own wife who happens to be Pārvatī's door-keeper. This woman, in turn, tells the stories to Pārvatī who is enraged that Śiva had told her a story that even her door-keeper knew. The erring attendant, Mālyavān, is cursed to be reborn on earth as Guṇāḍhya, where he will remain until he has spread the tale that he overheard far and wide. Thus, the story comes to earth and is told in the world of mortals by a narrator who is actually a celestial being.

Setting aside the questions that inevitably arise from the divine source of the Ocean of Stories, the text's own account of its subsequent earthly transmission presents us with a multiply fragmented corpus. On earth, Guṇāḍhya writes the *Bṛhatkathā* ('The Great Story'), i.e., all the seven tales that he heard from Śiva, on bark in his own blood using the *Paiśācī* language. This 'manuscript' is presented to a Sātavāhana king by Guṇāḍhya's students but the king rejects it because it is written in blood and in a crude and unsophisticated tongue. Crushed, Guṇāḍhya, the first earthly narrator (and the text's putative *ur*-author) burns the manuscripts of six of the seven tales that comprised the *Bṛhatkathā*. The one book that was salvaged from the proverbial flames was the adventures of the *vidyādhara* prince, Naravāhanadatta. When the Sātavāhana king heard this tale, he was entranced by it and decreed that it should be preserved.

The Sātavāhana monarch also added the *Kathāpīṭha* to the adventures of Naravāhanadatta, a preamble that tells the story of how Mālyavān was cursed, his life on earth as Guṇāḍhya and the role played by the king himself in the preservation of the last tale. In short, the *Kathāpīṭha* chronicles how the divine story came to be spread among humans. It is this *Kathāpīṭha* and the adventures of Naravāhanadatta that form the *Kathāsaritsāgara*. Naravāhanadatta's story, the skeleton that holds the multiplying stories of the *Kathāsaritsāgara* together, begins in the second book of the collection, the *Kathāmukha*. From this point on, in sixteen further books, the *Kathāsaritsāgara* unleashes its rivers and streams, tributaries and distributaries, lakes and seas of stories.

At its very start, then, the *Kathāsaritsāgara* points beyond itself to a larger collection of tales, the *Bṛhatkathā*, in a different and supposedly mythical language[3]. But even as it points to a larger text, it also states that the larger part of the larger text has been lost. Also in the *Kathāpīṭha*, we are confronted with a narrator, Guṇāḍhya, who acts within the story that he tells. This provides the perfect point-of-view twist to an already complicated myth of origins. What has been transmitted through this tortuous route into Somadeva's eleventh-century Sanskrit version is a mammoth set of wonderful tales, their origins shrouded in the smoke of Guṇāḍhya's fire. They are made all the more remarkable for the conspicuous lack of attention they have received from scholars and readers.

As in the case of other Indian texts, scholars have grappled with the authorship of the *Kathāsaritsāgara*. While

Somadeva may well be the 'author' outside the text, Śiva and Guṇāḍhya are the authors inside the text. If we accept that Somadeva was a historical person who put the tales together from a larger collection, we still have to contend with the 'authorship' of Guṇāḍhya who is a celestial born as a human with the express purpose of spreading the tale that he overheard, the tale of which we now have but a part. But before we investigate the issues of 'authorship' and divine origins, we should examine the material and linguistic history of the text we have in front of us.

The History and Language of the Text

The issue of the 'original' language of the stories, *Paiśācī*, has yet to be conclusively solved. A number of early Orientalists and some modern scholars believe that *Paiśācī* was a real language, spoken by a group of human beings known as the *piśācas* but with a wider currency as well[4]. It is likely, therefore, that *Paiśācī* was one of the many Prākrits that flourished all over the country, languages that were spoken by common people in everyday activity. For a long time, Prākrits were considered crude and unpolished (as their name suggests, *prākrit* meaning 'natural'), in relation to the highly developed grammatical constructs and aesthetic sophistication of Sanskrit. As if in direct anticipation of such a debate over the language of the text, the *Kathāsaritsāgara* contains a story in which a new grammar, the *Kātantra*, simpler and more pliable than Pāṇini's treatise, is produced by Kārtikeya and given to a Brāhmin to spread on earth.

Around the turn of the millennium, a number of Prākrits had developed literary traditions of their own, but *Paiśācī* seems not to have been one of them. In any event, Somadeva, true to his Brāhmin heritage and predilection, chose to preserve his collection of stories in Sanskrit. From the evidence in the *Kathāsaritsāgara* itself, J.A.B. van Buitenen believes that *Paiśācī* was a dialect in the north-western areas of the subcontinent[5]. An interesting twist to the whole issue of whether or not *Paiśācī* was a real language is the historical fact that the Sātavāhana kings, who ruled the western Deccan in the first centuries of the Common Era, were committed to a process of Aryanization. This meant that they encouraged the use and development of Sanskrit and Prākrits and rejected the local dialects which they referred to as *Paiśācīs*[6]. The geographical locales of the *Kathāsaritsāgara*, which become known to us through frequent references to the cities of Pratiṣṭhāna and Mālava and the forests of the Vindhyas, coincide with the boundaries and the administrative centres of the Sātavāhana kingdom. To add to this, as we have seen earlier, a Sātavāhana king definitely had something to do with the compilation of the text that we now know as the *Kathāsaritsāgara*, rejecting the manuscript in *Paiśācī* and then adding his mite to the multiple redactors that produced the current text.

F.W. Thomas suggests that *Paiśācī* had many variations, the earliest of which were related to the better known Prākrit Sauraseni[7]. He holds that *Paiśācī* was characterized mainly by peculiarities of pronunciation and that it was a dialect of travellers, traders and courtiers, people who came from different language regions and had, perforce, to communicate with each other. Thomas also thinks that since Guṇāḍhya's text was in this relatively old and unpracticed dialect which was deemed vulgar, and since it did not contain stories of the gods or of human heroes[8], it was not preserved like the *Rāmāyaṇa* and the *Mahābhārata*.

Such speculation, of course, assumes that there was an 'original' *Bṛhatkathā* written by a historical person named Guṇāḍhya and that his text was the basis for Somadeva's *Kathāsaritsāgara*. Assuming the factual existence of the *Bṛhatkathā* became more plausible when scholars discovered that there were other collections of stories that claimed to have the same source. Kṣemendra compiled the *Bṛhatkathāmañjarī* about thirty years before Somadeva presented his *Kathāsaritsāgara*. Kṣemendra's text is approximately a third as long as Somadeva's and 'inclined to poetic artifice.'[9] Buhler was sure that Somadeva and Kṣemendra had used the same source text for their separate collections but that they had worked independently of each other[10]. There was a fairly heated debate among scholars at the end of the nineteenth century about the literary merits of Kṣemendra's version over those of Somadeva's collection. Kṣemendra's supporters claim that Somadeva's text is dry and dull, with none of the poetic flourishes of simile and metaphor that adorn good Sanskrit writing. Other scholars criticize Kṣemendra's text for being all form and no substance.

The notion of a lost source text for the *Kathāsaritsāgara* received a further boost when a Frenchman, Felix Lacote, discovered a Nepali text by Buddhasvāmī. This *Bṛhatkathāślokasamgraha* seemed to have been written earlier than either Somadeva's or Kṣemendra's collections and claimed to be a Sanskrit version of the *Paiśācī Bṛhatkathā*. But even Buddhasvāmī's text was not complete, for though the manuscript that was found contained twenty-five thousand *ślokas*, it had only six out of twenty-six sections. Buddhasvāmī's collection is quite different from its Kashmiri siblings since it has far fewer stories, allowing the main narrative, the adventures of the prince Naravāhanadatta, to dominate.

Practitioners of textual studies commonly hold that the least complex version of any text is the oldest. Because Buddhasvāmī's *Bṛhatkathāślokasamgraha* has the least 'accretions,' (i.e., additional stories) its claims to being the closest to Guṇāḍhya's *Paiśācī* version are strengthened. Linguistic evidence also supports the claim that it is the earliest of the *Bṛhatkathā* texts. The language of the *Bṛhatkathāślokasamgraha* suggests that it was written as early as the eighth century CE, thus dating it a good three hundred years before the works of Somadeva and Kṣemendra. Buddhasvāmī's recension has many fans among scholars since the language used is 'lively and concise, observant and irreverent.'[11]

A combination of textual and extra-literary factors have promoted Somadeva's *Kathāsaritsāgara* as the best-known version of the *Bṛhatkathā*. On the basis of Lacote's study of the *Kathāsaritsāgara* manuscripts, N.M. Penzer believes that Kashmiri stories were added to Guṇāḍhya's collection of tales (as they were represented in Buddhasvāmī's version) and the Naravāhanadatta narrative was suppressed[12]. Thomas believes similarly, that the *Paiśācī* original was concerned mainly with the adventures of Naravāhanadatta, to which local and/or well-known stories, like the *Vetālapañcaviṃśati* (Twenty Five Tales of the *Vetāla*) and the Nala and Damayantī story, were added about two or three hundred years before Somadeva attempted his compilation[13]. It is worth reiterating that these theories of textual development are rooted in the hypothesis that the simpler versions and recensions of a text are more likely to be the earlier ones.

The history of the *Kathāsaritsāgara* recension used for this translation is not as contentious or as complicated as the history of the text itself. The *Kathāsaritsāgara* appeared on the Orientalist horizon through the work of H.H. Wilson who published a summary of the first five chapters of Somadeva's compilation in 1824. Brockhaus edited the first five chapters of the text in 1839 and by 1862, had published a complete edition of Somadeva's Sanskrit text from six manuscripts. The text had one hundred and twenty-four chapters (*tarangas* or 'waves' from the 'ocean of story') and Brockhaus divided these into eighteen *lambakas*, 'surges' or 'swells' in the 'ocean'. Between 1880 and 1884, Charles Tawney produced a complete English translation of the *Kathāsaritsāgara* that was published by the Asiatic Society of Bengal. Tawney used the Brockhaus edition as well as three other independent manuscripts for his translation. In 1889, the Nirnaysagar Press in Bombay published Durgadas' Sanskrit edition of the *Kathāsaritsāgara* that was compiled from the earlier Brockhaus edition and two other Bombay manuscripts. It is this edition that is commonly used for translations of Somadeva's *Kathāsaritsāgara*, including this one.

The History of the Authors

Working backwards from the existence and material history

of the text, we now have to contend with the issue of the authors, Guṇāḍhya and Somadeva. 'Authors' of Indian texts have always constituted a problem because the methods and practices of text production in ancient India were vastly different from what we have come to expect in our modern and (largely) Western-influenced publishing and writing world. Indian stories, tales, myths and legends were part of a rich and diverse oral tradition long before they were ever written. Even this oral tradition was hardly a homogenous, monolithic structure. Stories and tales varied from language to language, from region to region and, of course, from teller to teller.

'Texts' were compiled rather than created. They were redacted from the tales (sometimes written, most often oral) of several story-tellers rather than generated by the imagination of a single individual. Even the written *Kathāsaritsāgara* shows many hands and minds at work, for the Sanskrit varies greatly from story to story. Sometimes it is truly beautiful, punctuated with similes, metaphors and other rhetorical extravagance that make the reader pause to admire the use of the language as well as the skill of the composer. At other times, the language is purely functional, telling the story without frills and flourishes. At still other times, the Sanskrit is utterly pedestrian, indicating that the rhetorical tools of the language have been wielded by a person of lesser talents.

However, the genius of the compiler of a text, a Vālmīki, a Vyāsa, a Viṣṇu Śarmā, a Bharata, a Guṇāḍhya or a Somadeva, lies in the way random stories have been put together, have been made to cohere in a narrative that dips, and weaves and meanders and doubles back upon itself. While it may well be correct to assume that the personal name attributed to ancient Indian texts is that of the redactor rather than a creator of the stories, changing the concept of the producer of the text from 'author' to 'compiler' still leaves us with the question of whether these redactors/compilers were real, historical individuals who lived and breathed as they put the stories together or, whether names like Vyāsa, Vālmīki, Bharata and Guṇāḍhya are merely generic conventions that surround anonymous editors and story-tellers.

Most Indian composers/redactors appear as characters within the stories that they tell. In the case of Vyāsa, he not only tells the story of the *Mahābhārata,* he 'creates' it by fathering Pāṇḍu, Dhṛtarāṣṭra and Vidura. Vālmīki is moved to compassion by the death of two *kraunca* birds and his grief (*śoka*) inspires him to 'see' the story of Rāma and recite the *Rāmāyaṇa* in the *śloka* metre. But in the story that he tells, Vālmīki is also the sage who shelters Sītā in her banishment and raises the sons of Rāma. In fact, Lava and Kuśa recite Vālmīki's story of Rāma to Rāma and that is how we, the larger audience, get to hear the story. Viṣṇu Śarmā, the 'author' of the *Pañcatantra,* is the sage to whom the dull-witted princes are sent so that their 'minds can be awakened'. Guṇāḍhya, the source of our *Kathāsaritsāgara,* was once Śiva's *gaṇa* cursed to live on earth until he had spread the story narrated by Śiva far and wide.

Guṇāḍhya is perhaps the only 'author' of a well-known text who speaks in the first person. His story is told from his point of view, not by an unseen, omnipresent narrator as in the case of Vyāsa, Vālmīki and Viṣṇu Śarmā. But Guṇāḍhya appears with his story only in the *Kathāpīṭha* of the *Kathāsaritsāgara,* where having forsworn the use of Sanskrit and the known Prākrits, he wrote the story that he heard from Kāṇabhūti (who heard it from Vararuci) in his own blood in *Paiśācī.*

Was Guṇāḍhya a real person? Did he speak and write in a language called *Paiśācī?* Was there a human language called *Paiśācī* at all? Did the entire *Bṛhatkathā* (the adventures of all seven *vidyādhara* princes) exist at some point in time? Do we take the *Kathāpīṭha's* word and assume that Guṇāḍhya did exist? And if we do, how much of Guṇāḍhya's story do we believe? For Guṇāḍhya was not a mere mortal, he was none other than one of Śiva's faithful *gaṇas,* cursed by Pārvatī to live on earth. At what point do we suspend our disbelief about the divine origins of the 'author' of a text if we are determined to establish his historical existence? And finally, would it really matter if we were to argue that 'Guṇāḍhya' was only a literary device, a narrative ploy, created purely for reasons of structure and rhetoric?

Traditional *Kathāsaritsāgara* scholarship has assumed the real existence of Guṇāḍhya as a flesh and blood person but remains silent about his divine origins. van Buitenen believes that Guṇāḍhya wrote during the most prosperous time in Indian history, between the fourth and fifth centuries CE when the splendour of the merchant class and the trading wealth of India was known all over the world[14]. In a similar vein, Thomas suggests that Guṇāḍhya himself must have travelled a great deal, probably along the flourishing Indian trade routes that connected cities like Prayāga, Kauśāmbī and Ujjain. Guṇāḍhya compiled the stories that he heard in these cities and in the ports and attached to them a frame narrative that he created, the story of Naravāhanadatta[15].

The factual existence of Somadeva is easier to establish. Somadeva appears to have been a historical person since evidence for his existence comes to us from a time of recorded history and is supported by a historical chronicle, the *Rājataranginī*. He appears only in the epilogue of the Durgadas manuscript of the *Kathāsaritsāgara* where he praises his royal patrons, offers his compilation for their entertainment, and states that his stories contain the essence of the *Bṛhatkathā*. Somadeva sets himself apart from other Indian 'authors' by not acting in the story that he tells. This may be a clear indication of the fact that he was a compiler and a redactor rather than an 'author' in the modern sense of the word.

From what we know about him, Somadeva was a Kashmiri Brāhmin, the son of Rāmadevabhaṭṭa. R.C. Temple is firm in his belief that the *ur*-author of the *Kathāsaritsāgara*, Guṇāḍhya was not a Brāhmin and that all the Brāhmin predilections and behaviour (for example, in the story of Vararuci) that we find in the *Kathāsaritsāgara* are the work of Somadeva[16]. van Buitenen, in his comparison of the *Kathāsaritsāgara* and Buddhasvāmī's older text, comments that Somadeva was 'too much of a Brāhmin' to allow the kind of irreverence that enlivens the Nepali text to animate his collection[17]. What is important in this discussion is not the debate over Somadeva's puritanical Brāhmin streak but the underlying possibility that the collection of stories had a different flavour before Somadeva put his indelible mark on them.

The Orientation Of The Text

The eleventh century was a time of religious awakening in Kashmir and the distinctive philosophy of Kashmiri Śaivism was beginning to dominate the philosophical and intellectual landscape of the region. Vāsugupta had introduced the basic tenets of Kashmiri Śaivism about two-hundred-and-fifty years earlier, but the greatest philosopher of the school, Abhinavagupta, was probably Somadeva's contemporary. By the same period, Buddhism already had been pushed to the outer regions of the subcontinent and Kashmir was one of the few areas in the eleventh century where Buddhism had a real presence. Somadeva thus lived in a place and time in which multiple religious, social and cultural influences were prevalent rather than in a society that was homogeneous and unitary. That the *Kathāsaritsāgara* is nominally dedicated to Śiva could be attributed to two reasons: the religious preferences of Somadeva's royal patrons, and the general prevalence of Kashmiri Śaivism.

The *Kathāsaritsāgara* pays lip service to traditional Indian textual practices of invoking the gods, animating the outermost frame of the narrative with Śiva and Pārvatī and allowing the gods and other divine beings to flit in and out of the stories. Within the frames and the divine origins of the tale, the values that the collection of stories is concerned with are earthly power, glory and worldly pleasures. Hindus, Buddhists, Brāhmins, Kṣatriyas, merchants, Śūdras, tribals, fringe sects and ungodly beings are all a part of the universe of the text and there are few moral or religious teachings imparted by individual tales or by the text as a whole.

It has often been suggested that the *Kathāsaritsāgara* was written by and for the merchant class, for it celebrated their values, their way of life, their milieu. This idea is supported by the fact that the 'original' source text was written in a language other than Sanskrit and that the rules and regulations of Sanskrit poetics and prosody are largely disregarded. Hence, many scholars believe that the *Kathāsaritsāgara* could not have been written by or for Brāhmins whose social, economic, religious and aesthetic concerns would have been very different.

Comparative studies of *Kathāsaritsāgara* manuscripts with the available texts of Buddhasvāmī's and Kṣemendra's works indicate that it is very likely that the *Bṛhatkathā* (perhaps early versions of the *Kathāsaritsāgara* as well) was dedicated to Kubera, the god of wealth[18]. Kubera as the patron deity of a text that valorizes success and acquisition seems a logical choice. Supporting the hypothesis that the text was originally dedicated to Kubera is the fact that the name of the collection's hero is 'Naravāhanadatta', 'gift of Kubera.' As van Buitenen says, 'the hero is a prince with the name of a merchant.'[19] Based on Lacote's research, Penzer firmly believes that characters who were originally ordinary men and women, were elevated to the level of kings, princes and *vidyādharas* by the various re-tellings that led up to Somadeva's text[20].

It is here that the hypothesis of the text being 'Brāhminized' by Somadeva (or an earlier unseen and unnamed hand) becomes relevant. It is hard to see a Brāhminical overlay in the welter of stories that intersect, emerge from, and play into each other. In the *Kathāsaritsāgara*, a Brāhmin is just another kind of person that inhabits the stories. Brāhmins are not always clever, they are not always honourable and they are certainly not always religious or even pious. Many of the stories poke fun at Brāhmins; others do not even bother to describe them in any way other than by a simple caste name. Moreover, people from all castes and backgrounds, from kings to *piśācas*, retire to forest *āśramas* at the end of their lives. Rather than reinforcing a Brāhminical aspect, such stories work to democratize the values of Hindu society by privileging a contingent social dynamic over an 'ideal' one. Thus it is that the Brāhminical aspect of the

Kathāsaritsāgara is largely restricted to the language in which it appears.

What is of far greater interest than a supposed Brāhminical patina on the text is the discreet but unmistakable Buddhist element that creeps in. Among the many hundred stories that the *Kathāsaritsāgara* contains, one of them is the story of King Śibi and the dove, better known from the Buddhist Jātakas. In this story, King Śibi sacrifices himself for the bird because he is a *bodhisattva*. There are many other Jātaka stories included in the *Kathāsaritsāgara*, though most of them have been adapted to the needs of the text, and in that process, have become somewhat different from their Jātaka versions.

In Book X, there is a cycle of stories in which a merchant's son 'was born an incarnation of part of a *bodhisattva*' (*bodhisattva-aṃśa-sambhava*) but he behaves just like other virtuous characters in the text, displaying no specifically *bodhisattva* qualities. Eventually, he becomes a king and takes revenge on his estranged wife. But there are other stories in which young princes express a disinterest in the pleasures of royalty and retire to forests or to *āśramas*. The resonance with the life of Gautama Buddha are hard to miss in such stories. Further, a number of characters, from Vararuci to *vidyādhara* princes, express their belief in the basic Buddhist tenet that everything in the world is impermanent (*anitya*) and that worldly ties can lead only to sorrow (*dukha*). There is even a story in which a young man is explicitly converted to Buddhism from the Brāhminical religion that he follows.

It is clear from other historical records that Buddhism had a large following in the merchant communities of the subcontinent[21]. In the years when Buddhism spread like wildfire across the subcontinent and much of eastern Asia, its followers were largely traders, artisans and cultivators, communities that were growing in economic power at that time. If indeed, the *Kathāsaritsāgara* was directed towards the merchants, if it told their stories, then it is no surprise that Buddhist tenets should be an integral part of the text. Buddhism and Jainism were strong influences at the time when the stories that comprise the *Kathāsaritsāgara* were in circulation. Therefore, it is likely that religious tenets were picked up and retained alongwith the stories that contained them. Furthermore, at the time when Somadeva was compiling his text in the eleventh century CE, Buddhism still had a strong presence in Kashmir. A Buddhist milieu was, thus, present at two important times in the history of the text—when the stories were in circulation and when they were being compiled into a text seven hundred years later. In a tantalizing aside, F.W. Thomas states that *Paiśācī* was a language used by Buddhist sects[22], adding to the likelihood of a Buddhist milieu for the tales.

If we accept the idea that the text used a language that was associated with a specific religious group (in this case, Buddhism) the question arises of whether the text has a committed religious orientation. By default, the *Kathāsaritsāgara* has been considered a Hindu text because it came out of a period of Hindu dominance, because it was compiled by a Brāhmin in Sanskrit, and because Hindu ideas were contained in the stories. But we have just seen how the stories arose and were compiled at times when Buddhism was a major influence and how Buddhist ideas (if not a 'Buddhist' language) are also present within the text. The *Kathāsaritsāgara* contains stories and characters from many religions, sects and ways of life; it does not exclusively endorse the values and aspirations of any particular religion; in fact, it steers well clear of traditional religious goals by emphasizing the enjoyment of pleasure and power.

It is a persuasive idea that the collection's dedication to Śiva is conventional and incidental, rather than essential to the text's religious orientation. No doubt the gods that operate within the stories, Durgā, Pārvatī, Sarasvatī, Śiva and Kārtikeya, are Hindu, but their behaviour is generic to any divine being and does not betray their Hindu characteristics. Since the *Kathāsaritsāgara* has no single religious orientation, the most highly regarded beings in the stories are the *vidyādharas*, a relatively obscure class of celestials that seem to combine the features of *gandharvas* (celestial beings known for their beauty and their skill in music and dance) and *siddhas* (celestial beings who have magic powers because of their state of enlightenment). *Vidyādharas* are not essential to the divine hierarchy of any religion and appear in Hindu, Buddhist and Jain stories with equal frequency.

The religious multivalence of the *Kathāsaritsāgara* could be one of the reasons why the text did not fire the imaginations of the early Orientalists and has remained under-studied and under-appreciated to this day. An integral part of the Orientalist understanding was that Indian texts were primarily religious and that a complete disregard for material life and welfare characterized Indian life and culture. Faced with a text that did not endorse this, that, in fact, celebrated the worldly and the material, the Western scholarly establishment was happy enough to leave the *Kathāsaritsāgara* alone and treat it as trivial. Strangely, *The Arabian Nights,* that other great compendium of stories, was valorized by the same Orientalist establishment, perhaps precisely because it subverted traditional Islamic orthodoxy. The same subversive element in the *Kathāsaritsāgara* has led to its marginalization from the mainstream of Indian literatures even though it remains the nexus for different religions, different ideologies and different genres.

The Framed Narrative

Speaking of the *Kathāsaritsāgara,* van Buitenen was moved to comment that 'the main narrative has almost irretrievably got lost in a maze of stories that are added to it. At the slightest provocation, a speaker recalls a tale in which a speaker recalls another tale; and the banquet consists of nothing but *hors d'oeuvres.*' The pleasure of encountering a framed narrative is somewhat akin to the search for the heart of an onion; you peel away the layers and then reach a moment when you realize that the essence lies in the layers themselves.

Some of the most compelling and enduring stories in the world have a structural feature in common: they are framed narratives. The inner story (or stories, or, even sets of stories) has one or many outer frames that situate the story being told to us in a long line of narrators. The most familiar frame stories in Indian literature are the epics, the *Rāmāyaṇa* and the *Mahābhārata*. In both, the inner (main) stories are framed by a sequence of inverted commas which mark the story as told to so-and-so by so-and-so and then told again to so-and-so until it finally reaches the current reader/listener. In fact, the *Mahābhārata* calls itself *itihāsa*, which literally means 'thus it was said,' placing the text firmly within the oral tradition that passes a tale from one teller to the next through the generations and the ages.

On one level, framing is a narrative device that allows the teller of a tale to participate in the story that s/he is telling. The teller places her/himself at the centre as well as at the margin of the story being told. Both Vālmīki and Vyāsa act within the epics that they narrate as do Viṣṇu Śarmā and Guṇāḍhya. But along the way, as the text gets deeper and deeper into itself, we lose sight of the first story and the first teller as characters within stories begin to tell other stories and so on, even though everything is still contained within the first story. Though our reading may have left the first frame on the outer edge of the narrative, each inner story carries each and every frame with it through to the end of the text in the form of inverted commas.

The framed narrative has always been thought of as an eastern concept and device (supposedly linked to eastern ideas about non-linear time). Framed narratives that appear outside the subcontinent, (notably *The Arabian Nights, Decameron* and *The Canterbury Tales*) are all rooted in the *Kathāsaritsāgara*. There has been some debate (generated primarily by the travels of the *Pañcatantra*) about whether the frame narrative developed in the subcontinent or whether it was a Middle Eastern device. Those who believe that the frame narrative was a Middle Eastern contribution to story literature base their conclusions on the work of A.B. Keith who suggested this hypothesis in the early years of the twentieth century[23]. He claimed that the animal tales of the *Pañcatantra* travelled to pre-Islamic Persia and Arabia where they were framed in an outer story. When the tales travelled back to India, the frame came with them, whence it became an integral part of the text itself. Other texts adopted the device and it has now become a characteristic of rambling, multi-story Indian texts.

Keith's hypothesis is interesting but remains rather dubious. Framed narratives are such an integral part of Indian story-telling and Indian frames are so intensely complicated (more so than frames from other cultures) that it is hard to believe that the framing was not fundamental to Indian narrative structures or that it was a borrowed device. Indian textual frames provide a seamless link between the realm of the gods and the realm of humans and therefore, they cannot be simply unpacked. Framed texts do not merely insert the narrator into the story. Rather, the frames set up and encompass a world in which the magical is normal and the normal is magical. It is also very likely that the Indian epics were framed from the moment of their composition, a time that predates the travels of the *Pañcatantra* by at least three centuries.

The *Kathāsaritsāgara* has a relatively simple framing structure compared to the complexity and sophistication of the framing devices used in the Indian epics. There are several distinct and complete frames for the story of the adventures of Naravāhanadatta which is itself a frame for the multiple stories within it. The outermost frame is, of course, the incident in which Pārvatī demands a new story from Śiva and he tells the tales of the seven *vidyādhara* princes. This frame closes with the cursing of the *gaṇas* who now bring the story with them to earth. But the story at this point is not quite complete, since we have not yet been told the tale that caused all the fuss.

The second frame which is not exactly within the first, but is, rather, an extension of it, is the story of Puṣpadanta/Vararuci and Mālyavān/Guṇāḍhya who have to tell their adventures as well as the tale that Śiva narrated, to the *piśāca* Kāṇabhūti on earth. Once they have been released from their curses, their frame continues without them, moving Śiva's tale into the (human) hands of Guṇāḍhya's students and the Sātavāhana king. At the end of the *Kathāpīṭha*, this frame closes on the divine narrators and the 'main' story of Naravāhanadatta begins in the *Kathāmukha*.

But even the Naravāhanadatta frame, which in many ways, is *the* crucial skeletal structure for the stories within it, is not simple. It contains within itself several distinct cycles of stories (stories connected by a 'mini' frame of a single character in many lifetimes, for example, the Vikramāditya cycle) the largest of which are the Udayana and the Mṛgāṅkadatta cycles. Within the Naravāhanadatta frame, there are also independent story collections like the *Pañcatantra* and the *Vetālapañcaviṃśati*. Each of these, including the Naravāhanadatta frame, have clearly defined conclusions, usually the death of the hero (as in the Udayana cycle) or a 'happily ever after' situation. In a similar (though not identical) mini-frame closure, Guṇāḍhya slips out of the frame by writing down his stories and leaving them in the hands of others.

The difference between the *Kathāsaritsāgara* frames and those of the epics is that the outer frames of the *Kathāsaritsāgara* close at the beginning of the book—two of them close in the *Kathāpīṭha* and the early narrators cease to act in the stories that they tell. However, the Naravāhanadatta frame and all the stories within it continue to carry the inverted commas, the *parampara*, of Śiva telling it to Pārvatī, Vararuci telling it to Kāṇabhūti, Guṇāḍhya telling it to his students who tell it to the Sātavāhana king until the point that it reaches us through Somadeva.

It is through this structure (of the early frames closing in the beginning rather than being carried through to the end) that the *Kathāsaritsāgara* avoids the problem of the omniscient narrator (who is not omnipresent) faced by the *Rāmāyaṇa* and the *Mahābhārata*. In the epics, if Vālmīki and Vyāsa are acting in the story even as they relate it without using the first person pronoun, who is the person who narrates the outermost frame? Who says, 'Vyāsa said to Gaṇeśa' and who describes Vālmīki's outpouring of compassion at the death of the *krauñca* bird? Because we, the contemporary readers, know the *Kathāsaritsāgara* through

Somadeva who does not act in the story, he is the simple and uncomplicated omniscient narrator.

The magic moment in the framed narrative is the point at which the text turns into a Moebius strip, presenting one continuous unbroken surface to the reader, when the putative author of the text himself enters the story and at the same time, continues to tell it. The reader, at this point, is no longer sure what s/he is reading: is it still a report of events that happened in the past, or is it now an account of events being described as they happen or are they being made to happen by the creator/author?

This crucial narrative twist occurs in the *Kathāsaritsāgara*, a moment in which the frame flips upon itself and the reader is left wondering when the frame folded. In the opening verses of Book VI, we are told, 'Listen now to the divine adventures which Naravāhanadatta himself related from the very beginning, when he was asked by the *ṛṣis* and their wives about himself on some occasion after he had won the sovereignty of the *vidyādharas*.' When did Naravāhanadatta become the teller of his own tale? Who was telling it upto this point, if he wasn't? What happened to Guṇāḍhya and Vararuci and Kāṇabhūti as narrators?

The larger question that looms at this magic moment is this: if the frame is looped like this, what happens when the story reaches this point? If this were a real loop, the story would have to rewind itself at this point and go no further! Jorge Luis Borges expresses the paradox of the frame story telling itself when he writes about *The Arabian Nights*:

> This collection of fantastic tales duplicates and re-duplicates to the point of vertigo the ramifications of a central story in later and subordinate stories, but does not attempt to graduate its realities, and the effect (which should have been profound) is superficial, like a Persian carpet . . . The necessity of completing a thousand and one sections obliged the copyists of the work to make all manner of interpolations. None is more perturbing than that of

> the six hundred and second night, magical among all the nights. On that night, the king hears from the queen his own story. He hears the beginning of the story, which comprises all the others and also—monstrously—itself. Does the reader clearly grasp the vast possibility of this interpolation, the curious danger? That the queen may persist and the motionless king hear forever the truncated story of the *Thousand and One Nights*, now infinite and circular . . .[24]

Naravāhanadatta faces a similar problem in Book VI of the *Kathāsaritsāgara*, but the story continues in the third person, the narrator referring to himself as 'Naravāhanadatta', and relating a series of adventures and misadventures in which he is the hero. He also recalls all the tales within the tales, the stories told by story characters to other story characters.

The Content Of The Tales

Regardless of the mathematically 'dangerous' structure of the *Kathāsaritsāgara*, the 'main' narrative of the collection, Naravāhanadatta's adventures and his eventual coronation as the emperor of the *vidyadhāras*, is quite secondary to the profusion of stories that surround it. In fact, the story of Naravāhanadatta is fairly dull, consisting of a series of amorous encounters which culminate in marriage. This is followed by a string of battles in which he must defeat other *vidyādhara* kings before he can become undisputed emperor of the realm[25]. Naravāhanadatta appears every now and again between the other tales, in the company of his faithful ministers who tell him stories to while away the hours. Sometimes, the stories are told to his queens, or in the royal assembly. Quite often, someone that Naravāhanadatta meets will tell him their story that can cover several lifetimes. On other occasions, the stories the prince hears will have some bearing on the situation that he is in. For example, when he is pining for a lost love, he is told the story of the separation of Rāma and Sītā.

With the many types of stories that it contains, myths, legends, folk-tales, riddles, the *Kathāsaritsāgara* is a compendium of genres. The myth of Pururavas and Urvaśī rubs shoulders with a short-hand version of Pāṇḍu's curse, which nestles beside the tale of the birth of the Maurya kingdom which leads into a story about a talking bear who saved the life of a prince. One might say that the *Kathāsaritsāgara* is the locus for the intersection of the 'great' and the 'little' traditions, a place where pan-Indian, classical ideas and values meet local, regional forms and themes.

As with the *Rāmāyaṇa* and the *Mahābhārata*, there are forces beyond the characters that also act within the stories, for example, curses, boons, karma and fate (*daivam*, also called *vidhi*). Past lives are very important in the *Kathāsaritsāgara* stories. Often characters are given the boon of remembering their past lives even as they go forward into their next births. Similarly, when a curse ends, the cursed individual usually remembers all that which happened to him/her in the previous birth. But it is not only the memory of these lives that is important. In a literalistic karma, these past lives have direct consequences on current births. For example, a young *vidyādharī* who refuses to marry is cursed by her parents to be born on earth and have eight husbands; an arrogant young man is cursed to be born a lion with little intelligence. Relationships from past lives also operate in current births and often, husbands and wives from previous births will marry each other again. Friends from the past will also be friends in the current life.

Curses and boons abound and while curses usually relegate the individual to a 'lower' form of birth, boons are restricted to the gift of children and the passing on of important information. Śiva and Kārtikeya often intervene to give a man practising austerities some kind of knowledge. The goddess, usually Durgā/Cāmuṇḍī (though Sarasvatī also makes a few appearances), appears in dreams and directs her devotee to where s/he should be going next. The goddess also acts to save the lives of impetuous people who are ready to kill themselves for her (as in the case of Padmāvatī and the transposed heads) and in a few cases, restores the dead to life (as with Vīravara and his family).

Apart from bestowing boons (and sometimes curses), the pan-Indian gods and goddesses are largely absent from the stories. Their temples, however, abound and they usually respond to propitiation and worship with either directions or magic objects, but their presence is restricted to short, sharp interventions rather than to a sustained and steady influence. Of the gods in the stories, Kārtikeya bestows Vedic and religious knowledge, the goddesses act to protect their devotees, and Śiva, nominally the patron deity of the *Kathāsaritsāgara*, is the most otiose of all, invoked with regularity but decidedly detached from earthly events. Unlike in myth and epic (purveyors of the 'great' tradition), the great gods in the *Kathāsaritsāgara* act more as they would in folk genres where their intervention is limited to emergencies and is usually the result of propitiation. In folk genres, divine activity is usually the purview of local deities. In the *Kathāsaritsāgara*, the place of these local deities is taken by random *yakṣas*, *yoginīs*, *vidyādharas* and ascetics.

The other *deux ex machina* in the stories is *daivam* (used in the stories to mean 'impelled by destiny'), and makes the character do something that, while not contrary to the plot thus far, does move it along faster. For example, in the story of Anaṅgarati, her husband is 'impelled by destiny' to ask her for a song that lulls him to sleep. When he awakes, he finds that she has disappeared for she has to fulfil her curse of eight husbands. With the operation of *daivam*, the reader is encouraged to consider the possibility of what might have happened if her husband had not fallen asleep.

Past lives, boons, curses and *daivam/vidhi* are plot devices, which function to move the narrative along as well as to explain behaviour and events. The universe of the stories is one in which free will does not seem to operate, for all that happens and all that a character can accomplish is pre-determined. But what is not entirely clear from the stories is whether boons and curses act in conjunction with karma or whether they are used to interrupt the karmic cycle. Do boons and curses create the karmic events that an individual must endure? In either case, the pre-determined nature of a character's actions is not vitiated by karma, *daivam* or anything else, narrative destiny is firmly fixed.

The *Kathāsaritsāgara* does not appear to share the terror of caste impurities and miscegenation (*varṇasaṃkara*) of the *Rāmāyaṇa* and the *Mahābhārata*. Not only do all castes, sub-castes, outcastes and multicastes people the text, but characters do not necessarily behave in accordance with their caste *dharma*. Of course Brāhmins perform sacrifices, Kṣatriyas conquer kingdoms and merchants go on trading expeditions, but the stories have many cases of merchants becoming kings, Brāhmins becoming brigands and Kṣatriyas taking to trade. It is also quite common for individuals from one caste to marry into another caste. But the democracy of the textual universe is mitigated by the fact that every time there is an inter-caste marriage, one of the partners turns out to be a cursed celestial.

Apart from 'fringe' peoples like *pāśupatas*, Kapālikas, Śavaras, Bhīls, Mataṇgas, Pulindas and various kinds of ascetics, non-human creatures like *yakṣas, rakṣāsas, piśācas, vetālas*, a few *nagas, gandharvas, gaṇas, siddhas* and *apsarases* also find place in the stories. While *rakṣāsas* and *piśācas* are hardly differentiated, both being creatures that wander around at night and are given to eating human flesh, the *vetālas* get isolated from this general grouping primarily because of central role of the *vetāla* in the *Vetālapañcaviṃśati* cycle.

The most common English equivalent for *vetāla* is 'vampire', based on the fact that *vetālas* haunt cremation grounds and inhabit corpses. This is an unsatisfactory translation of the concept of *vetāla* because of the Transylvanian connotations of the word 'vampire.' *Vetālas* do not bite and suck blood from living beings and do not seem to possess bodies of their own. An English word closer in meaning to *vetāla* is 'zombie' but again, *vetālas* are not quite zombies because, unlike them, they appear to act independently of any outside control. Yet, mastery over the *vetālas* is obviously desirable as they can be of use to humans[26].

Of all the magical beings in the *Kathāsaritsāgara*, it is the *vidyādharas* that must engage our attention. No other Indian text accords the *vidyādharas* the importance that the *Kathāsaritsāgara* does, even though they are mentioned in the epics as well as in Jain and Buddhist tales. In other Indian stories, a *vidyādhara*, 'holder of knowledge,' is not particularly distinguished from either a *gandharva* or a *siddha* and constitutes a kind of generic semi-divine being that lives in the sky and has certain super-human powers, the most important of which is being able to fly.

John Dowson describes *vidyādharas* as,

> a class of inferior deities inhabiting the regions between the sky and the earth, and generally of benevolent disposition. They are attendants upon Indra, but they have chiefs and kings of their own, and are represented as inter-marrying and having much intercourse with men. They are also called kamarupin, 'taking shapes at will'; khechara and nabhas-chara, 'moving in the air'; and priyamvada, 'sweet-spoken'.[27]

E. Washburn Hopkins agrees with this basic definition and adds that *vidyādharas* 'gaze with astonishment at human prowess.'[28]

In the *Kathāsaritsāgara*, a *vidyādhara* named Śaktivega defines his own people as 'resolute souls, who, having propitiated Śiva either in this or in a former birth, obtain by his favour, the rank of *vidyādhara*. That rank, characterized by the possession of supernatural knowledge, a sword, a garland and so on, is of various kinds.'[29] This definition does not tell us much but it does indicate that *vidyādhara*-hood is something that humans can acquire through a series of acts coupled with the propitiation of Śiva. To become a *vidyādhara* is to receive a badge of merit from Śiva which includes access to certain useful powers. *Vidyādhara* powers have to be learned or bestowed as is indicated from various stories in which young *vidyādharas* are trained in the special arts and skills. These powers can also be taken away from individuals who misbehave and they do not carry over into other lives or through curses.

Even though *vidyādharas* seem to be unimportant in other texts, the *Kathāsaritsāgara* valorizes them as a kind of being to which humans can and should aspire. This adds to the evidence that the *Kathāsaritsāgara* is not about *mokṣa* or liberation from the cycle of births and deaths. It is about the aspiration to a higher realm of pleasure. A number of characters in the stories spend time in the *vidyādhara* realm and 'enjoy celestial pleasures' for a while, but only the chosen among them get to *become vidyādharas*. *Vidyādharas* are not immortal and thus, even the powers and pleasures that an individual can experience as a *vidyādhara* are time bound. When the individual's merit runs out, it's back to another life in another place.

Conclusion

The appeal of the stories in the *Kathāsaritsāgara* is ageless and apparently universal, judging from the many versions that the stories have taken in numerous languages and many cultures. There is a magical quality to the stories that goes well beyond the magic within them. *Yakṣas* and *yoginis* may become *djinns* and *afreets*, but the power of the stories themselves remains unchallenged. The attempt to understand the hold that stories have on the human imagination has taken many forms, from the analytic, structural theories of the Formalists to the more anthropocentric suggestions offered by Jung. But the mystery of the story, the point at which the listener is compelled to ask, 'What happened next?', and the hypnotic power of the story-teller have remained elusive.

This introduction raises many of the issues that surround the study of Indian texts and their translation. Whether we examine the problem of 'authorship' in the Indian tradition, or we discuss the religious orientation of the text, or we meditate on the structure of the text with its frames and its melding of the little and the great traditions, the search is for a cartography of an unbounded space that is the text. The issues raised by these discussions attempt to map the exploration of a relatively unknown text from within and without, from above and below.

Whether Guṇāḍhya was a real person and *Paiśācī* a real language, whether Somadeva 'Brāhminized' the stories, or whether Naravāhanadatta told his own story endlessly to a captive audience, does not have to impinge on the enjoyment of following Lohajaṇgha through his elaborate scheme to trick Makaradaṇṣṭrā or walking patiently with Vikrama as he ferries the mischievous *vetāla* back and forth through the cremation ground. But the possibility of the fictitiousness of the author of a fictional work in an allegedly fictional language, the potential for the story to be stuck in an endless instant replay, are all features that add dimensions to the stories within the stories and to the text. Wading through the framed narrative of the *Kathāsaritsāgara* has an allure, a potential for getting into something over one's head, of drowning in the magic and mystery of story-telling. Even as we duck in and out of the billows of individual tales in the Ocean of Story, there is some part of our mind that tries to hold onto the ever-receding frame, the shoreline that gets farther and farther as the waves in the ocean pull us away.

Foreword

'The Ocean of Story' is my very favourite collection of stories. It is a wonderful combination of simultaneously innocent and sophisticated folk common sense and highly sophisticated Sanskrit court style. It paints a vivid picture of a most particular part of India at one moment in history, and yet it tells stories that are the Indian variants—often the Indian sources—of stories told around the world. I can think of no one better qualified to capture these polarities than Arshia Sattar, who embodies in herself an unparalleled seat-of-the-pants brilliance and the subtle understanding of a cosmopolitan Indian woman who has lived, and lived well, in both India and the West ('the West' being in her case America, particularly the University of Chicago, where it was my great good fortune to encounter her). Her exuberance and her pleasure in the text spill out of every page of the introduction and infuse every page of the translation. She is a great storyteller herself, and a great appreciator of other peoples' stories.

The only competing English translation and edition of this text is the so-called Tawney-Penzer edition, a translation by C. H. Tawney, edited with copious notes by N. M. Penzer, and published in ten volumes, in London in 1924. But the present text has several virtues that the older edition lacks. First of all, it is in our language. Second, its author is a native of India. And, third, it is a selection, a book that one can read from cover to cover. Let me discuss this triad of virtues one by one.

One reason why it is necessary to retranslate a great classic every century at least is that our own language keeps changing, and each generation needs a new translation that reflects its own voice. This is why people did not stop translating Homer even after Chapman did it, and did it with genius, producing what may still be the most beautiful translation of Homer, just as many people regard the King James Bible as the most beautiful translation of the Bible. 'The Ocean of Story' requires such an updating even more than those other classics do, since it is such a now kind of book, so immediate, so worldly, so vernacular. (See the introduction for the ways in which scholars have regarded it as literally vernacular.) It cries out for a fresh voice, and it has found that voice in Arshia Sattar. A good test for a translation is just to read it aloud and see if it sounds like anything you have ever said but also if it says what it says in the way that the characters in the story are likely to have said it. Every single sentence of this translation passes that test, with flying colours.

A second virtue of this translation lies in the fact that Arshia Sattar is a native daughter. Sidestepping for the moment all the post-colonial, anti-Orientalist, hegemonic, subaltern discourse (did I miss anything?) about Western scholars who appropriate (ha! got another) Indian texts, it remains the case that there is a particular lilting, vital quality in the translation of an Indian text by a GOOD Indian translator. 'Good' is an important qualifier. It is generally the case, I think, that it is better for a translator to be native in the language *into* rather than the language *out of* which she translates. In the present instance this is the only possibility, since there are no longer any native speakers of Sanskrit; the next best thing would be a Hindi speaker (which Ms. Sattar is), since Hindi is is derived from Sanskrit. (Indeed, given the *Paiśācī* connection, the rhythms of Hindi might be even closer to the original than the rhythms of Sanskrit.) But a well-educated young Indian woman of the merchant class (the appropriate class to translate this merchant text; again, this describes Ms. Sattar) speaks English from birth, though such a woman, when educated in India rather than in England or America, retains certain deep native rhythms even in her English fluency. She also brings a native understanding of the substance of the text, of the way things smell and taste and sound in India, of the lay of land in which the text was written. This gives Arshia Sattar the inside track against any potential British or American competitors, over and above her particular advantage over Tawney/Penzer (and our good fortune in her) in that she is still alive, while they are long dead.

Finally, the selection. It is a Good Thing to have the whole translation of a great text made available for scholarly use, but there are things that a good selection can do that the full translation cannot. First of all, you can read it all. Who among us has read the entire *Mahābhārata*, or, for that matter, the entire Tawney/Penzer translation of 'The Ocean of Story'? Second of all, you can carry it around with you, take it to the beach, read it in the bathroom, give it as a present to your friends (especially if it has the democratic pricing of a Penguin; the Tawney/Penzer appeared in a magnificent elitist edition that bibliophiles bought, often never even cutting the pages). You can assign it to your students to read. More important, perhaps, the accessibility of a good, readable selection enables the text to enter into conversation with other texts in our contemporary tradition, a tradition which, in this Kali Yuga of mass culture, regards anything over 350 pages as 'heavy'. And, finally, a *good* selection—and this is a very good selection—allows even those few scholars who have the time, drive, leisure, and motive to read the original, enables even them to see the patterns and structures of the text that the full rendition obscures. Arshia Sattar has struck a perfect balance, including enough of the frame story so that we never lose sight of the structure of the work as a whole, but never allowing it to overwhelm the human detail of the individual stories contained within that frame; including enough of the famous stories so that we do not miss any of our old favourites, but also ferreting out enough obscure stories so that we learn something new on every page. She has somehow managed to reduce the length of the text without in any way reducing its texture or its total effect.

So we are triply in Ms. Sattar's debt for the translation.

As for her introduction, it is a masterful scholarly

achievement, full of wit and insight. It presents the reader with everything that anyone should know about the text, as well as with a great deal that the reader will enjoy knowing but might not necessarily need to know, and might not be told about by less imaginative scholars than Ms. Sattar. Ms. Sattar treats the Orientalists gently but mockingly, and judiciously doles out credit and blame in reviewing the use of the text as one of the foundation stones of the great Teutonic (and Finnish) edifice of Western folklore. She invokes the metaphor of the onion to illuminate the elusive nature of Indian storytelling, a metaphor all the more apt since anthropologists have used the onion to describe the Self in India, in contrast with the Western idea of the Self as an artichoke, in which you throw away the leaves and get down to the heart. For what should anyone have in the heart but a good story? Ms. Sattar also brilliantly employs the metaphor of the Moebius strip to explain the convolutions of the frame story—the leaves of the artichoke, it I may mix both metaphors and cultures. And she concludes her introduction by inviting us to drown with her in the ocean of stories. Who could refuse? Who, having read this far, will put the book down? What more can I say? You have a wonderful swimming companion. Dive in.

Wendy Doniger

Massachusetts
March 1994

Kathāpīṭha

May Śiva the blue-throated one, he who is ensnared by Pārvatī's noose-like glances, grant you prosperity.

May Gaṇeśa, who brushes away stars when he dances at twilight and who creates new ones from the spray of his trunk, protect you.

I worship the Goddess of Speech who is the light that illuminates everything, and here compose this collection of verses which are the essence of the *Bṛhatkathā*.

This book is exactly like the one from which it has been taken although the language has been modified so that this book is shorter. As far as possible, the connections between the stories have been maintained and the essence of the stories has been preserved. I have not undertaken this project out of a desire for fame as an original teller of tales. Rather, I have done this so that this vast web of stories, so different and so varied, be remembered.

Puṣpadanta And Mālyavān Are Cursed

Himavat is famous as the king of all mountains and is the dwelling place of *kinnaras, gandharvas* and *vidyādharas*, so glorious that Bhavānī, the mother of the three worlds, was born as his daughter. Himavat's mighty northern summit, with peaks that soar thousands of miles into the sky, is known as Kailāsa. Kailāsa laughs, 'Even Mt. Mandara did not become white when the ocean was churned[1], but I? I have become so without any effort!' Śiva, who is Pārvatī's beloved and the teacher of all living beings, lives on Kailāsa with *gaṇas, vidyādharas* and *siddhas* at his service. The new moon shines through Śiva's matted locks and joyfully turns the eastern peaks yellow in the twilight. Śiva pierced the heart of the demon Andhaka with his spear[2], but he pulled out the spear that had pierced the heart of the earth. The marks of Śiva's toe nails are reflected in the crest jewels of the gods and the demons as if he had blessed them with crescent moons.

One day, when Śiva and his beloved sat alone, she pleased him by singing hymns of praise. He placed her on his lap and said, 'What can I do that will make you happy?' and Pārvatī replied, 'Tell me a story that is new and amusing.' 'What is there about the past, the present and the future that you do not already know?' asked Śiva. But Pārvatī remained adamant, having become stubborn and wilful because of Śiva's affection and admiration.

Śiva wanted to keep Pārvatī happy and so he told her a short story about herself. 'Once Brahmā and Viṣṇu arrived at the foot of Himavat to visit me but instead saw a huge *liṅgam* of flame in front of them. One of them went up the *liṅgam* and the other went down but neither of them could reach its end and so they propitiated me with penance and austerities. After a while, I appeared before them and offered them boons. Brahmā demanded that I become his son and for his insolence he is no longer worthy of worship. Viṣṇu, on the other hand, begged that he be always devoted to me and as a result, he was embodied in you and became mine. You are that god, the all-powerful energy of the world. You were my wife in a previous birth as well.'

When Śiva finished this story, Pārvatī asked, 'How was that?' and Śiva replied, 'It happened a long time ago. Prajāpati Dakṣa had many daughters and you were one of them. He gave you to me in marriage and gave his other daughters to Dharma and the other gods. On one occasion, he organized a huge sacrifice and invited all his sons-in-law. For some reason, he left me out and when you asked him why I, your husband, had not been invited, he said, "Your husband wears a necklace of skulls. How can I invite him to an auspicious sacrifice?" His words pierced your heart like a poisoned needle and in a rage you said, "My father is a villain. I can no longer endure a body that is born from him!" and then, my beloved, you sacrificed your body. I was so angry that I destroyed Dakṣa's sacrifice.

'Then you were reborn as the daughter of Himavat the mountain, as the moon springs from the ocean. Remember how I came to these snowy mountains to perform austerities and how your father appointed you to serve me because I was his guest? The god of love was sent here to get a son from me to fight the demon Tāraka[3]. He was burned to ashes when he pierced me with one of his arrows at a vulnerable moment. Then I was won over by your penance and I agreed to your proposal of marriage for my own benefit, dear one.

'That is how you were my wife in a previous birth. What else can I tell you?' concluded Śiva. But Pārvatī flew into a rage and said, 'You are so deceitful! You have not told me a good story even though I asked for one! You worship Sandhyā and carry Gaṅgā on your head and care little for me!' Śiva promised to tell her a truly wonderful story and she calmed down. Pārvatī ordered that no one was to enter the room where they were seated and placed Nandi as a guard at the door.

Śiva began to speak. 'The gods are always happy and humans are always unhappy. But the adventures of divine people are amusing and so I will tell you tales of the *vidyādharas*.' Even as Śiva began the story, one of his favourite retainers, Puṣpadanta, the best among the *gaṇas*, arrived there. Nandi, who was guarding the door, did not let him enter the room. Puṣpadanta wondered why he was forbidden entry for no apparent reason. He was very curious and used his magic powers to slip through the door. He overheard the wonderful adventures of the seven *vidyādharas* that Śiva the trident-bearer, was narrating to his wife.

Puṣpadanta in turn told these stories to his wife, Jayā the door-keeper, for who can hide wealth or a secret from a woman? Jayā was filled with wonder and repeated the tales to Pārvatī. How can women be expected to restrain their speech? Pārvatī was enraged and accosted her husband, 'You did not tell me a story that no one had ever heard before!

Even Jayā knows this story!' Śiva discovered what had happened through his powers of prescience and explained to Pārvatī, 'Puṣpadanta heard this story when he entered the room with his magic powers and he then repeated it to his wife. No one else has heard it.' But Pārvatī grew even more angry and summoned Puṣpadanta.

As Puṣpadanta stood trembling before her, she cursed him to become a mortal for his disobedience. She also cursed Mālyavān, the *gaṇa* who tried to intercede on Puṣpadanta's behalf. The two retainers and Jayā fell at Pārvatī's feet and begged her to place a limit on the curse. Finally, the goddess spoke. 'There is a *yakṣa* named Supratīka who was turned into the *piśāca* Kāṇabhūti by Kubera's curse. He now lives in the Vindhya forests. When you see him and remember your origins, when you tell him this story, Puṣpadanta, you will be freed from the curse. And when Mālyavān hears the story from Kāṇabhūti, Kāṇabhūti's curse will end. Mālyavān will be released from his curse when he makes this story famous in the world.' As she finished speaking, the *gaṇas* disappeared as quickly as a flash of lightning disappears from before one's eyes.

In time, Pārvatī was filled with compassion for the cursed *gaṇas* and asked Śiva, 'Where have Puṣpadanta and Mālyavān been born on earth?' 'Beloved, Puṣpadanta has been born as Vararuci in the city of Kauśāmbī and Mālyavān has been born as Guṇāḍhya in Supratiṣṭha,' answered Śiva even as he experienced a momentary twinge of sadness as he recalled his two beloved servants.

Śiva and Pārvatī continued to live in happiness among the pleasure palaces of Kailāsa that were built from the wood of the *kalpavṛkṣa*, the wishing tree.

Puṣpadanta Becomes Vararuci And Learns The Vedas

Puṣpadanta wandered the earth as the mortal Vararuci, also known as Kātyāyana. When he had perfected his knowledge of the sciences and after he had served King Nanda as a minister, he grew weary of that kind of life and set off to visit the shrine of the goddess Durgā. Durgā was pleased with his penance and directed him in a dream to visit Kāṇabhūti in the forests of the Vindhyas.

Vararuci wandered through the Vindhya forests which were teeming with apes and tigers but had no human habitation and no water. At length, Vararuci came upon a *nyagrodha* tree and near it, he saw the *piśāca* Kāṇabhūti, himself like an enormous *sāla* tree, surrounded by hundreds of other *piśācas*. When Kāṇabhūti saw Vararuci, he rose and touched his feet. Vararuci sat next to him and said, 'You are obviously a person of good breeding. How have you become like this?' Because Vararuci had shown him such courtesy and affection, Kāṇabhūti said, 'I do not know how this happened to me but I will tell you what I heard from Śiva himself in the cremation ground at Ujjayini. Listen.

'When the goddess asked Śiva "How come you are so fond of skulls and spend so much time in cremation grounds?" Śiva answered, "Long ago, at the end of the *kalpa*, when the world was submerged in water, I pierced my thigh and let fall a drop of blood. When the blood touched the water, it turned into an egg. Puruṣa arose from the egg and from him, I generated Prakṛti of further creation. Thence arose the Prajāpatis who then created other beings. That is why, my dear, Puruṣa is known as the grandfather of the world. But after Puruṣa had created the moving and the unmoving things he became arrogant and I had to cut off his head. I undertook a mighty vow to atone for that, which is why I carry skulls and spend time in cremation grounds. The world itself is like a skull and sits in the palm of my hand. The two skull-shaped halves of the world are the earth and the sky."

'I was very curious about Śiva's story and wanted to hear more and so I lingered in the cremation grounds. I heard Pārvatī ask her husband, "When will Puṣpadanta return to us?" Śiva pointed to me and replied, "That *piśāca* you see over there was a *yakṣa* who used to be Kubera's retainer. He had a friend, a *rākṣasa* named Sthūlaśiras. Kubera did not like the fact that the *yakṣa* kept the company of *rākṣasas* and so he turned him into a *piśāca* and banished him to the

Vindhya forests. But his brother Dīrghajaṅgha fell at Kubera's feet and begged to know when his brother's curse would end. Kubera said that when the *piśāca* heard the *Bṛhatkathā* from Puṣpadanta who was also under a curse, and when the *piśāca* told that story to Mālyavān, he and the two *gaṇas* would be freed from their respective curses. Remember, my dear, you had fixed the same end to the *gaṇas* curses."

'When I heard that, I was overjoyed and came to this forest. I knew that I would be free of the curse when Puṣpadanta arrived,' said Kāṇabhūti. At that very moment, Vararuci remembered his origins and spoke as if he were waking from a deep sleep, 'I am that same Puṣpadanta. Listen to the story from me.' When Vararuci had finished relating the seven great stories in seven hundred thousand verses, Kāṇabhūti said, 'You are the very incarnation of Śiva. No one else knows this story. Thanks to you, the curse is already beginning to leave my body. If I am worthy of it, tell me your story from the moment of your birth, so that I can be further purified.' Kāṇabhūti bowed before him and Vararuci then told the *piśāca* his story from the moment of his birth in great detail. The story went like this.

'In Kauśāmbī, there lived a Brāhmin named Somadatta who was also known as Agniśikha. His wife, Vāsudattā, was the daughter of a divine seer. She was born on earth as the result of a curse. As the result of my own curse, I was born the son of Somadatta and Vāsudattā. My father died when I was very young, but my mother supported me with her hard work when I was growing up.

'One day, two Brāhmins covered with the dust of a long journey arrived at our house and asked to stay the night. While they were there, we heard the sound of a large drum. It made my mother think of her dead husband and as she sobbed she told me that my father's friend, the actor, was probably performing nearby. I volunteered to go and find out what was happening. "I will re-enact the whole performance for you, including the speeches," I said. When the two Brāhmins heard this, they were amazed but my mother said to them, "Don't doubt what my son is saying. He can repeat anything that he hears once." The Brāhmins recited a *pratiśākhya* to me to test my skill and I repeated it to them, syllable for syllable. The two Brāhmins and I went to the play and when we returned home, I re-enacted the whole performance for my mother. Once they were sure that I could really repeat anything after only one hearing, the Brāhmin named Vyāḍi humbly told my mother this story.

"In the city of Vetasā, there were two Brāhmin brothers, Devasvāmī and Karambhaka, who loved each other very much. I am the son of one of them and Indradatta here is the son of the other. It so happened that my father died and his brother followed soon after. Then our mothers died of grief and though we had become orphans, we still had a great deal of wealth. We decided to propitiate Kārtikeya with austerities in order to acquire knowledge.

"Kārtikeya appeared to us in a dream and told us to go to Pāṭaliputra, the city of King Nanda, where a Brāhmin named Varṣa would teach us everything. We left for Pāṭaliputra immediately but when we arrived there and made enquiries, people told us that there was a stupid Brāhmin named Varṣa in the city. Full of curiosity we went to Varṣa's house and found that it was in a terrible state. It was shaky, with cracked walls and a roof that afforded no shelter at all. It had become like an anthill for mice had ridden it full of holes. Indeed, it looked like the place where misfortune had been born.

"We saw Varṣa meditating outside and so we approached his wife who welcomed as with the honour due to guests. Her body was covered with dirt and her clothes were in tatters. She looked like the embodiment of poverty, drawn to that terrible place by her virtue. We bowed before her and told her about our search, including the reports about her husband's stupidity that we had heard. 'Children, what is there for me to be ashamed of? Come, I will tell you the whole story,' and that virtuous lady told us the following tale.

'An excellent Brāhmin named Śaṅkarasvāmī lived in this city and he had two sons, my husband and his brother,

Upavarṣa. My husband is foolish and poor, while his brother is exactly the opposite. Upavarṣa appointed his wife to look after his brother's house. In the rainy season, Brāhmin women make cakes in the shape of a *liṅgam* which taste disgusting. They are offered to Brāhmins to remove the discomfort of bathing in cold weather as well as the fatigue of bathing in the hot weather. But Brāhmins refuse to accept them because it is a repulsive practise. The *liṅgam* cake was given to my husband as an offering by my sister-in-law and he accepted it and brought it home. When I scolded him, he was deeply ashamed of his stupidity.

'He then went to worship at the feet of Kārtikeya who was pleased with his austerities and enlightened him with all the different kinds of knowledge. "You may reveal these when you meet a Brāhmin who can remember anything that he hears once," he said and my husband came home happily. Since then, he has remained immersed in meditation, repeating the name of god. You must find someone who can remember anything after hearing it only once and bring him here. Then your desire will definitely be fulfilled.'

"When we heard this story, we gave Varṣa's wife a hundred gold pieces to relieve her poverty and left the city. Since then, we have wandered the earth and had not found anyone with this talent until we came to your house today. Now that we have found this boy, let us take him with us so that we can acquire knowledge." My mother said, "I cannot doubt what you have said since it coincides with what I know. Long ago, when my son was born, a voice rang out from the sky, 'Behold this boy who will be able to remember anything that he hears only once. He will gain knowledge from Varṣa and will bring a new grammar into the world. He will be called Vararuci for only that which is excellent will interest him.' Ever since my son has grown up, I have been worrying day and night about where this teacher, Varṣa, might be. Now that I have heard your story, I am relieved. Take him with you and treat him like your brother."

'Once they had my mother's permission to take me away, the two Brāhmins were very happy and the night passed quickly for them. Vyāḍi gave my mother some money so that she could prepare a feast and quickly invested me with the sacred thread so that I could learn the Vedas. I tried to control the sadness that I felt on leaving my mother, but she cried copiously. Knowing that Kārtikeya's blessings had borne fruit, we left the city immediately. Soon we arrived at the house of my teacher, Varṣa. He, too, believed that I represented the physical embodiment of Kārtikeya's grace.

'The next day, our teacher sat down on sanctified ground and made us sit in front of him. He uttered the syllable *Om* in what sounded like a divine voice and at that moment, the Vedas and all the sacred knowledge that accompanied them flooded into his mind and he began to teach us. I learned everything after hearing it only once, Vyāḍi after hearing it twice and Indradatta after hearing it three times. All the Brāhmins of the city, who had never heard anything like this before, gathered around and watched with their mouths hanging open. They praised Varṣa and bowed before him. All of them, including Upavarṣa, had a great celebration in the city of Pāṭaliputra. Even King Nanda was impressed with Kārtikeya's favour and filled Varṣa's house with all kinds of wealth.

How The City Of Pāṭaliputra Was Founded

Vararuci continued his story in the forest and Kāṇabhūti listened intently.

'One day, after the recitation of the Vedas had been completed and the daily rituals had been performed, we asked our teacher, Varṣa, "How did this city become the home of wealth and learning?" He replied, "Listen and I will tell you the story.

"Where the Gaṅgā leaves the hills, there is a pilgrimage spot called Kanakhala. It lies at the point where the stream was brought down from Mt. Uśīnara, in the cleft made by the divine elephant, Kāñcanapāta. Once a Brāhmin from the south came there with his wife to perform penance. Three sons were born to them and in the course of time, the Brāhmin and his wife died. The three sons then went to the city of Rājagṛha to acquire knowledge. But even when they had learned everything, they were not satisfied and decided to go to the shrine of Kārtikeya in the south.

"They reached Cincini on the seashore and went to live in the house of a Brāhmin named Bhojika. Bhojika gave them his three daughters in marriage as well as all his wealth. Then, since he had no other children, Bhojika retired to the banks of the Gaṅgā to meditate and perform austerities.

"Once there was a terrible drought which caused a great famine. The three Brāhmins fled the area abandoning their virtuous wives, since concern for the families never touches the hearts of cruel men. When the women learned that the middle sister was pregnant, they sought shelter in the house of Yagnadatta who was their father's friend. Despite the terrible conditions under which they had to live, each one of them remained attached to her own husband, for women from good families do not forget their wifely duties even in adversity.

"Soon, the middle sister gave birth to a son and all three women vied with each other to shower him with affection. It so happened that once Śiva was wandering through the air at the time with Pārvatī on his lap. When Pārvatī saw the little boy she was filled with compassion and said to Śiva, 'Look, how attached those three women are to that boy! They rest all their expectations for the future in him! Let it happen so that he is able to look after them now, even though he is a child.' Śiva, the giver of boons, said to his beloved, 'This child is dear to me because in his last birth he and his wife were devoted to me. He has been born on earth to reap the fruit of his past austerities. His wife has been reborn as the princess Pāṭalī, daughter of King Mahendravarmā and in this life too, she will be his wife.'

"Then Śiva addressed the three women in a dream. 'Name this young boy Putraka. Every day when he wakes from sleep, you will find one hundred thousand gold pieces under his pillow. When he grows up, he will be a king.' The next morning, the boy awoke and the women found the gold pieces under his pillow. They were very pleased that their vows and prayers had borne fruit. With all that gold, Putraka soon acquired a large treasure and became a king, for the best fortune is the fruit of austerities.

"One day, Yagnadatta said to Putraka privately, 'Your father and uncles went away to another place because of a famine. You must start giving alms and wealth to Brāhmins so that your elders hear about it and return to the city. Listen and I will tell you the story of Brahmadatta.

'Long ago, King Brahmadatta lived in Vārāṇasī. One night, he saw a pair of swans flying through the air. They shone like gold and were surrounded by hundreds of white swans so that they looked like a streak of lightning in the midst of white clouds. The king was so desperate to see the golden swans again that he lost all interest in the usual pleasures of royalty. After consulting his ministers, he built a beautiful lake, a place where all living things could co-exist without fear of injury. Soon, the two swans that had so captivated him, arrived there and settled at the lake. When they had become tame, the king asked them about their golden plumage. They replied in human tongue, "We were crows in our last birth. One day, when we were fighting over the remains of the offering in the Śiva temple, we fell into the sacred pot and as a result, we have been born as swans with a memory of our previous birth." The king was able to admire them for as long as he wanted and was very pleased. Therefore, if you make a proclamation like King Brahmadatta did about a huge donation, you will be reunited with your father and uncles.'

"The three Brāhmins heard about Putraka's incredible distribution of gifts and arrived in his city. They were given much wealth and were reunited with their wives. It is quite astonishing that even after going through such adversity, those who are blind and undiscerning do not change their essentially wicked nature. Those three Brāhmins soon began to covet the kingdom for themselves and decided to kill

Putraka. They deceived him with plans of a pilgrimage and led him to the temple of Durgā.

"The three Brāhmins had already stationed assassins inside the inner chamber of the temple and they told Putraka to enter alone. When he saw the assassins, Putraka asked, 'Why do you want to kill me?' and the men told him that they had been hired by his father and two uncles. Putraka kept his wits about him and when he saw that the killers had been mesmerized by the goddess Durgā, he said to them, 'I will give you this valuable ornament if you leave me alone. I will keep your secret and go far away from here.' The killers took the jewel and lied to Putraka's elders that he had been killed. The three Brāhmins started for the city eager to take over the kingdom, but when they reached the city they were executed by Putraka's ministers for treason. How can the ungrateful ever prosper?

"In the meantime, Putraka, true to his word, entered the forests of the Vindhyas, thoroughly disillusioned with his own family. As he wandered through the forest, he saw two young men engaged in fierce hand-to-hand combat. He stopped and asked them who they were. 'We are the sons of the *asura* Maya and are fighting over our inheritance. A pot, a staff and a pair of shoes will go to whichever one of us is stronger.' Putraka was puzzled by this, but he smiled and asked why those objects were so precious. The young men said that the pot produced whatever food could be imagined, that whatever was written with the staff would become a reality and the shoes allowed the wearer to fly through the air.

"Putraka said, 'What is the use of fighting? These objects should go to the one who runs the fastest.' The two foolish fellows ran off in an attempt to obtain the magical objects while Putraka put on the shoes and flew into the air with the staff and the pot. In a flash he was far away. When he saw the beautiful city of Ākarṣikā, he came down from the sky. 'Courtesans are deceitful, Brāhmins behave like my father and uncles, and merchants are greedy for wealth. Whose house can I possibly stay in?' he wondered. Soon, he came upon an old derelict house and inside it, saw an old woman. He gave her a gift and began to live there with the old woman who looked after him respectfully.

"One day, the old woman spoke affectionately to Putraka. 'Son, I am concerned that you do not have a wife worthy of you. The king of this city has a young daughter named Pāṭalī and she is protected like a precious jewel in the innermost chambers of the palace." As Putraka listened to the old woman with his ears wide open, the god of love entered his heart through the unguarded path provided by his open ears. Putraka decided to see the young woman without delay and that very night, flew through the air with the help of the magic shoes. He entered the palace through a window that was as high as a mountain peak.

"There, in the secret inner chambers, he saw Pāṭalī lying asleep, caressed by moonlight. While Putraka stood there wondering how he should wake her, he heard a man singing outside. 'If he wakes the beauty while she sleeps in a secret place and if he embraces her even as she reproaches him gently when she opens her eyes, he will accomplish the goal of his life.' Taking courage, Putraka embraced the princess with trembling limbs and she awoke. When she saw Putraka she was both shy and curious, and her conflicting emotions made her glance at his face and then look away. Immediately, the couple went through the *gandharva* marriage ceremony and as they talked, they found their love growing while the night faded away. In the last watch of the night Putraka left his new wife, who already felt the pain of separation at his absence, and returned to the old woman's house.

"Every night, Putraka went to and from the palace in this manner until one day, Pāṭalī's guards found evidence of the secret meetings. They reported the matter to the king and a woman was appointed to secretly watch the inner chambers that night. When Putraka fell asleep beside his beloved, the woman marked his garment with red lac and in the morning, told the king what she had done. The king's spies found Putraka in the old woman's house, identifying him by the red mark on his clothes.

"Putraka was led into the presence of the king, but he put on his magic shoes and flew into the air. He reached Pāṭalī's apartments and said, 'Get up! We have been discovered and we must escape with the help of the magic shoes.' He picked her up in his arms and flew away. They alighted near the banks of the Gaṅgā and Putraka refreshed his weary beloved with food from the magic pot. When Pāṭalī saw the powers of the pot, she begged Putraka to show her more. With the magic staff, Putraka drew out a well-fortified city. He ruled the city and when he had become a powerful king, he conquered his father-in-law's lands and ruled over the whole of the earth that is surrounded by oceans. This is the city that along with its citizens was produced by magic. It is called Pāṭaliputra and is the home of wealth and learning."

'When Varṣa told us this wonderful story, Kāṇabhūti, it lingered in our minds for a very long time.'

Upakośā And Her Suitors

When Vararuci had finished telling this diversionary tale, he went back to the main story that he had been telling Kāṇabhūti in the forests of the Vindhyas.

'While I lived with Vyāḍi and Indradatta, I gradually learned all the sciences and grew into adulthood. Once, when we had gone to watch the celebrations during the festival of Indra, we saw a young girl who was beautiful enough to be the weapon of the god of love. I wondered who she was and Indradatta told me that she was the daughter of Upavarṣa and that her name was Upakośā. She had also made enquiries about me through her friends and when it was time for her to go home, she was deeply disturbed. She took my heart with her, bound in the web created by the loving glances she threw in my direction. Her face was like the full moon, her eyes like the blue lotus, her arms slim and graceful like lotus stalks. Her breasts were full, her neck long and slender and her lips like coral. She was even more beautiful than Lakṣmī. She was like the love god's treasure trove of beauty!

'My heart had been pierced by the arrows of love and that night, I could not sleep, thirsting for her red lips. When I finally fell asleep at the end of the night, I saw a woman in white garments who said to me, "Upakośā was your wife in your previous birth. She recognizes merit and virtue and will take no one other than you as a husband. You have nothing to worry about, my son, for I am Sarasvatī. I reside in your body at all times and I cannot bear your unhappiness." After saying this, she disappeared.

'Encouraged, I went and stood under the young mango tree that grew near my beloved's house. Her friend came to me and said that Upakośā had developed a fierce attachment to me. When I heard this, my unhappiness doubled and I said, "How can I marry Upakośā unless she is given to me willingly by her family? Death is better than dishonour. Make your friend's feelings known to her elders and we can expect a fortunate outcome from that. Dear friend, go and tell her family and save our lives." The friend went and told Upakośā's mother everything. The mother told her husband Upavarṣa who told his brother Varṣa who approved of the marriage. Varṣa sent Vyāḍi to bring my mother from Kauśāmbī for the wedding. We were married with all the appropriate rites and ceremonies and I lived happily with my wife and my mother.

'In the course of time, the number of Varṣa's students increased greatly and among them, one was a dull-witted fellow called Pāṇini. He grew tired of serving our teacher and so the teacher's wife sent him away. But Pāṇini still thirsted for knowledge and so he went to the Himalayas to perform austerities and propitiate Śiva. Because of his penances, he acquired a new grammar that is the source of all knowledge. He came back and challenged me to a debate and we argued for seven whole days. On the eighth day, when he had all but defeated me, a huge *Omkāra* from Śiva himself resounded through the heavens. That sound established the new grammar on earth and all of us who had been defeated by Pāṇini were regarded as fools.

'I was full of despair and decided to leave the city. I gave the merchant Hiraṇyagupta money to run my house and told Upakośā that I was going to the Himalayas to propitiate Śiva with austerities and fasts. Upakośā stayed at home and bathed in the Gaṅgā and performed all the fasts and rituals every day, for she was anxious to see me succeed. One day in the spring time, Upakośā went down to the Gaṅgā to bathe. Even though she was pale and thin like the new moon, she was still beautiful and capable of attracting admiring glances from men. That day, she caught the eye of the king's chief domestic priest, the city magistrate and the prince's secretary. The moment they saw her, they fell victim to the arrows of love. For some reason Upakośā took a long time over her bath that day. As she was returning home, the prince's secretary detained her roughly. However, she spoke to him calmly, "Dear one, I want this as much as you do. But I am the daughter of a respectable family and my husband is away. I cannot behave like this in public. If someone were to see us, our plans would meet with failure. Come to me during the first watch of the night of the Spring festival, when all the citizens are distracted." When she promised this, he let her go.

'She had hardly gone a few steps when her path was blocked by the priest. She set up a similar meeting with him for the second watch of the night of the Spring festival. He was persuaded to let her go, but that poor trembling woman had gone only a little further when the magistrate stopped her. With the third man, she made an appointment for the third watch of the same night. Fortunately, she was able to get away from him, too, and she reached home shaking with fright. She told her servants about the appointments that she had made. "It is better for a woman from a good family to die when her husband is away rather than to fall prey to the lustful glances of other men," she thought and her mind turned to me. She spent the night fasting and cursing her beauty.

'The next day, she sent one of her maids to the merchant Hiraṇyagupta to ask for some money so that she could honour the Brāhmins. He came to her in private and said, "Make love to me and I will give you the money that your husband left with me." She realized that the merchant was a wicked man and that she had no witness for the deposit that her husband had left with him. Even though she was overcome with grief at her plight, she made an appointment with the merchant for the last watch of the night of the Spring festival and he went away satisfied.

'Upakośā had her maids prepare a mixture of lampblack, oil and sweet perfumes in a large vat. She dipped four rags into the mixture and made her servants make a huge trunk which could be locked from the outside. On the night of the Spring festival, the prince's secretary arrived during the first watch, dressed in his best clothes. He entered the house without being seen and Upakośā said to him, "You cannot touch me before you have a bath. Go into that room and bathe." The foolish man was led into a dark inner chamber by the maids. They took off his jewels and his fine clothes, even his underclothes and gave him a single rag to wear as an undergarment. They rubbed the villain from head to toe with the mixture of lampblack and oil, pretending that they were using a perfumed ointment. While they rubbed it into his every limb, the second watch of the night arrived and with it the priest.

'The maids said to the secretary, "The king's priest who is a good friend of Vararuci has arrived. Quickly, climb into this," and they pushed the confused man, naked as he was, into the trunk and fastened it securely from the outside. The priest was also led into the dark inner chamber for a bath. The maids stripped him of his clothes and ornaments and rubbed him down with the oily mixture. When he was wearing nothing but the rag, the third watch of the night arrived, bringing the magistrate with it. The maids used his arrival as a means to scare the priest and pushed him into the trunk just like the prince's secretary before him. They locked him in the trunk and brought the magistrate into the room on the pretext of giving him a bath. They rubbed him with the oily mixture as they had done the others and also gave him a small rag to cover himself. While this was happening, the merchant arrived in the last watch of the night. The maids pushed the magistrate into the trunk and locked it from the outside, scaring him with the idea that the merchant might see him. Even though they could touch each other, the three men in the trunk dared not speak and cowered there in terror as if they were preparing themselves for a life in a dark dungeon.

'Meanwhile, Upakośā brought a lamp and led the merchant into the inner room. She said, "Give me the money that my husband left with you." When the wicked merchant saw that the room was empty, he said, "I told you I would give you the money that your husband deposited with me." As soon as he said that, Upakośā addressed the men hidden in the trunk, "Dear gods, listen to the words of Hiraṇyagupta." Then she blew out the lamp and the merchant was covered with the lampblack by the maids on the pretext of preparing him for a bath. Then, since the night was over, the maids took him by the neck and pushed him out of the house. Covered only by a small rag and the oily mixture, Hiraṇyagupta went home slowly, bitten by dogs along the way. He was so embarrassed that he was unable to look his servants in the face as they washed the oil off his body. Truly, the path of the wicked is not smooth.

'In the morning, Upakośā went to King Nanda's palace along with her maids without telling her parents. She told the king that the merchant Hiraṇyagupta was trying to take away her husband's money. The king had the merchant brought in so that he could investigate the matter. The merchant said, "Sir, I have nothing that belongs to this woman." Upakośā replied, "I have witnesses to prove this. When my husband left, he placed the family deities inside this trunk. This merchant admitted that the deposit was with him in front of them. Bring the trunk here and ask them yourself." The king was astonished to hear this and ordered that the box be fetched. Immediately, it was brought in carried by several men.

'Upakośā said, "Gods, tell the truth about what the

merchant said and then you can return to your own homes. If you do not tell the truth, I will either burn the box or open it up here." The men inside were terrified and replied that it was true, that the merchant had admitted that he had Vararuci's money in their presence. At a loss for words, the merchant confessed to his crime. But the king was overcome with curiosity and after asking Upakośā, had the box opened by breaking the lock. The three men were dragged out looking like lumps of darkness and it was with great difficulty that the king and his ministers recognized them. Everyone started laughing and the king, still curious, said to Upakośā, that virtuous woman, "What is all this?" and she related the whole story. All the people in the assembly praised Upakośā saying, "The behaviour of women from good families is above reproach because of their inherent virtue."

'Those four men, who had coveted another man's wife, were banished from the kingdom and their wealth was confiscated. How can the wicked ever prosper? The king affectionately made Upakośā his sister and gave her lots of wealth. Then she was allowed to return home. When Varṣa and Upavarṣa learned what had happened, they too, praised Upakośā and the whole city sang her praises.

The Two Nandas

'Meanwhile, Kāṇabhūti, I was performing severe penances on the snowy peaks of the Himalayas and had managed to propitiate Śiva, the giver of boons. He revealed Pāṇini's grammatical treatise to me and, following his command, I completed it. Then I returned home suffused with Śiva's grace, not feeling the strain of my efforts at all. I honoured my mother and the elders and heard about Upakośā's wonderful exploits. I was filled with joy and amazement as well as with affection and respect for my wife.

'Varṣa wanted me to recite the new grammar, but before I could do so, Kārtikeya revealed it to him. Vyāḍi and Indradatta asked Varṣa what fee they should pay him for teaching them and Varṣa replied, "Give me ten million gold pieces." The two Brāhmins came to me and said, "Dear friend, let us go and ask King Nanda for money to pay our teacher's fee. No one else can give us this amount of gold but Nanda since he has nine hundred and ninety million gold pieces. He made Upakośā his sister a while ago and that makes you his brother-in-law. We should get something from him on account of that." So the three of us set off for King Nanda's camp in Ayodhyā.

'The moment we arrived there, the king died. The kingdom was plunged into grief and we were very dismayed. At once, Indradatta, who was skilled in *yoga*, said, "I will enter the dead king's body. Let Vararuci present the request to me and I will give him the gold. Vyāḍi can guard my body until I return." Indradatta entered Nanda's body as planned and the king was restored to life. All his subjects celebrated and rejoiced. While Vyāḍi guarded Indradatta's body in an empty temple, I went to the king's palace.

'After honouring Yogananda, as Indradatta was now called, I asked for my teacher's fee. The king ordered Śakatāla, one of Nanda's ministers, to give me ten million pieces of gold. But when the intelligent minister saw the dead king come to life and a petitioner immediately gratified, he guessed that something was amiss, for nothing is unknowable to the wise. "I will do so, sir," he said but he thought to himself, "Nanda's son is still a boy and our kingdom is surrounded by enemies. I will let this person remain on the throne for now." He then ordered all the dead bodies to be burned at once. Indradatta's body was burned along with the others and Vyāḍi was thrown out of the temple where he had been guarding it.

'While this was going on, the king was insisting that the gold pieces be handed over to me quickly but Śakatāla was still suspicious and said, "The citizens are still rejoicing and celebrating. Let the Brāhmin wait a short while and I will give the gold to him myself." Suddenly Vyāḍi appeared in Yogananda's court shouting, "A Brāhmin who was in a yogic state left his body which has been burned by force while you were celebrating." Yogananda was greatly distressed when he heard this. And that crafty minister Śakatāla, once he realized that the body had been burnt and that the imposter was trapped, gave me the gold pieces.

'Yogananda spoke to Vyāḍi quietly in anguished tones. "Even though I was born a Brāhmin I have now become a Śūdra. What use have I of this regal splendour which is now all mine?" But Vyāḍi reassured him with some timely advice. "Śakatāla has understood what has happened. You should now watch him carefully for he is a great minister and will destroy you when it suits him. He will make Candragupta, the son of the previous Nanda, king. Make Vararuci your chief minister at once so that your kingship will be firmly established through his unique wisdom." Saying that, Vyāḍi went away to deliver the fee to his teacher and Yogananda appointed me his chief minister.

'I said to the king, "Even though your status as a Brāhmin has been snatched away irrevocably, your kingship will not remain unchallenged as long as Śakatāla retains his position. We must think of a way to destroy him." As soon as he heard my advice, Yogananda threw Śakatāla and his one hundred sons into a dark dungeon for the crime of burning a Brāhmin alive. One small plate of gruel and one small bowl of water were given to Śakatāla and his sons every day in the dungeon. Śakatāla said to his sons, "It is hard even for one man to live on this, let alone so many. So let one of us, the one who will take revenge on Yogananda, eat and drink every day." His sons replied, "You are the only one capable of that. Therefore, you should eat and drink." Revenge against one's enemies is dearer than life to the resolute. So Śakatāla would eat and drink every day, for those who are determined to succeed are cruel. As he watched his sons in the throes of death in that dark dungeon, Śakatāla thought, "A man who seeks his own advancement should not act rashly towards the powerful without first understanding their nature and gaining their confidence." Śakatāla's one hundred sons died before his eyes and he alone remained alive, surrounded by their skeletons.

'Meanwhile, Yogananda's rule took firm root. Vyāḍi came to see him after delivering the teacher's fee to Varṣa and said, "May you rule long, my friend! I came to say goodbye for I am going to perform austerities in an unknown place." Yogananda begged in a voice thick with tears, "Do not desert me. Stay here and enjoy the pleasures of my kingdom." "King, the body is destroyed in a moment. Which wise man would immerse himself in these fleeting pleasures? Material wealth is an illusion that does not deceive the wise," said Vyāḍi and left.

'Then, Kāṇabhūti, Yogananda went with me and his entire retinue to Pāṭaliputra, his capital city, to enjoy its pleasures. As Yogananda's minister, I became a prosperous man and lived there for a long time with my mother and elders, cared for by Upakośā. Propitiated by my austerities, the Gaṅgā gave me great treasures every day and Sarasvatī in embodied form told me what I needed to do.'

Śakatāla's Revenge

Vararuci continued his story.

'Gradually, Yogananda became a slave to his passions and like a rutting elephant, could not be restrained. Who would not be intoxicated by the sudden acquisition of abundant wealth? I began to think, "The king shows no restraint and by taking care of his affairs I am neglecting my own duties. I should release Śakatāla so that he can help me. Even if he is my enemy, he cannot do me much harm while I am still in office." I took the king's permission and pulled Śakatāla out of the dark dungeon, for Brāhmins are always compassionate. Śakatāla realized that it would be hard to defeat Yogananda while I, Vararuci, was still the king's chief advisor and so he decided to bide his time until the right moment came, like the reed that bends with the current of the river. At my request the cunning Śakatāla resumed his duties as chief minister.

Vararuci's Wisdom Causes Trouble

'On one occasion, Yogananda saw a hand rise out of the Gaṅgā with all five of its fingers pressed together. He summoned me at once and asked, "What is this?" I pointed two fingers towards the hand and it disappeared. The king was astonished and asked me again what this meant. "What can five united men not achieve in this world?" is what the hand meant to say by showing you its five fingers together. And I showed it two fingers indicating that even when two men are of the same mind, anything can be achieved. The king was very pleased when I solved this difficult riddle, but Śakatāla was disturbed because he realized that my superior intelligence would make his task difficult.

'One day Yogananda saw his chief queen leaning out of the window and talking to a Brāhmin guest. The king flew into a rage over this insignificant incident and ordered the Brāhmin's execution, for jealousy clouds a man's judgement. As the Brāhmin was being led to the execution ground, a dead fish in the marketplace laughed out aloud. This was reported to the king who immediately postponed the execution and asked me why the fish had laughed. "I will consider the matter and let you know," I said and left. As I was thinking over the problem alone, Sarasvatī came to me and said, "Hide in this palm tree tonight and you will learn the reason for the fish's laughter."

'I hid in the palm tree that night and saw a terrifying *rākṣasī* passing by with her young sons. When her children asked for something to eat, the *rākṣasī* said, "Tomorrow I will give you the flesh of a Brāhmin. He was not killed today." "Why wasn't he killed today?" they asked and she replied, "Because a dead fish laughed when it saw him!" "Why did the fish laugh?" asked the sons and the *rākṣasī* said, "All the queens are immoral, for there are men dressed as women in the harem and today, an innocent Brāhmin is being put to death! The fish knew about this and so it laughed. Dead spirits enter the bodies of all kinds of creatures so that they can laugh at the foolishness of kings." I left after I had heard this and in the morning, I told the king the reason for the fish's laughter. The men disguised as women were discovered in the harem and the king was impressed with my wisdom and pardoned the Brāhmin.

'When I witnessed this incident and other similar things as well as the king's lack of restraint, I was very disenchanted. At that time, a painter arrived at Yogananda's court. He made a portrait of Yogananda's chief queen that was so lifelike that it lacked only speech and movement. The king was delighted and gave the painter lots of money. He had the painting hung in his living quarters. One day when I was in the king's chambers, I realized that the picture did not have all the auspicious marks of a queen. Knowing where these marks should be, I assumed that there should be one on her waist, near her jewelled belt, I painted it in because I wanted the picture to be complete and then I left.

'Yogananda entered soon after my departure and noticed the new mark. He asked his attendant who had painted it in and was told that I had done it. "This mark is on a concealed part of the queen's body, a part that no one sees but me. How did this Vararuci know where it was? I am sure he has seduced my entire harem. That is how he knew about those men disguised as women!" raged the king as he grew more and more angry. Foolish men often construct such coincidences. He summoned Śakatāla and said, "You must have Vararuci put to death for seducing the queen." "As you command," said Śakatāla. But as Śakatāla left, he thought, "I do not have the power to kill Vararuci for he has an uncanny intellect. Besides, he rescued me from adversity. I will hide him and win him over to my side."

'Śakatāla told me about the king's irrational anger including the fact that he wanted me killed. "I will kill someone else so that a death is reported. But you must hide in my house and protect me from the king's anger." So I hid in his house and another man was killed in my place. Śakatāla's display of political acumen moved me to say to him with affection, "You are an excellent minister for not putting me to death. I cannot be killed for I have a *rākṣasa* for a friend. I have only to think of him and he will appear to devour the whole world. This king Yogananda is actually a friend of mine named Indradatta. He is a Brāhmin and should not be killed either." "Show me the *rākṣasa,*" said Śakatāla. The *rākṣasa* appeared as soon as I thought of him and Śakatāla saw him and trembled with fear. Then the *rākṣasa* disappeared and Śakatāla asked me how I had made friends with him. I told him how it had happened.

'There was a time when the chiefs of police would die one after another as they made their nightly rounds of the city. So Yogananda made me the police chief and as I walked through the city at night, I saw a *rākṣasa* wandering around. He asked me who the best looking woman in the city was. I started to laugh when I heard the question and replied, "Fool! Any woman is beautiful to the one who loves her!" "You are the only man to have beaten me," he said and I knew that I had escaped death by answering the question. The *rākṣasa* spoke again. "I am pleased with you. I will be your friend and will appear whenever you think of me." He disappeared and I returned to the palace. That is how the *rākṣasa* became my friend and my ally in times of need."

'Śakatāla then asked me to show him the goddess Gaṅgā in human form and she also appeared when I thought of her. When we had pleased her with hymns of praise, she disappeared and Śakatāla became my devoted ally. One day, when I was weary of being in hiding, he said to me, "You are so wise and know so much. How can you be depressed by these circumstances? You know that kings are whimsical and that soon you will be acquitted of all charges. Listen to this story.

The Wise Minister

"Long ago, King Ādityavarmā had a wise minister named Śivavarmā. It came to pass that one of the queens became pregnant and the king asked the harem guards, 'Two years have passed since I entered the harem. Tell me, how can this queen be pregnant?' The guards insisted that no other man had entered the harem except for the minister Śivavarmā who came and went without restriction. When the king heard that, he thought, 'This man is a traitor but if I kill him publicly, I will be criticized.' Ādityavarmā sent Śivavarmā to Bhogavarmā, the king of Sāmanta, the neighbouring state, on some pretext. He sent a messenger after him with a letter to Bhogavarmā asking him to have Śivavarmā killed. A week after the minister's departure, the pregnant queen was caught by guards while trying to escape with a man dressed as a woman. When this was reported to Ādityavarmā, he was filled with remorse. 'Why did I have a minister like Śivavarmā killed without reason?' he wailed.

"In the meantime, Śivavarmā reached the court of Bhogavarmā and the messenger with the letter came soon after. As fate would have it, Bhogavarmā told Śivavarmā in secret about the order to kill him. That excellent minister said to the king, 'You must put me to death otherwise I will kill myself.' Bhogavarmā was amazed and said, 'What is all this? I will curse you unless you explain it all to me!' and Śivavarmā replied, 'The land in which I am killed will not receive rain for twelve years.' Bhogavarmā began to worry. 'That wicked Ādityavarmā desired the ruin of my kingdom. He could have had this minister killed by secret assassins. We must not kill this minister and must also prevent him from killing himself.' Bhogavarmā then appointed guards for Śivavarmā and immediately sent him out of the country. Śivavarmā returned home alive because of his cunning and his innocence was proved without any effort from him, for goodness is always rewarded. In the same way, your innocence will also be established. Until then, Kātyāyana, stay in my house. This king will also regret what he has done." And I spent the days hidden in Śakatāla's house.

Betrayal Of Friends

'Then, Kāṇabhūti, it so happened that one day one of Yogananda's sons, Hiraṇyagupta, went hunting. He got carried far away into the forest alone because his horse was swift and soon, the day came to an end. He climbed up onto a tree for the night. At the same time, a bear who was being chased by a lion also climbed onto the same tree. When he saw how frightened the prince was, he spoke to him in a human voice. "Don't be afraid. You are my friend," and promised not to harm him. The prince trusted the bear and fell asleep, but the bear stayed awake. Soon, the lion spoke to the bear from under the tree. "Throw this man down to me and I will go away." But the bear replied, "Wicked one! I will not cause the death of my friend." Soon after, the bear fell asleep and the prince woke up. This time, the lion addressed the prince. "Man, throw me the bear." The prince was concerned for his own safety and wanted to please the lion and so he tried to push the bear out of the tree. Fortunately, the bear woke up and saved himself from falling. The bear cursed the prince to become insane for betraying a friend. The curse, the bear said, would not end until another person guessed what had transpired.

'When the prince reached his home the next morning, he went out of his mind. Yogananda was plunged into grief when he saw his son in that condition and cried, "If only Vararuci were alive! He would know what to do! How I regret my haste in having him killed!" Śakatāla heard this and at once thought, "Here is an opportunity to bring Kātyāyana out of hiding! He is a proud man and will not continue in the king's service after this insult. Then the king will put his faith in me." He begged the king's pardon and spoke, "Do not grieve, sir. Vararuci is alive. Have him summoned at once."

'I was brought before Yogananda and saw the prince in his terrible state. Through Sarasvatī's grace I was able to tell them exactly what had happened. "Sir, he has betrayed a friend," I said. At once, the prince was released from his curse and he praised and thanked me. The king asked me how I had known what had happened and I replied, "The wise infer everything through the sharpness of their mental faculties by observing and interpreting signs. I knew what had happened in this case in the same way as I knew about the auspicious mark on the queen." The king was deeply ashamed when he heard my words. I considered myself fortunate that I had cleared my name and went to my own home without accepting the king's gifts. To the wise, a good reputation is the greatest wealth.

Vararuci Retires To The Forest

'When I got home, all my servants stood weeping before me. I was disturbed by this and then Upavarṣa explained, "When Upakośā heard that the king had put you to death, she jumped into the fire and your mother died of a broken heart." I was overcome with grief and fell to the ground like a tree that has been knocked over by the wind. I released some of the sorrow I felt through loud lamentations, for who would not be scorched by the grief born from the loss of dear ones? "The only permanent thing in this world is impermanence. Since you know the world is an illusion, why are you fooled by it?" Varṣa said to me. With the help of this and other philosophical beliefs, I was able to recover my equilibrium. Disgusted with the world, I renounced all my worldly bonds and took solitude as my companion before going into the forest to practise asceticism.

The Story Of Cāṇakya

'The days passed and once, a Brāhmin from Ayodhyā came to where I was performing ascetic practices. I asked him how Yogananda was and full of sorrow, he said to me, "After you left Yogananda, Śakatāla realized that his chance for revenge had finally arrived. While he was plotting Yogananda's death, he came across a Brāhmin named Cāṇakya digging up the earth in his path. Śakatāla asked him what he was doing and Cāṇakya replied, 'This *darbha* grass pricked my foot and so I am digging it up.' Śakatāla realized that a man whose anger could produce such determination for revenge was the right man to use in his plot against Yogananda.

"After finding out his name, Śakatāla said, 'I appoint you to perform the thirteenth day rituals at the house of King Yogananda. I will pay you one hundred gold pieces as a fee and you shall be the chief priest. Meanwhile, come to my house,' and he took Cāṇakya with him. On the day of the ceremony, the king had no objection to Cāṇakya presiding over the rituals, and the Brāhmin took the seat of honour. But another Brāhmin, Subandhu, wanted the honour for himself. Śakatāla took the dispute to the king and Yogananda decided that Subandhu should preside over the ceremonies. Śakatāla reported the king's order to Cāṇakya, trembling with fear. 'It was not my fault,' he said. Cāṇakya blazed with anger and as he undid his topknot, he took a solemn vow. 'I will destroy this Nanda in seven days. When my anger has been appeased, I will retie my hair.' Yogananda was enraged when he heard this but Cāṇakya slipped away from there and took refuge in Śakatāla's house.

"Śakatāla secretly procured for him all that he required and Cāṇakya went to a secret place and performed a magic ritual. Yogananda developed a burning fever and died within seven days. Śakatāla killed Yogananda's son Hiraṇyagupta and installed the previous Nanda's son, Candragupta, as king. Candragupta made Cāṇakya, equal in wisdom to Bṛhaspati the adviser of the gods, his chief minister. Now that he had taken his revenge, Śakatāla felt that his life's goal had been accomplished and he went into the forest to grieve for his sons."

'Kāṇabhūti, I was very upset when I heard this story from the Brāhmin, for I realized that everything in the world is impermanent. That is when I came to Durgā's temple and it is through her grace that I have met you, dear friend, and have been able to recall my past birth. I have told you this great story through my divine knowledge and now that my curse is at an end, I will try and leave my body. You must remain here until a Brāhmin named Guṇāḍhya who has forsaken the use of Sanskrit, Prākrit and his own language, arrives with his students. He was an excellent *gaṇa* named Mālyavān and was cursed by Pārvatī when he tried to defend me. When you tell him this great story that was first narrated by Śiva, both you and he will be released from your curses.'

Vararuci set out for the sacred *āśrama* of Badarikā in order to give up his body. As he went along the banks of the Gaṅgā, he saw a hermit who lived only on fruit and vegetables and whose hand had been pricked by a blade of *kuśa* grass. Vararuci was curious about the state of the hermit's ego and so he turned the hermit's blood into sap. When the hermit saw the sap flowing from his hand he was filled with pride and exclaimed, 'I have attained perfection!' Vararuci smiled and said to him, 'I turned your blood into sap and I see, hermit, that you have not renounced your ego at all. Ego is a terrible obstacle in the path of true knowledge and without true knowledge, no one can be liberated, not even after a hundred vows. Those who desire true liberation are not distracted by the impermanent pleasures of heaven. So renounce your ego and strive for true knowledge.'

The hermit honoured Vararuci as his teacher and bowed to him. When he had taught the hermit this lesson, Vararuci proceeded towards the tranquil *āśrama*. He sought refuge with the goddess who would help him give up his body. She revealed her true form to him and gave him the secret for final renunciation that arises from the fire. Vararuci consumed his body with that meditation and reached his goal while Kāṇabhūti waited in the Vindhya forests for his encounter with Guṇāḍhya.

Mālyavān Becomes Guṇāḍhya And Has Many Adventures

Mālyavān, now named Guṇāḍhya, wandered the earth as a mortal. He had served king Sātavāhana and, in his presence had renounced Sanskrit and two other languages. Then he came to the shrine of Durgā for peace of mind. He took the goddess' advice and went to visit Kāṇabhūti where he remembered his origins as if waking from a deep sleep. He spoke in the *Paiśācī* language that was different from the three languages that he had forsworn and after telling Kāṇabhūti his name, Guṇāḍhya said, 'Quickly tell me the wondrous tale that you heard from Puṣpadanta so that we can both escape from our curses, my friend.' Kāṇabhūti was overjoyed and bowed before him. 'I will tell you the story. But first, I am consumed with curiosity about you so tell me about your adventures from the day of your birth.'

Guṇāḍhya began to speak. 'In the country of Pratiṣṭhāna, there is a city named Supratiṣṭha. Somaśarmā, a truly worthy Brāhmin, lived there and he had two sons, Vatsa and Gulma. He also had a third child, a daughter named Śrutārthā. In time, Somaśarmā and his wife died and the two sons were left to look after their sister. She suddenly became pregnant and Gulma and Vatsa began to suspect each other because no other man had passed that way. Śrutārthā understood what was going through their minds and said to her brothers, "Don't be suspicious of each other. Listen to my story.

"Kīrtisena is a young *nāga* prince, the son of Vāsuki's brother. He saw me one day as I was going to bathe. He fell in love with me and, after telling me his name and lineage, he married me by *gandharva* rites. He is a Brāhmin and he has made me pregnant." When they heard their sister's story, Vatsa and Gulma said, "How can we believe you?" Śrutārthā silently called the *nāga* prince to mind. He appeared at once and said to Vatsa and Gulma, "It is true that I am married to your sister. She is an *apsaras* who has fallen to earth because of a curse. And you are on earth for the same reason. A son will be born to her here and then you will all be released from your curses," he said and disappeared.

'In a few days, a son was born to Śrutārthā. I am that son, my friend. At the moment of my birth, a voice rang out of the sky and announced "This boy is a Brāhmin and the incarnation of a *gaṇa*. His name shall be Guṇāḍhya." The curse placed on my mother and uncles was over and they died, leaving me bereft. I overcame my grief and though I was still a child, I relied on my own capacities and went south to acquire knowledge. In time, I learned all the sciences and became famous. I returned to my own country to display my talents.

'When I entered the city of Supratiṣṭha with my students after a long absence, I saw a wonderful sight. In one place, the *Sāma Veda* was being chanted as it should be; in another place Brāhmins debated the interpretations of the Vedas; in a third place gamblers sang the praises of gambling in the following words, "He who knows the art of gambling has a treasure in his hands"; and in a fourth place, a group of merchants stood together discussing the art of making money in business. One of the men in the group began to tell others a story.

The Mouse Merchant

"It is not a great accomplishment if a thrifty man acquires wealth. I have become prosperous despite having absolutely nothing to start with! My father died while my mother was pregnant and my wicked uncles took away all my mother's wealth. Afraid for the safety of the child in her womb, my mother went to live in the house of Kumāradatta, my father's friend. I, who was to be the instrument of her future maintenance, was born there and my mother supported me by doing menial work. Though she was poor, she was deserving of charity and she persuaded a teacher to instruct me in writing and mathematics. 'You are the son of a merchant and you must go into business. There is a famous merchant called Viśākhila in this city and he is very rich. He gives money to men from good families as business capital. Go, and ask him to help you,' said my mother.

"I went to see Viśākhila and the moment I entered his house, I heard him say angrily to a merchant's son, 'See that dead mouse on the floor? A clever man would be able to use even that as a means to increase his wealth. I gave a stupid fellow like you many *dīnārs* and, far from multiplying the money, you have not even been able to keep what you had!' When I heard that, I said to Viśākhila, 'I will take this mouse from you as the capital investment for my business.' I then picked up the mouse, wrote him a receipt for it and left. The merchant burst out laughing and put the receipt in his safe.

"I sold the mouse as cat food to another merchant for two handfuls of gram. I ground up the gram and taking a pot of water, I went and stood under a shady tree at the crossroads outside the city. I offered the gram and the water humbly to a group of tired wood-carriers. Each of them gratefully gave me two pieces of wood. Next, I took the wood to the market and sold it. I used a little part of the money from the sale to buy some more gram and in the same way, the next day, I got some more wood from the carriers. I did this every day and soon had enough capital to buy all the wood-carriers' wood for three days. Suddenly, there was a great shortage of wood because of some heavy rains and I was able to sell my wood for a lot of money. I opened a shop with that money and became a merchant. I soon became a rich man through my own ability and acumen. I ordered a mouse of gold to be made and returned it to Viśākhila who gave me his daughter in marriage. I am known in the world as 'Mouse' because of this story. I have become a rich man without having had any money at all!"

'The other merchants were very impressed with this story, for who would not marvel at pictures suspended without walls?

The Brāhmin And The Courtesan

'Somewhere else, a Brāhmin who was a chanter of the *Sāma Veda* had been given eight gold pieces. A libertine gave him the following advice. "As a Brāhmin, you make enough to eat. You should use this money to learn the ways of the world." The foolish fellow asked, "Who will teach me?" "The courtesan named Caturikā. Go to her house," replied the libertine. "What shall I do when I get there?" asked the Brāhmin and the libertine told him to give the courtesan the gold and plead with her to teach him.

'The Brāhmin immediately went to the courtesan's house. She came to welcome him and he sat down in front of her and gave her the gold, stammering, "Teach me the ways of the world for this fee." The people who were sitting there began to laugh and the Brāhmin, after thinking a little, put his hands together into the shape of a cow's ear so that they formed a pipe. Like an idiot, he began to chant the *Sāma Veda* in a high-pitched voice and all the libertines gathered to laugh at him.[4] "How did this jackal get in here?" they asked. "Quickly, give him the half moon on his throat!"[5] The Brāhmin thought that the 'half moon' was the crescent-shaped arrow and afraid of having his head cut off, ran out of the house shouting, "I have learned the ways of the world!"

'The Brāhmin went back to the libertine who had sent him to the courtesan and told him what had happened. The libertine said, "When I used the word *sama* I meant that you should coax Caturikā into teaching you. Why did you bring the Veda into this? I suppose that people who fill their heads with Vedas have no room in them for anything else!" Laughing, he went to the house of the courtesan and said to her, "Give that two-legged animal his money back." She, too, burst into laughter and returned the money and the Brāhmin went home, as happy as if he had been born again.

'I saw more and more wondrous sights with each step that I took and finally, I reached the king's palace which rivalled Indra's in splendour. I entered with my students ahead of me so that they could announce my arrival, and then I saw the mighty king, Sātavāhana seated on a jewelled throne along with Śarvavarmā, surrounded by his ministers as Indra is surrounded by immortals. I blessed him and sat down. The king honoured me and the ministers sang my praises. "Sir, this man is famous on earth for his knowledge and is skilled in all the sciences. Because of that, he is named Guṇāḍhya, 'he who is rich in accomplishments', and the name fits him well." Pleased with this introduction, the king honoured me further and made me a minister. I lived there in happiness, took a wife, looked after the king's affairs and taught my students.

The Garden Of The Goddess

'One day, when I was wandering along the banks of the Godāvarī, I saw a beautiful garden known as Devīkṛti, which means 'created by the goddess'. It was an extremely beautiful place, like Indra's pleasure garden, Nandana, here on earth. I asked the caretaker of the garden how it had come to be there and he replied, "Sir, according to the story that the old people tell, there was once a Brāhmin who had taken a vow of silence and abstention from food. He came here and made this wondrous garden with a temple for the gods within it. All the people gathered to see it and when they asked the Brāhmin for his story again and again, he said, 'I was born a Brāhmin long ago in a place called Bharukaccha on the banks of the Narmadā. I was very lazy and nobody would give me alms even though I was poor. I left my home and gave up the life I had known. I wandered from one sacred pilgrimage spot to another and finally, I reached the shrine of Durgā. When I saw the goddess I thought to myself, "People please this goddess, this giver of boons, with offerings of animals. Why don't I, stupid animal that I am, kill myself here?" I picked up a sword to cut off my head and at that moment, the goddess herself spoke, "Son, you have attained perfection. Do not kill yourself, stay here with me!" So because of the goddess' boon, I acquired a divine nature and from that day on, my hunger and thirst have been destroyed.

'One day, the goddess said to me, "Son, go to Pratiṣṭhāna and plant a beautiful garden there," and she gave me celestial seeds with which to do it. I came here and made this beautiful garden with her power. You must look after this garden," he said and disappeared. That is how this garden was made by the goddess long ago."

'I was filled with wonder after hearing this story and went home slowly.'

How Sātavāhana Got His Name

Kāṇabhūti then asked Guṇāḍhya, 'Why was the king called Sātavāhana?'

'Listen and I will tell you,' said Guṇāḍhya.

'There was once a very powerful king called Dīpakarṇi. He loved his wife Śaktimatī more than his own life. One day when she was sleeping in the pleasure garden, she was bitten by a snake and died. The king, even though he did not have a son, took a vow of celibacy. Śiva came to him in a dream and said, "When you are out hunting you will see a boy riding a lion. Take him home with you. He shall be your son!" The king was filled with joy when he woke up and recalled his dream.

'One day while the king was out hunting, he was led far way into the forest. In the middle of the day, the king saw a young boy on the shores of a lake of lotuses, shining like the sun and sitting astride a lion. The lion was thirsty and set the boy down by the lakeshore. The king remembered his dream and killed the lion with a single arrow. The lion shed his body and took the form of a man. "What is all this?" cried the king in astonishment. The man said, "King, I am a *yakṣa* named Sāta and I serve Kubera. Long ago, I saw the daughter of a *ṛṣi* as she bathed in the Gaṅgā. She also fell in love with me and we got married by *gandharva* rites. Her relatives were very angry when they found out and they cursed us to become lions because we had followed our own desires. They said that her curse would end when she gave birth to a son and that mine would end when I was killed by your arrow. So we became a pair of lions. In time, she became pregnant and died after giving birth to this boy. I brought him up on the milk of other lionesses. Today, your arrow has freed me from my curse. I give you my son for this was ordained by those *ṛṣis* long ago." The *yakṣa* named Sāta disappeared and the king took the boy home. Because he had ridden upon Sāta, he was named Sātavāhana, "he who has Sāta as his mount". In time, Sātavāhana was placed on the throne and when King Dīpakarṇi retired to the forest, Sātavāhana became king of the earth.'

Now that he had answered Kāṇabhūti's question which had interrupted him in the middle of his story, the wise Guṇāḍhya returned to the main story that he was telling.

Guṇāḍhya's Adventures Continue—The King Learns Sanskrit

'One day during the Spring festival, King Sātavāhana came to the garden made by the goddess. He wandered around for a while, like Indra in Nandana and then entered the waters of the lake to amuse himself with his wives. He sprinkled them with water from his cupped hands and they splashed back at him. He looked like a male elephant being splashed by his female herd. His wives were beautiful, their eyes reddened by the collyrium which had run into them, their faces streaked with water, their wet clothes clinging to their bodies and revealing their curves. They splashed him with enthusiasm and the king made them flee into the nearby bushes. As the wind in the forest strips the leaves and flowers from the creepers, the king wiped the red marks from his wives' foreheads and stripped them of their ornaments.

'One of the queens, tired from the weight of her breasts, her body as tender as a flower, wearied of the game. She could not bear to be splashed any more and said to the king, "Don't splash me with water!" The king immediately ordered some sweets to be brought there and the queen burst out laughing as she said, "What are we going to do with sweets in the lake? I told you not to splash me with water. Don't you know how the words *'ma'* and *'udaka'* combine?[6] How can you be so stupid and not know this simple grammatical rule?" The king was deeply ashamed as his retinue burst into laughter when the queen, who was well-versed in grammar, pointed out his mistake. He gave up his games in the water and slipped away to his chambers full of despair, his pride crushed. He turned away from food and other pleasures and sat lost in his own thoughts, still as a picture. He would not answer even when he was spoken to. He realized that his only hope was to seek refuge either in learning or in death. He flung himself onto the couch and lay there, burning with shame and grief. His retainers had no idea what had happened when they saw him in that condition.

'When Śarvavarmā and I heard about the king's depression the day had almost ended. We saw that the king was still upset and called for one of his servants, a man named Rājahaṃsa. We asked him about the king and he replied, "I have never seen the king like this before. The other queens angrily told me that he had been shamed in public by that daughter of Viṣṇuśakti who pretends to be a scholar." Śarvavarmā and I were very disturbed when we heard this and tried to think of a solution. "If the king is suffering from a bodily disease, we can call the doctor but if it is something else, how can we find out the cause? He has no enemies and his subjects are loyal to him. Where did this sudden depression come from?" As we talked the matter over, the wise Śarvavarmā said, "I know the reason. The king is ashamed of his ignorance. He often calls himself stupid and craves knowledge. I have known this for a long time. We have just been told that the reason for his present condition is the insult from the queen." Śarvavarmā and I turned the problem over in our minds all through the night and in the morning, went to the king's apartments.

'No one was allowed to enter his chambers but I got in with some difficulty and Śarvavarmā slipped in quietly behind me. I sat down next to the king. "Why are you so depressed?" I asked but the king remained silent. Then Śarvavarmā said these extraordinary words. "Sir, a long time ago you told me to make you a learned man. Last night I cast a spell to produce a dream. In my dream, I saw a lotus that had fallen from the sky. A divine young man opened it and a celestial woman came out wearing white clothes. I saw her enter your mouth and then I woke up. I believe that woman was Sarasvatī and that she entered your mouth in her visible form." The king broke his silence when he heard this and he turned to me and said, "How long will it take a diligent man to become learned? How soon can you make me a scholar? All this wealth and power is useless to an idiot, like ornaments on a log!"

'"Sir, it usually takes a man twelve years to learn grammar, the door to all knowledge. But I will teach you that in six years," I said. Śarvavarmā was suddenly smitten with jealousy. "How can someone used to such an easy life endure hardship for such a long time? I will teach you all this in six months!" he vowed to the king. I was angry when I heard his impossible claim and said, "If indeed you teach the king all this in six months, I will renounce Sanskrit, Prākrit and the vernacular languages, in fact, all the three kinds of language that humans use!" "And if I don't accomplish this then I will carry your shoes on my head for twelve years!" countered Śarvavarmā. We both left but the king felt reassured because he knew that he would get what he wanted from one of us.

'Śarvavarmā realized that his promise was impossible to keep and he told his wife what he had done. "You have no other option but to appeal to Kārtikeya in a terrible situation like this," she said. Without eating, Śarvavarmā set out in the last watch of the night for Kārtikeya's shrine. I heard about this through my spies and in the morning, I reported it to the king. "What will happen now?" he wondered. A loyal noble named Siṃhagupta said to the king, "I was very upset when I heard about your terrible state and I went to Durgā's shrine outside the city prepared to offer her my head to secure your happiness. Then a voice came from the heavens and said, 'Wait! The king's wish shall be fulfilled.' So I feel sure that your aim will be accomplished." Siṃhagupta left and the king immediately sent two messengers to Śarvavarmā who, meanwhile, had been observing a vow of complete silence and was living on air at Kārtikeya's shrine.

'Kārtikeya was pleased with Śarvavarmā's physical mortifications and granted him his desire. The king's messengers came back and reported this to the king. He was overjoyed but I was full of despair. We were like the *cātaka* bird and the swan when they see the monsoon clouds, one full of joy, the other sadness. Śarvavarmā who had succeeded because of Kārtikeya's grace, came before the king and taught him all the sciences which presented themselves to him as he thought of them. At the very same moment they were revealed to Sātavāhana, for the pleasure of the gods can accomplish everything.

'The whole kingdom rejoiced when the people heard that the king had become learned and there were celebrations everywhere. Banners danced in the wind and Śarvavarmā was honoured with heaps of jewels. The king bowed before Śarvavarmā and called him his teacher and he was made regent of Bharukaccha on the banks of the Narmadā. Siṃhagupta, the man who first heard the news about Kārtikeya's boon to Śarvavarmā from the messengers, was also honoured and was made equal to the king. The queen, the daughter of Viṣṇuśakti who was the cause of the king's acquisition of knowledge, was raised above the other queens and the king affectionately anointed her with his own hands.

Guṇāḍhya's Vow Of Silence

'Still observing my vow of silence, I attended the king's court one day. A Brāhmin recited a Sanskrit *śloka* that he had composed and the king was able to respond in perfect Sanskrit. The people in the court were overjoyed and the king respectfully turned to Śarvavarmā and said, "Tell me in your own words how Kārtikeya showered you with his grace?" And Śarvavarmā told him the story of how it happened.

'"I took a vow of silence and abstention from food and left this city. When my journey was almost over I fell to the ground in faint, exhausted from my austerities. A man with a spear in his hand came up to me and said, 'Son, get up. Everything will go as you desire.' I felt as if I had been drenched in a shower of nectar as soon as I heard that and I revived, free from hunger and thirst, my health completely restored. I approached the temple burdened by the weight of my devotion and after bathing, I entered the inner sanctum with a feeling of anticipation. Kārtikeya appeared before me and then Sarasvatī entered my mouth in visible form. Kārtikeya recited the *sūtra* that begins 'the traditional doctrine of letters' and I was able to recite the *sūtra* that follows it with an ease and facility not natural to humans. Kārtikeya said, 'If you had not recited this *sūtra,* this grammatical treatise would have been even greater than Pāṇini's. It will now be known as *Kālāpaka,* after the tail of the peacock I ride and also as *Kātantra* because it is so brief,' and Kārtikeya revealed the short treatise on grammar to me.

'"Then Kārtikeya said further, 'Your king was a *muni* named Kṛṣṇa in his previous life. He was the pupil of the great Bharadvāja and was a man of fierce austerities. He fell victim to the arrows of the God of Love and fell in love with a *muni's* daughter who loved him in return. He was cursed by the other *munis* and that is why he is incarnate here on earth. The woman has been incarnated as his wife, the queen. Because Sātavāhana is the incarnation of a great sage, he will attain all this knowledge when he sees you and you bestow it on him. The highest truths are easily learned by men of great souls for they have already acquired knowledge in their previous births. They can recall everything with their powerful memories.' Kārtikeya said this and disappeared. I came out of the temple and the god's servants gave me rice. I set out and though I ate the rice on my journey every day, marvellous as it was, it did not become less." Śarvavarmā ended his story and Sātavāhana was pleased and went to take a bath.

'I was excluded from the proceedings by my vow of silence and so, bowing low to the king (who did not want to let me go) I left the town with two disciples, determined to perform austerities. I arrived at this shrine of Durgā and was directed by the goddess in a dream, so I came into these terrifying forests of the Vindhyas to find you. A Pulinda gave me a hint about a caravan passing this way and somehow, by good fortune, I managed to get here. I saw a huge gathering of *piśācas* and by listening to their conversation from a distance, I was able to learn the *Paiśācī* language which has allowed me to break my vow of silence. I learned that you had gone to Ujjayini and decided to wait until you returned. I honoured you in the fourth language, *Paiśācī*, when I saw you and then I was able to remember my origins. This is the story of my life in this birth.'

Kāṇabhūti said, 'Listen to how I heard about your arrival last night. My friend the *rākṣasa* Bhūtivarmā has divine sight. I went to him in the garden in Ujjayini where he lives and asked him when my curse would end. He said, "We have no powers during the day. Wait here till night falls and I will tell you." I waited there until nightfall. Then I asked him why the *rākṣasas* were rejoicing. Bhūtivarmā replied, "Listen and I will tell you what Siva said to Brahmā. *Yakṣas, rākṣasas* and *piśācas* have no power during the day because of the brightness of the sun and so they enjoy themselves at night. They also have power when the gods are not worshipped and when Brāhmins do not behave appropriately and when humans eat contrary to prescription. They do not go where a man abstains from eating meat and where a woman is virtuous. They do not attack the chaste, the courageous and those who are wise. Go now, for Guṇāḍhya, the means by which your curse will end, has arrived." And so I came here and I have seen you. Now I will tell you the story that Puṣpadanta told me. But I am curious about one thing. Why was he called Puṣpadanta and you Mālyavān?'

Devadatta Becomes Puṣpadanta

Guṇāḍhya said, 'On the banks of the Gaṅgā, there is a Brāhmin settlement called Bahusuvarṇaka. A learned Brāhmin named Govindadatta lived there with his wife Agnidattā who was devoted to him. In the course of time, they had five sons. They were all good-looking boys but they were stupid and they grew up arrogant and proud. One day a Brāhmin named Vaiśvānara, who resembled the god of fire, came to Govindadatta's house as a guest. Govindadatta was not at home and so the guest greeted his sons with respect, but they returned his greetings with laughter. The Brāhmin was so angry that he was about to leave when Govindadatta arrived. He asked the guest the reason for his anger and tried to appease him. But the Brāhmin said, "Your sons have become outcastes because of their stupidity and you have lost your caste by associating with them. I cannot eat in your house for I could not ever purify myself of that!" Govindadatta swore that he would never touch his wicked sons again. His wife, who was a hospitable woman, said the same thing and the Brāhmin was persuaded to be their guest.

'One of the sons, Devadatta, was filled with shame at his father's decision. He decided that his life was worthless if his parents felt like that about him and so he went to the *āśrama* of Badarikā to perform austerities. He first lived on leaves and then only on smoke in an unbroken series of ascetic practices in order to gain Śiva's favour. Śiva was pleased and revealed himself to Devadatta. The young man asked that he be allowed to serve Śiva all the time. "Acquire learning and enjoy pleasures on earth first, then your wish will be fulfilled," Śiva told him.

'Devadatta went as a student to the city of Pāṭaliputra and served the teacher Vedakumbha according to custom. Meanwhile, his teacher's wife was seized with a passion for him and made love to him. Women are always so fickle! So Devadatta gave up his studies which had been corrupted by the god of love and went to Pratiṣṭhāna without delay. There he sought an old teacher, Mantrasvāmī, who had an old wife, and learned all the sciences. When he had finished his studies, King Suśarmā's daughter, Śrī, saw that handsome young man the way the goddess Śrī saw Viṣṇu. Devadatta, too, noticed her standing at a window looking like the goddess of moon roaming through the air in a chariot. The look of love they exchanged was like an unbreakable chain that fastened them to each other. The princess beckoned Devadatta over with one finger and it seemed like a command from the god of love himself. When Devadatta came close, the princess emerged from the women's apartments and threw him a flower that she held between her teeth. He did not understand the sign and went back to his teacher's house wondering what he should do.

'Burning in the fires of love, Devadatta rolled on the ground and couldn't say a word and it was as though he were either deaf or distracted. But his wise teacher recognized the signs of love and asked him what had happened. With great difficulty, he got the story out of Devadatta and said to him, "By throwing down the flower that she held in her teeth, the princess was telling you that you should wait for her at the temple full of flowers called Puṣpadanta. You should go there at once." The young man forgot his grief and went to the temple. The princess came there on the excuse that it was the eighth day of the lunar fortnight and entered the inner sanctum alone to worship the deity. She saw the young man behind the door and he embraced her. "This is odd. How did you understand the meaning of the sign?" she asked and he replied that it was his teacher who had told him what it meant. The princess was enraged and said, "Let go of me! You are an idiot!" and ran out of the temple, afraid that her secret would be discovered. Devadatta also left the temple thinking about his beloved whom he had barely seen. Thereafter, he was so unhappy that he almost died of grief.

'Śiva, who had been pleased with Devadatta before, saw him in that state and ordered his *gaṇa* Pañcaśikha to help him obtain his heart's desire. Pañcaśikha came to Devadatta and consoled him. He made him dress as a woman and himself took on the disguise of an old Brāhmin. They then went together to King Suśarmā and the *gaṇa* dressed as a Brāhmin said to the king, "My son is travelling in another country and I am going to look for him. I want to leave my daughter-in-law in your care." The king was afraid of a Brāhmin's curse and believing that the young man was a woman, he placed him in his daughter's guarded chambers. After Pañcaśikha left, the young man lived in women's clothes and became the confidante of his beloved. One night he revealed himself to the princess and they married each other secretly by *gandharva* rites. When the princess became pregnant, the *gaṇa* appeared when he was remembered and carried them away at night without being seen.

'The next morning, Pañcaśikha stripped Devadatta of the women's clothes that he had been wearing, and dressed himself as before in the guise of an old Brāhmin and went to the king. 'I have found my son, king. Where is my daughter-in-law?' he asked. The king realized that the girl must have run away somewhere at night. Fearing a curse from the Brāhmin, he said to his ministers, "This man is not a Brāhmin. He must be some divine being who has come here to deceive me. These things are known to happen in the world. Listen to this story.

The Story Of King Śibi And The Dove

"In the old days, there was a king named Śibi who was generous, wise, compassionate, resolute and the protector of all creatures. Once, Indra took the form of a hawk to deceive him. He chased Dharma who had turned himself into a dove through magic. Terrified, the dove went to King Śibi for refuge. The hawk spoke to the king in a human voice. 'I am hungry. This dove is my food so release it to me. Otherwise I will die. Where will your justice be then?' Śibi then replied, 'This dove has come to me for protection and I cannot give it up. I will give you any other meat that is equal in weight.' 'If that is so, then I want your flesh,' said the hawk. The king agreed with pleasure. But as he cut off more and more of his own flesh, the dove appeared to get heavier and heavier on the scales. The king then threw his entire body onto the scales and a voice rang out from the sky, 'Bravo! Bravo! This is equal in weight to the dove!' and at that moment, Indra and Dharma threw off their hawk and dove bodies. They were very pleased with Śibi and restored his body to what it had been before. They gave him many boons and blessings and disappeared. In the same way, this is some god who has come to test me," said King Suśarmā.

Puṣpadanta Gets His Name

'Still fearful, Suśarmā addressed the *gaṇa* in the guise of a Brāhmin, falling on the ground before him. "Have mercy! Your daughter-in-law was carried away from here last night by magic even though she was guarded night and day." The Brāhmin took a long time to be convinced of this story and finally said, "Then give your daughter to my son in marriage." The king was still afraid of being cursed and gave his daughter to Devadatta and Pañcaśikha left.

'Devadatta had attained his beloved in public and he flourished in the power and glory of his father-in-law who had no other son. In time, the king appointed his grandson Mahīdhara his successor and retired to the forest. Devadatta also retired to the forest with the princess when he saw that his son was well taken care of. He again worshipped Śiva and by his favour, Devadatta gave up his mortal body and was made a *gaṇa*. Among the *gaṇas,* he was known as Puṣpadanta because he had not understood the sign from his beloved. His wife became the goddess' door-keeper, Jayā.

'That was the story of Puṣpadanta's name. Now listen to my story.

Somadatta Becomes Mālyavān

'I was Somadatta, the son of the same Brāhmin Govindadatta, who was Devadatta's father. I left home for the same reason as Devadatta and went to the Himalayas. I propitiated Śiva with offerings of many garlands. He was pleased and revealed himself to me. I rejected low pleasures and asked for the boon of serving him as a *gaṇa*. Śiva said to me, "Because you have worshipped me with garlands of flowers that grow in the deeper reaches of thick forests that you picked yourself, you shall serve me as a *gaṇa* and your name will be Mālyavān." Then I shed my mortal body and attained the divine state of God's servant. My name was given to me by Śiva as a mark of his favour. Kāṇabhūti, I have again become a mortal because of Pārvatī's curse. So tell me the story told by Śiva so that our curses will end.'

The End Of The Curse

In response to Guṇāḍhya's request, Kāṇabhūti narrated that wonderful tale made up of seven stories in his own language. It took Guṇāḍhya seven years to record the stories in seven hundred thousand couplets using the *Paiśācī* language. The great poet, afraid that the *vidyādharas* would steal his work, wrote the verses in the forest and in his own blood since he did not have any ink. The *vidyādharas, siddhas* and other divine beings came to listen as Kāṇabhūti told the tale. The area where Kāṇabhūti sat seemed as though it was covered with a canopy as the celestial beings hovered in the air above his head. When Kāṇabhūti had told the whole story to Guṇāḍhya he was released from his curse and returned to his home. The other *piśācas* that had accompanied him in his wanderings also ascended to heaven when the story was over.

Guṇāḍhya Writes The Bṛhatkathā

Guṇāḍhya began to think, 'I must spread this great story, the *Bṛhatkathā,* on earth since that is the condition Pārvatī placed for the end of my curse. How shall I make the tale popular? Who shall I give it to?' Guṇāḍhya had two students who had followed him, Nandideva and Guṇadeva. They said, "There is only one place for this great work and that is with Sātavāhana. He is a learned man and he will spread the tale far and wide as the wind spreads the fragrance of flowers." Guṇāḍhya agreed and gave the book to his two virtuous students and sent them to King Sātavāhana. He also went to Pratiṣṭhāna, the Sātavāhana's capital, but he waited outside the city in the garden made by the goddess and arranged to meet his students there.

The students showed the book to Sātavāhana and told him that it was Guṇāḍhya's work. The king was full of contempt when he saw their appearance and heard the *Paiśācī* language, for he had been made proud by his learning. 'Seven hundred thousand verses are proof of accomplishment but this *Paiśācī* language is crude. Besides, the manuscript is written in blood. Throw away this *Paiśācī* tale!' The two students took the book and returned to Guṇāḍhya and told him what had happened. Guṇāḍhya was very depressed, for who would not be upset when rejected by a knowledgeable person?

Guṇāḍhya then went with his students to a hill that was not very far away. It was a deserted but pleasant spot. There, he made a cavity for the sacred fire. One by one, he threw the pages of the book into the fire after he had read them aloud to the birds and the beasts. His students watched him and wept. But he kept one story of one hundred thousand verses, the one about Naravāhanadatta, because his students liked it particularly. While he was reading out and burning that wondrous story, the animals gave up their grazing and came there to listen with tears in their eyes. The deer, the boar, the buffalo and other wild animals came and stood around him in a circle.

In the meantime, Sātavāhana had fallen ill and the doctors said that his illness was due to eating bad meat. When the cooks were scolded, they said that the hunters brought them poor quality meat. When the hunters were questioned, they replied, 'Not far from here is a hill where a Brāhmin reads a page at a time and throws it into the fire. All the animals stand there and listen to him without eating. They do not wander around and graze and so their meat is poor.' The king was curious when he heard this and asked the hunters to lead him there. He saw Guṇāḍhya looking like a forest-dweller with long matted locks, grey like the smoke from a fire. The king recognized him as he sat in the midst of that circle of weeping animals. He bowed to him and asked him how all this had happened. The learned Guṇāḍhya told the king his adventures including the curse and the reason for the great story being on earth in the *Paiśācī* language.

The king realized that Guṇāḍhya was the incarnation of

a *gaṇa* and fell at his feet. He asked for the divine tale that Śiva had narrated. Guṇāḍhya said, 'I have already burnt six tales with six hundred thousand verses. There is only one tale of one hundred thousand verses left. Take that and my students will explain it all to you.' Then Guṇāḍhya bade the king goodbye and shed his earthly body with his yogic powers. Freed from his curse, Guṇāḍhya returned to his celestial home.

The king went back to his own city with the story that Guṇāḍhya had given him. It was called the *Bṛhatkathā* and contained the adventures of Naravāhanadatta. The students, Guṇadeva and Nandideva, were given lands, gold, jewels, mansions and still more wealth. Sātavāhana understood the story with their help and then composed a book called the *Kathāpīṭha* which narrated how the story came to be told in the *Paisacī* language. That story was so interesting that people forgot about the tales of the gods. First it spread in the city and then it spread throughout the three worlds.

Kathāmukha

This immortal story came from the mouth of Śiva, arising from his love for Pārvatī, just as the nectar of immortality arose when the ocean was churned by Mt. Mandara. Those who drink from the immortality of this story shall have their obstacles removed and shall be prosperous and Śiva's grace will bestow godliness on them, even as they live here on earth.

May Śiva's sweat protect you, that water which is fresh from his embrace with Pārvatī and that is Kāma's weapon against Śiva's fiery third eye!

In the kingdom of Vatsa, King Śatānīka ruled wisely and well from his capital city Kauśāmbī. He was descended from the heroic Pāṇḍavas, for he was the son of Janamejaya. Although he had two virtuous wives, the Earth herself and the queen Viṣṇumatī, the king had no sons. One day while he was out hunting, he met the sage Śāṇḍilya who gave him an oblation for his wife to consume and the prince Sahasrānīka was born. King Śatānīka, well-known for his valour, was called by Indra to help subdue the asuras. *He was killed in battle and Sahasrānīka became king. Because of his affection for Śatānīka, Indra invited Sahasrānīka to the great celebration that followed the victory over the* asuras. *When Sahasrānīka saw the beautiful celestial women in Nandana, Indra's paradise, he realized that he should get married. Indra told him that there was already a wife ordained for him since Sahasrānīka was none other than a cursed* vāsu. *His celestial love had also been born on earth as the princess Mṛgāvatī. But when Sahasrānīka was leaving Nandana, he inadvertently snubbed the beautiful* apsaras *Tilottamā by ignoring her and she cursed him to be separated from his beloved for fourteen years.*

Sahasrānīka married Mṛgāvatī and in time, she became pregnant. During her pregnancy, she had the urge to bathe in a tank of blood and while she was bathing, Garuḍa saw her and thought she was a piece of meat and carried her away. He left her on a mountain where she was rescued by an ascetic and her son Udayana was born in a hermitage. When the child was born, a disembodied voice announced that his son would be king of the vidyādharas. *Udayana grew up strong and brave and learned in all the sciences and his mother gave him his father's bracelet to wear. One day Udyana gave the bracelet to a hunter who had saved his life. The hunter sold the bracelet in the city and it was brought to the king's attention. The time for Sahasrānīka's curse of separation was at an end and he went to the mountain hermitage to meet his wife and son. With great joy, he brought them back to Kauśāmbī.*

Udayana was anointed crown prince and Yaugandharāyaṇa, Rumaṇvat and Vasantaka were appointed his ministers. King Sahasrānīka soon retired to the forest and Udayana ruled his kingdom wisely and well for some time. Gradually, he left all the administrative responsibilities to his ministers and began to spend more and more time in the pursuit of royal pleasures like wine, music and hunting. But soon he began to hear about the virtues and beauty of the princess Vāsavadattā and felt that she would be a suitable wife for him. Vāsavadattā's father, King Caṇḍamahāsena, was also interested in Udayana as a son-in-law and decided to take him prisoner so that he would marry Vāsavadattā. Udayana was taken prisoner while he was hunting and the king made him Vāsavadattā's music teacher. Meanwhile, Yaugandharāyaṇa and Rumaṇvat devised a plan to kidnap Udayana and Vāsavadattā so that they could be married, for they were already in love with each other.

When Udayana and Vāsavadattā had run away as a part of his ministers' plan, they were often despondent. On one such occasion, Vasantaka told a story for princess Vāsavadattā's amusement, a story that was funny and included a great many things.

The Courtesan Who Fell In Love

'There is a city named Mathurā, which is the birthplace of

Kṛṣṇa and a famous courtesan, Rūpiṇikā, lived there. Her mother Makaradaṅṣṭrā was an old madame and she appeared like a lump of poison to the young men who were attracted to her charming daughter. One day when Rūpiṇikā went to the temple at the time of worship to perform her duties, she saw a young man from a distance. That handsome young man affected her so deeply that she forgot all that her mother had taught her. She told her maid to urge the young man to visit her house that very day and the maid did as she was instructed. The man considered the invitation and then he said, "I am a Brāhmin named Lohajaṅgha and I have no money at all. What would I do in the house of Rūpiṇikā which is a place that only the rich can enter?" "My mistress does not want your money," replied the maid and Lohajaṅgha agreed to visit the house later.

'Rūpiṇikā was thrilled when she heard from her maid that Lohajaṅgha would come and see her. She went home and kept watch over the road that he would take and soon, Lohajaṅgha arrived. When Makaradaṅṣṭrā saw him she wondered where he had come from. Rūpiṇikā rose and went to welcome Lohajaṅgha herself with great respect. She put her arms around his neck and led him into her private apartments. She was completely overwhelmed by Lohajaṅgha's many virtues and felt that she had been born only to love him. She gave up the company of other men and Lohajaṅgha lived happily in her house.

'Makaradaṅṣṭrā, who had trained many courtesans, was very irritated with these developments and spoke to Rūpiṇikā privately. "Daughter, why do you keep the company of this poor man? A good courtesan would rather touch a corpse than a pauper! What can love possibly mean to a courtesan? Why have you forgotten this basic principle of your trade? The beauty of a sunset lasts only as long as the twilight and so also, the beauty of a courtesan is short-lived. A courtesan should be like an actress and feign love so that she can acquire wealth. Get rid of this poor man before you destroy yourself!" Rūpiṇikā replied in anger, "Stop talking like this! I love this man more than I do my own life! I have enough wealth already, what will I do with more? Mother, you must never speak to me about this again!" Makaradaṅṣṭrā was very angry when she heard her daughter's words and began to think of a way to get rid of Lohajaṅgha.

'One day Makaradaṅṣṭrā saw a nobleman coming down the road. He had lost all his wealth but was surrounded by his retainers who were carrying swords. She rushed up to him, took him aside and said, "My house has been occupied by a penniless lover. Come there today and behave such that he leaves at once. Then you can enjoy my daughter tonight!" The nobleman agreed and went into her house. Rūpiṇikā was at the temple at that time and Lohajaṅgha had gone out somewhere. Suspecting nothing, Lohajaṅgha came home a short while later and at once, the nobleman's servants fell upon him, kicking and beating him all over his body. They threw him into a filthy ditch and Lohajaṅgha escaped from there with great difficulty. Rūpiṇikā was overcome by sorrow when she learned of what had happened. The nobleman saw this and left the way he had come.

'Lohajaṅgha, who had suffered the old woman's intolerable atrocities, went to a pilgrimage spot, ready to give up his life for he could not bear to live without his beloved. He wandered in the desert, his heart burning with anger against Makaradaṅṣṭrā and his skin burning with the heat of the sun. He looked around for some shade but he could not see a single tree. He came upon the carcass of an elephant that had been stripped of all its flesh by jackals. The body was like a shell with only the skin remaining and Lohajaṅgha crawled into it and fell asleep. The breeze blew through the carcass and kept it cool. Suddenly, fierce clouds gathered and the rain began to pour down. The elephant's hide shrank and there was no longer a way out of it. Soon the area flooded and the hide was swept away by the force of the water. It was carried into the Gaṅgā and from there it floated into the ocean. A bird descended from the family of Garuḍa saw the hide and picked it up, carrying it to the other side of the ocean. It ripped it open to eat it but when it saw a man inside, it dropped it right there and flew away.

Lohajaṅgha In Laṅkā

'Lohajaṅgha was roused from his sleep by the bird pecking at the hide and he crawled out of the hole made by the bird's beak. He was astonished to find himself on the far shore of the ocean and was quite sure that he had dreamt everything. Then he saw two terrifying *rākṣasas* who were eyeing him from a distance with fear. They remembered how they had been defeated by Rāma and when they saw that Lohajaṅgha was another mortal who had crossed the sea, their hearts were filled with fear. They discussed the matter amongst themselves and then one of them went and reported the incident to King Vibhīṣaṇa. Vibhīṣaṇa, who had also seen Rāma's power, was equally frightened at the arrival of another human and said to the *rākṣasa*, "Go, my friend, and speak affectionately to that man. Tell him to honour me by coming to my palace."

'The *rākṣasa* cautiously went up to Lohajaṅgha and told him of Vibhīṣaṇa's invitation. Lohajaṅgha accepted calmly and went with the *rākṣasa* to Laṅkā and when he reached there, he was astonished at the number of golden buildings. He entered the royal palace and saw Vibhīṣaṇa who welcomed him. The Brāhmin Lohajaṅgha blessed the king and Vibhīṣaṇa asked him how he had got to Laṅkā. Lohajaṅgha cleverly replied "I am a Brāhmin named Lohajaṅgha and I come from Mathurā. I was very poor and so I went to Viṣṇu's temple and propitiated him with severe penances and fasts. Viṣṇu came to me in a dream and said, 'Go to Vibhīṣaṇa. He is my faithful devotee and he will give you much wealth.' I said that Vibhīṣaṇa lived in a place that I could not reach and then Viṣṇu said, 'You shall see Vibhīṣaṇa today!' When I awoke, I found myself on the other side of the ocean. I have no idea how I got here."

'Vibhīṣaṇa knew that Laṅkā was inaccessible so when he heard Lohajaṅgha's story, he thought to himself, "This man has divine powers!" and he said aloud to the Brāhmin, "Stay here and I will give you lots of wealth!" He placed Lohajaṅgha in the care of some man-eating *rākṣasas* and he sent others to the Svarṇamūla mountain to fetch a young bird born in the family of Garuḍa. He gave the bird to Lohajaṅgha so that he could get used to riding it in anticipation of his long journey back to Mathurā. Lohajaṅgha rode the bird around and rested in Laṅkā for some time, enjoying Vibhīṣaṇa's hospitality.

Why The Ground In Laṅkā Is Made Of Wood

'One day he asked Vibhīṣaṇa why the ground in Laṅkā was made of wood. Vibhīṣaṇa explained, "Listen and I will tell you about this since you are curious. Long ago, Garuḍa, the son of Kaśyapa, was eager to free his mother from slavery to the snakes that she had to endure to fulfil a promise[1]. He wanted to eat something that would increase his strength as he prepared to fetch the elixir which would release his mother. Garuḍa went to his father who said to him, 'Son, there is a huge elephant and a huge tortoise at the bottom of the ocean. They are in this form because they have been cursed. Go and eat them.' Garuḍa brought them out to eat and perched on a branch of the *kalpavṛkṣa*. The branch collapsed under his weight but Garuḍa held it in his beak out of respect for the *Vālakhilyas* who were practising austerities there. Afraid that if he dropped the branch human beings would be crushed, Garuḍa took the advice of his father and put it down in an uninhabited place. Laṅkā was built on that branch and the ground here is therefore wooden." Lohajaṅgha was very pleased with Vibhīṣaṇa's story.

Lohajaṅgha Outwits Makaradaṅṣṭrā

'Lohajaṅgha wanted to return to Mathurā and Vibhīṣaṇa gave him many valuable jewels. Since Vibhīṣaṇa was also a devotee of Viṣṇu who lived in Mathurā, he gave Lohajaṅgha a lotus, mace, discus and conch shell all made of gold to offer to the god. Lohajaṅgha took all that Vibhīṣaṇa had given him and climbed onto the bird that could travel one hundred thousand *yojanas*. He rose into the sky from Laṅkā and crossed the ocean, arriving in Mathurā with no trouble at all. He came down from the air near a deserted monastery outside the city and hid all his jewels there. He tied up the bird and went to the marketplace where he sold one of the jewels. He bought clothes and food with the money and returned to the monastery. He then ate and fed the bird and adorned himself with new clothes, flowers and sweet perfumes.

'When night came, he picked up the lotus, mace, discus and conch shell, mounted the bird and flew to Rūpiṇikā's house. He hovered in the air over the place that he knew so well and made a low sound to attract his beloved who was alone. Rūpiṇikā came out as soon as she heard the sound and saw, hovering in the night sky, a being shining with jewels who appeared to be Viṣṇu. "I am Viṣṇu and I have come here for your sake!" he said and Rūpiṇikā bowed her head and asked for his blessings. Lohajaṅgha came down from the sky and tied up his bird. Then he went with Rūpiṇikā into her private apartments. He stayed with her for some time and then he came out, climbed onto the bird and flew away through the air.

'The next morning Rūpiṇikā maintained a strict silence, thinking, "I am the wife of Viṣṇu. I can no longer speak to mere mortals!" Her mother asked her why she was behaving in this peculiar fashion and after much questioning, Rūpiṇikā placed a curtain between herself and her mother and recounted what had happened the night before and the reason for her silence. Makaradaṅṣṭrā did not believe a word of what her daughter said until that night when she saw Lohajaṅgha arriving on his bird. Early the next morning she went to her daughter, who was still behind the curtain, and said quietly, "Daughter, you have attained the status of a goddess here on earth because Viṣṇu has chosen you. I am your mother in this world! Grant me a favour for having given birth to you. Ask Viṣṇu to take me to heaven now, even in this tired old body."

'Rūpiṇikā agreed and when Lohajaṅgha came to her that night disguised as Viṣṇu, she asked him to fulfil her mother's wish. In the guise of the god, Lohajaṅgha said to his beloved "Your mother is a wicked old woman and I cannot take her to heaven in front of everyone. But the doors of heaven are open on the morning of the eleventh day and many of Śiva's *gaṇas* enter at that time, before anyone else. I can slip your mother in with them if she changes her appearance. Shave her head with a razor so that only five locks of hair are left and put a garland of skulls around her neck. Strip her of her clothes and cover her back with soot and her front with vermilion. Then she will look like a *gaṇa* and I will be able to push her into heaven easily." Lohajaṅgha stayed with Rūpiṇikā a little while longer and then he left.

'In the morning, Rūpiṇikā prepared her mother as she had been instructed and the old woman remained like that all day thinking about heaven. When Lohajaṅgha arrived that night, Rūpiṇikā handed her mother over to him. He took the old woman, naked as she was and made-up as he had directed, climbed onto his bird and flew away. From the air, he saw a huge stone pillar with a disc on top of it in front of a temple. He set the old woman down on top of the pillar. She held onto the disc for support and swayed in the wind like a banner that announced her mistreatment of Lohajaṅgha. "Stay here while I go and bless the world!" he said to her and disappeared.

'Lohajaṅgha saw that a crowd of people had gathered in the temple courtyard to maintain an all-night vigil before the temple festival. Lohajaṅgha addressed them from the sky. "Listen! Today, in this very place, the destructive goddess of smallpox shall fall upon you! Come, take refuge in Viṣṇu!" The people of Mathurā were terrified when they heard this voice from the sky and begged for Viṣṇu's protection and prayed that the calamity should not befall them.

'Lohajaṅgha came down from the sky, took off his godly disguise and slipped, unnoticed, into the crowd. Sitting on top of the pillar meanwhile, Makaradaṅṣṭrā began to worry. "The god has not returned and I have not yet reached heaven!" she thought. She could not hold any longer and began to slip off the pillar. "I am falling! I am falling!" she cried and when the people below heard this, they became hysterical with fear, believing that the smallpox goddess was about to descend on them, just as they had been warned. They began to shout, "Goddess! Do not fall! Do not fall!" The old and the young in Mathurā somehow managed to get through that long night, fearing each moment that the goddess would fall on their heads.

'When the night was finally over and morning came, they saw the old woman on top of the pillar in her wretched state. The people and even the king recognized her at once and they forgot their fear and burst into laughter. Soon Rūpiṇikā heard about the incident and came to the temple. When she saw that it was her mother who was on top of the pillar she was very embarrassed. She managed to bring her down with the help of the people gathered there. Everyone was dying of curiosity and asked Makaradaṅṣṭrā what had happened to her. She told them the whole story.

'The king, the Brāhmins and the merchants who were there were sure that all this had been the work of some magician or sorcerer. They announced that whoever had tricked the old woman should reveal himself and he would be honoured immediately. Lohajaṅgha came forward and when he was questioned, he narrated the whole story, right from the beginning. He offered the gifts sent by Vibhīṣaṇa to Viṣṇu and the people gazed at them in wonder and admiration. The citizens of Mathurā honoured Lohajaṅgha and by the order of the king, Rūpiṇikā was made a free woman. Now that Lohajaṅgha had taken revenge on Makaradaṅṣṭrā for all the troubles that he had to endure because of her, he lived happily in Mathurā with his beloved Rūpiṇikā, rich with the jewels he had brought back from Laṅkā.'

Lāvāṇaka

Hail to Gaṇeśa, the remover of obstacles, whose favour I seek, for even Śiva sought his favour so that he could create the world without hindrance.

The god of love conquers the world with his five arrows and even Śiva trembles at his command when he is embraced by his beloved!

When Udayana and the princess Vāsavadattā ran away together, King Caṇḍamahāsena agreed to let them marry each other and the wedding was celebrated with great joy and feasting in Kauśāmbī. Udayana was so much in love with his wife that he could not bear to be separated from her and once again, his ministers were left to rule the kingdom of Vatsa. Yaugandharāyaṇa, Rumaṇvat and Vasantaka undertook the conquest of neighbouring kingdoms on Udayana's behalf. Soon, Udayana married Padmāvatī, the princess of Magadha and both the queens, Vāsavadattā and Padmāvatī lived together happily. One day, Vasantaka told them the following story for their amusement.

Guhacandra And His Celestial Bride

'There is a famous city called Pāṭaliputra and it is so beautiful that it is the ornament of the earth. A great merchant named Dharmagupta lived there and once upon a time, his wife Candraprabhā became pregnant. She gave birth to a beautiful daughter named Somaprabhā. The moment she was born, Somaprabhā lit up the room with her beauty. She spoke clearly and was able to stand up and sit down. When Dharmagupta saw that the midwives were both astonished and a little alarmed, he was frightened and went himself to his wife's chambers. He bowed before the child and said to her quietly, "Honourable lady, who are you and why have you descended into my house?" She replied, "You must not give me away to anyone in marriage. As long as I am in this house, you shall prosper. What need is there for you to know any more?" Dharmagupta was frightened when she said this and hid her inside his house. He announced to the world that she was dead.

'In time, Somaprabhā grew up and though she had a human body, her beauty was quite divine. One day, while she was standing on the terrace of her house and enjoying the Spring festival, Guhacandra, the son of another merchant, saw her. His heart was struck by the arrows of love and he almost fainted. He returned to his home in a state of great agitation. He was tortured by love and when his parents begged him to tell them what the problem was, he made his friend tell them what had happened.

'His father Guhasena was deeply attached to his son and so he went to Dharmagupta's house to find out about the young woman. When he asked for her in marriage for his son, Dharmagupta turned him down saying, "My daughter is mad." Guhasena realized that Dharmagupta did not want to give his daughter to them and went home not knowing what to do next. He saw his son feverish with longing and he thought, "I will appeal to the king for I have done him a favour in the past. He will get this girl for my son who is at the point of death."

Guhasena went to the king with a gift of a priceless jewel and apprised the king of his problem. The king was fond of the merchant and called in the chief of police to help him. The two of them went to Dharmagupta's house and surrounded it with troops. Dharmagupta became tearful, convinced that his ruin was at hand. Then Somaprabhā said to Dharmagupta, "Father, give me away. Do not be ruined on my account. But my husband must never sleep with me. You must make this very clear to my father-in-law." Dharmagupta agreed to give his daughter in marriage to Guhasena's son after clearly stating that her husband was not to sleep with her. Guhasena agreed, but he laughed privately and thought to himself, "Let my son get married and we shall see what happens!"

'Guhacandra brought his bride home and his father said to him "Son, enjoy your wife. Is there anyone who renounces the pleasures of his own wife's bed?" Somaprabhā was very angry when she heard her father-in-law saying this. She turned around and pointed her finger at him as though it were a message of death. Guhasena saw that finger pointed at him and he was so terrified that all his breath left his body. When his father died, Guhacandra thought, "The goddess of destruction has entered my house as my wife!" He avoided the company of his wife who continued to live in his house. Thus, he remained celibate which was as difficult as standing on the edge of a sword. He was depressed and lost interest in all pleasures. He undertook fasts and the feeding of Brāhmins. His divinely beautiful wife maintained a strict silence but would always give alms to the Brāhmins after their meal.

'One day, an old Brāhmin arrived to eat there and he gazed with amazement at this woman who was a treasure trove of beauty. Very curious, he asked Guhacandra in private who his young wife was. When he persisted with his questions, Guhacandra sadly told him the whole story. The Brāhmin was sympathetic and gave him a *mantra* that would appease Agni so that his desires could be fulfilled. Guhacandra recited the *mantra* in secret and a man appeared out of the fire. Agni, in the guise of a Brāhmin, said to Guhacandra who had bowed at his feet, "Today, I will eat here and stay at your house for the night. I will show you the truth about your wife and then I will grant you your desire."

'The Brāhmin entered Guhacandra's house and ate with the others. At night, he lay down beside Guhacandra to sleep during the first watch. At that time, when the whole household was asleep, Somaprabhā, Guhacandra's wife, slipped out of the house. Immediately, the Brāhmin roused Guhacandra saying, "Come and see what your wife is upto." With his magic powers, he turned himself and Guhacandra into bees and as they left, he pointed to Guhacandra's wife who was walking out of the house.

'Somaprabhā went far outside the city and Guhacandra and the Brāhmin followed her. Guhacandra saw a beautiful *nyagrodha* tree, its branches spreading shade far and wide. He could hear the sound of heavenly singing and the sweet music of the *vīṇa* and the flute coming from underneath the tree. He saw a beautiful woman who looked like his wife near the trunk of the tree. She was sitting on a throne and was being fanned by white *chowrie* plumes. Her beauty outshone the moonbeams, as though she was the goddess of the moon herself.

'Guhacandra saw his wife climb the tree and sit down next to the woman, occupying one half of her throne. As he gazed upon those two women of equal beauty, Guhacandra felt as if the night had been illuminated by three moons. He was filled with curiosity and wondered if this was a dream or an illusion. He decided that this experience was the result of his good conduct and his association with the wise. Meanwhile, the two women ate the kind of food that was appropriate for them and drank heavenly wine. "Today, dear sister, a powerful Brāhmin has arrived in our house. It makes me nervous and so I must leave now," said Guhacandra's wife and climbed down from the tree. Guhacandra and the Brāhmin, still in the form of bees, flew ahead of Somaprabhā and reached home before she did. That celestial woman arrived later and entered the house without being seen.

'The Brāhmin said to Guhacandra, "You have seen now that your wife is some divine being and not a mortal. The other woman that you saw is her sister. Why would a divine creature like that desire any association with a human? I will give you a *mantra* that must be written above her door and I will tell you a scheme that must be employed outside to increase the power of the *mantra*. Fire burns in any case, but it burns better with the aid of the wind. So also, a *mantra* is effective by itself but is much more so when it is helped by an appropriate plan." The Brāhmin gave Guhacandra the *mantra* and instructed him in the required plan and then disappeared with the dawn.

'Guhacandra wrote the *mantra* over Somaprabhā's door and in the evening, embarked on the following plan to pique her interest. He put on his best clothes and in front of his wife, held a long conversation with a beautiful courtesan. His wife, who had been affected by the *mantra,* called to him and asked who the woman was. Guhacandra lied and said that she was a courtesan who was attracted to him and that he planned to visit her that day. Somaprabhā looked at him, her brow wrinkled in confusion and detained him with her left hand. She said, "So that is why you are all dressed up! Why do you have to go to her? Why don't you sleep with me? After all, I am your wife!" She begged him to stay, inflamed with desire as if she were possessed, because she was under the control of the *mantra.* Guhacandra was overjoyed and went into her chambers and slept with her. Though he was a mortal, he enjoyed celestial pleasures of a kind that he had never experienced before. Guhacandra then lived happily with his celestial wife who had been bewitched by the *mantra* and had given up her divine status for him.

'Thus, celestial women sometimes live in the houses of virtuous men as a reward for their devotion and charity. The gods and the Brāhmins are like Kāmadhenu, the cow that fulfils all desires, for anything can be obtained through them. All other means to attaining one's ends are secondary to this. Celestial beings fall to earth as a result of their misconduct as blossoms are felled by a storm.'

Indra And Ahalyā

When Vasantaka had said this to the queens, he continued. 'Listen to the story of Ahalyā.

'There was a great *muni* named Gautama and he had knowledge of the past, the present and the future. His wife Ahalyā was even more beautiful than an *apsaras.* Indra was captivated by her beauty and one day, he approached her secretly, for kings are often blind with power and seek forbidden things. Ahalyā, herself inflamed with passion, encouraged Indra. Gautama learned what was happening through his powers and arrived at the *āśrama*. Terrified, Indra turned himself into a cat.

'Gautama asked Ahalyā, "Who is here?" and she replied in Prākrit, "It is a cat," thus maintaining the truth of the situation. Gautama laughed and said, "It is indeed true that your lover is here!"[1] and he cursed her, but only for a short while as she had, in fact, told the truth. "Wicked woman! You shall become a stone until you see Rāma wandering in this forest!" He also cursed Indra. "A thousand vaginas shall appear all over your body for the vagina was the object of your desire. But when you set eyes on Tilottamā, the *apsaras* created by Viśvakarmā, the thousand vaginas will turn into a thousand eyes!" Gautama then returned to his performance of austerities but Ahalyā became a wretched stone. Indra's body was covered by vaginas, for misconduct shames everyone.

'Thus, misconduct has its own consequences, for one reaps the fruit of the seed that one has sown. Therefore, good people do not desire that which will harm those around them,' said Vasantaka as he concluded his story.

Udayana lived happily with his two queens. He planned a conquest of all the directions and decided to propitiate Śiva before he embarked on his journey. He fasted and performed penances and Śiva appeared to him and promised him a mighty son who would be the emperor of the vidyādharas. *Udayana conquered Vārāṇasī, Kaliṅga, the southern Cholas, the kingdom of Lāṭa in the west and Sindh. He defeated Mlecchas, Turuṣkas and Hunas and soon he had conquered the whole world. Udayana then returned to Kauśāmbī and his wives.*

Queen Vāsavadattā desperately wanted a son and Udayana told her to pray to Śiva. The mighty god appeared to her in a dream and promised her a son who would be the emperor of the vidyādharas. *In another dream, a mendicant gave her a fruit which she ate and soon after that, Vāsavadattā became pregnant. Meanwhile, virtuous and noble sons had been born to Udayana's ministers and to his faithful door-keeper, and they were named Marubhūti, Hariśikha, Tapantaka and Gomukha. At last, Vāsavadattā gave birth to the prince who was born the incarnation of Kāma himself, a beautiful child with all the auspicious marks of a great monarch. At his birth, a voice announced that he should be named Naravāhanadatta and that he would be an emperor of the* vidyādharas. *Showers of blossoms fell from the skies and the whole world celebrated the prince's birth with joy and feasting. Naravāhanadatta grew up strong and intelligent, in the company of the ministers' sons.*

Madanamañcukā

May Gaṇeśa protect you, he who scatters all obstacles by raising and lowering his head!

I worship the god of love whose arrows pierce even Śiva, making him bristle as if with thorns when he is in Pārvatī's embrace.

Now listen to the celestial adventures that Naravāhanadatta himself related, when he was once asked about his life by the seven *ṛṣis* and their wives after he had become sovereign of the *vidyādharas*.

Naravāhanadatta was carefully raised by his father, the king of Vatsa and he reached his eighth year. The prince learned the sciences and played in the gardens with the sons of his father's ministers. The queens, Vāsavadattā and Padmāvatī, were both very fond of him and devoted themselves to him day and night. This boy of noble stock grew, his body burdened by the weight of his virtues. But he filled out as he developed, like a bow made of excellent bamboo that straightens after the arrow is released. And his father looked forward to the time of his marriage, a time that was to arrive very soon. Now listen to what happened at this point in the story.

Ratnadatta Learns The Meaning Of Buddhism

There was a city named Takṣaśilā on the banks of the Vitastā. Its beautiful buildings and palaces were reflected in the river waters as if the city from the underworld had come to admire its own splendour. Takṣaśilā was ruled by King Kaliṅgadatta who was a devout Buddhist and all his subjects followed the same religion. The city shone with hundreds of jewelled Buddhist temples, as if with its horns proudly lifted, for it had no equal on earth. Kaliṅgadatta was like a father to his subjects and also acted as their teacher in spiritual matters.

There was also in that city a wealthy Buddhist merchant by the name of Vitastādatta, known for honouring Buddhist mendicants. He had a young son named Ratnadatta who was disgusted with his father and called him a wicked man. When his father asked him, 'Why do you criticize me?' the young man replied disdainfully, 'Father, you have renounced the religion of the three Vedas and now you practice an unrighteous faith. You ignore Brāhmins and honour Buddhist ascetics. Why are you interested in Buddhism which is the refuge of low caste people? They want to live free in a monastery, eat when they want, and have freedom from bathing and other rituals. They do not follow the prescribed Brāhminical style for their hair and seem quite content with a rag around their waists!'

When Vitastādatta heard this terrible distortion of his religion, he said to his son, 'There are many kinds of religion, some that include the world and others that transcend it. The religion of the Brāhmins also calls for the rejection of the passions, compassion for all beings and abstention from quarrels with one's family. You should not criticize the religion that I follow, which cares for all beings, because of the faults of a single individual! No one can denounce the merits of charity and what I do is care for all kinds of people. If I take pleasure in this doctrine, which preaches that non-violence leads to liberation, how can I be unrighteous?' But Ratnadatta refused to accept what his father said and became even more critical of him.

Full of regret, Vitastādatta went and told King Kaliṅgadatta, who was involved with the religion of his subjects, everything that had happened. The king summoned Ratnadatta to his assembly and pretending to be angry, called for the executioner. 'I have heard that this merchant's son is a wicked man and is habituated to crime. There is nothing to consider in this matter. Kill him at once for the crime of corrupting the kingdom!' But Vitastādatta interceded on his son's behalf and the king postponed the execution for two months so that Ratnadatta could be schooled in the right path. He placed Ratnadatta in his father's care and said that he should be brought back at the end of two months.

Ratnadatta was petrified and went back to his father's house thinking, 'What wrong have I committed against the king?' He worried constantly about his unjust execution that was to occur two months hence. He could not sleep at night nor during the day and grew weak from eating less and less. When the two months had elapsed, Ratnadatta, pale and thin, was taken by his father to the king. When the king saw him in that wretched condition, he asked, 'Why are you so weak? Did I ask you to stop eating?' Ratnadatta replied, 'I was so frightened that I forgot myself, let alone my food during this time. I have been thinking about my approaching death ever since I heard your command.' The king said, 'Son, I planned this so that you would learn the fear of death. All living creatures suffer from this fear and what higher value can there be than alleviating this fear for all beings? I demonstrated this to you so that you would learn the *dharma* and aim for the ultimate liberation. A wise man seeks liberation because he is afraid of death. Therefore, you must not criticize your father who clings to this *dharma*.'

Ratnadatta bowed to the king and said, 'By teaching me this *dharma*, you have inspired a desire for liberation within me. Teach me about that as well!' The city was celebrating a festival and was full of activity which could easily have distracted Ratnadatta. The king, therefore, gave him a bowl full of oil and said, 'Hold this bowl in your hands and walk around the city without spilling a single drop of oil. If you let it spill, these men will kill you at once!' The king sent Ratnadatta to walk around the city with the bowl and sent his soldiers with their swords drawn to accompany him.

Trembling with fear, Ratnadatta conscientiously avoided spilling the oil and walked around the city without too much trouble and returned to the king. The king noticed that the oil had not been spilled and he said to Ratnadatta, 'Did you see anyone when you were wandering through the city today?' The young man clasped his hands together and said, 'Truly, I did not see nor hear a single thing. I concentrated on not spilling a single drop of oil while I walked through the city for fear that these naked swords would descend upon me.' 'Because you were so intent on not spilling the oil you saw nothing. You should practice religion with the same concentration. A man who withdraws from outward distractions realizes the truth and will never again be caught in the web of action. Thus, I have taught you the essence of the doctrine of liberation.' The grateful young man fell at the king's feet and after being dismissed, returned to his father's house, full of joy, his goals fulfilled.

Kaliṅgadatta Has A Daughter

Kaliṅgadatta, who instructed his subjects in this manner, had a wife named Tārādattā. She was equal in birth to the monarch and because she was virtuous and sensible, she was a fitting ornament to the king, like language is to a poet who enjoys its many possibilities. She shone with virtue and auspiciousness and was to the king as moonlight is to the moon which contains the nectar of immortality. The king lived happily with his queen as Indra lives in heaven with Śacī.

After a while, Tārādattā grew heavy with her pregnancy. As the time for her delivery drew nearer, she appeared as pale as the eastern sky in which the new moon is about to rise. She soon gave birth to an incomparable daughter who was so lovely that she was the epitome of the Creator's ability to produce beauty. Even the lamps that affectionately blazed all night to protect the child from the evil eye were dimmed by her beauty. But the lamps faded as if in sorrow that the beautiful child was not a boy.

When Kaliṅgadatta saw his beautiful daughter, he was filled with disappointment. He understood that she was divine in some way, but he continued to despair for he had wanted a son. A son is joy incarnate while a daughter is nothing but grief. To distract himself, the king left the palace and went into a temple that was filled with images of the many Buddhas. In a corner of the temple, he overheard a religious discourse being given by a mendicant who sat among a group of people.

'The donation of wealth is the greatest ascetic practice in the world. Giving wealth is equal to giving life, because life depends on money. The Buddha was filled with compassion and he gave up his life for another as if it were a trivial straw. How much less is the value of wealth! It was through determined austerities that the Buddha gave up desire, acquired divine insight and attained the status of an Enlightened Being. A wise man should renounce selfish desires and do that which benefits others, even giving up his body in order to acquire the ultimate insight,' said the mendicant. He told the following story to illustrate his point.

The Seven Princesses

'Thus, long ago, a certain king named Kṛta had seven beautiful daughters born one after another. While they were still very young, they grew disinterested in life and left their father's house and went to the cremation grounds. When they were asked why they had done that, they said to their retainers, "This world is meaningless. In it, the body, union with lovers and other such joys are like a dream. The only thing that gives meaning to the world is working for the benefit of others. We have decided to use our bodies for the good of other beings and will fling our living bodies to those creatures that live on flesh. What use are these lovely bodies to us? Listen to this tale.

The Man With The Beautiful Eyes

"In the same way, long ago, there was a prince who, even though he was young and handsome, grew disinterested in the world and became a mendicant. One day, he went to the house of a certain merchant. The merchant's young wife was deeply attracted to the young man's eyes which were as long as lotus petals and she said to him, 'How is it that someone as handsome as yourself has undertaken such a difficult vow? I envy the woman whom your eyes gaze upon!' The mendicant pulled out his eye and holding it in his hand, he said, 'Mother, look at this eye for what it is! It is a revolting mess of flesh and blood. Take it if it pleases you! My other eye is also just like this. Tell me, what is so pleasant about them?' The merchant's wife was full of sorrow when she saw the eye and she said, 'Alas! I have done a terrible thing! I have caused you to pull out your eye!' The young mendicant said, 'Mother, don't be sad, for you have done me a favour. Listen and I will prove it to you.

The Sage And The King

'Long ago, a renunciant who wanted to experience all types of ascetic practices, lived in a beautiful garden. While he was performing his austerities, a king came there to amuse himself with the ladies of his harem. After a while, the king fell asleep because of all the wine that he had drunk. His queens uncaringly left him where he was and wandered around the garden. In a corner of the garden, they saw the sage meditating and out of curiosity, they formed a circle around him, wondering what he was. They were gone a long time and in the meanwhile, the king woke up. He could not see any of the women around and so he, too, strolled around the garden. He saw the queens in a circle around the sage and in a jealous rage, struck the sage with his sword. Power, envy, cruelty, drunkenness and insensitivity, each can cause a crime on its own, how much more so when they are all combined like the five sacred fires!

'The king left and although the sage had been stabbed, he remained free of anger. A god manifested himself in front of the hermit and said, "Great soul! If you so desire, with my powers, I will kill that wretched man who did this to you in anger!" But the sage replied, "Do not say that, for he has helped me in my duties. He has not hindered me in any way. In fact, it is because of him that I have learned forgiveness. If he had not acted this way, whom could I have forgiven? Which wise man would be angry over the fate of this body? To treat the pleasant and the unpleasant equally is to have attained the Absolute!" The god was pleased with the sage's words and he healed his wounds and disappeared.

'Just as the sage saw the king as his ally, so Mother, you have aided my ascetic practices by causing me to pull out my eye,' said the young hermit to the merchant's wife. She bowed to him with respect. The young hermit neglected his beautiful body and soon attained perfection.

"Therefore, though we are young and beautiful, what reason is there for holding on to our bodies? The wise know that the only good is to act for the benefit of others. We will give up our bodies for the benefit of the living beings in the cremation grounds which are the true home of happiness," said the seven princesses and they attained perfection.

'Thus, the wise have little interest even in their own bodies, let alone such trivial things as a wife, a son and retainers,' said the mendicant as the king listened to his discourse in the temple. He spent the day there and then returned to his palace where he was once again overcome with sorrow at the birth of a daughter. An old Brāhmin who lived in his house said to him, 'Why are you so sad about the birth of this pearl among women? Daughters are much better than sons, for they confer benefits in this world and the next. Why do great kings long for sons who covet kingship and devour their fathers like crabs? Kings like Kuntībhoja have been protected from sages like Durvāsas because of the virtues of daughters like Kuntī. One cannot gain the same fruits in the next world from a son as one can from the marriage of a daughter. Listen and I will tell you the story of Sulocanā.

Sulocanā Fulfils Her Father's Destiny

'A king named Suṣeṇa lived on Mount Citrakūṭa. He had been created as beautiful as the god of love to make Śiva jealous. He made such a beautiful garden at the foot of the mountain that the gods wanted to leave Nandana and live there on earth. In the middle of the garden was a lake full of blooming lotuses that was like a nursery for the lotuses that Lakṣmī plays with. The lake had jewelled steps leading into it and Suṣeṇa would lie there alone for a suitable bride could not be found for him.

'One day, the *apsaras* Rambhā passed that way as she wandered through the air after leaving Indra's palace. She saw Suṣeṇa amusing himself in the garden and he seemed like Spring itself walking among the blooming lotuses. "Can this be the moon that has descended into this garden in search of Lakṣmī who has fallen into the lotus lake? But this man has an unfading beauty! He must be the god of love who has come here to procure his flowery arrows! But then where is his companion Rati?" This was how Rambhā described Suṣeṇa as she descended from the sky. She took human form and approached the king.

'Suṣeṇa saw her coming and was astounded by her beauty. He thought to himself, "Who could this impossibly beautiful woman be? She must be divine for her feet do not touch the dust nor do her eyes blink. But I will not question her as she may fly away. Celestial beings who develop relationships with humans cannot bear their secret to be revealed." They soon began to converse and slowly, he embraced her and they made love in the garden. Suṣeṇa so captivated the *apsaras* that she forgot all about heaven. Love can be more attractive than one's home.

'Suṣeṇa's land was filled with heaps of gold as heaven is filled with the peaks of Mount Meru, for Rambhā's friends, the *yakṣiṇīs*, poured down wealth as if it were rain. In time, the beautiful *apsaras* became pregnant and gave birth to an exceedingly lovely daughter. When the child was born, she said to the king, "This was my curse and now it has ended. I am not an ordinary woman. I am the *apsaras* Rambhā and I fell in love with you the moment I saw you. Now that I have given birth to this child, I must leave you at once for that is the way it is with us. Look after our daughter for we shall meet again in heaven when she is married." Deeply distressed, Rambhā disappeared and the king was so upset that he wanted to kill himself. His ministers said to him, "Did Viśvāmitra kill himself even though he was devastated when Menakā returned to heaven after giving birth to Śakuntalā?" Slowly, the king was comforted by them and he recovered his equilibrium. His heart went out to his daughter who was to be the cause of his reunion with Rambhā. He became devoted to the child who was beautiful in all her limbs and he named her Sulocanā because of the beauty of her eyes.

'In time, Sulocanā grew into adulthood and one day, she was seen in the garden by a young ascetic named Vatsa, a descendent of Kaśyapa. Even though he had been made firm by his penance, he was overcome with love when he saw the princess. He thought to himself, "This girl's beauty is truly astounding. What could be the fruit of all my asceticism if it were not to obtain her as a wife?" As he was thinking this, Sulocanā noticed him, bright as a fire without smoke. Gazing at him with his beads and his water-pot, she immediately fell in love and thought, "Who is this man who appears to have self-control and is still so beautiful?" She approached him as if she were about to select him as a husband and threw her glance, which was like a garland of blue lotuses, around his neck. The ascetic was caught in the power of Love, a command that neither the gods nor the demons can disobey, and he blessed her. "May you obtain a husband."

'Sulocanā, whose modesty had been stolen away by the ascetic's extraordinary beauty, spoke with her eyes cast down. "If this is what you wish and if you are not merely making conversation with me, then speak to my father, the king, who has the right to give me away." After the ascetic had heard about her lineage from her retainers, he went to her father, King Suṣeṇa, to ask for her hand in marriage. Suṣeṇa was gracious to the ascetic, seeing that he was both handsome and self-controlled. He said, "This girl is my daughter by the *apsaras* Rambhā and when she is married, my love and I shall be reunited in heaven. This is what Rambhā told me when she left me to return to heaven. Tell me how this will be made possible?"

"When Menakā's daughter Pramadvarā was bitten by a snake, Ruru the ascetic gave her half his life and married her. Viśvāmitra carried Triśaṅku to heaven[1]. I, too, can spend the merits of my asceticism on this," thought the ascetic to himself and he said to the king, "This is not difficult." Then he addressed the gods in the king's assembly. "Let the king ascend to heaven in this very body by virtue of a part of my ascetic merit!" A voice rang out of the sky and declared, "So be it!" Suṣeṇa had his daughter Sulocanā married to Vatsa, the descendent of Kaśyapa, and went to heaven. There, he acquired a divine nature and lived in happiness with Rambhā who had been appointed his wife by Indra.

'Thus, Suṣeṇa was able to achieve his goal through his daughter. Daughters like this are born into the houses of people like yourself. Your daughter is probably an *apsaras* who has fallen from her position because of a curse, so do not despair at her birth,' said the Brāhmin to the king.

Kaliṅgadatta was reassured by the Brāhmin's story. He named his daughter, who delighted his eyes as if she were the new moon, Kaliṅgasenā. The princess grew up in her father's house along with her companions.

It so happened that the princess of Takṣaśilā, Kaliṅgasenā, set her heart on marrying Udayana, the king of Vatsa. Yaugandharāyaṇa decided that the marriage ceremony should be delayed so that Udayana would have a chance to consider the matter carefully. Kaliṅgasenā was installed in a palace in Kauśāmbī and waited for the auspicious day set for the wedding by the royal astrologers. As she waited in her palace, princess Kaliṅgasenā's friend Somaprabhā told her the following story.

Kīrtisenā Outwits Her Mother-in-law

'Long ago, in the city of Pāṭaliputra, there lived a merchant named Dhanalipta, and not without reason, for he was the richest of the rich. He had a daughter named Kīrtisenā who was very beautiful and she was dearer to him than life itself. Dhanalipta had his daughter married to a rich merchant from Magadha named Devasena. Devasena was a good man but he had a wicked mother who ran his house since his father was dead. When she saw that her son loved his wife dearly, she was inflamed with anger and ill-treated her daughter-in-law when Devasena was away. But Kīrtisenā said nothing of this to her husband, for a bride's position under a cruel mother-in-law is a difficult one.

'One day, Devasena was encouraged by his relatives to go to the city of Vallabhī for purposes of trade. As he was preparing for his journey, Kīrtisenā said to him, "I have not told you this for a long time, but your mother ill-treats me even when you are here. I do not know what she will do to me when you are away!" Devasena was confused when he heard this and, because he was fond of his wife and feared for her, he went to his mother and humbly said, "Kīrtisenā is in your hands, Mother, while I am away. Treat her with affection, for she is from a good family." Devasena's mother immediately called for Kīrtisenā and raising her eyes to heaven, she said to her son, "Ask her what I have done. This is the way she encourages you to create a rift in our home. Both of you are equal in my eyes." Devasena was reassured by her words and left the room, for who would not be fooled by the deceitfully sweet words of his mother? But Kīrtisenā stood there silently, smiling in confusion. The next day, Devasena left for Vallabhī.

'Kīrtisenā missed her husband terribly. By and by, her mother-in-law turned the servants against her. She made a plan with a female servant of hers and calling Kīrtisenā into a secret room, she stripped her naked. She said to her, "Wicked creature! You have taken my son from me!" and she and the servant attacked Kīrtisenā with their hands, feet and teeth. They threw her into an underground room that was securely fastened from the outside after they had taken out all the things that were in it. The wicked mother-in-law would give that poor girl half a plate of rice every evening. She thought to herself, "In a few days, I will say 'She died by herself while her husband was away. She was unfaithful to her husband.'" Poor Kīrtisenā who deserved happiness but was locked in that underground cellar, wept and thought, "I have a rich husband, I was born into a good family, I am fortunate and virtuous but despite all that I have to suffer like this because of my mother-in-law. This is why families are disappointed at the birth of a daughter for they can be tormented by mothers-in-law and sisters-in-law and are marked by misfortune!"

'As she was crying, Kīrtisenā found a small spade in the room and it was as though a thorn had been extracted from her heart by fate. She began to dig a tunnel from the underground room and as luck would have it, she ended up in her own apartments. She was able to look around the room by the light of a lamp that had been left there before, but she could have illuminated the room with her own virtue. She collected her clothes and her jewellery and at the end of the night, she secretly left the city. "I cannot go back to my father's house after all that has happened. What will I say and how would the people there believe me? I must find a way to reach my husband, for a husband is the only refuge for a virtuous woman," she thought.

'Kīrtisenā bathed in a tank and dressed herself like a nobleman and went into the marketplace. She got some money by selling a little gold and stayed the night in the house of a merchant. The next day, she made friends with a merchant named Samudrasena who wanted to go to Vallabhī. Still dressed as a nobleman, she set out with Samudrasena and his retainers in order to find her husband who had gone to Vallabhī earlier. She told the merchant that she had problems with her family and so she had decided to go to the other city.

'Along the journey, Samudrasena treated her with honour because he thought that she was from a royal family. Because the use of highways meant the payment of heavy tolls, the trading party used the road which led through the forests. In a few days, they reached the entrance of the forest. When they set up camp there in the evening, a jackal howled like a messenger of death. The merchant's retinue understood what that meant and, suspecting an attack by thieves, they all grabbed their swords and stood at the ready. The darkness advanced like a gang of thieves and Kīrtisenā in her man's clothes thought, "Alas! Evil deeds that have been committed in the past multiply like offspring! See! The suffering that my mother-in-law inflicted on me has borne fruit here as well! First I suffered my mother-in-law's anger that was like death itself. Then I entered that underground room that was like a second womb. Luckily, I escaped from there, as if I was born a second time and now here, my life is in danger again. If I am killed by thieves, my mother-in-law who is my sworn enemy, will definitely tell my husband that I ran off somewhere with another man. If someone tears off my clothes and learns that I am a woman, my honour is at stake. Death is better than that! I must save myself and not be concerned about this merchant who is my friend. For a virtuous woman must place the duties of a wife over all else, including friendship."

'She looked around and found a hollow in a tree, as if the earth had opened up for her out of sympathy. She slipped into the hollow and covered herself with leaves and twigs and stayed there, keeping her spirits up with thoughts of a reunion with her husband. In the middle of the night, a gang of thieves surrounded the trading party with their weapons raised. The fight that ensued was like a storm, the thieves howled like thunder, weapons flashed like lightning and blood rained on all sides. The thieves killed Samudrasena and his retinue and made off with all their wealth.

'Kīrtisenā heard all the noise and it was only by good fortune that she was not killed along with the others. The night passed and when the sun rose, she left the hollow of the tree. The gods themselves preserve the virtue of good women who are devoted to their husbands in times of trouble, for in that deserted forest, a lion saw Kīrtisenā and did not eat her, and an ascetic appeared out of nowhere. When she asked him for help, he calmed her and gave her water to drink and food to eat. After telling her which road to take, he disappeared. Then, refreshed as though by nectar and free of hunger and thirst, Kīrtisenā the devoted wife, set off down the road that the ascetic had pointed out.

Kīrtisenā Learns A Secret

'She saw the sun on the western mountain, its rays stretched out like fingers as though it were telling her to wait patiently for one more night. She slipped into a hollow in the root of a huge tree that was like a house and covered its opening with another bush. In the evening, she saw a terrifying *rākṣasī* coming by with her two young sons through a small hole in the bush. Kīrtisenā was very frightened, certain that she would be killed by the *rākṣasī* even though she had survived all the other calamities upto this point.

'The *rākṣasī* climbed into the tree and her sons followed her and said, "Mother, give us something to eat!" The *rākṣasī* said to them, "Little ones, even though I went to the main cremation grounds today, I did not get anything to eat. I begged the *yoginīs* for a share of their food, but they gave me nothing. Then I appealed to Śiva and he asked me for my name and my family. He said, 'You are well-born because you are descended from Khara and Dūṣaṇa. Go to the city of Vāsudatta which is not far from here. King Vāsudatta is a virtuous man and he wanders through the forests protecting them. He levies low tolls and punishes thieves and bandits himself. One day, when the king was tired after the hunt and was sleeping in the forest, a centipede crawled quietly into his ear. Slowly, it produced many other worms inside his head and this affected the king's muscles. The doctors have no idea what has caused this disease, but if it is not discovered soon, the king will die in the next few days. Eat his flesh when he dies and, by your magic powers, you will be free from hunger for six months.' Śiva has thus promised me an uncertain meal for which I must wait. What can I do, dear children?"

'Her children said, "Mother, if the disease is discovered,

will the king live? Tell us how such a disease can be cured."
"The king will definitely live if the disease is discovered. Listen and I will tell you how to cure this terrible sickness," replied the *rākṣasī*. "First, the king's head should be anointed with *ghee* and then warmed in the heat of the noon-day sun for some time. A fine bamboo tube should be inserted into his ear with its other end near a pot of cool water. The centipedes, bothered by the heat and the perspiration, will enter the tube to get near the water and will fall into the pot. Then the king will be free of his sickness."

'Kīrtisenā heard all that the *rākṣasī* had said to her sons from inside the tree trunk. She thought to herself, "If I get out of this place alive, I will go and save the life of the king, for he lives close to the forest in order to guard it and he levies low tolls on travellers and merchants. Many merchants travel this way because it is easier for them. This is what Samudrasena, who is now dead, told me. Maybe my husband will also pass this way. I will go to the city of Vāsudatta which lies at the edge of the forest and cure the king of his disease and then wait there for my husband's arrival." She made it through the night with great difficulty and then, in the morning, when the *rākṣasas* had left, she climbed out of the tree trunk.

'Still dressed as a man, she went slowly through the middle of the forest and in the afternoon encountered a virtuous cowherd. He was overcome by her beauty and saw that she had come from far away. When she asked him what country she was in, he replied, "The city before you is Vāsudatta and its king is also Vāsudatta. But he is about to die from a terrible sickness." Kīrtisenā said, "If someone takes me to the king, I know how to cure his illness," and the cowherd said that since he was going to that very city, he would point it out to her. Kīrtisenā agreed and the cowherd took her, dressed as a man, into the city.

Kīrtisenā Saves The King's Life

'The cowherd introduced the beautiful Kīrtisenā to the king's door-keeper and told him what had happened. The door-keeper reported everything to the king and Kīrtisenā was taken into his presence. Vāsudatta was suffering greatly from his sickness, but he felt better the moment he saw that incredibly beautiful woman, for the heart recognizes those who wish one well. Vāsudatta said to that woman disguised as a man, "Auspicious one, if you cure me, I will give you half my kingdom. I remember I had a dream in which a woman took a black blanket off me and so I feel that you will heal me." Kīrtisenā said, "The day has come to an end. Be patient, for tomorrow I will cure you of your sickness." She rubbed the king's head with *ghee* which relieved his pain and allowed him to sleep. All the people there praised Kīrtisenā saying that she must be a divine being who had come there as a result of the merit they had earned in a previous birth.

'The queen herself looked after Kīrtisenā and gave her a place to stay for the night as well as servants to attend on her. The next day, at noon, while all the ministers and courtiers watched, Kīrtisenā removed one hundred and fifty centipedes from the king's head through his ear in the manner that she had learned from the *rākṣasī.* After getting the centipedes into the pot of water, she calmed the king with milk and melted butter. The king recovered slowly and when the illness had left him, all the people looked at the worms in the pot with astonishment. The king looked at the horrid creatures that had so tormented him and was amazed and delighted and felt as if he had been born again. He bathed and ordered a great celebration and gave Kīrtisenā half the kingdom, heaps of gold, elephants, horses and villages even though she was not interested in any of these things. The queen and the ministers gave Kīrtisenā more gold and jewels and fine clothes, honouring her as the doctor who had saved the king's life. But Kīrtisenā was waiting for her husband and so she left the wealth with the king saying, "I have undertaken a vow for a short while."

'Kīrtisenā remained in her men's clothes and stayed in Vāsudatta's palace for some time, honoured by all the people.

While she was there, she heard that her husband, Devasena the merchant, was coming that way on his return from Vallabhī. As soon as she learned that his trading party had arrived in the city, she approached the caravan and saw her husband, experiencing the same joy as a peacock who beholds the monsoon clouds. She bowed before him, her tears of joy at the end of their long separation anointing his dusty feet. Devasena looked at her carefully and recognized her through her disguise, for she was hidden like the moon is hidden during the day because of the sun's rays. Devasena himself was like the moon and it was just as well that his heart did not dissolve like the moonstone when he was confronted by Kīrtisenā's moon-like face.

'When Kīrtisenā was revealed as a woman, her husband and the other merchants gathered there were astonished. The king arrived there for he, too, had heard of this amazing event. When he questioned Kīrtisenā, she related her adventures which were caused by her mother-in-law's cruelty, in front of her husband. Devasena was very angry with his mother when he heard the story but at the same time, he was filled with amazement and wonder. All the people there said joyfully, "Virtuous women who ride in the chariot of marital bliss and who are protected by the armour of their chastity and who carry the weapon of their intelligence will always win the battle." The king said, "This woman who has suffered for the sake of her husband is greater than even Sītā who shared Rāma's hardships. She has saved my life and from now on, she is my sister."

'Kīrtisenā said, "Give my husband the horses, elephants and villages that you gave me out of affection," and the king did as she asked. He also honoured Devasena, who with his treasury filled by the gifts that the king had given Kīrtisenā as well as by the wealth that he had acquired through trade, continued to live happily in the city of Vāsudatta with Kīrtisenā and avoided his mother. Kīrtisenā was delighted to be away from her mother-in-law and she, too, lived there happily, basking in the fame that her adventures had earned her.'

While Kaliṅgasenā was waiting to marry Udayana, a vidyādhara *prince named Madanavega was already in love with her and Śiva had promised him that she would become his wife. Madanavega visited Kaliṅgasenā at night in her palace, taking the form of Udayana with whom the princess was in love. Kaliṅgasenā married Madanavega by* gandharva *rites for she believed him to be Udayana. When Madanavega revealed himself, she realized that she loved him after all. Soon she was pregnant and gave birth to a beautiful daughter named Madanamañcukā, the incarnation of Rati, Kāma's wife. Udayana decided that Naravāhanadatta and Madanamañcukā should be married for she would make him an ideal wife. The two children grew up together and their attachment to each other increased with the passing months.*

Naravāhanadatta was anointed crown prince by his father and all the arts and sciences appeared in bodily form and entered his body. The young prince was taught the details and the subtleties of the art of governance by his ministers. And while this was happening, a vidyādhara *named Manasavega had fallen in love with Madanamañcukā. Her mother Kaliṅgasenā was anxious that the marriage of Naravāhanadatta and Madañamancukā be solemnized quickly so that her daughter would not be defiled by another man. Śiva appeared and announced that the marriage of the two would be good and suitable because Madanamañcukā was actually divine. She was the goddess Rati and therefore, had to marry Naravāhanadatta who was the incarnation of Kāma. The wedding was celebrated with great pomp and ceremony.*

Shortly after this, Naravāhanadatta was sojourning in the wooded hills where he met another vidyādharī, *Ratnaprabhā, who was also destined to be his wife. He married her and brought her back to Kauśāmbī where she lived happily with Madanamañcukā.*

Ratnaprabhā

May Śiva's head protect you, marked as it is by Pārvatī's nails as she playfully pulls his hair so that it appears studded with many moons.

May Gaṇeśa protect you, his curving trunk dripping with ichor so that it seems to be bestowing success.

When Naravāhanadatta had obtained Ratnaprabhā, his new vidyādharī *bride, he stayed with her in her house. The next day, his minister Gomukha and others came to visit. They were detained at the door by the door-keeper who allowed them to enter only after their arrival had been announced. They were welcomed with honour and Ratnaprabhā said to the door-keeper, 'Do not stop my husband's friends at the door like this again, for they are dearer to me than my life. I do not think that women's apartments should be guarded in this manner.' Then she said to her husband, 'Listen to what I have to say on the subject of the protection of women. I think that the custom of guarding them so carefully is useless. It arises from jealousy and serves no purpose at all. Well-born women protect themselves with chastity as their only bodyguard. But even the gods cannot protect the promiscuous, for no one can control a river or a lusty woman! Listen and I will tell you a story.*

The City Of Unchaste Women

'In the middle of the ocean there is an island named Ratnakūṭa. In the old days, it was ruled by a brave king who was a devotee of Viṣṇu and he was rightly named Ratnādhipati as he had several jewels in his possession. He wanted to conquer the world and make all the royal princesses his wives and so he undertook a great penance to propitiate Viṣṇu. Viṣṇu was pleased with Ratnādhipati and appeared to him in his manifest form and said, "Arise, for I am pleased with you. Listen to what I am going to say. In the country of Kaliṅga there is a *gandharva* who was cursed by a *muni* and has been born as a white elephant named Śvetaraśmi. Because of his penances in his previous birth and his devotion to me, Śvetaraśmi has divine wisdom. He can also fly through the air and remembers his past lives. In a dream, I instructed him to come here through the air and become your mount. You must ride that white elephant the way Indra rides Airāvata and fly through the air. Whichever king you visit thus will honour your presence and give you his daughter in marriage as a tribute for I will have already ordered them to do so in a dream. In this way you will conquer the entire earth as well as all its harems and you will marry eighty thousand princesses." After saying this, Viṣṇu disappeared.

'The king broke his fast and the next day, he saw the white elephant in the sky. He mounted him as Viṣṇu had instructed and conquered the entire earth and all the princesses. Ratnādhipati lived happily with his eighty thousand wives, enjoying himself as he pleased. Every day, he fed five hundred Brāhmins to please the pious elephant, Śvetaraśmi. One day, the king was mounted on his elephant and was roaming around the other islands. When he returned to his own island and was coming down from the air, a bird descended from Garuḍa struck that wonderful elephant with its beak. The king attacked the bird with his sharp elephant-goad and the bird flew away but the elephant fell to the ground in a faint. The king dismounted but the elephant, though he regained consciousness, was unable to stand despite all the efforts that were made and soon, he stopped eating. The elephant lay where he had fallen for five days and the king was so upset that he, too, stopped eating and prayed. "O guardians of the quarters, tell me the solution to this problem for otherwise I will cut off my own head and offer it to you!" He pulled out his sword and prepared to cut off his head when a voice rang out of the sky. "Do not act in haste. The elephant will rise only if he is touched by the hand of a chaste woman!"

'The king was delighted and called for his own wife and

chief queen, the carefully guarded Amṛtalatā. When the elephant did not rise at the touch of her hand Ratnādhipati called all his other wives. One by one they all touched the elephant but he did not rise, for not a single one of them was chaste. The king was terribly embarrassed when his eighty thousand wives were humiliated in public and so he called for all the women in his city and made each of them touch the elephant. But the elephant still did not rise and the king was shamed for there was not even one chaste woman in the entire city.

'Meanwhile, a merchant named Harṣagupta came to Ratnakūṭa from Tāmraliptī for he had heard what had happened and was filled with curiosity. Among his retinue was a servant woman named Śīlavatī who was devoted to her husband. When she saw what had happened, she said, "I will touch the elephant with my hand and if it is true that I have not even thought about a man apart from my husband, then it will rise." She touched the elephant and it stood up and began to eat. All the people gathered there were delighted to see Śvetaraśmi stand up and they shouted with joy and said, "Chaste women like this are hard to find, who, like Śiva, can create, preserve and destroy the world!" Ratnādhipati was also very pleased with the chaste Śīlavatī and gave her all kinds of wealth and jewels. He also honoured her master, Harṣagupta, and gave him a mansion near the palace. He decided to have nothing more to do with own wives and ordered that they be given only basic food and clothing.

'After the king had bathed, he sent for the chaste Śīlavatī and in private, in front of Harṣagupta, said to her, "If there is another girl in your father's family then give her to me in marriage for I know that she will be chaste and virtuous like you." Śīlavatī replied that she had a sister, Rājadattā, in Tāmraliptī and that the king could marry her if he so desired for she was very beautiful. The king agreed and, along with Śīlavatī and Harṣagupta, he mounted Śvetaraśmi and flew through the air on a personal visit to Tāmraliptī.

'Ratnādhipati went to Harṣagupta's house and that very day, he consulted astrologers for an auspicious time for him to marry Rājadattā. The astrologers made enquiries about the stars that the two of them had been born under and said "An auspicious conjunction for this wedding will arrive three months from now. If you marry Rājadattā under the present configuration she will definitely prove to be unchaste." Despite what the astrologers said, the king was eager to marry this beautiful woman for he was tired of living alone. He thought to himself, "Enough of all this debating! I want to marry Rājadattā today. She is the chaste Śīlavatī's sister and would never be unfaithful! There is an island in the middle of the ocean that is completely uninhabited. I will place her in the empty palace there and have her surrounded by women guards. How will she be unfaithful when she will not even see a man?"

'The king hastily married Rājadattā, who was given to him by Śīlavatī. After he had been received according to custom by Harṣagupta, he took his wife and Śīlavatī, mounted Śvetaraśmi and returned through the air to Ratnakūṭa where the people eagerly awaited his arrival. He richly rewarded Śīlavatī who had now fulfilled all her desires because she had reaped the fruits of her virtue. Ratnādhipati placed his wife on that elephant which could fly through the air and took her to the island which was inaccessible to men. There, he placed her in the empty palace and sent whatever she needed through the air with the elephant because he was so distrustful. He was deeply attached to Rājadattā and so he spent every night with her but returned to Ratnakūṭa during the day to perform his royal duties.

'One day, the king had an ill-omened dream and so he indulged in a drinking game with Rājadattā to get over his discomfort at the dream. Rājadattā was drunk and did not want Ratnādhipati to leave but he returned to Ratnakūṭa to attend to the royal affairs, for kingship requires great dedication. He transacted his business but all the while, his mind was uneasy, dwelling on the fact that he had left his wife alone in a drunken state. Meanwhile, Rājadattā was truly alone in that inaccessible place, for her servants were busy with their domestic chores. Suddenly she saw a man enter the door, like destiny that was determined to undo all the precautions taken to guard her. She was filled with astonishment when she saw him and because she was a little drunk, she went up to him and asked who he was and why he had come to that isolated place.

The Story Of Rājadattā's Lover

'That man, who had endured many hardships, said to Rājadattā, "I am the son of a merchant from Mathurā and my name is Pavanasena. When my father died, I was left an orphan and my family took away all my wealth. I went to another country and had to resort to the indignity of serving another man. With great difficulty, I managed to collect a little wealth through trading but once when I was travelling, I was raided by thieves along the way. Then I wandered as a beggar with others like myself and finally came to a mine of jewels known as Kanakakṣetra. I was contracted to pay the king of the area his share but even after digging for a whole year, I did not find a single jewel. While the other men that I was with were overjoyed with the jewels that they had found, I was overcome with sadness and went to the seashore and began to gather firewood. As I was collecting the wood to build a funeral pyre for myself, a merchant named Jīvadatta came that way. He was a compassionate man and he persuaded me not to kill myself. He fed me and as he was going to the island of Svarṇadvīpa the next day, he took me with him.

"After we had been sailing on the ocean for five days, huge clouds suddenly appeared. Torrential rain began to fall and the wind spun the ship around as if it were the head of a rutting elephant. The ship sank in a moment but I was lucky enough to grab a plank just as we were sinking. I climbed up on it and, at that very moment, the storm abated. Impelled by destiny, I came to this island and reached a forest. When I saw this rest-house, I entered it and here I saw you who are like a shower of nectar to my weary eyes." Rājadattā, impassioned by love and wine, pushed him onto the couch and took him in her arms. Where the five fires of womanhood, drunkenness, solitude, lust for a man and lack of self-control exist together, what chance does good conduct have? That a woman in the throes of love has no discretion is proved by the queen's attachment to that repulsive and unfortunate creature.

Ratnādhipati Learns The Truth

'Meanwhile, Ratnādhipati, the king of Ratnakūṭa, was eagerly on his way to the island, mounted on the sky-flying elephant. He entered the palace and saw his wife Rājadattā in the arms of another man. He was completely repulsed by the sight of that man and wanted to kill him, but he did not do so, for the man fell at his feet and cried piteously. Ratnādhipati saw that his wife was really frightened despite her drunken state and he thought to himself, "How can a woman who is addicted to wine, that chief cause of lust, ever be faithful? It is not possible to control a lustful woman even if she is guarded. Can one expect to hold a whirlwind in one's arms? This is the result of my ignoring the astrologers' predictions. Those who ignore the words of the wise are left with a bitter taste in their mouths. When I learned that Rājadattā was Śīlavatī's sister I forgot that the *kālakūṭa* poison was born along with the elixir of immortality. Besides, man can never match the workings of Fate!"

'Thinking thus, the king was not angry and spared the life of his wife's lover after asking him his life story. When the merchant's son was dismissed from there, he had few options left. He saw a ship coming in from afar and he climbed onto his plank and while drifting in the sea, he cried out, "Save me! Save me!" A merchant named Krodhavarmā was aboard the ship and he pulled the merchant's son out of the water and took him as a helper. The act which is appointed for a man's destruction follows him wherever he may go. For this idiot was discovered by Krodhavarmā in a secret relationship with his wife and was cast into the sea where he drowned.

'Meanwhile, Ratnādhipati made Rājadattā and her servants climb onto Śvetaraśmi and without any anger, brought her back to Ratnakūṭa and handed her over to Śīlavatī. He narrated the incident to his ministers and said, "What sorrow I have suffered as a result of my attachments to these meaningless and insubstantial pleasures! I will now go to the forest and take refuge with Viṣṇu so that I am never again the vehicle for such pain!" His ministers and Śīlavatī tried to dissuade him but the king was disillusioned with the world and would not change his mind. The king renounced all pleasures and gave half his wealth to the virtuous Śīlavatī and the other half to the Brāhmins. He made over his kingdom in the prescribed fashion to a superior Brāhmin named Pāpabhañjana. While his subjects watched with tears in their eyes, he called for Śvetaraśmi so that he could retire to an *āśrama* in the forest.

'As soon as the elephant was brought in, it renounced its body and a divine-looking man emerged wearing a necklace and a bracelet. The king asked him who he was and what all this meant. The man said, "There were two *gandharva* brothers living on Mount Malaya. I am Somaprabha and my elder brother was named Devaprabha. My brother had only one wife and he loved her dearly. Her name was Rājavatī. One day, when he was roaming through the air with her in his arms and I was also with them, we reached a place called Siddhavāsa. We worshipped Viṣṇu in his temple there and sang hymns of praise. Soon a *siddha* arrived there and could not take his eyes off Rājavatī who was singing beautifully. My brother grew jealous and angry and said to the *siddha*, 'How is it that despite being a *siddha* you are gazing lustfully at another man's wife?' The *siddha* was outraged and cursed him. 'Idiot! I was admiring the song, not your wife! For that, you will be born in a human womb as will your wife, and you will have to see her in the arms of another man with your own eyes!'

"I was angry when I heard the curse and in my immaturity, I hit the *siddha* with a toy elephant that I had in my hand that day. Then he cursed me as well. 'You will be born an elephant like the one with which you just hit me!' But the *siddha* was compassionate and when he was propitiated by my brother, he pronounced an end to our curses. 'Devaprabha, even though you shall be mortal, through Viṣṇu's favour you shall become the king of an island and your brother shall come to you as an elephant that is worthy of the gods. You shall obtain eighty thousand wives and shall learn of their unchasteness in public. After that, you shall marry the woman that your present wife has become and you shall see her in the arms of another man. You shall become disgusted with the world and shall give your kingdom to a Brāhmin. When you retire to the forest, your brother shall be released first from his curse as an elephant. Then you and your wife shall also be released from your curses.' This was the end of the curse that the *siddha* pronounced and we were all born as a result of our acts in our earlier births. Now the end of our curse has arrived!"

'After Somaprabha had said this, Ratnādhipati recalled his previous birth and said, "Indeed, I am that very Devaprabha and Rājadattā is my earlier wife Rājavatī." Then he and his wife gave up their human bodies and turned into *gandharvas* in a moment. In front of all the people, they rose into the air and returned to Mount Malaya, their home. Śīlavatī grew prosperous because of her virtues and went back to Tāmraliptī where she continued her life of good deeds.

'Thus it is true that a woman cannot be guarded by force in this world. But young women from good families are protected by their own virtue. Jealousy causes pointless pain and is irritating to others. Instead of protecting women, it creates desire within them.'

Naravāhanadatta and his ministers were very pleased when they heard this sensible story from Ratnaprabhā.

Naravāhanadattta's minister, intending to reiterate the lesson of Ratnaprabhā's story, said, 'Chaste women are hard to come by and there are several unchaste women who can never be trusted. Listen to this story which will prove that.

Niścyadatta Meets A Vidyādharī

'In Ujjayini there is a town that is famous all over the world. A merchant's son named Niścayadatta lived there. He lived by gambling but he was a generous man and every day, he would bathe in the Śiprā and worship Śiva. He would then give alms to the Brāhmins and the poor, eat his meal and would go to the cremation ground near Śiva's temple and anoint himself with sandal paste. Niścyadatta had smeared ointment on a stone pillar there and he would anoint his back by rubbing it against the pillar. Soon, the pillar became smooth and highly polished.

'One day, a painter and a sculptor came that way. When they saw the smooth pillar, the painter drew a picture of Pārvatī on it and the sculptor carved out the figure with his chisel. After the two of them had left, a *vidyādhara's* daughter passed that way in order to worship Śiva and saw the image of Pārvatī. The image was so clear that she felt that the goddess must be close by and after her prayers, she sat inside the pillar to rest.

'The merchant's son, Niścayadatta, came there and was astonished to see the image of Pārvatī carved on the pillar. He rubbed his limbs with the paste and then moved the paste to another part of the pillar so that he could anoint his back by rubbing against it. The beautiful *vidyādharī* inside the pillar saw him and was captivated by his good looks. She thought to herself "How can it be that such a handsome man has no one to anoint his back? I will do it for him!" She pushed her hand out of the pillar and rubbed his back for him lovingly. The merchant's son felt her touch and heard the tinkle of her bangles. At once, he caught hold of her hand. The *vidyādharī* was invisible but she spoke from inside the pillar. "What harm have I done you? Please let go of my hand!" and Niścayadatta replied, "I will release your hand if you reveal yourself and tell me who you are!' The *vidyādharī* agreed and he let go of her hand.

'She emerged from the pillar and revealed herself, beautiful in every limb. She sat down next to him and gazing at his face, she said, "In the Himalayan peaks there is a city named Puṣkarāvatī and it is ruled by a *vidyādhara* named Vindhyāpara. I am his daughter and my name is Anurāgaparā. I came here today to worship Śiva and then decided to rest. I saw you come to the pillar and rub your back against it to anoint yourself and you seemed like a weapon from the God of Love. My heart was filled with love for you and then my hand was covered with your paste as I rubbed your back. You know what happened after that. Now I must return to my father's house."

'The merchant's son said to her, "Beautiful lady, you have taken possession of my heart. How can you leave without returning it to me?" The *vidyādharī* was flooded with love for him and said, "I will marry you if you come to my city. It is not hard for you to reach and you will certainly be successful in your efforts for nothing is impossible for the adventurous." Having said this, Anurāgaparā flew into the sky and Niścayadatta returned to his home but his mind stayed with her. He thought of the hand that had come out of the pillar like a shoot from a tree and sighed. "Even though I grasped her hand, she got away from me! I will go to Puṣkarāvatī to see her and either I will die in the process or fate will help me!" He spent the day tormented by love and the next morning set out in a northerly direction.

Niścayadatta Subdues A Yakṣinī

'As he travelled, three other merchants' sons who were going in the same direction joined him as companions. They travelled through cities and villages and forests until at last they reached the northern regions which were inhabited by Mlecchas. Niścayadatta and his companions were captured by a Tajika who sold them to another Tajika. He, in turn, sent them in the care of his servants as a gift to a Turuṣka named Muravara. When the servants learned that Muravara was dead, they gave Niścayadatta and the other three to his son. Muravara's son thought, "These people have been sent as a gift by my father's friend so I must send them to my father by throwing them into his grave in the morning." He then had the four young men bound in chains until the morning so that they could not escape.

'While they were tied up at night, Niścayadatta spoke to his friends who were suffering from a terrible fear of death. "What is the point of being depressed? Pull yourselves together, for misfortunes run away in fear from those who are resolute. Concentrate your minds on the incomparable Durgā and she will help us through this!" He reassured them thus and prayed to Durgā. "I honour you, O goddess and I worship your feet that are dyed red as if with the blood of the demon Mahīṣa! You control even Śiva and thus, you rule the three worlds which live and move in you! You protected the three worlds, O slayer of Mahīṣa. Protect me now for I need your assistance, O you who care for your devotees!" They praised the goddess in these words and then they all fell asleep out of exhaustion.

'The goddess appeared in a dream and said to Niścayadatta and his companions, "Rise up, sons, and leave this place for your bonds have been loosened!" The young men woke in the middle of the night and saw that indeed, their bonds had come undone by themselves. Delighted, they told each other about the dream and quickly left the place. After they had gone a long way, the night ended and the merchants' sons who had been through such terrible things, said to Niścayadatta, "Dear friend, we have had enough of this region that is inhabited by Mlecchas. We have decided to go to the Deccan, but you can do as you please." Niścayadatta did not detain them and let them go where they wanted. He continued his long journey alone, drawn by the noose of love that Anurāgaparā had thrown around him.

'As he went along, Niścayadatta met four Pāsupata ascetics and crossed the river Vitastā with them. After that, they ate a meal and as the sun caressed the western mountains, Niścayadatta and the ascetics entered a forest that lay in their path. They met some wood-carriers who said to them, "Where are you going at the end of the day? There are no villages ahead. There is only a deserted Śiva temple in the forest but whoever stays there at night, whether inside or outside, is eaten by a *yakṣinī* named Śṛṅgotpādinī. She causes horns to grow on the foreheads of her prey and then, after they have been bewitched, consumes them as if they were sacrificial victims." The four ascetics who were Niścayadatta's travelling companions said, "What can a wretched *yakṣinī* do to us? We have spent many nights in various cremation grounds all over the place!"

'Niścayadatta went with the ascetics and when they reached the deserted Śiva temple, they all went in, prepared to spend the night there. The courageous Niścayadatta and the ascetics made a circle of ashes in the temple courtyard and lit a fire inside the circle. They remained in the circle, chanting *mantras* to protect themselves. Later that night, they saw the *yakṣinī* approaching. She was dancing and playing a musical instrument made of bones. She stared at one of the ascetics and recited a *mantra* as she danced outside the circle. Horns appeared on his forehead and he was bewitched. He began to dance and soon danced himself into the fire. The *yakṣinī* dragged his half-burnt body out of the fire and ate him with great delight. Then she stared at the second ascetic and recited the *mantra* that produced the horns and bewitched him. He, too, was made to dance and fell into the fire. She dragged him out and ate him in front of the others. In the same way, she managed to bewitch and eat all four ascetics one by one that night.

'As she was eating the last of the four, she grew drunk with all the flesh and blood and laid her musical instrument on the ground. Niścayadatta had kept his wits about him and he quickly picked it up. He began to dance around as he fixed his eyes on the *yakṣinī,* laughing and reciting the *mantra* that produced the horns which he had learned from hearing it so often. The *yakṣinī* was bewitched by the *mantra* and as the horns were just about to appear on her head, she fell at Niścayadatta's feet and begged for her life since she was afraid of death. "Do not kill me, great one! Have mercy on a woman! I come to you for protection so stop reciting the *mantra*! Save me for I know all about you and what you desire! I can help you! I will take you to the place where Anurāgaparā is!" When Niścayadatta heard her plea, the courageous man stopped reciting the *mantra*. He then climbed onto the *yakṣinī's* shoulder and she carried him through the air to find his beloved.

'When morning arrived, they had reached a wooded mountain where the *yakṣinī* bowed to Niścayadatta and said, "Now that the sun has risen, I no longer have the power to fly through the air. Spend the day in this forest. Eat the delicious fruit and drink the clear water here. I will go now to my own house and return at night and take you to Puṣkarāvatī, that jewel of the Himalayas and into the presence of Anurāgaparā." The *yakṣinī* set him down from her shoulder and taking his permission, went away, promising to return later. After she had left, Niścayadatta saw a beautiful clear lake but it was touched with poison. The sun pointed it out to him with its long rays as an example of what the heart of a passionate woman can be like. Niścayadatta knew by the smell that the lake was poisoned and after bathing, he wandered around the mountain, greatly afflicted with thirst.

The Lover Who Was Turned Into A Monkey

'As he wandered in search of water, he saw, at a height, two shining objects that gleamed like red rubies. He dug up the earth there and put it aside and then he saw the head of a monkey. It was alive and its eyes shone like rubies. While he stared in amazement and wondered what this might be, the monkey addressed him in a human voice. "I am a man that was turned into a monkey. I am also a Brāhmin. If you get me out of here, I will tell you my whole story!" Niścayadatta was even more surprised, but he moved the earth aside and freed the monkey. The monkey fell at his feet and said, "You have given me back my life by pulling me out of the earth! Eat and drink for you must be tired and now, thanks to you, I can also end my long fast." The monkey led Niścayadatta to the banks of a distant mountain river with shady trees and delicious fruit. Niścayadatta bathed and ate and then he said to the monkey who had also eaten, "If you are a man, how did you become a monkey? Tell me!" And the monkey said, "Listen and I will tell you.

'In Vārāṇasī, there was an excellent Brāhmin named Candrasvāmī. His virtuous wife gave birth to a son. That is me, my friend. My father named me Somasvāmī. In the course of time, I mounted the rutting elephant of love and my passion was hard to control. At that time, the merchant Śrīgarbha lived in Vārāṇasī and his beautiful daughter Bandhudattā was married to the merchant Varāhadatta of Mathurā. Bandhudattā had come to stay in her father's house and one day, when she was looking out of her window, she saw me passing by. She was attracted to me at once and sent me a message through her confidante, asking that we should meet. Her friend met me in secret and I, blinded by love, went with her to her house. She hid me there and went to fetch Bandhudattā whose enthusiasm made her forget her modesty. She threw her arms around my neck, for love is the only passion that creates daring in a woman. Thus, everyday, Bandhudattā would slip out of her father's house and meet me at her friend's.

"One day, Bandhudattā's husband arrived from Mathurā to take her back to her own home from which she had been away a long time. Her husband was anxious to take her away and her father gave her permission to leave, but Bandhudattā asked her friend for a second favour. 'My husband is definitely going to take me away to Mathurā but I cannot live without Somasvāmī. Tell me, what is the solution to this situation?' Her friend Sukhaśayā was a *yoginī* and had magical powers so she said, 'I have two *mantras*. One will turn a man into a monkey when a string is tied around his neck and the other will turn him into a man again when the string is unfastened. But the man will remain intelligent even when he is in monkey form. If you so desire, dear friend, you can keep your lover Somasvāmī for I can turn him into a monkey. You can take him to Mathurā as a pet. I will teach you the two *mantras* so that you can turn him into a monkey when you are in company and into your beloved when you are alone.' Bandhudattā agreed and she sent for me in secret and affectionately told me about the plan. I consented and in a moment Sukhaśayā turned me into a monkey by tying a string around my neck and reciting the *mantra*. Bandhudattā took me in that form to her husband and said, 'My friend gave me this little animal to play with.' Her husband was very pleased when he saw me in her arms as a pet for even though I was a monkey, I was intelligent and was able to speak. I stayed there, laughing to myself and thinking, 'What wonderful creatures women are!' for love will sway anyone.

"As promised, Bandhudattā's friend taught her the *mantra* and the next day, she left her father's house to go to Mathurā with her husband. Out of love for her, Bandhudattā's husband had one of his retainers carry me on his back during the journey. In three days we reached a forest that lay in our path and which was inhabited by hordes of wild monkeys. When the wild monkeys saw me, they attacked us in groups from all sides, calling to each other in their shrill voices. The excited monkeys came and bit the servant who was carrying me on his shoulder and deeply agitated, he threw me onto the ground and ran away in fear and the monkeys picked me up. Out of her love for me, Bandhudattā, her husband and all the retainers attacked the monkeys with sticks and stones, but they could not drive them away. And the monkeys, as though enraged at this assault, pulled out each and every hair from my body with their nails as I lay there in a faint.

"Finally, I recovered my strength and loosened my bonds. I was able to get away from the wild monkeys because of the string around my neck and because I prayed to Śiva. I ran into the dense jungle and disappeared from their sight. Gradually, wandering from forest to forest, I reached this wood. 'How could lusting after another man's wife have resulted in my being turned into a monkey in this very birth? I have even lost Bandhudattā!' I thought to myself as I wandered around this place in the rains, burning in the fires of grief. But my troubles were not yet over, for a female elephant found me and picked me up with her trunk. She threw me onto an anthill that had become muddy with the rains. I know that she must have been some goddess impelled to do this by Fate, for even though I tried hard, I could not extricate myself from the mud. Fortunately, I did not die and as I meditated on Śiva, I gained true knowledge. I felt neither hunger nor thirst and today, dear friend, you have extricated me from this dry mud. Although I have gained knowledge, I do not have the power to liberate myself from this monkey-form. I shall become a man if someone unties the string around my neck and recites the correct *mantra*. This is the story of my life. But how did you happen to come to this forest? Tell me your story now, friend," said the monkey.

'Niścayadatta told the Brāhmin Somasvāmī who was now in monkey-form, the story of his adventures, how he had come from Ujjayini in search of a *vidyādharī* and how he had overcome a *yakṣinī* who had brought him there at night. Somasvāmī was still wise, even though he now bore the form of a monkey and he said to Niścayadatta, "Like me, you, too, have endured a great deal for the sake of a woman. But women, like good fortune, are fickle. Their love is brief like the twilight, their hearts are twisted like river beds. They cannot be trusted like snakes and like lightning, they are unpredictable. Anurāgaparā the *vidyādharī*, even though she is in love with you now, will drop you when she finds one of her own kind, for you are only a human being. Stop your efforts to obtain this woman for you will be left with a bitter taste in your mouth! Do not go onwards to Puṣkarāvatī, the city of the *vidyādharas*. Climb onto the *yakṣinī's* back and return to Ujjayini. Listen to my words, for when I was in the throes of passion, I did not listen to a friend's advice and I am suffering as a result of that! When I was in love with Bandhudattā, a dear friend of mine, Bhavaśarmā the Brāhmin, tried to dissuade me by saying, 'Do not fall under the spell of a woman for women are hard-hearted. I will tell you a story to prove my point. Listen.

The Battle Of The Yoginīs

"In Vārāṇasī there lived a young Brāhmin woman Somadā, who was beautiful and lascivious, but she was also secretly a *yoginī*. As luck would have it, I got involved in a secret relationship with her and as we spent time together, my attachment to her grew. Once, I hit her in a fit of jealousy but that cruel creature endured it silently, hiding her anger for that moment. The next day, she placed a string around my neck as if in play and I immediately turned into an ox! She sold me to a man who kept camels when she received the right price. He loaded me with burdens and seeing me suffer, a *yoginī* named Bandhamocinī was moved to compassion. She learned through her magic powers that Somadā had turned me into an animal and when my master was not looking, she slipped the string off my neck. I returned to the form of a man and my master thought that I had escaped and looked all over for me.

"I was leaving that place with Bandhamocinī when, as luck would have it, Somadā passed that way and saw me from a distance. She was extremely angry and said to Bandhamocinī, 'Why have you freed this wicked man from his animal state? You shall face the consequences of this terrible deed! Tomorrow I will kill both you and this wretched man!' She went away, but Bandhamocinī, to counteract Somadā's powers, said to me, ' She will come in the form of a black mare to kill me and I will take refuge in the form of a brown mare. When we have begun to fight, you must come upon her from behind with your sword and hit her hard. That is how we shall kill her. Come to my house in the morning,' and she showed me where she lived.

"When she entered the house, I returned to my own home, feeling that I had lived through more than one life in this birth. I went to Bandhamocinī's house in the morning with my sword in hand and Somadā arrived there in the form of a black mare. Bandhamocinī took the form of a brown mare and they began to fight, kicking with their heels and biting with their teeth. I hit that wicked creature Somadā with my sword three times and she was killed by Bandhamocinī. I was now free from fear and from the danger of being turned into an animal and I made up my mind to avoid the company of wicked women who usually share these three failings—fickleness, rashness and a desire for the company of *yoginīs*. 'Bandhudattā seems to associate with *yoginīs*, why do you then chase her? If she does not love her husband, why do you think that she loves you?'

"Even though my friend Bhavaśarmā gave me this advice, I did not listen and now I am in this condition. So listen to me and give up your passion for Anurāgaparā. She will reject you the minute she finds a lover from her own race. Like a bee that wanders from flower to flower, a woman always desires new men. You will suffer like me, my friend!" But even though Somasvāmī who had been turned into a monkey spoke these words, they did not enter Niścayadatta's heart which was already full of love. He said to the monkey, "Anurāgaparā will not desert me for she is born in the refined family of a *vidyādhara* king."

Niścayadatta Marries The Vidyādharī

'While they were talking, the sun sank into the western mountain in hues of red as if to please Niścayadatta. The night came like a messenger from the *yakṣinī* Śṛṅgotpādinī and soon after, she herself arrived. She placed Niścayadatta on her shoulder and took him towards his beloved after he had said goodbye to the monkey who begged to be remembered. In the middle of the night, they reached Puṣkarāvatī, the city of Anurāgaparā's father. Anurāgaparā had learnt through her magic powers that Niścayadatta was coming and she came to greet him the moment they arrived. The *yakṣinī* put him down and pointing to Anurāgaparā, she said, "Here comes your beloved like another moon to please your eyes at night. I must leave now." She bowed to Niścayadatta and left.

'Anurāgaparā was delighted to see her lover after such a long separation and she embraced him and welcomed him eagerly. He returned her embraces and being overjoyed after so many troubles, he felt as though he had left his own body and entered hers. He immediately made her his wife by *gandharva* rites and she created a magic city with her powers. Niścayadatta lived with her in that city which lay outside Puṣkarāvatī and her parents knew nothing of this for she had bewitched them. Niścayadatta told her about all his adventures and troubles and she honoured him and gave him all the pleasures that he could imagine. He told her the wonderful story of Somasvāmī who had been turned into a monkey and said, "If you can release my friend from his animal condition through your powers, you will have performed a worthy deed." Anurāgaparā replied that the *mantras* of *yoginīs* lay outside her powers but that she would fulfil Niścayadatta's wish with the help of her friend Bhadrarūpā, a witch. Niścayadatta was very pleased and said, "Let us go and visit my friend." The next day, she put Niścayadatta on her lap and they flew through the air and arrived in the forest where the monkey lived.

'Niścayadatta saw his friend in his monkey form and approached him with Anurāgaparā who bowed to him and asked after his health. The monkey welcomed them and said to his friend, "Today I am well for I see that you are together with Anurāgaparā!" and he blessed the *vidyādharī*. They all sat down on a beautiful stone and talked about Somasvāmī's previous adventures that Niścayadatta had already related to Anurāgaparā. Then Niścayadatta and his wife left and she carried him in her arms through the sky to their own house.

'The next day, Niścayadatta wanted to see his friend, the monkey, again and this time, Anurāgaparā said, "Go by yourself today. I will teach you how to fly as well as how to ascend and descend from the sky," and so saying she bestowed the skill on him. Niścayadatta went through the sky to meet his friend. He stayed with him a long time and while he was there, Anurāgaparā went out into her garden. She was sitting there when a young *vidyādhara* who was wandering aimlessly through the air arrived. He realized through his powers that Anurāgaparā was a *vidyādharī* with a human husband, but he was overcome with love for her and came up to her. When she looked up, she saw that he was young and handsome and she asked him softly who he was and where he had come from. "I am a *vidyādhara* named Rājabhañjana and I am known for my mastery over *vidyādhara* skills and powers," he replied. "Lady with doe-like eyes, I fell in love with you the moment I saw you and have become your slave. End your relationship with this mortal who lives on earth and take me, for I am your equal, before your father finds out about this!" She looked at him shyly and that fickle woman thought to herself, "This man is right for me!" He knew that he had convinced her and made her his wife, for secret love needs nothing more than the union of two hearts.

'Niścayadatta returned after his meeting with Somasvāmī and the *vidyādhara* had already left. But Anurāgaparā no longer had any love for her human husband and she did not share his embrace saying that she had a headache. But that foolish man was so confused by love that he could not tell that she was lying and spent the day thinking that she was ill. The next day he went to see his friend with the new skills that he had learnt but he was depressed. When he had left, Anurāgaparā's lover returned, having spent a sleepless night without her. She was waiting for him eagerly and he embraced her but because he had not slept the night before, he soon fell asleep in her arms. Anurāgaparā hid her sleeping lover with her powers and because she too had not slept at night, she fell asleep as well.

The Monkey Displays His Wisdom

'Niścayadatta, meanwhile, was with the monkey who welcomed him warmly and asked him why he seemed depressed. Niścayadatta replied, "Anurāgaparā is not at all well and that is why I am depressed for I love her more than my life." The monkey who had special knowledge said, "She is sleeping now so go to her and take her in your arms.

Bring her to me through the air with the skills that she taught you and I will show you something truly amazing." Niścayadatta flew through the air and carefully lifted Anurāgaparā who was still asleep but he did not see the *vidyādhara* sleeping in her arms since she had made him invisible. In a moment, he had brought her to the monkey. The monkey gave Niścayadatta a *mantra* by which he could, through supernatural sight, see the *vidyādhara* who was clasped in Anurāgaparā's arms. "What does this mean?" cried Niścayadatta and the monkey, who could see the truth, told him everything.

'Niścayadatta flew into a rage and meanwhile the *vidyādhara*, his wife's lover, flew away into the sky and disappeared. Anurāgaparā also awoke and when she realized that her secret had been discovered, she stood there, ashamed, her eyes downcast. His eyes full of tears, Niścayadatta said to her, "Wicked one! How could you do this to me? I trusted you! We know of ways to control mercury which is the most restless of all substances, but there seems to be no way to control a woman's heart!" Anurāgaparā could not answer and stood there weeping softly. She flew back to her home through the air.

'Then the monkey said to his friend, Niścayadatta, "Even though I tried to convince you not to, you chased this beautiful woman and the pain that you are now suffering is the fruit of uncontrolled passion. How can one trust either good fortune or fickle women? Enough grief, quiet yourself now. Even the gods cannot master destiny!" Niścayadatta was calmed by the monkey's speech and he controlled his grief and sought refuge in Śiva. Thereafter, he stayed in the forest with the monkey.

'It so happened that a female ascetic named Moksadā passed that way. Niścayadatta bowed to her and she asked, "How is it that even though you are a man, you have a monkey as a friend?" He told her his own sad story and then he related the curious adventures of his friend and said, "If you know any *mantras* that will effect this, please release my friend, this wonderful Brāhmin, from his animal condition!" The woman agreed and recited a *mantra* and loosened the string around the monkey's neck. Somasvāmī gave up his monkey body and became a man like before. The ascetic disappeared in a flash like lightning and in the course of time, Niścayadatta and the Brāhmin Somasvāmī attained liberation after performing many austerities.

'Thus, women are naturally restless. Their behaviour can lead a man to a chain of events that result in true discrimination and even an indifference to worldly pleasures and matters. But, among them, one can occasionally find a truly virtuous woman who adorns her family as moonlight does the night sky.'

When Naravāhanadatta and Ratnaprabhā heard this wonderful story from Gomukha, they were very pleased.

On another hunting trip, Naravāhanadatta met and married the princess Karpūrikā. The expanding royal family lived together happily in Kauśāmbī. One day, the vidyādhara *Vajraprabha came to visit his future emperor. He assured the company that Naravāhanadatta would unite both the northern and southern* vidyādhara *territories under his rule.*

Alaṅkāravatī

We bow to Gaṇeśa before whom even the mountains bow when he dances for they stoop with the weight of Niśumbha.[1]

Naravāhanadatta Falls In Love With Alaṅkāravatī

Naravāhanadatta, the son of the king of Vatsa, lived in his father's palace and listened with amazement to the tales of the vidyādharas. *One day, while he was hunting, he sent back his entourage and entered a vast forest with Gomukha as his only companion. His right eye began to flutter, indicating good fortune and soon, he heard singing and the sound of the* vīṇā. *He proceeded in the direction of the music and not far away, he came upon a Śiva temple. He tethered his horse and entered the temple. He saw a celestial woman inside, surrounded by her attendants, praising Śiva with her music. The moment he set eyes on her, Naravāhanadatta's mind was disturbed as the waters of the ocean are disturbed by the reflection of the moon. Despite her natural modesty, the young woman returned his gaze with passion and love and as a result, she was unable to play another note on her* vīṇā.

Gomukha understood what was passing through Naravāhanadatta's mind and asked one of the attendants who the young woman was. At that very moment, an older vidyādharī *who resembled the younger woman in looks, descended from the skies preceded by a ray of red-gold light. She sat down beside the younger woman who rose and touched her feet. The older woman blessed her and said, 'May you obtain a husband who will be a king of the* vidyādharas.' *Naravāhanadatta approached the older woman and bowed before her. After she had blessed him, he asked softly, 'Mother, who is this girl?' and the older woman replied, 'Listen and I will tell you.'*

Alaṅkāravatī's Story

'On a mountain as high as Himavat, there is a city named Sundarapura where the *vidyādhara* king Alaṅkāraśīla used to live. That generous and virtuous king had a wife named Kāñcanaprabhā. When a son was born to them, the goddess Pārvatī told the king in a dream that the boy should be named Dharmaśīla because he would be devoted to righteousness. In time, the prince grew into a young man. The king taught him all the sciences and anointed him the crown prince. The prince was so righteous that his subjects loved him even more than they had loved his father.

'Then Kāñcanaprabhā became pregnant again and this time, she gave birth to a daughter. When the child was born, a voice spoke, "She will be the queen of Naravāhanadatta, the ruler of the three worlds." The child was named Alaṅkāravatī and as time passed, she grew into a young woman as beautiful as the new moon. When she was old enough, her father taught her all the arts and sciences himself. She was devoted to Śiva and wandered from temple to temple worshipping him. Meanwhile, her brother, Dharmaśīla, even though he was still young, grew disinterested in worldly matters. He said to his father, "These worldly pleasures are impermanent and do not appeal to me. Is there anything in the world that does not turn bitter at the end? Have you heard a sage's words on this subject, 'All created things are destroyed, all that is raised high falls, all unions end in separation, all life ends in death.' How can the wise enjoy momentary pleasures? Neither wealth nor earthly pleasures are of any use in the world beyond. Only righteousness stays as a friend, every step of the way. I am going into the forest to perform penances and austerities until I attain the highest truth."

'Alaṅkāraśīla was deeply disturbed by his son's words. With his eyes full of tears, he said to the boy, "My son, why are you so convinced of this even though you are so young? Good people desire a life of peace and solitude after they have enjoyed their youth. This is the time for you to be married and to rule the kingdom justly and enjoy worldly pleasures, not renounce the world." In reply to his father's entreaty, Dharmaśīla said, "Age does not determine periods of abstinence or periods of enjoyment. Even a child can attain self-control if he is favoured by the gods, but no evil person, even though he is old, can aspire to the same peace. I have no interest in the kingdom or in taking a wife. I have only one purpose in life and that is to please Śiva with austerities."

'When Dharmaśīla said this, the king realized that whatever efforts he made, the boy would not change his mind. Weeping, he said, "My son, you display total detachment even though you are so young. Why shouldn't I, who am so much older, also take refuge in the forest?" The *vidyādhara* king went into the world of mortals and gave away huge quantities of gold and jewels to Brāhmins and to the poor. Then he returned to his own city and said to his wife Kāñcanaprabhā, "I order you to stay in our city and look after our daughter Alaṅkāravatī. The auspicious time for her marriage will be on this very day, a year from now. Then I will give her to Naravāhanadatta. Our son-in-law will come to our city and rule the three worlds." The king made his wife take an oath that she would abide by his wishes. Though she wept, he sent her back with their daughter, and went into the forest with his son.

'Kāñcanaprabhā lived in the city with her daughter, for which virtuous wife would ignore her husband's wishes? Meanwhile, Alaṅkāravatī went from one Śiva temple to another and her mother accompanied her out of affection. One day, the science of *prajñāpti* directed Alaṅkāravatī thus: "Go and worship Śiva at Svayambhu in Kashmir and you will easily obtain Naravāhanadatta, king of the *vidyādharas,* as a husband." Alaṅkāravatī went to Kashmir with her mother and worshipped Śiva at all the holy places, Nandikṣetra, Mahādevagiri, Amaraparvata, the Sureśvarī mountains, Vijaya and Kapaṭeśvara. After they had completed this pilgrimage, Alaṅkāravatī and her mother returned home.

'Fortunate one, know that this girl is that same Alaṅkāravatī and that I am her mother Kāñcanaprabhā. She came to this Śiva temple today without telling me but through the science of *prajñāpti*, I knew that she was here and I also knew that you would arrive here. Accept my daughter in marriage as ordained by the gods. Tomorrow is the day appointed for her wedding by her father. Return to your city Kauśāmbī today. We shall also leave and tomorrow, when king Alaṅkāraśīla returns from the *āśrama*, he will himself give you his daughter in marriage.'

Alaṅkāravatī and Naravāhanadatta were very upset when they heard this. Their eyes filled with tears for they could not bear to be separated even for a night, like cakravāka *birds at the end of the day. When Kāñcanaprabhā saw their distress, she said, 'Why are you so upset at the idea of being separated for one night? Those of firm resolve are able to bear indefinite separation. Listen to the story of Rāma and Sītā.*

Sītā's Banishment

'Long ago, King Daśaratha of Ayodhyā had a son named Rāma who was the older brother of Lakṣmaṇa, Śatrughna and Bharata. Rāma was the incarnation of a part of Viṣṇu[2] and was born for the destruction of Rāvaṇa. Rāma's wife was Sītā, the daughter of King Janaka and she was dearer to him than life. Bound by destiny, Daśaratha bestowed the kingdom on Bharata and sent Rāma into the forest with Sītā and Lakṣmaṇa. Rāvaṇa abducted Rāma's beloved Sītā with his magic powers and took her away to Laṅkā, his own city, killing Jaṭāyu along the way. The bereaved Rāma killed Vālī and made an alliance with Sugrīva. Then he sent Hanumān to fetch news of his wife. When Hanumān found Sītā imprisoned on the island of Laṅkā, Rāma crossed the ocean by building a bridge over it and killed Rāvaṇa. He left Laṅkā in the care of Vibhīṣaṇa and brought Sītā back with him. He returned to Ayodhyā from the forest and while he was ruling the kingdom that Bharata bestowed upon him, Sītā became pregnant.

'One day, Rāma was wandering through the city with a small entourage so that he could learn what the people wanted. He saw a man throwing his wife out of the house because she had been with another man. The woman wailed, "Lord Rāma did not reject his wife even though she had been in the house of a *rākṣasa*. My husband is superior to him since he is throwing me out for having been in the house of a relative!" When Rāma heard the woman say this to her husband he was very disturbed and returned to his palace. Fearing the people's gossip, Rāma abandoned Sītā in the forest. To a successful man, the pain of separation is preferable to infamy.

'Burdened by her pregnancy, Sītā reached the *āśrama* of the sage Vālmīki. He comforted her and persuaded her to stay there. The other sages at the *āśrama* said to each other, "Sītā must be guilty otherwise her husband would not abandon her like this. We are becoming polluted by being with her all the time. But Vālmīki will not ask her to leave the *āśrama* out of pity. He overcomes the pollution of her presence by the power of his austerities. We had better go to another *āśrama*." Vālmīki understood what was happening and said, "Have no fear. I have seen with my meditative powers that this woman is pure and innocent."

'Even after this assurance the other sages were still doubtful and so Sītā said to them, "Test my chastity by any means you like and if I prove to be guilty you can cut off my head." The sages felt sorry for her and said, "There is a lake named Ṭiṭṭibhasāra in this great forest. In the old days, a woman named Ṭiṭṭibhī was falsely accused by her husband of having an affair with another man. She called upon the Earth and the *lokapālas* and they created this lake to prove her innocence. Let Rāma's wife prove her chastity there."

'Sītā went with the sages to the lake and, on its shores, the chaste woman said, "Mother Earth, if I have never thought about another man even in a dream, let me reach the other side of the lake!" and entered the waters. The Earth appeared and lifted Sītā onto her lap and carried her to the other side. The sages honoured Sītā when they saw that and wanted to curse Rāma for abandoning her. But Sītā, who was a devoted wife, said to them, "Do not think ill of my husband. Curse me instead for I am the wicked one!" The sages were pleased with her and blessed her with the birth of a son. She continued to live at the hermitage and in time, she gave birth to a boy. Vālmīki named him Lava.

'One day, Sītā took the child with her when she went to bathe. When Vālmīki saw the empty hut, he was worried. "Sītā always leaves the child here when she goes to bathe. Where can he be? He must have been carried away by a wild animal. I had better create another child or Sītā will die of grief when she returns from her bath." Vālmīki took a blade of *kuśa* grass and created an infant that looked exactly like Lava and left him in the hut. When Sītā came back and saw the child, she asked the sage, "My child is with me. Where did this one come from?" Vālmīki told her what had happened. "Accept this second child also, for I made him from a blade of *kuśa* grass with my powers." Sītā brought up both the boys, Lava and Kuśa, and Vālmīki performed all the sacred ceremonies for them. The two Kṣatriya boys learned the martial arts and all the sciences from Vālmīki.

'Once, the two boys killed a deer that belonged to the *āśrama* and ate its flesh. On another occasion, they made a toy out of a *liṅgam* that Vālmīki used for worship. The sage was angry but Sītā interceded on their behalf and Vālmīki allowed the boys to perform a penance to make up for their misdeeds. "Let Lava bring golden lotuses from Kubera's lake as well as some of the *mandāra* flowers that grow in Kubera's garden. When both the brothers have worshipped the *liṅgam* by offering these flowers they will have atoned for their bad behaviour." Lava, though still a boy, went to Kailāsa and entered Kubera's garden and his lake. He killed the *yakṣas* who were there and picked the lotuses and the flowers. On his way back, he was tired and rested under a tree along the path. Meanwhile, Lakṣmaṇa came by looking for a man with all the auspicious marks for Rāma's human sacrifice. He challenged Lava to fight according to Kṣatriya custom and, after stunning him with a stupefying arrow, he tied him up and carried him to Ayodhyā.

'At the *āśrama*, Sītā was worried about Lava's absence but Vālmīki comforted her. He knew what had happened and said to Kuśa, "Lava has been captured by Lakṣmaṇa and taken to Ayodhyā. Go there and free him after you have defeated Lakṣmaṇa with these," and he gave Kuśa divine weapons. Kuśa laid siege to the sacrificial grounds at Ayodhyā and defeated Lakṣmaṇa in single combat with the divine weapons. When Rāma advanced to meet him, he found that he, too, could not defeat the boy who had Vālmīki's power. Rāma asked him who he was and why he had come there.

'Kuśa said, "Lakṣmaṇa has captured my older brother and brought him here. I have come to set him free. Our mother Sītā has told us that we, Lava and Kuśa, are the sons of Rāma," and he related her story. Rāma broke into tears and had Lava brought before him. He embraced both the boys, saying, "I am that wicked Rāma." The citizens gathered and when they saw the two boys, they praised Sītā. Rāma acknowledged the boys as his sons. He had Sītā brought to Ayodhyā from Vālmīki's *āśrama* and after handing over the responsibilities of the kingdom to his sons, he lived happily with her.

'Resolute people can endure long separations like this. How is it that the two of you cannot bear it for even one night?' said Kāñcanaprabhā to Naravāhanadatta and her daughter Alaṅkāravatī who was eager to be married.

She rose into the air with her daughter and promised to return the next day. Naravāhanadatta went back to Kauśāmbī with a heavy heart.

The very next day, Naravāhanadatta and Alaṅkāravatī were married in a grand ceremony with all the vidyādharas *in attendance. Naravāhanadatta went and spent some time in his father-in-law's city, Sundarapura, and then returned with his new wife to Kauśāmbī.*

One day, Gomukha told Naravāhanadatta the following story.

The Princess Who Refused To Marry

'There is a city on earth appropriately named Śūrapura for it is the dwelling place of heroes. King Mahāvarāha, destroyer of his enemies, ruled there. Because he had propitiated Pārvatī, his wife Padmarati bore him a daughter named Anaṅgarati. As Anaṅgarati grew up, she became proud of her beauty and though many kings asked for her hand, she refused to get married. She said, "I will only marry a man who is courageous and handsome and accomplished in at least one thing."

'Four young men from the south, who had heard about Anaṅgarati and had the qualities that she desired, arrived in Śūrapura to seek her hand. They were announced by the door-keeper and in Anaṅgarati's presence, Mahāvarāha asked them, "What are your names and what are your backgrounds? What are your skills?" The first one said, "I am a Śūdra named Pañcapaṭṭika and I can weave five sets of garments every day. I give one to a Brāhmin, the second I offer to Śiva, the third I wear myself, the fourth I would give to my wife if I had one and the fifth I sell and live off the proceeds."

'The second one said, "I am a Vaiśya named Bhāṣājña and I know all the languages of all the birds and animals." The third one said, "I am a Kṣatriya named Khaḍgadhara and no one wields a sword better than I." The fourth one said, "I am a Brāhmin named Jīvadatta and by the grace of the goddess, I can bring a dead woman back to life." Then the Śūdra, the Vaiśya and the Kṣatriya praised their own courage, good looks and skill but the Brāhmin praised only his courage and his skill, saying nothing about his looks. The king told the door-keeper to take the four young men to his house so that they could rest.

'Mahāvarāha asked Anaṅgarati, "Daughter, which of these four young men do you like?" and she replied that she did not like any of them. She said, "One is a Śūdra and a weaver. What is the use of his virtues? The second is a Vaiśya. Of what value is the knowledge of the language of birds and others? I am a high born Kṣatriya woman, how can I be given to him? The third one, the Kṣatriya, is equal to me in rank but he is poor and lives by selling his services. I am a princess, how can I marry him? The fourth one, the Brāhmin Jīvadatta, I do not like at all. He is ugly and he is unrighteous. He has fallen from his exalted position because he has rejected the Vedas. You should punish him instead of offering me to him as a wife! As a king, you are the protector of the four castes and the four stages of life. A king who upholds righteousness is far better than a king who wins battles. The king who upholds righteousness will rule over thousands of heroic kings who win battles." The king sent his daughter back to her chambers and went to have a bath.

'The next day, the four young men wandered around the city, satisfying their curiosity. Just then, a vicious elephant named Padmakabala broke out of the stables and ran amok, trampling the people who came in his way. When the great elephant saw the four young men, he charged towards them to kill them and they in turn advanced towards him with their weapons ready. Khaḍgadhara, the only Kṣatriya among them, went ahead of the others and attacked the elephant alone. With a single blow, he cut off the trumpeting elephant's trunk as easily as if it were a lotus stalk. He displayed his swiftness by escaping between the elephant's feet and dealt him another blow from the back. With the third blow, he cut off the elephant's feet and the animal fell down with a groan and died. The townspeople were amazed at this display of courage and the king was very impressed when he heard about it.

'The next day, the king went out hunting with Khaḍgadhara and the other young men. The king and his entourage killed tigers, deer and boars. Angry lions rushed towards them when they heard the trumpeting of elephants, but Khaḍgadhara split a lion that attacked them in half with a single blow of his sharp sword. He killed a second lion by grasping it by the foot with his left hand and smashing it onto the ground. Bhāṣājña, Jīvadatta and Pañcapaṭṭika also killed a lion each by dashing it to the ground. The four young men killed lions and tigers with ease even though they were on foot, and the king was full of admiration for them. When the hunt was over, he returned to his city and the young men went to the door-keeper's house.

'The king reached his chambers and, even though he was tired, he summoned his daughter and told her about the accomplishments of the four young men. She was suitably impressed so the king said to her, "If Pañcapaṭṭika and Bhāṣājña are low caste and Jīvadatta, even though he is a Brāhmin, is ugly and dabbles in forbidden practices, what is wrong with the Kṣatriya Khaḍgadhara? He is handsome and noble and he is known for his strength and courage. He killed the mad elephant, he takes lions by the foot and dashes them to the earth and kills other lions with a single stroke of his sword. If you find fault with him for being poor and serving others, I can make him into a man served by others. Please, daughter, choose him as your husband."

'Anaṅgarati said, "Bring the men here and ask the astrologer what he thinks." The king had the young men summoned and in their presence, he asked the astrologer, "Find out whose horoscope matches Anaṅgarati's and set an auspicious time for the wedding." The astrologer asked the young men what stars they had been born under and after considering the matter for a long time, he said to the king, "If you will not be angry with me, I will tell you the truth. None of these men suit your daughter. Nor will she be married here. She is a *vidyādharī* who is on earth because of a curse. The curse will end in three months. Let these men wait here for three months and if she does not return to her own world, the wedding can take place." They all accepted the astrologer's advice and waited.

'When the three months had passed, the king called the four young men, the astrologer and Anaṅgarati. Mahāvarāha saw that his daughter had grown more beautiful and he was very pleased but the astrologer felt sure that the time of her death had arrived. As the king was asking the astrologer what should be done now that the three months had passed, Anaṅgarati remembered her previous birth and covering her face with her upper garment, she gave up her human body. "Why is she doing this?" thought the king, but when he uncovered her face, he saw that she was dead, like a frost-bitten lotus. Her eyes, which had been like black bees, had ceased to move, her flower-like face was pale and her sweet voice was silenced like the song of a swan. Overcome with grief, the king fell to the ground, like the mountains which fell when Indra had clipped their wings[3]. The queen also fainted and as her ornaments fell from her body like blossoms, she seemed like a flowering tree felled by an elephant. The courtiers wailed loudly and the four young men were very upset.

'When King Mahāvarāha recovered his senses, he said to Jīvadatta, "This is your moment. None of the others have the appropriate skill. You declared that you could bring a dead woman back to life. Revive my daughter and I will give her to you in marriage." Jīvadatta sprinkled the princess with water over which he had read some *mantras* and chanted the following verse. "Cāmuṇḍā, goddess who laughs loudly and wears a garland of skulls, you who are not to be looked at, help me!" Despite all his efforts, the princess remained lifeless and Jīvadatta was overcome with despair. He said, "This skill that was bestowed upon me by the goddess has proved fruitless. Since I am now an object of scorn, I have no interest in living." He got ready to cut off his head with a sword when a voice spoke from the sky. "Wait, Jīvadatta! Do not act in haste! Listen! This young woman is a *vidyādharī* who has been a mortal for so long because of her celestial father's curse. Now she has renounced her human body and returned to her realm in her own body. Go back and worship the goddess. You will win back this noble *vidyādharī* through her favour. Neither you nor the king should grieve for her because she is enjoying celestial pleasures." The king performed the funeral rites for his daughter and he and his wife got over their sorrow. The other three young men returned to where they had come from.

Jīvadatta Wins The Vidyādharī

'Jīvadatta felt somewhat reassured and went to worship and

propitiate the goddess with austerities. She appeared to him in a dream and said, "I am pleased with you! Get up and listen to what I have to say. In the city of Vīrapura in the Himalayas, there is a *vidyādhara* king called Samara. His queen Anaṅgavatī gave birth to a daughter named Anaṅgaprabhā. Anaṅgaprabhā was so proud of her youth and beauty that she refused to take a husband. Her parents were very angry and cursed her: 'You shall become a mortal and not experience the joys of marriage even in that state. When you are sixteen years old, you will give up your human body and return here. A mortal who is ugly because he was cursed for falling in love with a *muni's* daughter and who has a magic sword will take you back to the world of humans against your will. You will be unfaithful to him and will be separated from your husband. Because your husband took away the wives of eight men in his previous birth, he will experience enough sorrow for eight births. You will lose your memory and take many human husbands because you persisted in rejecting the husband chosen for you. You rejected Madanaprabha who wanted to marry you and was equal to you in birth. He shall also be born as a human king and shall become your husband. Then you shall be freed from your curse and return to your own world and you shall marry a suitable man.'

"Anaṅgarati was that *vidyādharī* who was cursed by her father. She has now returned to her parents and is Anaṅgaprabhā once again. Go to Vīrapura and obtain that girl for a bride by defeating her father in battle even though he is protected by his skills and his heritage. Take this sword that will make you fly through the air and invincible in battle." After saying so, the goddess vanished and when Jīvadatta awoke, he saw that the magic sword was in his hand. Jīvadatta was very happy and praised the goddess. By the nectar of her grace, the fatigue from his long austerities disappeared and he was refreshed. He flew around the Himalayas with the sword in his hand till he reached Vīrapura, the city of the *vidyādhara* Samara.

'Jīvadatta defeated Samara in battle and then married his daughter Anaṅgaprabhā and lived in Vīrapura, enjoying celestial pleasures. After he had lived there for some time, he said to his father-in-law and to his beloved Anaṅgaprabhā, "Let both of us visit the human world. I long for it. The land of one's birth is always the dearest, even if it is inferior." Samara agreed, but the prescient Anaṅgaprabhā was persuaded to go with great difficulty. Jīvadatta took Anaṅgaprabhā into his arms and descended to the human world from the sky. Anaṅgaprabhā was tired and when she saw a pleasant mountain, she said, "Let us rest here," and Jīvadatta alighted there with her. He produced food and drink with his magic powers. Impelled by his destiny, Jīvadatta said to Anaṅgaprabhā, "Beloved, sing me a sweet song." She began to sing a hymn of praise to Śiva and Jīvadatta fell asleep as he listened.

Jīvadatta Wakes Up

'Just then, a king named Harivara came that way, tired from his hunt and in search of some water. He was drawn to the singing as if he were a deer and leaving his chariot, he walked in the direction of the song. His right eye fluttered so he knew that something good was going to happen and then he saw Anaṅgaprabhā, shining like the brightness of the god of love. While his heart was held by Anaṅgaprabhā's voice and her beauty, the god of love pierced it with an arrow. Anaṅgaprabhā, too, was deeply attracted to this handsome man and said to herself, "Who is this man? Is he the god of love without his flowery bow? Or is he Śiva's grace incarnate because the god is pleased with my song?" She asked him in a voice that quivered with passion, "Who are you? Why have you come to this forest?" Harivara told her how he had come there. He then asked her who she was and who it was that slept beside her. She replied, "I am a *vidyādharī* and this is my husband who has a magic sword. But I fell in love with you the moment I saw you so let us leave this place quickly before he wakes up. Then I will tell you my story in detail." Harivara was so delighted, it was as if he had gained the sovereignty of the three worlds!

'Anaṅgaprabhā wanted to take Harivara in her arms and fly to her celestial world, but at the very moment, she was stripped of her magic powers because she had betrayed her husband. Then she remembered her father's curse and was very upset. Harivara noticed that she was disturbed and said, "This is not the time for grief. Your husband may wake up. Besides, you should not grieve over something like this which is a matter of destiny. Who can escape the shadow of one's own head or the course of one's fate? Let us go!" Anaṅgaprabhā agreed and Harivara picked her up in his arms as happy as if he had found a great treasure and carried her to his chariot. His entourage welcomed him joyfully. He reached his city in his chariot which travelled as swiftly as thought. When his subjects saw him with a woman, they were filled with curiosity. Harivara dwelt in the city named after himself, enjoying celestial pleasures in the company of Anaṅgaprabhā. Anaṅgaprabhā stayed there happily with him, having forgotten all her powers because of the curse.

'Meanwhile, Jīvadatta awoke alone on the mountain and saw that Anaṅgaprabhā and his sword were both missing. "Where is Anaṅgaprabhā? Where is my sword? Could she have gone away with it? Have they both been carried off by someone?" he wailed. As he tried to understand what had happened, he searched all over the mountain for three days, burning in the fires of love. Then he came down and wandered in the forest for ten days but he could not find her anywhere. "Oh cruel fate! You gave me both the sword and Anaṅgaprabhā with such difficulty and now you have carried them both away!" He wandered around thus, wailing, without food or water until he reached a village and entered the imposing house of a Brāhmin. When the beautiful lady of the house, Priyadattā, saw him, she immediately ordered her maidservants, "Quickly, wash Jīvadatta's feet. This is the thirteenth day that he has gone without food or water, grieving over the separation from his beloved." Jīvadatta was amazed when he heard this and thought to himself, "Is Anaṅgaprabhā here or is this woman a witch?" When his feet had been washed and he had eaten, he humbly asked

Priyadattā, "Tell me how you knew all that had happened to me? And then tell me, where are my sword and my beloved?"

'Priyadattā, who was a devoted wife, said, "There is no one in my heart, not even in my dreams, except for my husband. I see all other men either as sons or as brothers and no one leaves my house without hospitality. Because of this, I have the power to know the past, the present and the future. Anaṅgaprabhā was carried off by a king named Harivara. While you were asleep, he passed by, drawn by fate and attracted by her song. He lives in a city named after himself and you cannot get Anaṅgaprabhā back because he is very strong. But that promiscuous woman will leave him for another man. The sword was given to you by the goddess only so that you could obtain Anaṅgaprabhā. Since that task is over, the sword has returned to the goddess by its own power and the woman has been carried away. Have you forgotten what the goddess told you in a dream about Anaṅgaprabhā? Why are you so upset about something that was bound to happen? Renounce this series of acts that lead again and again to grief! What use is that woman to you who is now attached to another man and who has lost all her powers because of her infidelity?"

'Jīvadatta was now disgusted by Anaṅgaprabhā's behaviour and lost all interest in her. He said, "My attachment to Anaṅgaprabhā has been destroyed by your words of wisdom, for who would not benefit by associating with good people? All this has happened to me because of my previous misconduct. So I will go to the holy pilgrimage spots and wash away my past. Why should I be hostile to others because of Anaṅgaprabhā? One who conquers anger conquers the world." While Jīvadatta was saying this, Priyadattā's hospitable and righteous husband came home. He, too, welcomed Jīvadatta and helped him forget his grief. After Jīvadatta had rested he bade them goodbye and left on his pilgrimage.

Jīvadatta Is Released

'In the course of time, Jīvadatta visited all the pilgrimage centres on earth, enduring many difficulties and living on fruits and roots. Then he went to the shrine of the goddess and performed severe penances, going without food and sleeping on a bed of *kuśa* grass. The goddess was pleased and manifested herself to him and said, "Rise, my son, for you are my fourth *gaṇa*, Vikaṭavadana. The other three are Pañcamūla, Caturvaktra and Mahodaramukha. Once, you all went to the banks of the Gaṅgā to enjoy yourselves and while you were there, you saw Cāpalekhā, the daughter of the *muni* Kapilajaṭa, having a bath. All of you fell in love with her and begged for her attention. She replied, 'I am a virgin. Go away!' Your three companions fell silent, but you grabbed her by the arm and she cried, 'Father, save me!' Her father, who was nearby, came there in a rage and you let go of her hand when you saw him. Still, he cursed all of you. 'Be born as humans, you evil fellows!' You asked him when the curse would end and he said, 'When you have asked for princess Anaṅgaprabhā in marriage and when you have gone to the world of the *vidyādharas,* then the three of you will be free of your curse. But you, Vikaṭavadana, will win Anaṅgaprabhā when she becomes a *vidyādharī* and lose her again and then endure great suffering. When you have propitiated the goddess for a long time, then your curse will end. This will happen to you because you touched Cāpalekhā's hand and because you have taken the wives of so many others.'

"You four *gaṇas* who had been cursed by the sage were born as four young men Bhāṣājña, Pañcapaṭṭika, Khaḍgadhara in the southern region. When Anaṅgarati returned to her world, the other three came here and were released from their curse by me. Now that you have propitiated me, your curse is also at an end. Consume your earthly body with this fiery meditation and rid yourself of the bad acts that otherwise would take eight births to wear off." The goddess disappeared and Jīvadatta burned up his mortal body and all his bad actions. He was at last freed from his curse and became the best among the *gaṇas*. Even the gods have to suffer for being attracted to other men's wives. Why should inferior beings not suffer for the same thing?

Anaṅgaprabhā's Adventures Continue

'Anaṅgaprabhā, meanwhile, had become Harivara's chief queen and lived happily in his city. The king was with her day and night and left the affairs of the kingdom to his minister Sumantra. Once, a new dancing teacher named Labdhavara came to Harivara's kingdom from Madhyadeśa. When the king saw his skill in music and dance, he appointed him teacher to the ladies in the harem. Labdhavara made Anaṅgaprabhā into such a good dancer that even her rival queens expressed their admiration. Anaṅgaprabhā fell in love with her teacher because she spent so much time with him and also because she enjoyed his teaching. The dancing teacher, attracted by her youth and beauty, suddenly learned a new kind of dance from the god of love.

'One day, desperately in love, Anaṅgaprabhā went to the dancing teacher when he was alone and said, "I am deeply in love with you and cannot live a moment longer without you. The king will not tolerate this if he finds out. Let us leave this place and go to where he will not find us. The king has given you gold, horses and camels because he was pleased with your dancing and I have my jewels. Let us go quickly to a place where we can live without fear!" The dancing teacher was pleased with her attentions and agreed to the plan. Anaṅgaprabhā put on a man's clothes and went to the dancing teacher's house, accompanied only by a woman servant who was completely devoted to her.

'They left the city on horseback with all their wealth strapped onto a camel. First Anaṅgaprabhā gave up the glories of being a *vidyādharī*, then she rejected the pleasures of royalty and then she took refuge in the fortunes of a dancer! Truly, women are fickle! Anaṅgaprabhā and the dancing teacher reached the distant city of Viyogapura where they lived together happily. The dancing teacher felt that by being with Anaṅgaprabhā, his name, Labdhavara, 'one who has attained a prize', had been justified.

'When Harivara found out that Anaṅgaprabhā had left, he wanted to die of grief. But the minister Sumantra consoled him and said, "Why don't you understand this? Think it over yourself. Anaṅgaprabhā left her husband, who had obtained the powers of a *vidyādhara* by means of a sword, the moment she saw you. Why would a woman like that stay with you? She has left for something trivial because she does not desire the good, like someone who is enamoured of a blade of grass believing it to be a heap of jewels. She has definitely gone with the dancing teacher for he is nowhere to be seen and I heard that they were in the dance hall together in the morning. Since you know all this, why are so you attached to her? A promiscuous woman is like the sunset which has a moment of glory every evening."

'The king mulled over what the minister had said and thought to himself, "This wise man has spoken the truth. A relationship with a promiscuous woman can never be lasting for she changes every moment. In the end, such a relationship leads to revulsion. A wise man never submits to the current of a river or to the power of a woman for both will drown him even as they playfully continue on their way. Those who are detached from pleasure, who are not interested in material wealth and who face danger bravely, they are the ones who have conquered the world." So Harivara renounced his grief and lived happily in the company of his other wives.

'Meanwhile, Anaṅgaprabhā lived with the dancing teacher in Viyogapura for some time. As fate would have it, the dancing teacher struck up a friendship with a young gambler named Sudarśana. The gambler managed to take away all the dancing teacher's remaining wealth from under Anaṅgaprabhā's very nose. Anaṅgaprabhā pretended to be angry because of that and left the dancing teacher who was now penniless and went away with Sudarśana. The dancing teacher had lost his wife and his wealth. Disgusted with the world, he matted his hair and went to perform austerities on the banks of the Gaṅgā. But Anaṅgaprabhā, who kept taking new lovers, stayed with the gambler.

'One night, Sudarśana was robbed of all his wealth by thieves who entered his house. When Sudarśana noticed that Anaṅgaprabhā was upset about their poverty, he said, "Let us go to my friend Hiraṇyagupta. He is a wealthy merchant and we can borrow something from him." Impelled by destiny, the gambler went with Anaṅgaprabhā to ask Hiraṇyagupta for a loan. When the merchant and Anaṅgaprabhā saw each other, they fell in love. "Tomorrow I will give you the money, but today, you must eat here," said the merchant. But Sudarśana sensed the bond between the other two and said, "I did not come here today to dine with you." The merchant replied, "Do as you wish, my friend, but let your wife eat here since this is the first time she has come to my house." Sudarśana was silent and the merchant went into his house with Anaṅgaprabhā.

'Hiraṇyagupta and Anaṅgaprabhā ate and drank and made merry together, for she was relaxed with all the wine that she had drunk. Sudarśana waited for his wife outside the house but a servant came and gave him a message from the merchant. "Your wife has eaten and left. Why are you still waiting here? You must not have seen her leave. Go home!" Sudarśana told the servant that he knew Anaṅgaprabhā was still inside the house and that he would not leave. The merchant's servants drove him from the gate with kicks and blows. Sudarśana was very dejected as he left, and he thought to himself, "Can this merchant, who is my friend, have taken my wife away from me? Or am I reaping the fruits of my actions in this birth itself? What I did to another man has been done to me. How can I be angry with the merchant when my own actions must have elicited the same feeling? I will end this chain of actions right here so that I am not humiliated further." Sudarśana renounced his anger and went to Badarikā and performed severe penances.

'Anaṅgaprabhā was as pleased as a bee on a flower to have found such a handsome husband in Hiraṇyagupta. In the course of time, she gained complete control over the wealth and the heart of the merchant who was deeply in love with her. King Vīrabāhu, even though he knew that this beautiful woman lived in his city and was deeply attracted to her, did not carry her off and remained within the bounds of virtue. Slowly, the merchant's wealth began to decrease, for in the house of a promiscuous woman, neither prosperity nor virtue have a place. One day, Hiraṇyagupta put together some goods and went to the island of Suvarṇabhūmi to trade. He took Anaṅgaprabhā with him because he did not want to be separated from her. They reached the city of Sāgarapura where Hiraṇyagupta made friends with a local fisherman named Sāgaravīra who lived near the sea. Anaṅgaprabhā and the merchant travelled with Sāgaravīra to the seashore where they boarded a boat to set sail for the island.

'As they were sailing along, a terrible cloud appeared with lightning that flashed as if it were its eyes and it filled the travellers with dread. Rain poured down, the wind rose and the ship began to sink beneath the waves. All the passengers started wailing and crying and Hiraṇyagupta, as the ship shattered like his hopes, girded his loins. He gazed at Anaṅgaprabhā and cried, "Dear one, where are you?" and plunged into the water. He managed to swim along and as luck would have it, he saw another trading ship and climbed onto it. Meanwhile, Sāgaravīra had tied some planks together with rope and placed Anaṅgaprabhā on them. He climbed onto the raft and he paddled with his arms as he comforted the terrified Anaṅgaprabhā. As soon as the ship had been destroyed, the cloud disappeared and the sea was calm like a man after his anger has passed. Hiraṇyagupta's ship was pushed by the wind as if it were destiny and reached the shore in five days. He was depressed at being separated from his beloved but he realized that he could not fight fate. He went slowly back to his own city and because he was a resolute man, he regained his composure, made some more money and lived happily.

'Anaṅgaprabhā was brought to the shore in one day on the planks paddled by Sāgaravīra. He comforted her and took her to his own house in Sāgarapura. Anaṅgaprabhā treated Sāgaravīra like a hero for saving her life. He was also wealthy, good looking and in the prime of his life and he fulfilled all her wishes. She decided to marry him. A promiscuous woman does not distinguish between high- and low-born men. So Anaṅgaprabhā lived happily with Sāgaravīra, enjoying the wealth that he gave her. One day, from the roof of her house she saw a handsome young Kṣatriya named Vijayavarmā walking down the street. Attracted by his good looks, she went to him and said, "I was drawn to you the moment I saw you. Make love to me!" Vijayavarmā was elated when he heard this invitation from an exceedingly beautiful woman who had approached him of her own accord and he took her back to his house. Sāgaravīra was very upset when he learned that his beloved had left him and went to the banks of the Gaṅgā to renounce his body through ascetic practices. His grief was great, but how could such a low-born man have held on to a *vidyādharī*?

Anaṅgaprabhā's Last Husband

'Anaṅgaprabhā continued to live in the same town, enjoying herself with Vijayavarmā. One day, King Sāgaravarmā toured his city mounted on an elephant. As he was admiring the beautiful city that was named after him, he went past Vijayavarmā's house. Anaṅgaprabhā knew that the king was coming that way and she climbed up onto the roof to see him. The moment she set eyes on the king, she fell in love with him and boldly asked the elephant driver, "I have never ridden an elephant. Give me a ride on yours so that I can know what it is like." The elephant driver turned to the king. The king noticed Anaṅgaprabhā who was so beautiful it was as if she were the moon come down to earth. He gazed at her as if he were a *cakora* bird and knowing that he could have her, said to the elephant driver, "Take the elephant over there and gratify her desire. Let this beautiful woman sit on the elephant." The driver did as he was told and as soon as the elephant was close enough, Anaṅgaprabhā threw herself into the king's lap. How could it be that this woman, who had shown such an aversion to the idea of a husband, now had an insatiable appetite for them? Her father's curse must have brought about this change in her.

'Anaṅgaprabhā clung to the king's neck as though she were afraid of falling and he was delighted by her touch. Dying to kiss her, he carried that woman, who had approached him through artifice, off to the palace. The king placed her in the harem and made her his chief queen after she told him her story and revealed that she was a *vidyādharī*. When Vijayavarmā found out that Anaṅgaprabhā had been taken away by the king, he came and attacked the king's servants outside the palace. He fought bravely and died there, for men of honour do not suffer insults because of women. Vijayavarmā was lifted out of the world of humans by celestial women who said to him, "What do you need this awful woman for? Come to Nandana with us!"

'Now that she was with the king, Anaṅgaprabhā strayed no further, as rivers come to rest in the ocean. She believed herself lucky to have found such a husband and the king felt that his life's goal had been accomplished when he got her for a wife. Soon, Anaṅgaprabhā became pregnant and gave birth to a son. The king named him Samudravarmā and gave a great feast to celebrate his birth. The boy grew into a fine young man, known for his strength and courage, and the king anointed him crown prince. Soon, the prince brought Kamalāvatī, the daughter of king Samaravarmā, to court in order to marry her. When he got married, his father bestowed his kingdom upon the prince because he was impressed with his virtues. Samudravarmā knew his duties as a Kṣatriya, so when his father gave him the kingdom, he bowed to him and said, "Father, let me go and conquer the earth, for a king who does not conquer is as effeminate as a woman.

The only prosperity and fortune that are genuine are those won by the conquest of other kingdoms. What use is kingship to those rulers who oppress the poor? They eat their subjects like greedy cats who eat their offspring."

"Sāgaravarmā said to his son, "You have just become king. Establish yourself here first, for there is nothing wrong with ruling your own subjects well. Also, a king should not seek battle before estimating his own strength. You are courageous and your army is mighty, but fortune in battle is fickle and you cannot be assured of victory." Even though his father used this and other similar arguments, Samudravarmā convinced him to let him go. In time, he conquered the four directions and established his rule over neighbouring kings. He came back to his city with elephants and horses and all the wealth given to him as tribute. He fell at his parents' feet and honoured them with precious stones from various countries. Obeying their instructions, the prince gave horses and elephants and gold and jewels to Brāhmins as well. He also gave wealth to his servants and to his subjects so that the word "poor" became meaningless in his kingdom. When the old king who lived with Anaṅgaprabhā saw his son's success, he felt that his life had been fulfilled.

'While they were celebrating, the king said to his son in the presence of all his ministers, "I have done what I had to do in this life. I have enjoyed the pleasures of kingship, I have remained unconquered and now I have seen you invested with sovereignty. I have nothing left to strive for so I will go to an *āśrama* while I still have the strength. The roots of age whisper in my ear, 'Why do you still live in your house when this body will soon be destroyed?'" Even though his son protested, Sāgaravarmā went with his beloved Anaṅgaprabhā to Prayāga, for all his goals had been fulfilled. His son escorted them there and returned to the city where he ruled wisely and well.

Anaṅgaprabhā's Curse Is Finally Over

'Sāgaravarmā and Anaṅgaprabhā worshipped Śiva in Prayāga. Śiva appeared in a dream to Sāgaravarmā and said, "I am pleased with the penances that you and your wife have performed. Listen. Both you and Anaṅgaprabhā are *vidyādharas*. Tomorrow your curse will end and you will return to your own world." Sāgaravarmā woke up and learned that Anaṅgaprabhā had the same dream. Anaṅgaprabhā was very happy and said, "I remember everything about my past birth. I was the daughter of the *vidyādhara* king Samara in Vīrapura and my name was Anaṅgarati. My father cursed me and I lost my powers. I was born a mortal woman and forgot my *vidyādharī* nature but now I remember it all."

'As she was speaking, her father descended from the sky. Sāgaravarmā welcomed him with honour and Samara said to his daughter, "Take back your powers, for your curse has ended. You have suffered the pain of eight lives in one life!" He took her onto his lap and restored her powers to her. He said to Sāgaravarmā, "You are a *vidyādhara* prince named Madanaprabha. I am Samara and Anaṅgaprabhā is my daughter. Earlier, when she was of marriageable age, she had many suitors but she refused to take a husband because she was proud of her looks. You, who are her equal in virtues, were keen to marry her but she refused you as well. Because of that, I cursed her to be born in the world of humans. But you were in love with her and begged Śiva that she be your wife in the human world. You gave up your *vidyādhara* body by your magic powers and became a man and Anaṅgaprabhā became your wife. Now, both of you can return to your own world as a couple."

'Sāgaravarmā then remembered his previous birth, renounced his body in Prayāga and became Madanaprabha. Anaṅgaprabhā recovered her brightness with the restoration of her powers and when she became a *vidyādharī*, her body shone brighter than ever. Madanaprabha and Anaṅgaprabhā were attracted to each other in their celestial bodies and were very happy. Along with Samara, they flew into the air and went to Vīrapura. Samara married his daughter to Madanaprabha with all the appropriate rites. Madanaprabha took his beloved, whose curse had now ended, to his own city and they lived there in peace.

'Thus, celestial beings can fall to earth because of curses. Their misconduct brings them to the world of humans and after they have suffered the consequences, they return to their own world because of their previous merit.'

When Naravāhanadatta heard this story from Gomukha, he and Alaṅkāravatī were very pleased and proceeded with the tasks for the day.

Naravāhanadatta continued to live in happiness with his wives. One day, when he was out hunting, he reached a great forest. Soon after, four celestial men arrived and carried him away to meet Viṣṇu who sent Naravāhanadatta to retrieve four apsarases *that Indra had taken from him. When Naravāhanadatta had accomplished the task, Viṣṇu gave the four* apsarases *to him as wives. Naravāhanadatta stayed with his four new wives for some time, enjoying the celestial delights that they presented him with and then he returned with them to his earthly kingdom. His family was glad to see him after so long and welcomed his new wives warmly.*

Śaktiyaśas

We worship Gaṇeśa's trunk which is red with vermilion and is like a sword that cuts down arrogance, irresistible to its enemies.

"May Śiva's third eye protect you, the one that blazed forth as he prepared his arrow to burn the city of Tripura[1], even as his other eyes rolled in anger.

"May Narasiṃha's curved claws, red with his enemies' blood and his fiery eyes, destroy your troubles.

The King's Bracelet

Naravāhanadatta, the son of Udayana, lived happily in Kauśāmbī with his wives and his ministers. Once, a merchant who lived in the city came to Udayana as the king sat in his assembly. The merchant's name was Ratnadatta and when the door-keeper had announced his arrival, he came and bowed to the king and said, 'Sir, there is a poor coolie named Vasudhara who has suddenly begun to eat and drink well and give away alms. I was curious about this and so I took him to my house and gave him as much food and drink as he wanted. When he was drunk, I questioned him about his newly-acquired affluence and he answered thus. "I picked up a jewelled bracelet from the door of the king's palace and I sold one gem from it for one hundred thousand dīnārs *to the merchant Hiraṇyagupta. That is how I can afford to live in such comfort these days." Then he showed me the bracelet which was marked with the king's name. I came here to tell you that this has happened.'*

The king had the coolie and the gem merchant brought in with due courtesy and when he saw the bracelet, the king thought to himself, 'I remember now that the bracelet slipped off my arm when I was on a tour of the city.' The courtiers asked the coolie why he had hidden the fact that he had found a bracelet with the king's name on it. 'I make my living by carrying loads. How would I know the letters of the king's name? I kept it because I was oppressed by poverty,' said the coolie. Then the gem merchant was asked why he had not returned the bracelet and he said, 'I bought it freely in the marketplace and there was no mark on it. Now you say it has the mark of the king on it. This man has taken five thousand dīnārs *from me and I have the balance of the payment.' Yaugandharāyaṇa, who was also there, said, 'No one is at fault. How could the illiterate coolie read the king's name? Poverty makes thieves and who would give up what they find unclaimed? And the merchant who bought it fairly is also not at fault.'*

The king agreed with his prime minister's analysis. He took back the jewel from the merchant and gave him the five thousand dīnārs *that he had given the coolie. He let the coolie off without punishment. The coolie, who had spent the five thousand* dīnārs, *went back home without any worries. Even though the king hated the merchant Ratnadatta for being wicked and treacherous he honoured him for the service he had performed. When everyone had left, Vasantaka approached the king and said, 'When one is cursed by fate, then even the wealth one has disappears. The coolie has just had an experience like that of the wood-cutter and the magic pot.*

The Magic Pot

'Long ago, in the city of Pāṭaliputra, there lived a man named Śubhadatta. Every day, he would gather a load of wood and sell it in the market and supported himself and his family. One day, he went into a distant forest where, as it happened, four *yakṣas* lived. The *yakṣas,* who were wearing their celestial ornaments and clothes, saw that Śubhadatta was terrified of them and they therefore approached him very courteously. When they learned that he was poor, they felt sorry for him and said, "Stay here in our house and work for us and we will look after your family without them asking for any support from you." Śubhadatta stayed with the *yakṣas* and brought them all they needed for their ritual baths and did other small tasks for them. When it was time to eat, the *yakṣas* said to him, "Give us food from this magic pot." Śubhadatta saw that the pot was quite empty so he hesitated but the *yakṣas* smiled and said, "Śubhadatta, you don't understand! Put your hand in the pot and you will find whatever you wish to eat. This pot gives you whatever you want." Śubhadatta put his hand inside the pot and he found all the food and drink that anyone could possibly want. He fed the *yakṣas* from the pot and then ate something himself.

'Śubhadatta served the *yakṣas* in this way with devotion and some fear, but he worried about his family and wondered how they were getting on. The *yakṣas* reassured Śubhadatta's grieving family in a dream and Śubhadatta was touched by their kindness. After a month had passed, the *yakṣas* said to Śubhadatta, "We are pleased with your devotion. Tell us, what can we give you?" 'If you are truly pleased with me then you should give me this magic pot," replied Śubhadatta. The *yakṣas* said, "You will not be able to keep it, for if the pot breaks it will leave you immediately. Ask for some other boon." Despite their warnings, Śubhadatta would ask for nothing else and so they gave him the magic pot. Śubhadatta was very happy. He bowed to them, took the pot and went back to his home where his family was overjoyed to see him.

'Śubhadatta produced food and drink from the magic pot but because he wanted to keep it a secret, he put the food in other vessels and ate and drank with his family. He gave up carrying wood for a living and enjoyed himself with fine food and drink. One day, when he was drunk, his relatives asked him, "Where did you get the money to indulge in all these pleasures?" That foolish man was too proud to tell them plainly and so he picked up the pot and placed it on his shoulder and began to dance. As he was dancing, he tripped over in his drunkenness and the pot fell from his shoulder onto the ground and broke into pieces. However, it immediately regained its original shape and returned to its former owners but Śubhadatta sadly found himself as poor as before.

'The minds of people who are slaves to drinking and

other vices, are destroyed and so they cannot retain wealth even after they have got it.'

When the king of Vatsa had heard this funny story about the magic pot from Vasantaka he went to bathe and perform his other daily duties. Naravāhanadatta also bathed and ate with his father and then, at the end of the day, he went with his companions to his own house. At night, he was unable to fall asleep and Marubhūti, his minister, said to him, 'I know that it is because you desire this slave that you haven't called for your wives. But you haven't called for the slave either and so you cannot sleep. Why do you still fall in love with courtesans even though you know better? They have no compassion. Listen to a story about this.

The Courtesan's Tricks

'There is a beautiful and prosperous city called Citrakūṭa and a very rich merchant named Ratnavarmā, the richest of the rich, lived there. He propitiated Śiva and a son was born to him and he was named Īśvaravarmā. The boy studied all the sciences and when Ratnavarmā, who had no other son, saw that Īśvaravarmā was growing up, he thought to himself, "God has created courtesans who are both beautiful as well as wicked to steal the hearts and wealth of young men who are intoxicated with their youth. I will give my son to an experienced courtesan so that he can become familiar with their ways and not be deceived by them." So he took his son to the mansion of a courtesan named Yamajivhā.

'Ratnavarmā and Īśvaravarmā saw the old courtesan with her jowly cheeks, huge teeth and stubby nose teaching her daughter thus: "Everyone honours riches, especially courtesans but the courtesan who falls in love gives up her chance at wealth. A courtesan must forsake love, for love brings darkness to her as the twilight brings the night. A well-trained courtesan displays affection like an actress. First she gains a man's affections and then his wealth. If he is ruined, she should reject him but if he regains his money, she should take him back. A courtesan is like a sage for she treats all men, young, old, ugly or deformed, in the same way. Thus, she attains the highest purpose of her life."

'When Yamajivhā had finished this lecture, Ratnavarmā approached her and she honoured him as a guest. He sat down and said, "Teach my son the ways of courtesans so that he may know them well. I will gave you a thousand *dīnārs* for your work." The old courtesan agreed. Ratnavarmā gave her the money and left his son with her and came home. In a year, Īśvaravarmā had learned all the skills of the courtesan in Yamajivhā's mansion and came back to his father's house.

'When Īśvaravarmā turned sixteen he said to his father, "Money is both religion and love for people like us and from money comes respect." Ratnavarmā was pleased when he heard this and since he agreed with his son, he gave him five crores of gold coins to start a business. On an auspicious day, Īśvaravarmā collected a caravan and set out for Svarṇadvīpa. On his way there, he reached the city of Kāñcanapura and set up camp in a garden outside the city. After bathing and eating, the young man entered the city and went to the temple to see a performance. He saw a young dancer named Sundarī who moved like a wave of beauty tossed by the winds of youth. He fell in love with her the moment he saw her and everything the old courtesan had taught him slipped out of his mind, as though in anger at his foolishness. At the end of the performance, he sent the dancer a message through a friend and she bowed low and said that she was indeed honoured to be of service to him.

'Īśvaravarmā left his camp in the care of guards and went to Sundarī's house. When he got there, Sundarī's mother, Makarakaṭī, honoured him with the appropriate rituals. At night, she took him into a room with a bed which had a canopy of glittering jewels. Īśvaravarmā spent the night there with Sundarī who was a skilled dancer and whose name aptly described her nature. She lavished him with affection and never left his side so, the next day, he was unable to tear himself away from her. In those two days, the merchant's son gave her twenty-five lakhs worth of gold and jewels. "I already have a lot of wealth but I have never had a man like you! What do I need this money for when I have you?" said Sundarī with feigned affection as she refused all his gifts.

'Sundarī was her mother's only child and so Makarakaṭī said to her daughter, "From now on, all our wealth is as much his as his own and so you must take whatever he gives you. There is nothing wrong with that." Sundarī began to accept gifts with a false unwillingness and the foolish Īśvaravarmā thought that she was in love with him. Enchanted by her beauty, her dancing and her songs, the merchant stayed on at her house and soon, two months had gone by. In that time, he had given her two crores.

'One of Īśvaravarmā's friends, Arthadatta, came to him and said, "What happened to all that you learned from the old courtesan with so much difficulty? Has it proved useless now that you are in that very situation, like knowledge of weapons is useless to a coward in battle? How can you believe that a courtesan is truly in love with you? Is there really water in desert mirages? Let us leave this place before all your wealth is exhausted, for if your father finds out, he will be very angry." Īśvaravarmā said to his friend, "It is true that one cannot count on the affections of courtesans, but Sundarī is not like the others. She would die if she lost sight of me for even a moment! You go and tell her that we have to leave." Arthadatta spoke to Sundarī in front of Īśvaravarmā and Makarakaṭī. "You have an unusual affection for Īśvaravarmā but the time has come for him to go on to Svarṇadvīpa to trade. He will make a lot of money and come back here and stay with you happily. Let him go, dear friend." Sundarī's eyes filled with tears and she pretended deep sadness and said to Arthadatta, "What can I say when you know best? Who can foresee the end of an event? I resign myself to my fate." Her mother said, "Be brave and stop grieving. Your lover will achieve his ends and come back to you."

'As Makarakaṭī consoled her daughter, she made a plan with her in secret. They spread a net in a well that was on Īśvaravarmā's path. Meanwhile, Īśvaravarmā was terribly distressed at the thought of the separation from his beloved and Sundarī also hardly ate or drank, as if out of sadness. She took no interest in singing or dancing either and Īśvaravarmā reassured her with his love. Īśvaravarmā set out on the day chosen by his friend and Makarakaṭī prayed for his success. Sundarī wept copious tears and followed him with her mother until they reached the well outside the city. Īśvaravarmā sent Sundarī back from there and went on his way but Sundarī threw herself into the well where the net had been spread. At once her mother and her retainers began to wail, "Oh dear daughter!" "Oh beloved mistress!"

'Īśvaravarmā and his friend turned around when they heard the wailing and were told that Sundarī had thrown herself into the well. Īśvaravarmā was stunned. Makarakaṭī continued to wail and grieve loudly but she sent her servants, who were very attached to her, quietly into the well. They went down with ropes and cried out, "By a miracle, she is alive, she is alive!" and they brought Sundarī out of the well. Sundarī pretended as if she were nearly dead and called out Īśvaravarmā's name. When he came to her, she began to cry softly. Īśvaravarmā was delighted and comforted her and took his beloved back to her house and went there himself with all his retainers. He decided that Sundarī really loved him and that by securing her love, he had attained the true goal of his life. He no longer wanted to go on his journey and made up his mind to stay with Sundarī. Arthadatta said to him, "Friend, why have you destroyed yourself with this relationship? You cannot believe that Sundarī loves you just because she threw herself into a well! The schemes of courtesans are too devious even for the gods. What will you say to your father when you have spent all his money? Where will you go? Leave this place immediately for your own good if you still have your wits about you!"

The Golden Monkey

'But Īśvaravarmā ignored his friend's advice and stayed in Sundarī's house for another month in which time he spent the last of the money that his father had given him as capital. Makarakaṭī had him thrown out of Sundarī's house when he had nothing left. Arthadatta returned quickly to Citrakūṭa and told Īśvaravarmā's father what had happened. Ratnavarmā was very upset and went to Yamajivhā, the old courtesan. "You took a great deal of money from me to teach my son, but Makarakaṭī has taken everything from him!" and he described all that had happened to his son. Then Yamajivhā said to him, "Send your son here as soon as possible and he will be able to get everything back from Makarakaṭī." Ratnavarmā immediately sent Arthadatta to bring Īśvaravarmā home and also sent his son some money for expenses.

'Arthadatta went to Kāñcanapura and gave Īśvaravarmā the message from his father. He added, "You would not listen to me and now you have seen for yourself that courtesans are cruel and unsympathetic. After you had given Sundarī and her mother five crores of gold coins, they threw you out of the house! Which wise man would look for love with a courtesan or try to extract oil from sand? Why are you blind to this fact? A man is brave and wise and fortunate only as long as he steers clear of women's wiles. So go back to your father and make him happy." Arthadatta persuaded Īśvaravarmā to return with these words and took him back to his father.

'Ratnavarmā spoke to Īśvaravarmā kindly because he loved his only son, and took him to Yamajivhā's house again. Arthadatta told her the whole story, including the part where Sundarī threw herself into the well and how, consequently, Īśvaravarmā lost the last of his wealth. Yamajivhā said, "I am the one at fault because I forgot to teach him this trick. Makarakaṭī had spread a net inside the well and Sundarī jumped into it so that she would not be killed. But there is something in this, too." She made her servants bring her a monkey named Āla. She gave the monkey a thousand *dīnārs* and said, "Swallow these," and the monkey did so since that is what he had been taught to do. "My little one, give this man twenty and this man twenty-five and this man sixty and this man one hundred!" said Yamajivhā and each time the monkey produced exactly the amount of money that she had asked for.

'After Yamajivhā had displayed the monkey's talents she said to Īśvaravarmā, "Take this monkey with you and go back to Sundarī's house. Every day, ask him for money that you have already made him swallow in secret. When Sundarī sees this monkey, which is like the stone that makes wishes come true, she will give you all she has in order to procure the monkey for herself. After you have got all her wealth, make the monkey swallow enough money for two days and quickly go as far from the city as you can." She gave Īśvaravarmā the monkey and made his father give him two crores as capital. He took them and went to Kāñcanapura.

'Sundarī welcomed Īśvaravarmā back as if he were the means to all her ends and embraced him and his friend. When Īśvaravarmā had gained her confidence, he said to Arthadatta, "Go and fetch Āla," and the monkey was brought in. The monkey had already swallowed a thousand *dīnārs* and so Īśvaravarmā said to him, "Dear little Āla, give us three hundred *dīnārs* today so that we can eat and drink well and another hundred for our other expenses. Give one hundred to Makarakaṭī, one hundred to Brāhmins and the hundred left from the thousand to Sundarī." The monkey did as he was told. Every day for a fortnight, Āla gave Īśvaravarmā money for his expenses. Makarakaṭī and Sundarī thought that the wishing stone had arrived in the shape of this monkey who provided a hundred *dīnārs* a day. "If only Īśvaravarmā would give us the monkey, all our wants would be fulfilled," they thought. Sundarī and her mother talked the matter over in private and one day, Sundarī said to Īśvaravarmā, "If you really love me, give me Āla." Īśvaravarmā replied with a smile, "He belongs to my father and is everything to him. It would not be appropriate for me to give Āla away." But Sundarī persisted. "If you give him to me, I will give you five crores!" she said.

'Īśvaravarmā spoke as if he had considered the matter and came to a decision. "If you were to give me everything you had or even this whole city I would not give him to you, least of all for these few crores." Sundarī begged, "I will give you everything I have but you must give me this monkey or my mother will be angry with me!" and she fell at Īśvaravarmā's feet. Then Arthadatta said, "Give it to her. Let whatever has to happen, happen." Īśvaravarmā promised Sundarī the monkey and he spent the next day with the delighted woman. He secretly made the monkey swallow two thousand *dīnārs* before giving him to Sundarī and Makarakaṭī. He took all their wealth as a price for the monkey and went to Svarṇadvīpa to trade.

'Sundarī was overjoyed because for two days, the monkey gave her a thousand *dīnārs*. But on the third day, even though she asked him kindly, he gave her nothing. Sundarī then hit the monkey with her fist. The monkey was beside himself with anger and scratched and bit Sundarī and Makarakaṭī. Makarakaṭī, whose face was streaming with blood, beat the monkey with a stick till he died. When they saw that he was dead and realized that all their wealth was gone, the mother and daughter wanted to kill themselves. All the townspeople laughed when they heard the story and said, "Makarakaṭī took everything that a man had because of her trick with the net but he has taken everything from her through his monkey. She laid a trap for him but did not see the one he had laid for her!" Sundarī and her mother, their faces bruised and their wealth all gone, had to be restrained by their relatives from killing themselves. Īśvaravarmā returned from Svarṇadvīpa to his father's house with a huge amount of wealth. His father was delighted and rewarded Yamajivhā and had a grand celebration. Īśvaravarmā realized the folly of associating with courtesans and got married and stayed at home with his wife.

'Thus, the heart of a courtesan is filled with lies and treachery, so the man who wants to be rich should not associate with them any more than he should cross a deserted forest with only a caravan.'

When Naravāhanadatta and Gomukha had heard Marubhūti's tale about Āla and the net, they laughed long and hard. When Marubhūti finished his story about the unsympathetic nature of courtesans, the wise Gomukha related the story of Kumudikā, whose lesson was the same.

How The Courtesan Used The King

'Vikramasiṃha was the king of Pratiṣṭhāna. He had the courage of a lion, so his name truly reflected his nature. His beloved queen was from a good family and she was so beautiful that the only ornaments she needed were her looks. Her name was Śaśilekhā. One day, when Vikramasiṃha was in his city, five or six of his relatives got together, went to his palace and surrounded it. Mahābhaṭṭa, Vīrabāhu, Subāhu, Subhaṭṭa and Pratāpāditya were all powerful kings and Vikramasiṃha's minister tried unsuccessfully to dissuade them from making war. Vikramasiṃha went out to confront them. The armies exchanged showers of arrows and Vikramasiṃha, confident of his strength, mounted an elephant and joined the battle. When the five kings saw him turning back the enemy forces with only a single bow, the united armies attacked and Vikramasiṃha's forces were scattered as they were fewer in number.

'Vikramasiṃha's minister, Anantaguṇa, was at his side and said, "Our army has been routed and there is no chance of victory here. You went into this battle despite my advice, so now listen to what I am saying so that we can remedy the situation. Get off this elephant and mount a horse so that we can leave this place. If you stay alive, you can defeat your enemies later." The king listened to this advice, left his army and went away with the minister. Vikramasiṃha and Anantaguṇa disguised themselves and reached Ujjayini. They went to the house of Kumudikā, a courtesan famous for her wealth. When she saw Vikramasiṃha enter her house, she thought, "Who can this distinguished man be? His regal bearing and the marks on his body suggest that he is some great king. Surely I can use him as a means to the fulfilment of my desire!" She rose and went down to welcome them and treated them as greatly honoured guests. The king was tired and immediately, Kumudikā said to him, "I am fortunate, for the good deeds of my past lives have come to fruition today. You have sanctified my house by coming here yourself. Your favour has made me your slave. My two hundred elephants and horses and this house full of jewels are for you to use." She provided the king and his minister with all they needed for their baths and other refreshments.

'King Vikramasiṃha lived happily with Kumudikā in her house and she placed all her wealth at his disposal. He used her money and even gave it away but instead of being disturbed by that, Kumudikā seemed pleased. The king was delighted and felt sure that she was in love with him, but Anantaguṇa said to him in secret, "Courtesans are not to be trusted but I must confess I have no idea why Kumudikā pretends to be attached to you." The king said, "Kumudikā would lay down her life for me! I will prove it to you if you don't believe me!" The king then embarked on this charade. He ate and drank very little and emaciated his body so that soon, he seemed almost dead. He lay on the ground without moving and the attendants came to carry him away to the cremation grounds, weeping as they did so. Anantaguṇa displayed a grief that he did not feel. Kumudikā climbed onto the funeral pyre with the king even though her relatives tried to stop her. Once the king saw that Kumudikā had followed him onto the pyre, he sat up and yawned before the fire was lit. All the people gathered there shouted, "He is alive! It is a mircale! A miracle!" and they took the king and Kumudikā back home.

'They had a great celebration and the king was restored to his usual health. He whispered to Anantaguṇa, "Did you see Kumudikā's affection for me?" and the minister replied, "I still do not trust her. There must be some other reason for her behaviour and we will just have to wait and see. But we should tell her who we are so that we can gather an army from her and from your friends and kill our enemies in battle." Meanwhile, a spy Anantaguṇa had sent out returned and said that Vikramasiṃha's enemies had taken over the kingdom and that queen Śaśilekhā had heard a rumour that the king was dead and had killed herself. The king was very upset when he heard this and began to cry saying, "Dear queen, O virtuous lady," over and over again.

'Kumudikā found out what the trouble was and came to console the king. She said, "Why didn't you tell me all this before? Now, with my wealth and my forces, you can conquer your enemies!" Vikramasiṃha put together a large army with her wealth and went to a powerful king who was his friend. With both armies, he killed the five kings in battle and took over their kingdoms as well as his own. He said to Kumudikā, "I am very pleased with you. What can I do for you in return?" Kumudikā said, "If you are really pleased with me then remove the thorn that has been in my heart for a long time. In Ujjayini, I have a lover named Śrīdhara, the son of a Brāhmin. The king has put him in prison for a very small offence. Release him for me! When I saw you and noticed your auspicious marks, I knew that you would be successful. So I served you with devotion. I climbed onto the pyre with you because I thought I would never attain my objective without you. And life without my lover was not worth living." The king said to her, "Beautiful lady, I will do this for you, do not despair!" Then he remembered his minister's words and thought to himself, "Anantaguṇa was right when he told me not to believe in a courtesan's affections! But I must satisfy this wretched woman's wish," and he went to Ujjayini with his army. He had Śrīdhara released, gave him lots of wealth and reunited him with Kumudikā who was delighted. Then he returned to his own city and from then on, always heeded the advice of his ministers. Soon, he conquered the whole earth.

'So a courtesan's heart is dark and deep,' said Gomukha as he finished his story.

Then Tapantaka said, in the presence of Naravāhanadatta, 'You should never trust women in general for they are all fickle, the married ones and the ones who live in their father's houses as well as courtesans! I will tell you an amazing thing that happened here.

The Unfaithful Wife

'There was a merchant in this city named Balavarmā and his wife was named Candraśrī. She saw Śilahara, another merchant's son, from her window one day. She sent her friend to invite him into her house. She began meeting him there in secret every day and her friends and family soon found out about her affair. Only Balavarmā did not know about her infidelity, for often husbands are blind to their wives' faults because of affection. One day, Balavarmā developed a high fever and was soon very ill. But despite this, his wife would go every day to her friend's house to meet her lover. One day, her husband died while she was there. When she heard the news, she left her lover and climbed onto her husband's funeral pyre even though her friends, who knew the truth, tried to stop her. Women are impossible to understand. They fall in love with other men and then cannot live without their husbands.'

The Wicked Wife

Then, another one of Naravāhanadatta's ministers, Hariśikha, said. 'Do you know what happened to Devadāsa?'

'In a village a long time ago, there lived a man named Devadāsa and with good reason, he had a wife named Duḥśīlā, 'of bad character,' for she was in love with another man. One day, Devadāsa left the village because he had some business at the king's court. His wife wanted to have him killed so while he was away, she hid her lover on the roof of the house. She made her lover kill her husband in the middle of the night while he slept and then she sent her lover away and remained silent until the end of the night. In the morning, she ran outside and began to scream, "My husband has been killed by thieves!" Her husband's family came there and saw his body and asked, "If he was killed by thieves, how come they didn't steal anything?" They then asked Devadāsa's young son, "Who killed your father?" He replied clearly, "During the day, a man climbed up onto the roof and at night, he came down and killed my father before my very eyes. But before that, my mother left my father's side and took me away." Devadāsa's family realized that he had been killed by his wife's lover. They found the lover and had him killed. They banished Duḥśīlā and adopted the young boy. A woman who loves a man other than her husband will definitely kill him one day, as would a snake.'

After Hariśikha's story, Gomukha spoke again. 'Why tell stories about other people! Listen to the absurd thing that happened right here to Vajrasāra, King Vatsa's servant.

The Cuckolded Husband

'Vajrasāra was brave and handsome and had a beautiful wife from Mālava whom he loved more than his own self. One day, her father arrived from Mālava with his son, eager to see his daughter and invited his daughter and her husband to Mālava. Vajrasāra entertained his father-in-law and then took permission from the king and went to Mālava with his wife. He stayed in his father-in-law's house for a month and then came back here to serve the king but his wife stayed with her people. The days went by and then, suddenly, Vajrasāra's friend Krodhana came to him and said, "Why have you destroyed your family by leaving your wife at her father's house? That wicked woman is having an affair with another man! I was told this today by a reliable person who came from Mālava. Don't disbelieve the story, punish your wife and marry someone else!"

'Vajrasāra was stunned when he heard this story and he thought, "This must be true for she did not return even when I sent someone to bring her back. I will go and bring her back myself and see what is going on there." He went to Mālava and after taking permission from his parents-in-law, he took his wife and left the city. After they had gone a long way, he slipped away from his retainers and entered a deep forest with his wife. When they were alone, Vajrasāra said to her, "I have heard from a reliable friend that you are having an affair with another man. You did not come back when I sent for you. Tell me the truth now or I will punish you!" She replied, "If you have made up your mind, why are you questioning me? Do what you like with me!" Vajrasāra was outraged when he heard her indifferent words and tied her to a tree and began to beat her with creepers. He stripped off her clothes but when he saw her naked, his lust for her was aroused and he asked her to make love to him. She said, "I will, if you let me tie you up and beat you with creepers like you did to me." Inflamed with passion, Vajrasāra agreed and she bound him firmly by his hands and feet to a strong tree. Then she cut off his nose and ears with a sword. She took the sword and his clothes and that wicked woman dressed herself as a man and left immediately.

'Vajrasāra remained tied to the tree with his nose and ears cut off, having lost a lot of blood as well as his self-respect. An ascetic who had come to the forest in search of medicinal herbs saw him and felt sorry for him. He untied him and took him home. He restored Vajrasāra to health and then Vajrasāra returned to his own home. Even though he searched for his wicked wife, he could not find her anywhere. He told Krodhana all that that had happened and Krodhana in turn went and told the king. All the people who heard the story agreed that his wife had done the right thing by taking his clothes and punishing him since he had lost all manliness and was, indeed, like a woman. But despite their insults, Vajrasāra is still here, unashamed.

'How can you trust a woman?' asked Gomukha. Then Marubhūti said, 'Listen to this story about how women's minds are unsteady.

The Unsuitable Lover

'In the south, there lived a king named Siṃhabala. His wife was Kalyāṇavatī, the princess of Mālava and she was dearer to him than all the women in the harem. He ruled his kingdom with her until, one day, he was overthrown by his relatives. The king left for Mālava with Kalyāṇavatī, a few weapons and a few retainers. Along the way, a lion charged towards them but the king cut off its head with his sword. Then a wild elephant attacked them, trumpeting loudly, and the king killed it by cutting off its trunk and feet. He scattered a gang of thieves single-handed, as if they were lotuses and he trampled them with his feet as an elephant tramples water lilies. And thus he displayed his uncommon valour along the journey. When they reached Mālava, the king, this ocean of courage, said to Kalyāṇavatī, "Don't tell anyone in your father's house what happened on the journey. It would be shameful to talk about it, for there is nothing remarkable about the courage shown by a Kṣatriya."

'He entered his father-in-law's house and when he was asked the reason for his arrival, he said that he had been overthrown. His father-in-law honoured him and gave him horses and elephants and Siṃhabala went to a powerful king named Gajanika for help. Determined to defeat his enemies, he left his wife at her father's house. The days went by and once, as Kalyāṇavatī stood at the window, she saw a handsome man and lost her heart to him. Full of love, she thought, "I do not know anyone more handsome or braver than my husband but I am still drawn to this man. I must meet him," and she confided in her servant. She had her servant bring the man into the women's quarters at night, pulling him up through the window with a rope. When the man entered the room, he did not sit on the couch beside Kalyāṇavatī, but sat some distance away.

'Kalyāṇavatī was very disappointed, for she realized that he was probably from a low caste. At that very moment, a snake came down from the roof. The man sprang up in fear and killed the snake with an arrow. As it fell dead, he picked it up and threw it out of the window and the coward then danced with joy. Kalyāṇavatī was disgusted when she saw him dancing and thought, "What am I doing with this wretched man?" Her friend, who was very perceptive, saw that she was upset and so she left the room and then returned, pretending to be frightened. "Your father is coming! Let this young man go back to his home the same way he came here!" The young man left through the window. He was so frightened that he fell, but fortunately, he was not killed.

'Kalyāṇavatī said to her friend, "My dear, you did the right thing by getting rid of this base fellow. You understood what I was feeling. My own husband, even after killing lions and tigers will not speak of it and this fool dances with joy after killing a snake! How can I leave my husband and be attracted to a man like this? I curse my fickle mind, in fact, I curse the nature of women who are like flies, ignoring camphor to rush towards impurities!" The queen spent the night full of regret and then waited for her husband in her father's house. Siṃhabala had, meanwhile, defeated his wicked relatives with the help of Gajanika's army. He got back his kingdom and fetched his wife from her father's home after giving his father-in-law much wealth. Siṃhabala ruled the earth for a long time, unopposed.

'Thus, even the minds of virtuous women are fickle. Even though their husbands are brave and handsome, their minds wander. Good women are hard to find.'

When Naravāhanadatta, the son of King Udayana, heard this story from Marubhūti, he fell asleep.

One day, when Naravāhanadatta was amusing himself in the royal gardens, he saw a horde of vidyādharīs. *One of them, Śaktiyaśas, was more beautiful than all the others and Naravāhanadatta was instantly attracted to her. When he approached her, she told him that she was destined to marry him a month from that day and returned to her home, promising to come back on the appointed day.*

When Gomukha saw that Naravāhanadatta was downcast, he said, 'Listen and I will tell you an enchanting tale.

The Princess With The Parrot

'In the old days, King Sumanas ruled in the beautiful city of Kāñcanapuri. He dwelt there in great majesty after conquering the inaccessible forts and lands of his enemies. One day, as he sat in his assembly hall, the door-keeper announced that a Niṣāda princess, Muktalatā, and her brother, Vīraprabha stood at the door with a parrot in a cage. The king allowed them to enter the assembly and when the people there saw the Niṣāda woman's beauty, they thought, "This woman is not mortal. She must be a celestial being!" The woman bowed to the king and said, "This parrot knows the four Vedas and is named Śāstragañja. He is also a poet, knows all the sciences and the arts and is very learned. I have brought him here for you on the orders of King Maya." She handed over the parrot and the door-keeper gave him to the king whose curiosity had been aroused. The parrot recited the following verse, "King, it is appropriate that the dark smoke of your courage is fanned by the sighs of your enemies' widows but it is strange that the flame of your courage blazes strongly in all directions despite the floods of tears they weep at their defeat."

'Then the parrot said, "What proof would you like of my erudition? Tell me which *śāstra* I should recite from." The king was amazed but his minister said, "I am sure that this parrot has been cursed. He must have been a sage in his past life. He remembers his former birth because of his good deeds and so he can recall all that he learned." The king asked the parrot, 'I am curious, tell me about yourself. How is it that though you are a parrot, you are so learned in the *śāstras?* Who are you?" The parrot spoke through his tears and softly said, "It is a sad story, but since you command me, listen and I will tell you.

The Parrot's Tale

"Near the Himalayas, there is a *rohinī* tree. It is like the Vedas, for many birds shelter in its branches that spread across the sky, as Brāhmins take refuge in the various branches of learning. A pair of parrots had made their home there and I was born to them because of my misconduct in my previous life. My mother died when I was born but my aged father took me under his wing and nurtured me. My father remained in the *rohinī* tree and ate the fruits left over from other parrots and fed me with them as well.

"One day, a terrifying army of Bhīls arrived, blowing on their cow horns and making a loud noise. The entire forest became like an army in defeat as the animals ran helter-skelter, with terrified antelopes leaping like fluttering dust-stained war banners and the tails of frightened deer like *chowrie* plumes. When the tribe had spent an entire day in bloody hunting, they went back to their village with all the flesh they had gathered. But one old man had no meat at all. It was evening and he was hungry and when he saw the *rohinī* tree, he climbed it. He pulled parrots and other birds from their nests, killed them and threw them onto the ground. When I saw him coming closer, like the messenger of death, I hid under my father's wing out of fear. He came to our nest and killed my father by wringing his neck and threw him to the ground. I fell with my father but I slipped out from under his wing and quietly crawled into the undergrowth. The Bhīl came down from the tree, cooked and ate some of the parrots and carried the rest away to his village.

"I was no longer frightened but the night seemed long because of my grief. The next morning, when the sun was high in the sky, I was thirsty and stumbled along the ground to a lake covered with lotuses. As a result of my previous good deeds, I saw the *muni* Marīci, who had just finished bathing, on the banks. He revived me by splashing water onto my face and put me onto a leaf and carried me to his *āśrama* out of pity. The head of the *āśrama*, Pulastya, saw me and laughed out loud. The other ascetics there asked him why he had laughed and Pulastya, who had divine vision, said, 'I laughed out of sorrow when I saw this cursed parrot. After I finish my morning prayers, I will tell you his story and that will make him remember his previous births.' When he had finished praying, the other ascetics reminded him of his promise and Pulastya told my story.

'From the city of Ratnākara, King Jyotiṣprabha ruled the earth firmly and well. Śiva gave the king a boon because he was pleased with his austerities and a son was born to his queen, Harṣavatī. In a dream, the queen saw the moon entering her mouth and so the king named his son

Somaprabha[2]. The boy grew up with all the virtues of the moon and was dearly loved by his subjects. Jyotiṣprabha saw that he was brave, virile, well-loved and capable of looking after the empire and so he anointed him crown prince with great joy. He made the virtuous Priyaṃkara, son of his own minister Prabhākara, Somaprabha's minister. One day, Mātali, Indra's charioteer, came down from the sky with a celestial horse and said to Somaprabha, "You are a *vidyādhara* and a friend of Indra's. He has sent you this horse, Aśruśravas, the son of his own horse Ucchaiḥśravas, because of his previous affection for you. When you mount this horse, you will be unconquerable by your enemies." Mātali gave Somaprabha that wonderful horse and after being honoured, returned to the sky.

'Somaprabha spent the day celebrating and the next day, he said to his father, "A Kṣatriya desires conquest, so give me permission to go out and conquer the regions." His father was pleased and made all the necessary arrangements. Somaprabha bowed to his father and, on an auspicious day, he mounted Indra's horse and set out on his conquests with an army. As he was now invincible, Somaprabha defeated great kings with that wonderful horse and collected heaps of jewels from them. When he bent his bow, the heads of his enemies also bent but even after his bow was straightened, his enemies could not raise their bowed heads.

'On his return, Somaprabha took a path that went by the Himalayas. While his army camped, he went into the forest to hunt. As fate would have it, he saw a bejewelled *kinnara* and chased it on the horse given to him by Indra. The *kinnara* disappeared inside a mountain cave and Somaprabha was carried far away by his horse. When the sun had spread its light over the whole world and reached the western peaks to meet the twilight, the tired prince managed to turn around. He saw a lake at a distance and decided to spend the night on its shores and dismounted. He watered his horse and then drank and ate fruits himself. He felt less tired and then suddenly, he heard music. Out of curiosity, he went in the direction of the sound and close by, he saw a young celestial woman singing in front of a *śivaliṅgam*. "Who could she be?" he said to himself in amazement. The young woman saw that he was noble and welcomed him as a guest and asked, "Who are you and how did you come to this inaccessible place?" The prince told her his adventures and said, "Tell me, who are you and what are you doing in this forest?" The woman replied, "If you want to hear my story, listen!" and she spoke in a voice full of tears.

The Story Of Manorathaprabhā

"On a plateau in the Himalayas there is a city named Kāñcanābha where the *vidyādhara* king Padmanābha lives. I am his daughter, Manorathaprabhā by his queen Hemaprabhā, and my father loves me more than he does his own life. Using my magic powers, I would visit islands, mountains, forests and gardens with my friends. We would play there every day but I would always return to my home at mealtimes, in the third watch of the day. One day, when I was wandering on the lake shore, I saw the son of a *muni* who was there with his friend. Attracted by his good looks, I sent him a message with my friend and approached him. He welcomed me with his glance and I sat down near him.

"My friend understood our feelings and asked the young man's companion, 'Tell me who you are?' The companion replied, 'Not far from here is the *āśrama* of *muni* Dīdhitimān. He is celibate but once, when he came to this lake to bathe, he was seen by the goddess Śrī. She could not sleep with him in the flesh because of his vow of celibacy, but she desired him greatly and gave birth to a son by the sheer power of her passion that she felt for Dīdhitimān. She gave the son to Dīdhitimān since she had conceived him by looking at the *muni*, and then disappeared. The *muni* gladly took the child and named him Raśmimān. Slowly, the boy grew up and the *muni* invested him with the sacred thread and lovingly taught him all the sciences. This young man is Raśmimān, the son of Śrī, and he has come here with me to enjoy himself.'

"The young man's companion asked my friend all about me and she told him my name and my lineage as I have told you. The young man and I were more and more attracted to each other, especially after hearing about each other's families. Just then, a retainer came to me and said, 'Get up, for your father is waiting for you in the dining-hall of his palace.' I promised to return quickly and leaving the *muni's* son, went to my father's house. I did not eat very much and when I came out of the room, my friend came to me and said, 'Raśmimān's companion is at the front gate and he is very agitated. He told me that Raśmimān sent him here, giving him the power to fly through the air which he inherited from his father. Apparently Raśmimān is deeply in love with you and cannot live another moment without you by his side."

"When I heard this, I left my father's house with my friend and Raśmimān's companion who showed us the way. I reached here to find that Raśmimān, unable to bear our separation, had given up his life with the rising of the moon. I was bereft and wanted to throw myself into the fire with his body. But at that very moment, a man with a body of fire descended from the sky, lifted Raśmimān's body and went away. I wanted to throw myself into the fire anyway when a voice rang out, 'Manorathaprabhā, don't do this. At the appropriate time, you will be reunited with the *muni's* son!' So I wait here for him, full of hope, worshipping Śiva. I have not seen Raśmimān's companion again."

'Somaprabha asked Manorathaprabhā, "Why are you alone? Where is your friend?" to which she said, "The *vidyādhara* king Siṃhavikrama has an incomparable daughter, Makarandikā. She is my dear friend and shares my sorrow. She sent her attendant here today to ask about me and I sent my friend back with her. That is why I am alone."

'As she spoke, she showed Somaprabha her friend who was coming down from the sky at that moment. After

Manorathaprabhā and her friend had talked, she made her friend give Somaprabha a bed and grass for his horse. The night passed and in the morning, they saw a *vidyādhara* descending from the sky. His name was Devajaya and he sat down and said to Manorathaprabhā, "I have a message for you from King Siṃhavikrama. His daughter, your friend, because of her affection for you, has refused to marry until you do. He wants you to go there and persuade her to marry soon." Manorathaprabhā prepared to go there out of love for her friend and Somaprabha said to her, "I am curious about the world of the *vidyādharas*. Take me with you. With enough grass to eat, my horse can stay here while I go with you." Manorathaprabhā agreed and flew through the air with her friend while Devajaya carried Somaprabha in his arms.

Somaprabha Meets His Future Bride

'They were welcomed as guests and Makarandikā, when she saw Somaprabha, said, "Who is this?" Manorathaprabhā told her his story and Makarandikā's heart went out to him. Somaprabha felt as though he had found the goddess incarnate and thought to himself, "Who is the lucky man destined to marry Makarandikā?" Manorathaprabhā asked Makarandikā in private, "Why don't you want to get married?" and Makarandikā replied, "How can I do that until you choose a husband, for you are dearer to me than my own life!" Manorathaprabhā affectionately told her friend that she had already chosen a husband and that she was waiting to see him again. After hearing this, Makarandikā agreed to get married.

'Manorathaprabhā understood what was going through her friend's mind and said, "Somaprabha has wandered all over the earth and has come here as your guest. You should honour him as one." "I have offered him everything except my body," said Makarandikā. "He can have that as well if he likes." Manorathaprabhā went and told the king about Somaprabha and Makarandikā's love and had their wedding arranged. Somaprabha was delighted and said, "I must return to your *āśrama* since my army, led by my minister, has probably come there looking for me. If they do not find me, they will suspect the worst and turn back. I will get news of my forces and then come back to marry Makarandikā on an auspicious day." Manorathaprabhā then took him back, making Devajaya carry him in his arms.

'Meanwhile, Somaprabha's minister, Priyaṃkara, had followed him and arrived at the *āśrama* with the army. While Somaprabha was telling him all his adventures with great delight, a messenger arrived from his father with a letter asking him to return at once. On his minister's advice, he went back to his city with his army so as not to disregard his father's wishes. He told Manorathaprabhā and Devajaya that he would come back after seeing his father. Devajaya went and reported this to Makarandikā and she was plunged into grief at the separation. She no longer enjoyed strolling in the garden, nor singing, nor the company of her friends, nor the sweet songs of the parrots. She would not eat nor take pleasure in adorning herself. Despite her parents' efforts, her spirits did not improve. She left her couch of lotus stalks and wandered around like a mad woman, causing her parents great distress.

Makarandikā Is Cursed

'Her parents tried to comfort her, but when she refused to listen, they grew angry and cursed her. "You shall fall among poverty-stricken Niṣādas for a short time. You shall have the same body but you shall not remember your past birth!" Makarandikā entered a Niṣāda's house and became a Niṣāda woman. Her parents regretted the curse and died of grief. That *vidyādhara* king had been a *ṛṣi* in his former birth and had known all the *śāstras* but has now become a parrot because of some misdemeanours in his previous life. His wife was born as wild pig. This parrot remembers what he learned in his past life because of the austerities he had performed.

'I laughed because I knew the wondrous consequences of one's deeds. He will be released as soon as he tells the tale in a king's court. Somaprabha will find Makarandikā, the parrot's daughter, who is now a Niṣāda woman, in his *vidyādhara* birth. And Manorathaprabhā will also be united with Raśmimān, the *muni's* son, who is now a king. Somaprabha met his father and returned to the *āśrama* and now propitiates Śiva so that he can be with his beloved again.'

"This was the story the sage Pulastya told and when I heard it, I remembered my former birth and was both happy and sad. Then Marīci, the *muni* who had found me and brought me to the *āśrama,* reared me. When my wings developed, I flew all over the place, as is natural to birds, displaying my talents. I fell into the hands of a Niṣāda and came here to your court. And now, the misdeeds that made me into a bird have been destroyed."

The Lovers Are Reunited

'When the learned parrot finished his story in the assembly hall, King Sumanas' heart filled with wonder and love. In the meantime, Śiva was pleased with Somaprabha's austerities and said to him, "Stand up and go to the court of King Sumanas where you will find your beloved! Makarandikā became a Niṣāda woman, Muktalatā, because of her father's curse. She has gone there with her father who has become a parrot. When she sees you, she will remember her life as a *vidyādharī* and you will be joyfully reunited when you recognize each other." Śiva, who is merciful to his devotees, then said to Manorathaprabhā who also lived in the *āśrama,* "The *muni's* son, Raśmimān, whom you had chosen as a husband, has been reborn as Sumanas. Go to him and when he sees you, he will remember his former birth." Somaprabha and Manorathaprabhā were directed separately in their dreams and went at once to Sumanas' court. When Makarandikā saw Somaprabha, she recalled her former birth and was released from her curse. She them recovered her celestial body and embraced him. Somaprabha, who had obtained the *vidyādharī* princess, the very incarnation of celestial pleasures, by Śiva's favour, felt that he had fulfilled his life's goal and embraced Makarandikā. King Sumanas remembered his former birth when he saw Manorathaprabhā and re-entered his former body which fell from the sky. He became Raśmimān and embraced his beloved for whom he had longed. He went to his *āśrama* and Somaprabha went with his beloved to his city. The parrot gave up his bird body and went to the home he had earned from his austerities.

'Thus human beings who are destined to meet again are reunited, even though they are far apart in the world.'

Naravāhanadatta heard this romantic story from Gomukha when he was pining for Śaktiyaśas and felt much better.

Then Gomukha, who had finished the tales of the two vidyādharīs, *said to Naravāhanadatta, 'Some people, even though they are inclined towards worldly pleasures, resist the temptation of love and passion. Listen to this story and you will understand why.*

The Man Who Controlled His Anger

'King Kuladhara had a servant named Śūravarmā who was from a good family and was famous for his courage. One day, Śūravarmā entered his house unannounced and found his wife alone with his best friend. He controlled his anger and restrained himself thinking, "What is the use of my killing an animal who has betrayed a friend? Or of punishing this wicked woman? What is the point of my burdening myself with these misdeeds?" He did not harm the couple but he said to them, "I will kill you if I see you again. I do not want to see either of you as long as I live." He let them go and they went far away. Śūravarmā married again and lived happily. Thus, a person who conquers anger will never experience sorrow and the one who is discriminating will not be afflicted by adversity. It is discretion and not courage that leads to success, even among animals. Listen to this story about the lion, the bull and the other animals.

The Bull Frightens The Lion

'The son of a rich merchant lived in a certain city. Once, he went to Mathurā to trade and a bull named Sañjīvaka that was pulling a loaded cart dragged hard on his yoke and broke it. The path was muddy because of floods in a nearby mountain stream and the bull slipped and fell, injuring himself. The merchant's son tried to rouse the bull for a long time but when he saw that the bull was immobilized by his injuries, he left him there and continued on his way. But fortunately, the bull recovered. Sañjīvaka rose and ate the tender grass that grew more there and slowly, he regained his former condition. He went to the banks of the Yamunā and as he ate the fresh grass there, he grew healthy and strong. He wandered where he pleased, his hump full and proud, digging up ant-hills with his horns and bellowing loudly, like Nandi.

'A lion named Piṅgalaka lived in a forest close by. He was brave and fierce-looking. That king of the beasts had two jackals named Damanaka and Karaṭaka as his ministers. One day, the lion went to the shores of the Yamunā to drink water and heard Sañjīvaka bellowing loudly. Piṅgalaka had never heard a sound like that before and thought, "What kind of sound is this? Surely some great animal lives here and if it sees me, it will either kill me or hound me out of this forest!" The lion quickly went back to the forest without drinking water, terribly frightened. But he hid his fear from his followers. Damanaka, the clever jackal, said quietly to Karaṭaka, the other minister, "How is it that our master has returned so soon without drinking any water? We should ask him what the matter is." Karaṭaka replied, "How does it concern us? Haven't you heard what happened to the monkey that pulled out the wedge?"

The Curious Monkey

"In a certain town, a merchant decided to build a temple and had collected a lot of wood for that purpose. The workmen cut through the upper portion of a plank, wedged it apart and went home. A monkey came there and mischievously jumped onto the plank which was being held apart by the wedge. He sat across the part that had been wedged as if he were in the mouth of death. He pulled out the wedge and his genitals were crushed by the two parts of the plank which crashed together and the monkey fell down and died.

"Therefore, a person can be destroyed by interfering in things that do not concern him. Why should we get involved in what the lion is thinking?" said Karaṭaka. But Damanaka insisted, "We should try and understand our master's feelings at all times. Which servant would be content with merely filling his belly?" To which Karaṭaka responded, "Servants should not interfere in their masters' affairs merely to satisfy themselves!" Damanaka then said, "Stop that! Each one is satisfied with what suits him. A dog is happy with a bone but a lion pursues an elephant." "But if the master gets angry, where is your advantage?" asked Karaṭaka. "Masters are like mountains, rough, resolute, inaccessible and surrounded by monsters." Damanaka agreed but added that the wise servant gains influence over the master by slowly understanding his character.

'Karaṭaka challenged Damanaka to win the lion's confidence and Damanaka approached Piṅgalaka. The lion welcomed him and Damanaka sat down and said, "My family has served you for generations. You should seek out the people who desire your welfare even if you do not know them well and those who wish you ill should be rejected. When a cat is acquired with money it is precious, but a mouse that has been reared on food from your own house is killed. A king who wants to succeed must listen to the advice of those who wish him well and they, in turn, must give him the right advice, even without being asked. So, if you will not be angry or offended by my presumption, and if you trust me and do not wish to hide your feelings from me, may I ask you a question?"

'Piṅgalaka said, "I trust you because you are devoted to me. Ask me your question," and Damanaka said, "You were thirsty and went to drink water. Why did you return so disturbed?" The lion thought, "He has guessed my feelings. Why should I hide anything from this devoted servant?" and he said aloud, "I cannot conceal anything from you, so listen. When I went to drink water, I heard a sound that I had never heard before. I think it must be the roar of an animal greater than myself, for the sound that an animal makes usually reflects its might. That is the way animals have been created. Now that this beast has come here, neither the forest nor my body are my own. I must leave for some other forest."

'Damanaka replied, "You are brave, why do you want to give up this forest? Flowing water can break bridges, rumours can end friendships, lack of discrimination destroys good advice and cowards are frightened by mere words. Even machines make terrible noises until we know what they are. You should not be afraid of this unfamiliar sound. Listen to the story of the jackal and the drum as proof of what I am saying.

The Jackal And The Drum

"In the old days, a jackal lived in a certain forest. He was wandering around looking for food when he came to a battlefield. There, he heard a loud noise and when he looked around, he saw a drum lying on the ground. He had never seen a drum before and wondered, 'What kind of being is this that makes such a sound?' He came closer and saw that it did not move and so he concluded that it was not an animal. He observed that the sound was produced when the wind moved an arrow that was stuck in the drum. The jackal realized that there was nothing to fear and climbed into the drum to find something to eat. But it was empty. There was nothing there but wood and skin.

Sañjīvaka And Piṅgalaka Become Friends

"So, do not fear this sound! If you like, I will go and investigate," said Damanaka and the lion said, "Go, if you have the courage!" and the jackal went to the banks of the Yamunā. He walked in the direction of the sound and came upon the bull eating grass. He went closer and introduced himself and then went back and reported everything to the lion. Piṅgalaka was very pleased and told Damanaka that if he had really made friends with the bull, then he should fetch the animal so that the lion could see him. Damanaka went back and invited the bull into the lion's forest. The bull refused the invitation because he was afraid. So the jackal went back to the lion and made him promise that the bull would be safe. When Damanaka assured Sañjīvaka that he would come to no harm, the bull went with him to the lion.

'The bull bowed before the lion and Piṅgalaka said gently, "Stay here with me without fear from now on!" The bull agreed and in the course of time, the bull and the lion became such good friends that the lion ignored his other retainers. Damanaka was very displeased at this and said quietly to Karaṭaka, "Look, our master is so dominated by Sañjīvaka that he has lost interest in us! He eats alone and does not give us a share. And the fool is now advised by the bull! It is all my fault because I brought the bull here! I will take steps to destroy him and free our master of this attachment." Karataka said, "Friend, you will not be able to do this now." But Damanaka replied that he would accomplish his plan by his intelligence. "The one who keeps his wits about him even in adversity can accomplish anything! Listen to the story of the crab that killed the crane," he said.

The Crab Who Killed The Crane

"A crane lived by a tank that was full of fish. The fish would flee in fright when they saw the crane and he was unable to catch and eat them. So he made a plan and said to them, 'There is a man with a net who wants to catch fish. He will come here soon and kill you. If you trust me, listen to what I have to say. There is a clear lake in a deserted place that the local fishermen do not know about. I will take you one by one so that you can live there.' The silly fish were so frightened that they said to the crane, 'We trust you. Please take us there!' The crane took them away one by one to a rock where he killed and ate many of them. A crab saw the crane carrying the fish away and asked him where he was taking them. The crane told the crab what he had told the fish and the crab was so frightened that he begged the crane to take him away as well. The crane was tempted by the smell of his flesh and picked up the crab and flew through the air to the rock. But the crab noticed the bones of the fish that the crane had eaten and realized that the crane ate those that trusted him. The moment they alighted on the rock, the wise crab calmly bit off the crane's head. He went back and told the remaining fish what had happened and they honoured him as their saviour. Intelligence is power and power is of no use to one without intelligence. Listen to the story of the lion and the hare.

The Hare Who Tricked The Lion

"A lion lived in a certain forest. He was brave and undefeated and he killed all the creatures that he saw. The animals had a conference and said to the lion, 'We will send you an animal for your food. Why do you want to damage your own interests by killing us indiscriminately?' and the lion agreed. He ate an animal a day and one day, it was the hare's turn to be eaten. The hare was sent off by the other animals, but the wise creature thought the matter over with a clear head. 'An intelligent person does not panic even in adversity. Now that death stands before me, I will come up with a plan.' The hare delayed going to the lion and when he finally got there, the lion said, 'Why have you come so long after my mealtime? What punishment can I give you that is greater than death, you rascal!' The hare bowed and said, 'It is not my fault! I was not in control of my actions today for another lion delayed me when I was on my way. I was able to escape only after a long time!' The lion's eyes turned red with anger and he waved his tail and said, 'Who is this other lion? Show him to me!' The hare asked the lion to come with him and took him to a far away well. 'He lives here,' said the hare. 'Look, you can see him!' The lion roared in anger and looked into the well. He saw his own reflection in the clear water and heard the echo of his own roar. The king of the beasts thought that there was another lion in the well who roared louder than himself and jumped into the well to kill him. The foolish lion was drowned and the hare, who had escaped death because of his intelligence, went back to the other animals and entertained them with his story.

Damanaka Sows The Seeds Of Suspicion

"Thus, intelligence and not might is the greatest strength. The hare used intelligence to kill the lion. I will also attain my goal through intelligence," said Damanaka and Karataka was silent. Then Damanaka went to his master and sat there as if he were deeply depressed. When Piṅgalaka asked him what the matter was, he said to him quietly, "I will tell you, for it is not right to remain silent if one knows something significant. If one desires the welfare of one's master one should speak even if one is not asked. Listen to what I have to say and do not doubt my word. The bull Sañjīvaka wants to kill you and take over the kingdom. While he was a minister he decided that you were a coward. Even now he is tossing his horns, his natural weapons, with which he intends to kill you. He says to the other animals in the forest, 'When I have killed this meat-eating king of the beasts then all of you can live in peace under me for I eat only grass.' Reconsider your opinion of this bull, for you shall never have peace of mind as long as he is alive."

"What can that grass-eating bull do to me? I am brave and powerful!" said Piṅgalaka. "But how can I kill an animal who has come to me for protection and to whom I have promised safety?" Damanaka said to his master, "Don't say that! No one can be the king's equal! The goddess of fortune cannot place one foot each on two people and keep her balance. She has to abandon one of them. A king should not dislike a servant who wishes him well and honour a bad servant. Such a king will be shunned by the wise as a wicked patient is shunned by good doctors. Fortune goes where there is a giver of advice and a listener. Even if that advice seems distasteful in the beginning it is worthwhile in the end. He who listens to bad advice and ignores the good will experience misfortune. What is the meaning of this love that you have for the bull? What does it matter if he came to you for protection or if you promised him freedom from harm? Besides, if you keep him near you all the time, you will get worms from his shit. The worms will enter your body which is covered by scars from the tusks of angry elephants! The bull may have planned to kill you by cunning artifice! A clever person can decide not to hurt another actively but damage can occur by association with the wicked. Listen to a story as proof of this.

The Bedbug And The Flea

"A bedbug lived in the mattress of a certain king. She had crept in there, undetected, from somewhere else and her name was Mandavisarpiṇī. One day, a flea named Ṭiṭṭibha entered the mattress, brought there by the wind from some other place. When Mandavisarpiṇī saw the flea, she said, 'Go away! Why have you come into my home?' and Ṭiṭṭibha answered, 'I want to drink the king's blood because I have never tasted it before. Let me stay here!' Mandavisarpiṇī let the flea stay but warned him, 'Friend, you must not bite the king at any time that you please. You must bite him gently only when he is sleeping soundly,' to which Ṭiṭṭibha agreed and waited. But that night, Ṭiṭṭibha bit the king as he got into bed. The king jumped up, shouting, 'I've been bitten!' The clever flea hid himself quickly and the servants found the bedbug and killed her.

"So Mandavisarpiṇī was killed because of her association with Ṭiṭṭibha. Similarly, your association with Sañjīvaka cannot turn out well. If you don't believe me, you will soon see him yourself, confidently tossing his horns which are as sharp as spears!" Damanaka managed to change Piṅgalaka's feelings towards the bull with these words and the lion was convinced in his heart that Sañjīvaka should be killed. Assuring himself of the lion's feelings, Damanaka went to meet the bull. He sat down beside him quietly and the bull asked him what was wrong and if he was unwell. "How can a servant ever be well? No one is dear to a king forever, for time affects us all. All dependents are ultimately despised," said Damanaka and Sañjīvaka asked again, "My friend, tell me why you are so upset today." Damanaka then said, "I speak from affection, so listen to me. Piṅgalaka, the king of the beasts, has turned against you. He has no regard for your friendship and wants to kill and eat you. His evil retainers have encouraged him in this." The bull believed Damanaka because he had trusted him before, and was very dejected. He said, "An unworthy master is swayed by his unworthy servants and though he can be won over by loyalty, he soon becomes a stranger. Listen to this story as proof.

How The Camel Was Tricked

"There was a lion named Madotkaṭa in a certain forest and he had three retainers, a panther, a crow and a jackal. One day, the lion saw a camel that had escaped from a caravan and wandered into the forest. The lion had never seen a camel before and he asked his companions what kind of creature it was. The crow, who had been to many countries, said that it was a camel. The lion was curious about the new creature and after having approached him, promised the camel that he would come to no harm. The camel became his companion and stayed there with him. One day, the lion got into a fight with an elephant and was badly wounded. He grew weaker and stopped eating even though he was surrounded by his hungry companions whom he was responsible for feeding. The lion was exhausted and as he wandered in search of food, he asked all his companions except the camel what he should do. They replied, 'We must give you advice that is appropriate for such an adverse situation. What friendship do you have with the camel? Why don't you eat him? He is a grass-eater and is therefore meant to be eaten by carnivores like ourselves. Why should one not be sacrificed to feed the many? And if you are concerned that you promised him safety, then we will devise a plan by which he offers you his body himself.'

"The crow took the lion's permission and went to the camel. He said, 'Our master is distracted by hunger but he says nothing to us. We have decided to offer ourselves to him to be in his good graces. If you want him to think well of you, you should do the same.' The innocent camel agreed and went to the lion with the crow. The crow said to the lion, 'Eat me for I am alone.' The lion said that there was no point in eating such a small animal. So the jackal said 'Eat me!' but the lion rejected him as well. Then the panther said, 'Eat me!' but the lion would not eat him either. At last, the camel, deceived by their words, said, 'Eat me!' and the others fell upon him and killed him. They divided him among themselves and ate him.

"In the same way, some animal has turned Piṅgalaka against me without reason. Now Fate will decide what happens next. It is better to be in the service of a vulture with swans as retainers than to serve a swan with vultures as courtiers. Worst of all is a king like this with courtiers like this!" said Sañjīvaka. Damanaka said, "Patience can accomplish anything. Listen to this story.

The Bird Who Challenged The Ocean

'A *ṭiṭṭibha* bird lived on the seashore with his wife. The female was about to lay eggs and she said to her husband, 'Let us go somewhere else, for if I lay my eggs here the sea may wash them away.' Her husband replied, 'The sea cannot challenge me!' to which his wife said, 'How can you compare yourself with the sea? You must follow good advice otherwise we will be ruined! Listen to this story:

The Turtle And The Geese

'In a certain lake, there was a turtle named Kambugrīva and two swans named Vikaṭa and Saṅkaṭa were his friends. One day, the lake dried up in a drought and the swans wanted to go to another lake. The turtle asked his friends to take him along with them and the swans said, "The lake we want to go to is very far away but if you want to come with us, you have to do exactly as we say. You have to hold with your teeth a stick that we will carry between us. You must not utter a word along the way, otherwise you will fall and die." The turtle agreed and held the stick with his teeth. The swans flew into the air with the two ends of the stick in their beaks and reached the area where the lake was. They were seen by some townspeople who wondered aloud what the swans were carrying. The turtle heard the noise they were making and asked the swans what it was. He let go of the stick to speak and fell to the ground where the men killed and ate him.

'Thus people who relinquish good sense are destroyed like the turtle who relinquished the stick,' said the female *ṭiṭṭibha*. Her husband retorted, 'That may be true, but listen to this story.

The Fish Who Took Timely Action

'Three fish named Anāgatavidhātā, Pratyutpannamati and Yadbhaviṣya lived in a lake near a river and were good friends. One day they heard passing fishermen say, "There must be fish in this lake." Anāgatavidhātā was afraid that they would be killed by fishermen and he swam into the current of the river and went to another place. Pratyutpannamati stayed where he was, unafraid, and decided that he would leave if danger approached. Yadbhaviṣya also stayed there, resigning himself to his fate. A few days later, the fishermen arrived and threw a net into the lake. Pratyutpannamati fell into the net but wisely lay there without moving, as if he were dead. The fishermen were killing the fish caught in the net but they did not kill Pratyutpannamati because they thought he was already dead. He took advantage of the situation, jumped into the current and swam away to another place. But Yadbhaviṣya, the foolish fish, struggled in the net and so the fishermen killed him.

'I, too, will make a plan when danger is at hand. I will not leave now for fear of the sea,' said the male *ṭiṭṭibha* to his wife and stayed where he was in his nest. But the sea had heard his arrogant words. In a few days, his wife laid her eggs and the sea came and carried them away with his waves. The sea was curious about what the male *ṭiṭṭibha* would do next. The female wailed to her husband, 'The tragedy that I had predicted has taken place!' The male *ṭiṭṭibha* was unmoved and said to his wife, 'Wait and see what I do to that wretched sea!' He called together all the birds and told them what had happened. They went crying to Garuḍa, the king of birds, and begged for his protection. They told him that the sea had carried away their eggs and that even though Garuḍa was their protector, they were vulnerable. Garuḍa appealed to Viṣṇu who dried up the sea with fire and made him return the eggs.

The Battle Between The Lion And The Bull

"One must be wise and determined in an adverse situation. Now a battle with Piṅgalaka stands before you. When he raises his tail and stands with his four paws together, you know that he is about to attack. You must toss your head and gore him in the stomach with your horns. Kill your enemy by pulling out his entrails!" said Damanaka to the bull and then went to Karaṭaka and told him that he had managed to create a rift between the lion and the bull.

'Sañjīvaka approached the lion quietly, trying to ascertain his feelings by observing his face and movements. He saw that the lion was ready to attack since he had his paws together and his tail in the air. Piṅgalaka saw that the bull was tossing his head in fear. The lion lunged at the bull with his claws and the bull attacked with his horns and the battle between them began. When the saintly Karaṭaka saw this, he said to Damanaka, "Why have you brought this tragedy on our master for your own selfish purposes? Wealth obtained by oppressing people, friendship obtained by deceit and a beloved obtained by violence will not last long. But enough of this, for those who speak to a person who disregards good advice will come to a bitter end, like Sūcīmukha and the monkey.

The Bird Who Interfered

"Once, a group of monkeys were wandering in the forest in winter and they saw a firefly. They mistook it for a real fire and so they covered it with grass and leaves and tried to warm themselves. One of them fanned it with his breath. A bird named Sūcīmukha saw the monkey and said, 'This is not fire, this is a firefly, so don't exert yourself.' The monkey did not stop even though he had heard what the bird said. So Sūcīmukha came down from the tree to persuade him. The monkey grew angry and threw a stone at the bird and crushed him.

"So there is no point in talking to those who will not accept good advice. Why should I say more? You created a rift by deceit and you know that anything done with bad intentions cannot turn out well. Listen to this story.

The Man Who Outsmarted Himself

"A merchant had two sons and their names were

Dharmabuddhi and Duṣṭabuddhi. They left their father's home and went to another country in order to make money. Somehow, they managed to make two thousand *dīnārs* and returned to their own city. They buried the money under a tree but kept one hundred *dīnārs* which they divided equally between them and lived happily in their father's house. One day, Duṣṭabuddhi went to the tree alone and dug up the money for himself, for he had extravagant ways. After a month had passed, he went to Dharmabuddhi and said, 'Come, let us divide the money, for I have expenses.' They went to where they had buried the *dīnārs* and dug up the place. When they found no money there Duṣṭabuddhi called his brother a cheat and said, 'You have taken all the money. Give me my half!' but Dharmabuddhi replied, 'I did not take it. You must have done it!' They began to fight and in the process, Duṣṭabuddhi hit Dharmabuddhi on the head with a stone and dragged him to the king.

"Each brother told his story to the king's officers but they were unable to resolve the dispute. While they prepared to arrest them both for trial Duṣṭabuddhi said, 'The tree under which the money was buried will stand as a witness and confirm that Dharmabuddhi took the *dīnārs*.' The officers were surprised to hear this but they agreed to ask the tree the next day. The brothers were released on bail and they returned home. Duṣṭabuddhi told his father the whole story and secretly gave him the money and said, 'Hide in the tree and speak as my witness!' The father agreed and they went at night and he hid himself inside the tree's large hollow.

"The next day, the king's officers went with the two brothers and asked the tree who had taken the money. 'The *dīnārs* were taken by Dharmabuddhi,' said the father from inside the tree. 'This is impossible! Duṣṭabuddhi must have hidden someone inside the tree to speak on his behalf!' said the officers. They directed smoke into the tree's hollow and the father suffocated and fell out of the tree dead. The officers understood what had happened and made Duṣṭabuddhi return the money to his brother. They cut off Duṣṭabuddhi's hands and tongue and banished him from the city. Then they honoured Dharmabuddhi as a man who lived up to his name.

"Thus, an injustice can lead to terrible things. One should always act righteously, like the crane and the snake.

The Crane And The Snake

"A snake would come and eat a crane's fledglings as soon as they were born. On the advice of a crab, the crane spread pieces of fish from the opening of a mongoose's lair all the way to the snake's hole. The mongoose came out and followed the fish trail, eating as he went, to the snake's hole. Eventually, he killed the snake and its children.

"One can therefore certainly succeed by devising a scheme. Listen to this story.

The Mice That Ate Iron

"There was once a merchant's son who had only his father's weighing scale left as property. The scale was made of a thousand *palas* of iron and the man left it in care with a fellow merchant when he went to another city. When he returned and asked for his balance, the merchant told him that it had been eaten by mice. 'It is quite possible. That iron was particularly tasty and the mice loved it,' said the merchant sadly though he was laughing in his heart. The merchant's son asked him for some food and because the merchant was in a good mood, he agreed. The merchant's son went to bathe, taking the other man's young son with him. He persuaded the boy to come along by giving him some *āmalaka* fruit. After they had bathed, the clever merchant's son hid the boy at the house of a friend and returned alone. When the merchant asked where his son was, he replied, 'A bird came down from the sky and carried him away.' 'You have hidden my son!' shouted the merchant in anger and took the merchant's son to the king.

"There, the merchant's son said the same thing. 'This is impossible! How can a bird carry away a boy?' said the people in the royal assembly and the merchant's son replied, 'In a country where mice can eat a huge iron balance, a kite can carry off an elephant, let alone a small boy!' Curious, the people asked for the whole story and when they had heard it, they made the merchant return the balance and the merchant's son gave back the boy.

"Thus, the intelligent are able to achieve their ends by scheming. But you have brought our master into danger by your rashness," said Karaṭaka. But Damanaka laughed when he heard this and said, "Have you ever heard of a lion being defeated by a bull in battle? There is a great difference between a lion whose body is scarred with wounds from elephants' tusks and a bull whose body has only been prodded by a stick!"'

'As the jackals were talking, Piṅgalaka killed Sañjīvaka. After the bull's death, Damanaka recovered his position as minister along with Karaṭaka and they lived happily for a long time with the king of the beasts.

Naravāhanadatta was pleased with this story from Gomukha for it contained a wealth of information on statecraft and was full of wise counsel.

The next night, which was the night of the full moon, Gomukha told Naravāhandatta the following story.

The Bodhisattva Who Became A King

'In a certain city, a merchant's son was born and was an incarnation of a part of the *bodhisattva*. His mother died and his father married again. He sent his son away and the young man went to live in the forest with his wife. His younger brother was also asked to leave the house by their father, but he was not as calm by nature as his older brother. So they parted ways and the younger brother went in a different direction.

'In the course of their wanderings, the older brother and his wife reached a huge desert that had no water, no trees and no grass. The sun's rays were strong and soon, they ran out of food and water. For seven days they wandered through the desert and the young wife grew tired and thirsty. Her husband kept her alive by feeding her portions of his flesh and slaked her thirst by letting her drink his blood. On the eighth day, they reached a mountain pasture full of grass, running water and the cool shade of fruit trees. The young man refreshed his wife with fruits and water and went down to bathe in the river.

'While he was bathing, the young man noticed a man with his hands and feet cut off being carried away by the river's current. He seemed in need of help and though the young man was exhausted by his journey, he jumped into the water and rescued the crippled man. He brought him onto the shore and, filled with compassion, he asked him, "Who did this to you?" "My enemies cut off my hands and feet and threw me into the river so that I would die slowly and painfully. But you have saved my life." The young man bandaged the cripple's wounds and gave him food and water. It was only after that that he bathed and ate himself. The young man, who was a part of the *bodhisattva*, continued to live in that forest with his wife, eating roots and fruits and performing austerities.

'One day when he had gone to gather fruit, his wife fell in love with the cripple whose wounds had now healed. She decided to kill her husband and hatched a plot with the cripple. That evil woman pretended to be ill and pointed to a plant that grew in an inaccessible valley across a river that was hard to ford and said to her husband, "I will live only if you bring me that very plant which was pointed out to me in a dream by the gods." The husband let himself down into the valley by a rope that was made of grass and fastened to a tree. His wife untied the rope and the man fell into the river and was swept away by the strong current. The river carried him far away and threw him up onto the shore near a certain city. He was unharmed because of the merit he had accumulated through his good conduct in the past. He climbed out of the water and rested under a tree, for he was tired after his experience, and he thought about his wife's unpardonable behaviour.

'It so happened that the king of that city had died suddenly. The city had a custom by which, when the king died, an auspicious elephant was driven through the streets and any man that the elephant picked up with his trunk was anointed king. The auspicious elephant reached the young man and, as if pleased with his calm nature, picked him up and placed him on his back. The young man, who was a merchant's son but a part of the *bodhisattva*, was taken to the city and anointed king by the people. Once he became king, the young man did not waste his time with women. Instead, he practised the virtues of compassion, non-violence and generosity.

'His wife thought that her husband had been drowned and she wandered around with her crippled lover on her back without any fear of her husband. She went from city to city and village to village begging for alms, saying that the cripple was her husband and that his hands and feet had been cut off by his enemies. Eventually, she reached the city where her real husband was king. She begged there as usual and the townspeople honoured her and gave her alms, believing that she was a devoted wife. News of her virtue reached the ears of the king. He had the woman brought to him with the crippled man on her back. When she arrived, he recognized her and asked, "Are you the devoted wife?" and the woman, who did not recognize her husband, surrounded as he was by the glory of royalty, replied, "I am." Then the king, who was an incarnation of a part of the *bodhisattva*, laughed and said, "I have seen the fruit of your devotion. I fed you on my own flesh and blood, which you devoured like a human *rākṣasī*, and was still unable to keep you. How is it that this man, who has neither hands nor feet, has not only kept you but makes you carry him around like this? Did you carry the husband that you threw into the river on your back? It is that vicious deed that you are paying for now with this burden!"

'The woman recognized her husband when he revealed her past actions and she fainted with fright and seemed to be lifeless. The king's ministers asked him eagerly, "Tell us why you said that," and the king told them the whole story. When the ministers heard that the woman had tried to kill her own husband, they had her nose and ears cut off and banished her from the kingdom along with the cripple. Thus, fate appropriately paired the cripple with the woman who had her ears and nose cut off and the man who was a part of the *bodhisattva* with the majesty of kingship.

'A woman's heart is full of hate and she is unable to tell right from wrong. Women are led by their senses and are hard to understand. But good fortune comes to the noble, the calm and the virtuous unexpectedly, as if it were pleased with them.'

After Gomukha had finished this story, he began another one.

The Bodhisattva And The Creatures In The Well

'There was once a young man who was very noble. He was a part of the *bodhisattva* and his heart was ruled by compassion. He built a hut in the forest and lived there performing austerities. He rescued animals who were in pain and appeased even *piśācas* and other cruel beings by giving them gifts of water and jewels. One day, while he was walking through the forest in order to help those in need, he came upon a huge well. He peeped into it and a woman spoke loudly from inside. "Sir, there are four of us in here, me, a lion, a bird with a golden crest, and a snake. We fell into the well during the night. Take pity on us and pull us out!" "I can believe that the three of you fell in because of darkness," said the man to the woman, "but how did the bird fall in?" The woman replied that the bird had fallen in because he had been caught in a fowler's net. The man tried to pull them out of the well with his ascetic powers but he could not, and realized that his powers had left him. "This woman must be wicked and my powers have left me because I spoke to her. I had better try some other means to get them out," he thought and plaited a rope of grass. He pulled all four of them out of the well with the rope and they all thanked and praised him. Completely amazed, he said to the lion, the bird and the snake, "Tell me, how is it that you all speak in human voices?" The lion said, "We can all speak in human tongue, we remember our past births and we are all enemies. We will tell you our stories one by one. Listen," and the lion began his own story.

The Lion's Tale

"There is a beautiful city in the mountains called Vaidūryasṛṅga and the *vidyādhara* prince Padmaveśa lives there. A son named Vajravega was born to him but the boy was conceited and while he lived in the world of the *vidyādharas,* he picked fights with everyone, relying on his courage and martial skills. Padmaveśa tried to stop his son but he would not listen and so Padmaveśa cursed Vajravega to be born into the world of men. Oppressed by the curse, Vajravega wept, his powers and his pride both gone. He asked his father when his curse would end and, after thinking for a while, Padmaveśa replied, 'You will be born a Brāhmin's son on earth and you will be conceited in that birth as well. Your father will curse you and turn you into a lion and you will fall into a well. A good man will rescue you out of kindness and when you have repaid him, you will be free of the curse.'

"So Vajravega was born as the son of the Brāhmin Haraghoṣa, in Mālava and he was named Devaghoṣa. In that birth, too, he was proud of his valour and fought with many people. Haraghoṣa told him not to make so many enemies and when he did not listen, his father grew angry and cursed him. 'You will become a lion who is proud of his strength but has little intelligence.' As a result, Devaghoṣa, who was really a *vidyādhara,* was born as a lion in the forest. I am that very lion. I was wandering here at night and impelled by destiny, I fell into this well. You have pulled me out of it. I will leave now but I will return whenever you think of me.

I will repay you for this kindness and shall be freed from my curse."

'The lion left and the *bodhisattva* asked the bird to relate his story.

The Bird's Tale

"In the Himalayas, there is a *vidyādhara* king named Vajradaṅṣṭra whose wife gave birth to five daughters one after another. The king propitiated Śiva and finally a son was born to him. The king named him Rajatadaṅṣṭra and loved him more than his own life. He was so fond of his son that he bestowed *vidyādhara* powers on him while he was still a boy and Rajatadaṅṣṭra grew up the apple of his family's eye. One day, his older sister, Somaprabhā, was playing on a musical instrument. In his childish way, Rajatadaṅṣṭra kept asking her to give it to him and when she did not listen, he mischievously snatched it from her hand and flew into the air with it, as if he were a bird. Then his sister cursed him. 'Since you snatched my instrument and flew away with it, you shall become a bird with a golden crest.' Rajatadaṅṣṭra fell at his sister's feet and begged her to pronounce an end to the curse. She said, 'Foolish boy, when you are a bird, you will fall into a deep well. A good man will rescue you out of compassion and when you repay him, you will be released from the curse.'

"I am that bird and I fell into this well at night. Now that you have rescued me, I will leave but I will return whenever you think of me. If you are in trouble and need my help, I will repay your kindness and shall be free of my curse."

'The bird flew away and the snake began his story.

The Snake's Tale

"I was the son of a *muni* in the *āśrama* of Kaśyapa and I was friends with another *muni's* son. One day, my friend went down to the lake to bathe. I stayed on the shore where I saw a snake with three hoods and decided to trick my friend. I fixed the snake right there on the banks of the lake by means of a *mantra* in order to frighten my friend. He returned from his bath and when he saw the snake, he was so frightened that he fainted. I brought him back to consciousness but he knew what I had done through his powers of meditation and he cursed me in anger. 'Go and become a three-hooded snake like this one!' I pleaded with my friend to place an end to the curse and he said, 'As a snake, you shall fall into a well and a man will pull you out. Your curse will end when you have done him a favour,' and I became a snake. Today, you have pulled me out of the well. I will come to you when you think of me and help you. Then my curse will end."

'So saying, the snake went away and the woman began her story.

The Woman's Tale

"I am the wife of a Kṣatriya who serves the king. He is young and handsome, brave and generous and well-respected. I had an affair with another man and when my husband found out, he decided to punish me. I heard about this from my friend and I fled into this forest. But it was night and I fell into this well. Then you pulled me out and, because of your kindness, I can start another life elsewhere. I hope there will come a day when I can repay you."

'The wicked woman said this to the *bodhisattva* and went to the city of King Gotravardhana. She asked for a job and was appointed as a maid to the chief queen.

The Bodhisattva Needs Help

'Meanwhile the *bodhisattva* lost his powers because he had spoken to the wicked woman and was unable to gather roots and fruits for his food. Exhausted by hunger and thirst, he thought about the lion. At once the lion appeared and fed him on the flesh of forest animals. In a short time, the *bodhisattva* was strong again and the lion said, "My curse is at an end. I will leave you now." The *bodhisattva* agreed to let him go and the lion became a *vidyādhara* and returned to his own world.

'Soon after that, the man who was an incarnation of a part of the *bodhisattva* suffered again because he had no food and thought about the golden-crested bird. The bird appeared the moment he was remembered and when the *bodhisattva* told him his troubles, the bird brought him a basket full of jewels. "This wealth will last you a lifetime. I have done my duty towards you and my curse has ended. I will leave now. May you always be happy!" The bird then became a *vidyādhara* youth and returned to his home in the sky and took over his father's kingdom.

'As the *bodhisattva* roamed through the land trying to sell the jewels, he reached the city where the woman he had rescued from the well lived. He left the jewels with an old Brāhmin woman who lived in a deserted part of the city. As he was going to the market, he saw the woman that he had rescued from the well coming towards him. They began to chat and the woman told him about her job as the queen's attendant and he told her about all that had happened to him, even about the basket of jewels that he had got from the bird. He took her to the old woman's house and showed her the jewels. The woman went and told the queen about them.

'The clever bird had stolen the basket of jewels from the queen's chambers, from under her very nose. When the queen heard from her servant that the same basket was now in the city, she went at once and told the king. The king made the woman identify the *bodhisattva* and had him brought from the old woman's house with the jewels. The king asked him how he had got the jewels and even though he believed his story, he confiscated the jewels and threw the *bodhisattva* into prison.

'The *bodhisattva* remembered the snake's promise while he was locked up and the snake, who was an incarnation of a *muni's* son, appeared at once. When the snạke learned what the problem was, he said to the good man, "I will go and coil around the king and I will not let him go until you tell me to. You must announce from prison that you can free the king of the snake and when you speak to me, I will release the king and he will give you half his kingdom." The snake went and coiled around the king and placed his three hoods on his head. The people cried, "This is terrible! The king has been swallowed by a snake!"

'As planned, the *bodhisattva* announced that he could free the king and when the servants heard this, they rushed and reported it to the king. The king had the *bodhisattva* brought to him. He said, "If you free me from this snake, I will give you half my kingdom. My ministers will ensure that I keep my word," and the ministers agreed. The *bodhisattva* then said to the snake, "Release the king immediately!" and the snake obeyed. The king gave the *bodhisattva* half his kingdom and so he became a rich man in an instant. The snake became a young hermit since his curse had ended. He related his story in front of everyone and then returned to his *āśrama*.

'So you see that fortune favours the virtuous and misconduct leads to suffering, even for the great. You cannot trust a woman for if she will not be moved even if someone rescues her from death, what else will move her?'

And when he had finished this tale, Gomukha said, 'Listen and I will tell you more stories about stupid people.

The Monk Who Was Bitten By A Dog

'In a certain Buddhist monastery, there was a novice monk who was rather dull-witted. One day as he was on the way to the city, he was bitten on the thigh by a dog. He went back to the monastery and thought, "Everyone will want to know what happened to me and if I tell each person individually, it will take me a long time. I had better think of a way to tell them all at once." He then climbed to the roof of the monastery and sounded the prayer gong. His fellow monks were puzzled when they heard the gong and asked the novice why he had rung it at an unusual hour. He showed all the other monks his thigh and said, "I was bitten by a dog and I thought that it would take a very long time to tell each of you such a long story. Therefore, I called you all here so that I could tell everyone what happened. Listen to the story now and look at my thigh."

'The other monks laughed till their sides ached and said, "What a huge fuss he has made over such a little thing!"

'Now that you have heard the story of the foolish monk, listen to the story of the miser.

The Miser And His Kheer

'There was once a wealthy but foolish merchant who was a miser. He and his wife ate rice gruel without salt every day and as a result, he did not know the taste of any other food. Impelled by destiny, he said to his wife one day, "I feel like eating *kheer* today. Cook some for me." His wife started cooking the *kheer* and the miser went and lay on his bed inside his house so that no one would see him and visit him as a guest. Meanwhile, a friend of his, who was rather mischievous, came by the miser's house and asked the wife where her husband was. She did not answer him and went inside to tell her husband that his friend had arrived. Her husband said to her, "Sit here and cling to my feet. Start weeping and tell my friend that your husband has died. He will go away and we can eat the *kheer* together happily."

'The woman sat down and began to wail. The friend came in and asked her what was wrong and she replied that her husband was dead. The friend thought to himself, "But I saw her happily cooking *kheer* just now. How is it that her husband has suddenly died without any illness? I am sure they saw me coming and enacted this little farce. I am not going to leave." The clever fellow sat down there and joined in the wailing. The neighbours and the miser's relatives heard the noise and came in to take the miser to the cremation ground since he was still pretending to be dead.

'Fearing that this would actually happen, the miser's wife

came and whispered in her husband's ear, "Get up before these people take you away and burn you!" The miser whispered back, "No! That scheming fellow wants to eat my *kheer*. I cannot get up because it was when he came into the house that I pretended to be dead. People like me are more attached to their possessions than they are to their lives." Meanwhile, the mischievous friend and all the relatives carried the miser away. He remained unmoving all the way to the cremation ground and did not say a word even when he was being burned. So the foolish man gave up his life and the others enjoyed the wealth that he had earned through hard work.

'Now that you have heard that story, listen to the one about the students and the cat.

The Monks And The Cat

'In a monastery in Ujjayini, there lived a stupid teacher. He could not sleep at night because mice would run around the room and disturb him. He told his friend about the problem. His friend was a Brāhmin and said to him, "Get a cat and it will eat up all the mice." The teacher said he had never seen a cat before and did not know what it was or where he might find one. His friend said, "A cat's eyes are like glass, it is brown in colour, and it has fur on its back and it strolls down the streets. You can identify a cat by these characteristics. Have one brought in, my friend," and after advising his friend thus, the Brāhmin returned to his home.

'The teacher said to his students, "You were all here and heard what my friend had to say. You should be able to recognize a cat. Go and look for one on the streets." The students went wandering around looking for a cat. They could not find one anywhere and at length, they saw a young Brāhmin renunciant walking towards them. His eyes were like glass, his skin was brown and he had a deer-skin on his back. When the students saw him, they said, "He fits the description. We have found a cat," and took him to their teacher.

'The teacher saw that the renunciant had all the characteristics that his friend had enumerated and locked him inside the monastery at night. When the renunciant heard the description of a cat, that silly fellow thought that he must, indeed, be one. It so happened that the renunciant was a student of the Brāhmin who had described the cat to the teacher. When the Brāhmin came there the next morning and saw the young man, he asked those foolish students how he had got there. "We brought him here as a cat after we heard your description," said the teacher and the students. The Brāhmin burst out laughing. "There is a world of difference between a foolish fellow and an animal with four feet and a tail!" The idiots let the boy go and said, "Let us go and look for a cat as it has now been described to us in detail."

'Everyone laughed at their stupidity, for lack of knowledge makes one foolish.

'You have heard the story of the cat and the fools. Now listen to the next one.

The Bull From Heaven

'In a monastery full of fools, there was one man who was the most foolish of them all. He once read in a religious text that a man who built a temple tank would earn great merit. Since he was a rich man, he constructed a large tank close to his own monastery. One day, when he went to admire his tank, the greatest of all fools saw that the sand on its banks had been dug up by some creature. When he went there the next day, he saw that another part of the bank had been dug up. He was very confused and thought to himself, "Tomorrow morning I will come here early and keep watch the whole day to see who is doing this."

'He came there early the next day and saw that a bull came down from the sky and dug up the banks with his horns. The fool thought, "Why don't I go up to heaven with this bull?" and he caught hold of its tail. The heavenly bull lifted the man clinging to his tail and carried him through the air. In a moment, they had reached Kailāsa, the bull's home. The foolish man lived there for a while, eating celestial sweets and drinking and enjoying himself. He observed that the bull would keep going down to earth and returning and that chief of fools, impelled by destiny, thought, "I can hold onto the bull's tail and go and visit all my friends and relatives. I can tell them this wonderful story and then I can come back again." He hung onto the bull's tail when he was leaving and reached the surface of the earth.

'He went to the monastery and his friends there hugged him and asked him where he had been. He told them all that had happened to him. They begged to be allowed to go with him so that they, too, could enjoy celestial pleasures. The foolish man consented and the next day, he took them all to the tank. The bull arrived as usual and the foolish man caught hold of his tail. Another man caught hold of the fool's feet, another man took hold of the second man's feet and so on until they had formed a chain. The bull rose up into the air with the men.

'While they were flying through the air clinging to the bull's tail, one of the men asked the fool, "Tell us, how big were those sweets that you ate in heaven, the ones of which there is an unending supply?" The foolish man's concentration was disturbed and he let go of the bull's tail and put his hands together in the shape of a lotus and said, "This big."

'The next minute, he and all the other men fell from the sky on to the ground and were killed. The bull reached Kailāsa but the people on earth laughed and laughed when they saw what had happened. Fools will do harm to themselves by asking questions and giving answers without prior thought.

'You have heard the story about the fools who flew through the air. Now listen to the tale of yet another fool.

The Fool In The Tree

'A foolish man was walking down a road when he suddenly forgot the way to the village he wanted to reach. He asked passers-by for directions and they said, "Take the road that goes up by the tree on the banks of the river." When the idiot reached the tree, he climbed it for he had been told that his path went that way. He climbed higher and higher until the branch at the very top bent with his weight. He had to hold on to it tightly to keep from falling off. While he was holding on for dear life, an elephant that had been drinking water at the river passed by the tree with a rider on its back. When the fool saw them, he said humbly to the elephant driver, "Sir, help me down!" and the elephant driver let go off the hook with which he controlled the elephant. He took hold of the man to take him down from the tree but the elephant continued on its way. The driver was left holding onto the man who was holding onto the tree.

'The fool said to the elephant driver, "Quickly, sing a song so that the villagers hear it and come to take us down. Otherwise we will fall into the river and will be swept away." The elephant driver began to sing so sweetly that the fool was very pleased and wanted to clap. He forgot his situation and let go of the tree so that he could applaud properly with both hands. Immediately, both he and the elephant driver fell into the river and were drowned, for the company of fools does no one any good.'

After Gomukha had told Naravāhanadatta this tale, he went on to tell the story of Hiraṇyakṣa.

Hiraṇyakṣa And Mṛgāṅkalekhā

'In the lap of the Himalayas lies the country of Kashmir, the crest jewel of the earth and the home of all the arts and sciences. King Kanakākṣa ruled in the city of Hiraṇyapura. His wife was named Ratnaprabhā and when the king propitiated Śiva, she gave birth to a son named Hiraṇyakṣa. One day, when the young prince was playing ball, he intentionally threw it at a female ascetic who was passing that way. The woman who had magical powers and had conquered her anger, laughed at the prince and said, "If your youth and your virtues make you so arrogant, what will happen to you if you get Mṛgāṅkalekhā as a bride?" The prince begged her forgiveness and asked, "Who is this Mṛgāṅkalekhā?"

'The female ascetic said, "In the Himalayas, there is a famous *vidyādhara* king named Śaśitejas and Mṛgāṅkalekhā is his incomparably beautiful daughter. She is so lovely that her beauty keeps the *vidyādhara* princes awake at night. She will make an appropriate wife for you and you will suit her as a husband." Hiraṇyakṣa then asked the female ascetic how he could win her for himself and the ascetic replied, "I will go and talk to her about you to find out how she feels. Then I will return and take you there. Tomorrow morning, you will find me in the temple of the god Amareśa which I visit every day." The ascetic then flew into the air with her magic powers and went to visit Mṛgāṅkalekhā in the Himalayas. She praised Hiraṇyakṣa's many virtues and soon, Mṛgāṅkalekhā eagerly asked the ascetic, "How will I get a husband like that? My life will be worthless if I don't!" That day, love was kindled in the young woman's heart and she spent the night talking to the female ascetic.

'Meanwhile, Hiraṇyakṣa thought about Mṛgāṅkalekhā all the time. One night, Pārvatī came to him in a dream and said, "You are a *vidyādhara* who has become mortal because of a *muni's* curse. You will be released from your curse by the touch of the female ascetic's hand and then you will marry Mṛgāṅkalekhā. You have nothing to worry about on this account for Mṛgāṅkalekhā was your wife in your previous life as well." The goddess disappeared and when the prince awoke, it was morning and he went to take a purifying bath. Then he went to the temple of Amareśa and sang his praises, for that was the meeting place appointed by the female ascetic.

'In her own palace, Mṛgāṅkalekhā finally fell asleep. Pārvatī appeared to her in a dream and said, "Don't be sad. Hiraṇyakṣa's curse is at an end and he will become a *vidyādhara* again by the touch of the female ascetic's hand." When Mṛgāṅkalekhā woke in the morning, she immediately told the ascetic her dream and the ascetic returned to earth. She said to Hiraṇyakṣa who was in the temple compound, "Son, come to the world of the *vidyādharas*!" Hiraṇyakṣa bowed before her and she picked him up in her arms and flew into the air. At once, Hiraṇyakṣa's curse ended and he became a *vidyādhara* and remembered his past birth. "I was a *vidyādhara* king named Amṛtatejas in the city of Vajrakūṭa in the Himalayas. Long ago, a *muni* cursed me for ignoring him and I was born into the human world where I was to remain until I was touched by your hand. My wife abandoned her body out of grief and has now been reborn as Mṛgāṅkalekhā. I have loved her before. Now I will go with you and win her again, for I have been cleansed by your touch and my curse has ended," said Amṛtatejas as they travelled through the air to the Himalayas. He saw Mṛgāṅkalekhā in her garden and she observed that the prince was exactly like the female ascetic had described. How wonderful that these two lovers should have entered each other's hearts through the ears and now through the eyes!

'The ascetic, who was very outspoken, said to Mṛgāṅkalekhā, "Go and tell your father all this so that you can get married." Mṛgāṅkalekhā cast her eyes down in embarrassment and went to her father. She made her friend tell him all that had happened. Her father had also been spoken to by Pārvatī in a dream and he welcomed Amṛtatejas with honour and organized the wedding of his daughter with all the appropriate ceremonies. Amṛtatejas returned to Vajrakūṭa with his wife. He asked the female ascetic to bring his mortal father Kanakākṣa to Vajrakūṭa so that he might enjoy celestial pleasures for a while. After some time, he sent Kanakākṣa back to earth while he continued to live happily with Mṛgāṅkalekhā.

'Thus, one's former actions determine one's destiny making things that seem to be out of reach easy to attain.'

When Naravāhanadatta heard this story from Gomukha, he was able to fall asleep even though he was still pining for Śaktiyaśas.

Finally, after a month of waiting and pining, Naravāhanadatta married the vidyādharī *Śaktiyaśas in a glittering ceremony that involved days of feasting and merriment. His other wives welcomed*

Śaktiyaśas and they all lived together happily. Shortly after that, Naravāhanadatta was approached by two heroic princes from the city of Vaiśākha who wanted him to marry their sister, Jayendrasenā. Naravāhanadatta was pleased to take her as his wife and formed an alliance with the princes.

Although Naravāhanadatta had so many wives, Madanamañcukā was his chief queen and his favourite, for he loved her more than he loved his own life. One night, Naravāhanadatta dreamed that a celestial woman had carried him away to her home in the sky. He woke up to find that he really had been transported to the vidyādhara *realm by Lalitalocanā, for she, too, was destined to marry him. Naravāhanadatta married Lalitalocanā and stayed with her in Mount Malaya for some time.*

Śaśāṅkavatī

One day, as Naravāhanadatta was wandering alone in the beautiful mountain groves, he was seized with a desperate longing for Madanamañcukā. He was so unhappy that he swooned in grief. A passing ascetic, Piśaṅgajaṭa, revived him and told him the story of Mṛgāṅkadatta who also was separated from his beloved for a long time and had to undergo many trials before he could win her.

The Story Of Mṛgāṅkadatta

'The virtuous and heroic prince Mṛgāṅkadatta was born in Ayodhyā and grew up in the company of his ten wise ministers. One night, one of the ministers had a dream in which a *vetāla* told him that Mṛgāṅkadatta would marry the beautiful and virtuous princess Śaśāṅkavatī of Ujjayini. Mṛgāṅkadatta then had a dream in which Śiva promised him that he would be successful in his endeavours after a period of trial and tribulation. Mṛgāṅkadatta decided that he would win his bride through diplomacy rather than war and set off for Ujjayini with his ministers, all of them disguised as *pāśupata* ascetics. Along the way, in a huge forest, Mṛgāṅkadatta and his ministers angered a *nāga* who cursed them to be separated from each other for a short period. Bewildered by the curse, the young men wandered off in different directions and Mṛgāṅkadatta was left alone in the forest. But he decided to make his way to Ujjayini in any case. As he travelled through the forest, he made friendships and alliances with the various tribes that lived there—Śavaras, Bhīls, Pulindas and Mātaṅgas. After a while, his ministers began to reappear one by one and each would tell Mṛgāṅkadatta the story of his adventures while they had been apart.

'As Mṛgāṅkadatta was on his way to Ujjayini, he saw his minister, Vikramakesarī. Overjoyed, they embraced one other and the minister began to relate the story of his adventures. "When I was cursed by the *nāga*, I was wandering around and came to a little village where I met a Brāhmin who seemed determined to commit suicide. With kind words and clever arguments, I dissuaded him from doing so. When he had heard the story of my adventures, he said, "Son, I am grateful to you for saving my life. I will give you a *mantra* by which you can charm *vetālas*". "But what will I do with something like that?" I asked. The Brāhmin laughed and said, "Don't you know what happened to King Vikrama once he had gained mastery over *vetālas?* Listen to this story as proof of what a *vetāla* can do for you.

King Vikrama And The Mendicant

"The country of Pratiṣṭhāna lies on the banks of the Godāvarī. In the old days, the famous King Vikrama lived there. He was the son of Vikramasena and was Indra's equal in might. Every day, when King Vikrama was in his audience chamber, a mendicant would arrive and give him a fruit. And every day, the king would hand the fruit to his treasurer. Ten years passed in this way.

"But one day, when the king received the fruit from the mendicant, he gave it to a baby monkey that had escaped from its keepers. The monkey bit into the fruit and as it split open, a priceless jewel of unparalleled excellence fell out of it. The king picked it up and asked his treasurer, 'I have been giving you the mendicant's fruit for ten years now. What have you done with all of it?' The poor treasurer trembled and replied, 'Sir, I used to throw it into the treasury through the window. If you like, I can open up the treasury and see what is in there.' With the king's consent, he rushed to the treasury and came back with the news that all the fruit had rotted away and in its place, there lay a heap of shining jewels. The king was pleased to hear this and gave all the jewels to the honest treasurer.

"The next day, when the mendicant arrived with his customary gift, the king said, 'You have been greeting me every day with this great display of wealth. I will not accept the gift today unless you tell me why you have been doing this for the last ten years.' The mendicant then spoke to the king privately and said, 'I need the help of a brave man for a *mantra* that I want to procure and I thought that you would be the right man to help me.' The king agreed to help. The mendicant was pleased and said, 'The first day of dark fortnight of the moon is approaching. At nightfall, on that day, I will wait for you under the banyan tree in the cremation ground. Meet me there!'

"When the dark half of the lunar fortnight arrived, the honourable king remembered the mendicant's request and his own promise. When night fell, he put on dark clothes and covered his head with a black turban. Picking up his sword, he slipped, unseen, out of the palace and made his way to the cremation ground. It was a truly ghastly place, covered with the dense smoke from burning funeral pyres, their flames leaping into the air and illuminating the countless human skulls and bones that lay around. The king could hear ghosts and ghouls and vampires feasting and frolicking among the corpses. Jackals howled in the distance and it seemed as though Śiva had arrived in his destructive form to claim the earth. The king remained unafraid and walked on towards the banyan tree. Under it, he saw the mendicant engrossed in drawing a *maṇḍala*. 'I am here, mendicant. Now, tell me what I can do for you,' he said. The mendicant was overjoyed to see the king and said, 'Thank you for coming. You have done me a great favour. Listen to what you have to do. Walk south from here and you will see a lone *aśoka* tree. From it hangs a corpse. Bring it to me.'

"'So be it,' said the king and began to walk in a southerly direction. His path was lit only by the dying embers of the funeral pyres but he walked on through the darkness to fetch whatever it was that the mendicant needed from the *aśoka* tree. The king reached the tree which was covered with smoke and stank of burning flesh. He looked up and saw that there was a corpse hanging from the upper branches. He climbed the tree and cut the rope that held the corpse. As the corpse fell to the ground, it let out a terrible scream as though it were in great pain.

"The king hurriedly climbed down, thinking perhaps the body still held some life. He stretched out his hand and gently stroked the body to ease its pain. As soon as he did that, the corpse let out a chilling laugh that echoed all around. The king quickly realized that the dead body had been taken over by a *vetāla*. 'Why do you laugh?' he asked without the slightest trace of fear. But even as he spoke, he saw that the corpse had left the ground and was back on the upper branches of the tree. Undaunted, he went up the tree again and threw the corpse over his shoulder. He climbed down and started to walk back to the banyan tree and the mendicant. As he trudged along in silence, the *vetāla* that had inhabited the corpse spoke. 'It is a long walk. I will tell you a story to pass the time. Listen.'

"And the *vetāla* began to tell King Vikrama a series of stories that were in the form of riddles. At the end of each one, he said to the king, 'If you know the right answer and hide it from me, your head will split into a hundred pieces! So consider well before you reply.

The Wise Friend

'The holy Gaṅgā flows around the city of Vārāṇasī like a garland around its neck. The city is Śiva's home and is inhabited by virtuous people. In the old days, King Pratāpamukuṭa, who consumed his enemies the way fire consumes a forest, ruled there. His son, Vajramukuṭa, crushed the pride of his enemies with his valour and crushed the god of love with his good looks.

'The prince's dearest friend was Buddhiśarīra, the son of a minister, and the prince loved him more than his own life. One day, when the prince and the minister's son were amusing themselves, they got engrossed in chasing a deer and were drawn far away into the forest. The prince went along cutting off the maned heads of lions as though they were mere plumes on the heads of horses. Soon, they reached a beautiful grove, suitable for the god of love himself. It was filled with the song of birds and the trees waved their blossoms like fans. The prince and the minister's son then saw a lake that was like a matchless ocean covered with different kinds of lotuses. As they approached the lake to bathe, they saw a young woman of divine beauty surrounded by her attendants. She seemed to fill the lake with waves of her beauty and it was as though a lotus sprang up wherever her glance fell, creating a new forest. She was more enchanting than the full moon, more beautiful than any lotus. The prince was smitten the moment he saw her and wondered who she might be. She was equally captivated by the prince and forgot her modesty. Pretending to play, the young woman made signs to tell the prince who she was and where she came from. She took a lotus from the flower garland around her neck and put it in her ear. Then she twisted it into the ornament known as the 'the tooth[1].' She then put the lotus on her head and placed her hand on her heart. The prince understood nothing of the signs but the perceptive son of the minister understood all that she had said.

'The young girl was soon led away by her attendants. When she reached home, she lay on a couch dreaming about the prince for whom she had made the signs. The prince, too, was bereft without the young woman, like a *vidyādhara* without his magical powers. By the time he reached his own city, he was miserable. One day, the minister's son told him that the young woman was easy to find. "What is her name? Where is her village? What is her lineage? We cannot find her unless we know all this! Why do you torment me with these false promises?" cried the prince, losing his patience. "Did you not see what she was telling you by her signs?" asked his friend. "By putting the lotus in her ear, she said that she lived in the land of King Karṇotpala[2]. When she made it into the ornament known as "the tooth', she told you that she was the daughter of an ivory carver. When she lifted the lotus upwards, she said that her name was

Padmāvatī and by putting her hand on her heart, she proclaimed her love for you. Now, there is a king named Karṇotpala in the land of Kaliṅga and one of his favoured retainers is a famous ivory carver. This man, Sangrāmavardhana, has a daughter named Padmāvatī, a jewel of the three worlds, whom he loves more than his own life. I was able to understand her signs because I keep in touch with the common people."

'The prince was delighted to hear this and felt sure that he would be able to attain the object of his desires. Pretending to go on a hunt, the prince and his friend set off in the direction of the lake to find the young woman. The prince's swift horse soon left his entourage behind and he reached Kaliṅga with only the minister's son in attendance. The two young men came to the city of King Karṇotpala and located the ivory carver's mansion. They found an old woman's house nearby where they could stay. The minister's son fed and watered the horses and after hiding them, asked the old woman, "Mother, do you know an ivory carver named Sangrāmavardhana?" The old woman replied humbly, "Certainly. I was his nurse and now he has appointed me as a companion to his daughter Padmāvatī. I don't go there very often these days since all my good clothes have been taken away. You see, my son is a gambler and he takes away my finery as soon as he sees it." The minister's son was pleased with this information and immediately gave his upper garment to the old woman. Then he said, "You are like our mother so do what we ask without telling anyone. Go to the ivory carver's daughter and tell her that the prince she saw at the lake has arrived in this city because he loves her. Tell her that he has sent you there with a message."

'The old woman agreed, enticed by the gifts from the minister's son. She went to Padmāvatī but returned almost immediately and said, "I told her about your arrival in secret, but when she heard that, she threatened me and hit me on my face with her hands smeared with camphor. I was so upset with her behaviour that I have been crying all the way home. Look, you can see the marks of her hands on my face." The prince was terribly downcast and lost all hope of attaining his beloved. But the wise minister's son comforted the prince in private. "Don't be disappointed. Your beloved kept the message to herself and by striking the old woman's face with camphor-smeared fingers she has sent you a message. These ten nights of the bright lunar fortnight are not suitable for a meeting." The minister's son went to the market and sold some gold that he had hidden away. With the money, he had the old woman cook them a wonderful meal that all three of them enjoyed.

'When the ten days had passed, the minister's son sent the old woman to Padmāvatī again. The old woman had got used to all the fine food and drink and was eager to please her guests. After her visit, she said to the young men, "Today I went there and stood silently. When Padmāvatī saw me, she accused me of carrying a message from you. Then she hit me on my breast with three fingers dipped in red dye. Look at this!" Again, the minister's son reassured the prince, "Don't worry! By hitting the old woman on the breast with three fingers stained in red dye, your beloved is telling you that she has her period for the next three days and cannot receive you."

'When the three days had passed, the old woman was sent back to Padmāvatī's house. This time, Padmāvatī greeted her with respect and entertained her lovingly with wine and various foods. When the old woman got up to return home in the evening, there was a fearful commotion in the street below. They heard people shouting, "A mad elephant has broken loose and is trampling people!" Padmāvatī cautioned the old woman, "Don't take the public road where this elephant has run amok. Instead, we will let you out through this big window on this seat tied with a rope into the garden. Climb the tree, cross the wall and go to your own house." The old woman sat on the seat and was let down into the garden by the maids. She went home by the path pointed out to her and related everything to the prince and the minister's son. The minister's son said to the prince, "Your goal has been accomplished. Padmāvatī has shown you how to get to her. Go there and wait until nightfall. Then enter your beloved's chambers."

'The prince went into the garden by climbing the wall the old woman had shown him. He saw the seat with a long rope attached to it. He looked up and noticed a group of maids in the window who seemed to be expecting him. When they saw him climb onto the seat, they pulled him up by the rope and the prince entered his beloved's room through the window. Padmāvatī's face shone like the moon scattering moonbeams in all directions. She welcomed the prince eagerly with warm embraces and sweet endearments. The prince immediately married Padmāvatī by the *gandharva* ceremony and remained hidden in her chambers for days, fulfilling all his desires.

'One day, the prince said to his beloved, "My dear friend and helper, the minister's son, is also here. In fact, he is staying in your companion's house. Let me visit him and I will come back here." The shrewd Padmāvatī said, "Noble prince, those signs that I made for you, did you understand them or was it your friend, the minister's son?" "I did not understand any of them. The minister's son deciphered them. He is known for his wisdom," replied the prince. The beautiful woman considered this for a while and then said, "You should have told me this before. Your friend is like my brother and I should honour him above all other people." The prince left her house and went to visit his friend. As they were talking, the prince mentioned that he had told Padmāvatī who had really deciphered the signs. The minister's son did not approve of what the prince had done. They talked until dawn and after the morning prayer, Padmāvatī's friend arrived bearing betel leaves and fine things to eat. She honoured the minister's son and gave him fine food making sure that the prince got none of it. She told them that her mistress awaited them at a banquet and then left. "Look, I'll show you something strange," said the minister's son and he gave all the food to a dog. As soon as the dog ate the food, it fell over dead. Shocked, the prince said, "What is all this?"

"Now that your beloved knows that I am the clever one who deciphered the signs, she has tried to kill me with this poisoned food. She is deeply in love with you and thinks that you will never place her first in your affections and, that under my influence, you may even leave her and return to your own city. Don't be angry with her. Just convince her to leave her family and I will devise a plan to carry her away from here." "You really are wisdom incarnate," said the prince in admiration.

'At that very moment, they heard people shouting outside, "The king's infant son is dead, alas, alas!" The minister's son seemed pleased to hear this. He gave the prince a trident with sharp points and said, "Tonight, go to Padmāvatī's house and ply her with drink until she passes out. While she sleeps, brand her on the hip with this red hot iron and run away with all her jewels. Leave her chambers through the window, using the seat tied with rope. Trust me, I will make everything turn out for the best." The prince went as before to his beloved, for princes should not doubt the advice of their wise ministers. He made his beloved senseless with wine, marked her hip, carried off her jewels and returned to his friend. When he showed him the jewels and told him he had done as he was told, the minister's son was sure that his aim had been achieved.

'The next morning, the minister's son went to the cremation ground disguised as an ascetic and made the prince play the part of his disciple. He said to the prince, "Take this necklace from among your beloved's jewels and try and sell it in the marketplace. But price it so high that no one is willing to buy it. Wander around the market displaying it so that many people get a chance to see it. If the police catch you, say it was given to you by your guru for sale." The prince went to the market and wandered around, displaying the necklace. Soon, he was arrested by the police who had been informed about the theft at the ivory carver's house. They took the prince to the city magistrate who questioned him courteously, thinking that he was an ascetic. "Sir, the ivory carver's daughter's jewels were stolen last night. Where did you get that necklace from?" The prince, disguised as an ascetic, said, "My guru gave it to me. Come and question him." So the magistrate went to the guru and said, "Sir, where did you get the necklace that is in your disciple's hand?"

'The wily minister's son took the magistrate aside and said, "You know that I am an ascetic and wander here and there. By chance, I was in the cremation grounds one night when I saw a group of witches. They had the king's son with them. They offered the boy's heart to Bhairava as they invited the god to their ceremony. One of them was very drunk and tried to snatch away my prayer beads. She had magic powers and distorted her face terribly. But when she went too far, I heated my trident with the power of my asceticism and branded her on the hip. I grabbed this necklace from her body and now I am trying to sell it for food."

'The magistrate went and reported the matter to the king who felt sure that the necklace belonged to the ivory carver's daughter. He sent a trusted old woman to see if her hip was marked. The old woman returned and confirmed that it was. The king was now sure that the ivory carver's daughter was the witch who had taken away his son. He went to the minister's son, who was still disguised as an ascetic, and asked him how Padmāvatī should be punished. In accordance with his advice, Padmāvatī was banished from the city despite her parents' lamentations. She fled into the forest. Even though she had been stripped naked and was very agitated, she believed that all this was part of the minister's son's plan. In the evening, while she was still crying, the prince and the minister's son arrived, having shed their disguises. They placed her on a horse and returned to their kingdom where she and the prince lived happily. But the ivory carver thought that his daughter had surely been eaten by wild animals in the forest and died of grief. His wife followed soon after.

"When the story ended, the *vetāla* said to King Vikrama, 'I have a doubt about this story. Why don't you resolve it for me? Who was to blame for the death of Padmāvatī's parents, the minister's son, the prince or Padmāvatī? You are the wisest of men. If you know the truth and don't tell me, your head will split into one hundred peices.' The king had worked out the answer and, afraid of the *vetāla's* curse, replied, 'What is so difficult about this? None of the three are guilty. The fault lies with King Karṇotpala.'

"Why is it the king's fault? Those three young people were instrumental in the death of the old couple. Why should the crow be blamed when the swan eats the rice?' asked the *vetāla*. 'None of the three young people are at fault. The minister's son was furthering the desires of his master. The prince and Padmāvatī were consumed by love and were intent on being with each other and so were not aware of any crime they might have committed. But King Karṇotpala was ignorant in the science of government because he did not keep in touch with what the common people were saying through spies and other means. He is guilty of an ill-considered act and should therefore take the blame for the old couple's death.'

"When the *vetāla* heard this answer with which the king had broken his long silence he disappeared from the king's shoulder to test his persistence. But the king was undaunted and went off in pursuit of him.

"King Vikrama went again to the *aśoka* tree to fetch the *vetāla*. When he got there, he saw by the light of the funeral pyres that the corpse was lying on the ground and groaning. The king picked up the corpse animated by the *vetāla* and placed it on his shoulder. He began to walk back quickly and in silence. The *vetāla* spoke from his shoulder. 'King, this situation does not become you, so listen, and I will tell you a story that will entertain you.

The Brāhmin Who Brought His Beloved Back To Life

'There is a Brāhmin settlement on the banks of the Yamunā called Brahmasthala. A Brāhmin named Agnisvāmī, who had fully mastered the Vedas, lived there. His daughter,

Mandāravatī was so beautiful that after she was born, her creator lost interest in all the divine maidens that he himself had created before that. When she grew up, three young Brāhmins, all equally virtuous and accomplished, arrived from Kanyakubja, a neighbouring city. Each of them wanted to marry her and swore to Agnisvāmī that he would die if she were given to any other man. Her father did not want any of them to die and so gave her to none of them and she remained unmarried. But the three Brāhmins stayed in Brahmasthala, drinking in the beauty of her face which was like the full moon, as though they were *cakora* birds who live on moonbeams.

'One day, Mandāravatī suddenly developed a burning fever and died. The young Brāhmins were overcome with grief but they bathed and adorned her and took her to the cremation ground. After she had been cremated, one of them built a hut on that very spot. He made a bed of her ashes and began to live off alms. The second one took her bones to the Gaṅgā while the third became a renunciant and began to wander through the land.

'In his wanderings, the third young man reached a village called Vajraloka and went to the house of a Brāhmin. The Brāhmin treated him with courtesy and gave him food. But while the young ascetic was eating there, a child began to cry loudly and incessantly. The child's mother tried to pacify it, but nothing would make the child stop crying. The mother grew so angry that she picked up the child and threw it into the blazing fire. The fire consumed the child's tender flesh in a moment and turned it into ashes. The young ascetic was so horrified by what he saw that his hair stood on end. "My goodness! I seem to have entered the house of a *brahmarākṣasa*. To eat here would be a sin!" he exclaimed.

'The householder reassured him, "Watch! I have the power to bring the dead back to life with the recitation of a *mantra*." He then read a *mantra* from a book over some dust and threw the dust into the fire. The child came back to life at once and seemed none the worse for its ordeal. The young ascetic calmed down and continued his meal as the householder put the book away on a shelf. The householder went to bed after he had finished eating. The ascetic spent the night there but as soon as the householder had fallen asleep, he quietly stole the book because he wanted to restore his beloved to life.

'He travelled day and night with the book and soon, he reached the cremation ground where his beloved had been burnt. At the same time, the Brāhmin who had taken her ashes to the Gaṅgā also arrived there. Together, they found the third Brāhmin who had built a hut and slept on a bed of her ashes. The ascetic said to the other two, "Move this hut so that I can revive my beloved from her ashes with the power of this *mantra*!" and recited the *mantra* over dust and threw it on the ashes and Mandāravatī rose out of the fire, her body like gold, more beautiful than before. The three Brāhmins were overcome with love when they saw her alive again and began to fight among themselves. One of them said, "She is my wife because I brought her back to life with my *mantra*!" Another said, "She is my wife because I brought her back to life by visiting the sacred pilgrimage spots!" The third one said, "She is my wife because I looked after her ashes and brought her back to life with my penance!"

'King Vikrama, you be the judge of their dispute,' said the *vetāla*. 'Tell me, whose wife should that girl be? If you know the right answer and you don't tell me, your head will split open!' The king replied, 'The one who restored her to life is like a father to her and not her husband because he gave her the gift of life. The one who took her bones to the Gaṅgā should be considered her son. The one who slept on her ashes out of love and practised austerities in the cremation ground is the one fit to be her husband because his actions were motivated by true love.'

"When the king had broken his silence by speaking thus, the *vetāla* disappeared from his shoulder. But the king was determined to accomplish the mendicant's mission and decided to fetch him again. Men of firm principles keep their promises even if they have to lose their lives in the bargain.

"Then King Vikrama went again to the *aśoka* tree to fetch the *vetāla*. He found him in the same corpse and lifted him onto his shoulder. Once again, he began the journey back in silence. As he was walking the *vetāla* said, 'It is odd that you are not tired by this going back and forth. I will tell you another story for your amusement.

The Wiles Of Women

'Pāṭaliputra is a famous city and in the old days, King Vikramakesarī ruled there. The gods had made him a storehouse of virtues as well as of wealth. Among his possessions was a parrot who had been born that way because of a curse. His name was Vidagdhacūḍāmaṇi and he was learned in all the *śāstras*. On his advice, the king married a woman of equal status, the princess of Magadha named Candraprabhā. By coincidence, the princess owned a myna bird named Somikā who was also very learned. The parrot and the myna shared a cage and placed their wisdom and learning at the service of the king and queen.

'One day, the parrot, who was very attracted to the myna, said, "We share the same bed, the same perch and the same food. Why don't you marry me, dear one?" The myna replied, "I don't want to get involved with you because all males are wicked and ungrateful." "Males are not wicked," said the parrot. "It is females who are hard-hearted." And so the two of them began to argue. Finally, they decided that if the myna won the argument, the parrot would be her slave and if she lost, she would become the parrot's wife. They went to the king for the resolution of their dispute. The king was in his father's judgement hall and when he heard the opposing points of view, he said to the myna, "Tell me, why are males ungrateful?" "Listen to this story," said the myna and she told the following story to prove her point about the failings of males.

The Vice-ridden Husband

"A rich merchant called Arthadatta lived in the city of Kāmandakī and he had a son named Dhanadatta. After his father died, the young man became very self-willed and unrestrained. He began to spend time with all kinds of undesirable people which led, in the course of time, to his downfall. Truly, the root of corruption is the company of evil people. In a short time the young man had squandered all his wealth on his vices and, embarrassed by his poverty, he left Kāmandakī and began to wander from place to place. In his wanderings, he reached a place called Candanapura. He was hungry and so he approached the house of a merchant. The merchant saw that Dhanadatta was obviously well-bred and asked him about his family. When he heard about his background, the merchant made Dhanadatta his personal assistant and gave him his daughter Ratnāvalī in marriage along with a large dowry.

"Dhanadatta lived in his father-in-law's house and as the days passed in happiness, he forgot about his earlier misfortunes. Once again, his desire for his vices arose. He badly wanted to return to Kāmandakī to indulge in all his old habits. Somehow, that deceitful young man managed to persuade his father-in-law to let Ratnāvalī accompany him, laden with jewels, even though she was his only daughter. Dhanadatta set out for Kāmandakī with his wife and an old woman as their companion.

"After a while, the three reached a remote forest. Feigning a fear of bandits, Dhanadatta took his wife's jewels into his safe-keeping. How hard-hearted and ungrateful are males addicted to gambling and vices! That wretched man had intended to kill his virtuous wife for the sake of her wealth, but instead, he threw her and the old woman into a deep pit and went on his way. The old woman died from the fall, but Ratnāvalī got caught in a bush. She climbed out of the pit by clinging to tufts of grass and creepers (for she was not yet destined to die), weeping piteously all the time. That poor young woman, her limbs bruised and painful, asked for directions at every step and finally reached her father's house. Her parents were perturbed when they saw her arriving so unexpectedly and they questioned her eagerly. Weeping bitterly, the good woman said, 'We were attacked by bandits during our journey. They tied up my husband and led him away. The old woman died but I fell into a pit and survived. A kindly traveller pulled me out and it is by good fortune that I have reached here.' Her parents comforted her and the virtuous Ratnāvalī stayed with them, thinking about her absent husband.

"In the meantime, Dhanadatta had reached Kāmandakī and had again lost all his money because of his vices. 'I will go back to my father-in-law and fetch some more money. I will tell him that I have left his daughter in my house here,' he thought. As he approached his father-in-law's house, Ratnāvalī saw him coming from a distance. She ran and fell at his feet for a good woman's feelings for her husband do not change even if he is a rogue. Dhanadatta was terrified when he saw her there, but she quickly told him the story about the bandits that she had invented for her parents. Reassured, Dhandatta entered his father-in-law's house and was greeted with joy. 'Thank goodness he was left alive by the bandits!' said the father-in-law to his friends at the great celebration party. Then Dhanadatta lived happily ever after with his wife, enjoying his father-in-law's wealth. One night, that cruel fellow, (and I must say this for the sake of the story, even though it is too horrible), killed his wife while she slept in his arms and took away her ornaments. He ran off to Kāmandakī with them! This story proves that males are villains,' said the myna.

"Now you say your piece," said the king to the parrot and the parrot spoke.

The Thief Who Saw It All

"Females are intolerably reckless, wicked and immoral. Listen to a story that proves this. An extremely wealthy merchant named Dharmadatta lived in the city of Harṣavatī. He had an incomparably beautiful daughter named Vāsudattā whom he loved more than his life. He gave her in marriage to a man of equal rank and virtue, Samudradatta, who lived in the city of Tāmraliptī. Samudradatta was so handsome that the young women of the city gazed at him with love like the *cakora* bird gazes at the moon. One day, when Vāsudattā was in her father's house and her husband was in Tāmraliptī, she saw a handsome young man from a distance. That fickle woman was deeply attracted to the stranger and sent him a message through her friend. They became secret lovers and from that time onwards, she spent night after night with him.

"One day, Vāsudattā's husband came to her house and her parents were delighted to see him. Vāsudattā adorned herself in all her finery for the celebration but would not speak a word to her husband despite her mother's pleadings. She lay on her bed in silence. Even when her husband spoke to her, she pretended to be asleep because her affections lay with another. Eventually, tired from his journey and drowsy with wine, her husband yawned and fell asleep. As everyone slept, overcome with eating and drinking, a thief entered the living quarters through a hole. At that very moment, Vāsudattā got up and slipped out for her appointment with her lover without seeing the thief. But the thief saw her go and was deeply disappointed. He thought to himself, 'She has gone out in the dead of the night wearing the very ornaments that I came here to steal. Let me see where she goes,' and so he followed Vāsudattā, keeping her in sight but remaining unseen.

"Vāsudattā went to her meeting with her lover in a nearby garden carrying flowers and sweet ointments, accompanied only by one friend. When she got there, she saw her lover hanging dead from a tree. The city guards had mistaken him for a thief and had hanged him. Vāsudattā was overcome with grief and fell on the ground, wailing, 'I am finished, I am finished!' Vāsudattā went to the tree and brought down her lover's body and adorned it with flowers and sweet ointments. Blinded by passion and grief, she gathered him into her arms. But as she raised his dead face to kiss him, her lover, whose body had been taken over by a *vetāla*, bit off her nose. Vāsudattā dropped the body and ran away in confusion and pain, but she soon returned to make sure that her lover was truly dead. She saw that the *vetāla* had left his body and that he was lifeless. She went away, weeping softly with fear and humiliation.

"The thief meanwhile had seen everything and thought, 'What has this wicked woman done? Alas, a woman's heart is as black and deep as a well. I wonder what she will do next?' and so, out of curiosity, he followed her at a safe distance. Vāsudattā went back to her own house and entered the room where her husband was still sleeping. She began to wail loudly, 'My nose has been bitten off by this evil fellow who pretends to be my husband! I have done nothing to deserve this!' The servants, her father and her husband all woke up when they heard her shouting and were thoroughly confused. When her father saw that indeed her nose had been bitten off, he had Samudradatta tied up accusing him of being a wife-beater. The husband did not say a word even as he was being bound, for he saw that his father-in-law, the servants and all those who had been listening had turned against him. The thief slipped away quietly and the night which had been disrupted by all this commotion slowly came to an end.

"Samudradatta was taken to the king, along with his wife with her bitten-off nose. When the king heard the story, he rejected Samudradatta's explanation with contempt and ordered his execution on the grounds that he had maimed his own wife. Samudradatta was led to the execution ground accompanied by the beating of drums. Suddenly, the thief appeared and spoke to the king's men. 'Don't execute this man without knowing what really happened. Take me to the king so that I can tell him everything.' The thief was taken to the king and he fearlessly told him all that had happened that night, right from the beginning. 'If you want proof of my story, you will find this woman's nose in the corpse's mouth,' said the thief. The king sent his retainers to see if the thief's story was true and once it was confirmed he pardoned Samudradatta. He had Vāsudattā's ears cut off and banished her from the kingdom. He even punished her father. The king was pleased with the thief and made him the city magistrate.

"Thus, women are deceitful and wicked by nature." As the parrot said this, Indra's curse ended and he became Citraratha the *gandharva* and ascended to heaven in his divine form. At that same moment, the myna was also released from her curse and became the divine maiden Tilottamā and went to heaven. Their dispute remained unresolved in the assembly.'

"When the *vetāla* had finished this story, he said to King Vikrama, 'So, sir, who is worse, males or females? If you know the answer and do not tell me, your head will split into pieces.' The king replied, 'Females are wicked. Males sometimes behave badly but females are wicked always and everywhere.' When he said this, the *vetāla* left his shoulder and disappeared and the king set off again in an effort to retrieve him.

"That night in the cremation ground, King Vikrama went again to the *aśoka* tree. The corpse inhabited by the *vetāla* laughed loudly, but the king placed it on his shoulder without fear and walked back in silence. As they went along, the *vetāla* spoke again. 'King, why do you make so much effort for this wicked mendicant? You don't seem to care that this labour is fruitless. Let me tell you a story to entertain you.

The Devoted Servant

'There is a beautiful city on earth appropriately named Śobhāvatī for it is filled with beauty. King Śūdraka ruled there and his spirit of valour was kept burning by the *chowrie* fans waved by the wives of his conquered enemies. The Earth was so glorious during his reign that she forgot all her other great rulers, including Rāma. One day, a Brāhmin called Vīravara from Mālava came to King Śūdraka for a job. Vīravara's family consisted of three people, his wife Dharmavatī, his son Sattvavara and his daughter Vīravatī and he had three weapons: a sword by his side, a dagger in one hand and a shield in the other. Even though he had such a small family, Vīravara asked the king for a salary of five hundred *dīnārs* a day. The king saw that he was a noble person and agreed to give him the high salary. But the king was curious about how Vīravara spent the gold coins since he had such a small family. So he had Vīravara followed by spies.

'Vīravara would go and see the king every morning and then stand, sword in hand, at the palace gate all afternoon. Then he would go to his own house and give his wife one hundred *dīnārs* of his salary for food. With one hundred he bought clothes and the materials needed for sacred rituals. After bathing, he would put away one hundred *dīnārs* for the worship of Viṣṇu and Śiva. He gave away two hundred in charity to poor Brāhmins and this was how he spent five hundred *dīnārs* a day. Then he would worship the fire and eat his food. Every night, he would go and stand at the palace gate with his sword. When the king heard from his spies that Vīravara lived in this righteous manner, he was well-pleased and told his spies to stop their surveillance, for he considered Vīravara worthy of the highest honour.

'Vīravara endured the summer when the sun's rays were at their hottest. Then the monsoon came, brandishing a sword of lightning as if to compete with Vīravara, and the rain poured down. Huge clouds rained day and night, but Vīravara stood as always, unmoving, at the palace gate. One day, the king saw him standing there in the morning and climbed to the palace roof at night to see if he was still there. The king shouted, "Who stands there at the palace gate?" and Vīravara replied, "I am here, sir!" "Ah!" thought the king, "This Vīravara is a man of great forbearance and he is truly devoted to me. I must give him a higher appointment." He climbed down from the palace roof and went to bed in the inner chambers.

'The next day it rained heavily again and a thick darkness covered the skies. The king climbed to the palace roof like before and called out, "Who is that at the palace gate?" and again, Vīravara replied, "I am here!" Even as the king marvelled at Vīravara's devotion to duty, he heard the sound of a woman crying in the distance. "There are no poor, no oppressed or unhappy people in my kingdom," thought the king. "Who is this woman who is weeping alone at night?" The king said aloud, "Listen, Vīravara, there is a woman crying in the distance. Go and find out who she is and why she is weeping." "So be it!" said Vīravara and set out with his sword in his hand and his dagger strapped to his side. He did not mind the darkness or the blinding rain on that night which was as dark as a *rākṣasa*, the bolts of lightning like rays from its eyes. The king was curious and also felt sorry for Vīravara who was going out alone on such a terrible night. He climbed down from the roof and picking up his sword, he followed Vīravara.

'Vīravara walked in the direction of the weeping until he came to a tank outside the city. In the middle of the tank, he saw the weeping woman who wailed, "O brave man, O generous one, how can I live without you?" Amazed, Vīravara asked her, "Who are you and why are you weeping?" "My son, I am the Earth and King Śūdraka is my rightful husband. He is going to die three days from now. Where will I get another husband like him? I am weeping out of grief for him and for myself." Vīravara was alarmed and said, "Honoured lady, why will such a thing happen? Isn't there some way in which the death of this protector of the world can be prevented?" The Earth replied, "There is one way in which this can be done and you are the only one able to do it." "Tell me at once so that I can do it. What use is my life otherwise?" said Vīravara. The Earth replied, "Who is there braver and more devoted to his master than you? Listen. The king has built a temple to the goddess Caṇḍīkā near the palace and she is always eager to favour her devotees. If you sacrifice your son Sattvavara to her, the king will live another hundred years. You must do this at once or the king will be dead in three days." The heroic Vīravara declared, "Goddess, I will do this at once!" The goddess blessed him and disappeared. The king, who had followed Vīravara, overheard this exchange between the goddess and his servant.

'Vīravara went quickly in the darkness to his house while the king followed him secretly. Vīravara woke his wife Dharmavatī and told her that he had to sacrifice his son to save the king. Dharmavatī said, "We must do what benefits the king. Wake our son and tell him." Vīravara woke the sleeping boy and told him what had happened. "My son, you must be sacrificed to the goddess Caṇḍikā so that the king can live. Otherwise he will die in three days." Even though he was young, the boy lived up to his name by being tremendously resolute and, with a fearless heart, said to his father, "If the king should live by the sacrifice of my life, then I will have fulfilled my purpose. I will have at least repaid him for all the food that I have eaten. What are we waiting for? Take me to the goddess' temple now and sacrifice me so that the king can be at peace." When he heard this from Sattvavara, Vīravara said, "You are truly my own son!" The king had heard all this while he was standing outside Vīravara's house and he thought, "There is no one to equal them in courage!"

'Vīravara placed his son on his shoulder and his wife took their daughter Vīravatī by the hand and the family went to the temple of the goddess Caṇḍikā. The king followed them unobserved. When they reached the temple, the boy was placed in front of the goddess by his father. Sattvavara bravely bowed before her and said "Goddess, by the sacrifice of my head may King Śūdraka live, may he rule for another hundred years unopposed!" Vīravara cried, "Bless you, bless you!" and cut off his son's head and offered it to the goddess. "May the king live by the sacrifice of my son's head!" he cried. At once, a voice rang out of the sky. "Bravo! Who is more devoted to his master than you, Vīravara! By sacrificing your only son, you have bestowed both life and a kingdom upon King Śūdraka!"

'Vīravatī embraced her dead brother's head and broke into sobs. Overcome by grief, she died of a broken heart. Weeping, Dharmavatī said, "Now that the king's prosperity has been assured, I want to say something. This innocent young girl died of grief for her brother. Both my children are dead. What meaning can there be in my life? I could not ensure the king's prosperity by giving my own head to the goddess so give me permission to now offer my body. I will enter the fire with the bodies of my children!" "Perform this blessed act, noble lady, for there can be nothing in your life now except grief for your lost children. But do not grieve that you could not sacrifice yourself. Would I not have sacrificed myself to the goddess had any other means been available? Just wait until I build a pyre with these pieces of wood," said Vīravara.

'Vīravara built the pyre, placed the bodies of his children on it and lit it with the flame of a lamp. Dharmavatī fell at her husband's feet and then prayed to the goddess, "May this noble man be my husband in my next life as well and may the sacrifice of my body ensure his master's welfare!" The virtuous woman then threw herself into the fire from which flames rose like strands of hair. Then that courageous Vīravara thought, "The disembodied voice testified that I have fulfilled the king's needs. Why should I cling to life now that I am all alone? It does me no honour to stay alive when my whole family, for whose welfare I am responsible, has sacrificed itself. Why don't I please the goddess by offering myself to her?" He stood in front of the goddess and sang this hymn of praise:

"Hail to you, slayer of the demon Mahīṣa, oppressor of the demon Ruru; you who hold a trident in your hand,
Hail to you who causes rejoicing, who supports the three worlds and are the best of all mothers,
Hail to you whose feet are worshipped by the whole world, you who are the refuge of the devoted,
Hail to you who wears the rays of the sun and dispels the darkness,
Hail Kālī, carrier of skulls, wearer of skeletons. Hail to Śiva.
Be gracious to King Śūdraka with the sacrifice of my head!"

'Then he swiftly cut off his head with his sword.

'The king had been watching all this from his hiding place and was completely amazed. "No one anywhere could have heard or seen anything like this! Look at what this noble family has done for me! Though the world is wide and varied, where is the man who would do something like this for the good of his master and not talk about it? My life and my power would be like that of an animal's if I do not repay this act!" So saying, the king drew his sword and went up to the goddess. "O goddess, take my head and give me a boon. Let this Brāhmin, Vīravara, whose deeds reflect his name, who sacrificed his life for me, be brought back to life along with his family." As he said this prayer and prepared to cut off his head, a voice was heard, "Do not act in haste. Your valour has pleased me and look, your dead servant Vīravara has been restored to life!" The voice then fell silent and Vīravara and his family came back to life unhurt. The king hid himself again and gazed at them through tears of joy.

'Vīravara felt as though he had just woken up from a deep sleep and when he saw his beloved wife and children, he was completely confused. He asked each one of them by name, "How is it that you are alive after being burnt to ashes? How is it that I am alive after I cut off my own head? Is this an illusion or is it the goddess' mercy?" His wife and children answered, "It is due to the goddess' favour that we are alive." Vīravara worshipped the goddess and went home with his family, having accomplished his aim. He left his wife and children at the house and went immediately to stand at the palace gate as he always did. The king who had seen it all and knew all that had happened, left his chambers and climbed to the palace roof. He called out, "Who is there at the palace gate?" and Vīravara answered, "I am standing here, master. As you ordered, I went off in the direction of that woman but she disappeared like a *rākṣasī*." The king was astonished at Vīravara's reply because he had himself seen what had happened. "This man is as noble and brave as the ocean is deep. Even though he has performed an extraordinary deed, he does not speak about it." Deep in thought, the king descended to the inner rooms and slept for the rest of the night.

'The next morning, when Vīravara came to present himself at the king's audience, King Śūdraka recounted the events of the night to the ministers with delight and they were all astounded. In gratitude and affection, the king gave Vīravara and his son the lands of Lāṭa and Karṇāṭa to rule. Then the two kings Śūdraka and Vīravara who were equal in power, lived happily, helping each other.

"When the *vetāla* had completed this wonderful story, he asked King Vikrama. 'Tell me, king, who was the bravest of them all. Keep the curse in mind before you answer!' Vikrama replied that King Śūdraka was the bravest of them all. 'Why not Vīravara? There in no one as brave as him born on earth! And was his wife not braver, who had to see her son being sacrificed like an animal? And why was his son Sattvavara not the bravest of all who, even though he was a child, displayed such courage? Why do you say that Śūdraka was the bravest of them all?' asked the *vetāla*.

"The king replied, 'It is not as simple as that. According to the traditions of his family, Vīravara had taken a vow that his life and those of his family were for the protection of their master. For his wife, a virtuous woman born in a good family, her husband is her only god. She has no duty higher than following her husband. Sattvavara was like them because he was their son. A web is like the threads that produce it. But Śūdraka is special because he gave up his life to save the lives of those whose duty it was to protect his life.'

"Hearing Vikrama's reply, the *vetāla* left his shoulder unseen and went back to his tree with his magic powers. But the king was not perturbed and took that familiar path to fetch him again.

"King Vikrama went back to the *aśoka* tree and saw that the *vetāla* had again entered the corpse that was hanging there. He took the corpse down and with a great display of displeasure, he turned around and started to walk back. As he walked in silence in that huge cremation ground, the *vetāla* spoke from his shoulder. 'King, you have undertaken a thankless task, but since I am fond of you, I will tell you a story to amuse you.

The Three Suitors

'In Ujjayini there lived a virtuous Brāhmin named Harisvāmī. He was the beloved minister of King Puṇyasena. Harisvāmī's wife was equal to him in birth and by her, he had a virtuous son named Devasvāmī. A daughter of matchless beauty, Somaprabhā, rightly named, was also born to him. When the time came for Somaprabhā to be married, she had grown proud of her beauty and sent a message to her father and brother through her mother. "If you value my life, you will give me away to a man who has courage or prescience or magic powers and to no one else." When Harisvāmī heard this he began to worry about finding her a husband who would fit into one of these categories. While he was immersed in worry, he was sent by King Puṇyasena as an emissary to the king of the Deccan to forge an alliance.

'When Harisvāmī had finished his work in the Deccan, he was approached by a Brāhmin who had heard about his daughter's beauty and wanted to marry her. "My daughter will not marry a man who does not have courage or prescience or magic power. Tell me, sir, which one of these do you have?" The Brāhmin replied "I have magic powers." "Show me!" said Harisvāmī. At once, the man created a chariot that could fly through the air. He placed Harisvāmī in the magic chariot and took him around heaven and the three worlds in a moment and brought him back again, delighted, to the very place where he had been sent to do business. Harisvāmī promised his daughter to the man with the magic powers and fixed the wedding for seven days hence.

'But meanwhile in Ujjayini, another Brāhmin had asked Somaprabhā's brother, Devasvāmī, for her hand in marriage. Devasvāmī said that Somaprabhā wanted a man with courage or prescience or magic powers as a husband and the man declared that he had great courage. He displayed his skills with missiles and combat weapons and Devasvāmī promised him his sister in marriage. With the advice of astrologers, he set the marriage date seven days hence. At the same time, Harisvāmī's wife was approached by a third Brāhmin intent on marrying her daughter. "My daughter will only marry a man who has courage or prescience or magic powers," said the mother and the man told her that he was prescient. After she had questioned him about the past and the future, she promised her daughter to him on that same day, seven days hence.

'The next day, Harisvāmī came home and told his wife and son all that had happened and that he had fixed the date of his daughter's wedding. Both of them in turn told him what they had arranged and Harisvāmī grew agitated as three bridegrooms had been invited on the same day. On the appointed day, the three bridegrooms arrived at Harisvāmī's house. At that very moment, a strange thing happened. The bride, Somaprabhā, disappeared and no one knew where she had gone. Harisvāmī was completely bewildered and asked the prescient man, "Tell me, where is my daughter now?" The man replied, "She has been abducted by the *rākṣasa* Dhūmraśikha and he has taken her to his home in the forests of the Vindhyas." Harisvāmī was very frightened and cried, "This is terrible! How will we get her back? How will she be married?" The man with the magic powers said, "Have courage! I can take all of you to the place where this man says Somaprabhā is." In a moment, he produced a magic chariot equipped with all kinds of weapons and when all the men had climbed into it, the chariot rose into the air. In a moment, they had reached the forests of the Vindhyas where the prescient man had told them the *rākṣasa* lived.

'The *rākṣasa* was very angry when he saw the men in the chariot and he attacked the courageous man. A wondrous fight took place between the man and the *rākṣasa*, like the fight between Rāma and Rāvaṇa who had also fought over a woman. In a moment, the courageous man had cut off the *rākṣasa's* head with his crescent arrow. Once the *rākṣasa* was dead, the men found Somaprabhā in his house and they climbed into the chariot with her. When they returned to Harisvāmī's house, the marriage ceremony could not be completed even though the auspicious moment had arrived, because a huge dispute arose between the three bridegrooms. The prescient man said, "If I had not told you where the girl was, how would you have found her? She should be given to me!" The man with the magic powers said, "But I made the chariot that flies through the air. How could you have gone through the skies and returned in a moment like the gods? How could you have fought the *rākṣasa* who had his own chariot, without this chariot? Therefore, I deserve to marry this girl!" The courageous man said, "But I was the one who killed the *rākṣasa* in battle!" As they argued Harisvāmī remained silent and confused.

'King, tell me, which one should she be given to? If you know the answer and don't tell me, your head will split!' said the *vetāla*. The king broke his silence and replied, 'She should be given to the courageous man because he won her back by the strength of his arms. He killed the *rākṣasa* in battle at the risk of his life. The prescient man and the one with magic powers only acted as instruments.' "When the *vetāla* heard Vikrama's answer, he left his shoulder and went as before, to his tree.

"King Vikrama went again to the *aśoka* tree to fetch the *vetāla*. He placed him on his shoulder as before and began to walk in silence. As he walked along the path, the *vetāla* said, 'King, you are wise and brave and I am fond of you. So I will tell you a tale for your amusement. Listen carefully to my question.

The Heads That Got Switched

'King Yaśaḥketu was famous throughout the world. His capital city was called Śobhāvatī and it had a splendid temple consecrated to Pārvatī. To the south of the city was a lake called Gaurītīrtha. Every year, during the bright lunar fortnight in the month of *Āṣāḍha*, huge crowds from different parts of the world came there to bathe. Once, on that auspicious day, a washerman named Dhavala from the village of Brahmasthala came there. While he was performing the rituals, he saw Madanasundarī, the daughter of a washerman called Śuddhāpaṭa. He was captivated by her beauty which exceeded that of the full moon. He found out her name and details about her family and went back to his house deeply in love. He would not eat and could not sleep. When his mother asked him what the matter was, he told her about his love. She in turn told her husband, Vimala, and when he saw his son's condition, he said, "Why do you grieve over something that is easy to attain? I know Śuddhāpaṭa and he will give his daughter to you in marriage if I ask him. We are equal to him in status, wealth and deeds." Vimala thus reassured his son, persuaded him to eat something and took him the very next day to Śuddhāpaṭa's house.

'Vimala asked for Śuddhapāṭa's daughter's hand in marriage for his son Dhavala and Śuddhāpaṭa agreed. The auspicious day for the wedding was fixed and Madanasundarī, equal in birth to Dhavala, was married to him the very next day. Dhavala went back to his father's house with his wife who had fallen in love with him the moment she saw him. While they were living there happily, Madanasundarī's brother came to visit. He was received courteously and his sister embraced him and welcomed him while the family asked after his welfare. When he had eaten and rested, he said, "My father has sent me here to ask Madanasundarī and her husband to join us in celebrating the festival of the goddess."

'The next morning, Dhavala set out for his father-in-law's house with Madanasundarī and his brother-in-law. When the three of them reached the city of Śobhāvatī, they saw the great temple of Pārvatī. Dhavala said to his wife and brother-in-law, "Come, let us visit the shrine of the goddess!" But his brother-in-law hesitated and said, "How can we approach the goddess empty-handed?" "Then I will go alone. You can wait outside," said Dhavala and went into the temple.

'After he had worshipped and meditated on the goddess, who with her eighteen arms had crushed terrifying demons and had trampled the buffalo-demon under her lotus feet, he was filled with pious thoughts. "People worship the goddess with different kinds of sacrifices. Why should I not sacrifice myself to her so that I can obtain salvation?" From the deserted inner sanctum, Dhavala took a sword that had been offered to the goddess by some travellers a long time ago. He then fastened his head by his hair to the chain of the temple bell and cut off his head. When he did not return for a long time, his brother-in-law went into the temple to look for him. He saw his sister's husband's head lying on the ground and was horrified. In grief, he picked up the same sword and cut off his head.

'Madanasundarī was very agitated when even her brother did not return and she went towards the temple. When she entered and saw her husband and her brother dead, she wailed, "Oh dear, what is all this? I am ruined!" and fell onto the ground. Soon, she stood up and grieving for those two young men who had died so suddenly, she thought, "What is the use of my living now?" She addressed the goddess, "Dear goddess, you who are the most blessed, chaste and holy and who occupy half of your husband Śiva's body, you who are the refuge of women and who take away grief, why have you taken my husband and my brother at the same time? This is not fair since I have always worshipped you exclusively. I have always come to you for refuge, so listen to this pathetic request of mine before I prepare to abandon my ill-fated body. Wherever and whenever I am born again, O goddess, let these two be my husband and my brother." She praised and worshipped the goddess and bowed before her. Then she fashioned a noose from creepers and tied it to an *aśoka* tree. As she placed her neck through the noose, a loud voice resounded through the air. "Do not act in haste, daughter! I am pleased with the courage you display despite your youth. Throw away that noose! Attach the heads of your husband and brother to their bodies and by my grace, they will rise up again alive!"

'When Madanasundarī heard this, she slipped off the noose and ran to the corpses. In her excitement and joy, she attached her husband's head to her brother's body and her brother's head to her husband's body. Both the men rose up alive and without injury but because their heads had been exchanged, their bodies were mixed up. There was joy all around as they told each other what had happened. After praising the goddess the three of them continued their journey. But as they went along, Madanasundarī noticed that the men's heads had been exchanged. Thoroughly confused, she wondered what she should do.

'So tell me, king, which of the two mixed up people was her husband? You know that if you do not speak the curse will befall you!' "When the king heard the *vetāla's* story and the question, he answered, 'The one with the husband's head is her husband because the head rules the limbs and personal identity depends on the head.' "When he said this, the *vetāla* left his shoulder unnoticed.

"King Vikrama went again to the *aśoka* tree to fetch the *vetāla* and placed him on his shoulder. As they went along the path, the *vetāla* said, 'King, to make your toil a little easier, I will tell you a story, listen.

The King Repays A Debt

'There was a city named Tāmraliptī on the eastern shore of the ocean and its king was named Caṇḍasiṃha. He rejected his enemies' wives but not the battlefield. He stole away the prosperity of his enemies but not the wealth of his neighbours. One day, a nobleman from the south named Sattvaśīla came to the king's gate. He announced himself to the king and because of his poverty, he became a dependent of the king and stayed there. He served the king diligently but never received any reward from him. "If I was born in a royal family, how come I am poor like this? And being poor, how come the Creator has made my desires so vast? I have served the king but my attendants are oppressed, and I have long been hungry, but the king has not even noticed me."

'While the poor man thought thus, the king went out to hunt. He went into the forest with his horses and his foot soldiers while the poor man ran in front of him with a stick. The king chased a huge boar and was soon in another forest that was very far away. The boar escaped among the trees and the shrubs and the king lost his way. In a little while, he was completely exhausted. Even though the king had been riding a horse as swift as the wind, the poor man had kept up with him on foot, uncaring of his own life and afflicted by hunger and thirst. When the king saw that the poor man had followed him in that condition, he spoke to him kindly, "Do you know how we got here?" The poor man put his hands together and bowed. "I don't. But rest here for a little while. Right now, the sun is shining with all its might, like a jewel in the centre of the sky-bride's girdle." The king said gently, "Then will you go and find me some water?" "I will," said the poor man and climbed up a tall tree. From there he saw a river and climbing down, he led the king to it. He took the saddle off the horse and let it roll around. He refreshed the animal by giving it water and grass.

'When the king had bathed, Sattvaśīla took sweet *āmalaka* fruits out of his upper garment, washed them and offered them to the king. When the king asked him where he had got the fruit, he bowed and said, "I have lived like this for ten years, eating fruits and worshipping the gods, like a hermit who fulfils his vows despite being a part of society." "You are rightly named Sattvaśīla!" remarked the king. The king thought to himself, "Shame on the kings who do not know which among their servants is unhappy and which not, and a curse upon those courtiers who do not give the king this information." Sattvaśīla said, "Why don't you have some?" and the king took two fruits from his hands. After eating them and drinking some water, the king rested for a while. Then he mounted his horse which Sattvaśīla had prepared for him and the poor man ran in front to point out the way. Even though the king begged him to climb up on the horse behind him, Sattvaśīla refused. The king met his entourage on the way and finally reached his own city. The king praised the poor man's devotion and gave him all kinds of wealth and lands and still felt that he had not rewarded him as he deserved. Sattvaśīla was released from the position of being a dependent on the king and became a prosperous man. But he remained close to King Caṇḍasiṃha.

'One day, Sattvaśīla was sent to the Siṃhala island to ask for the princess' hand for the king. He had to go by sea and so he propitiated his personal deity and boarded the vessel along with the Brāhmins that the king had appointed. When the ship was halfway to Siṃhala, a banner arose from the waters that excited and stunned everyone. It was so high that its top touched the clouds, it was made of gold and had many colours. Within a moment, rain poured down from a huge bank of clouds and the wind blew fiercely. The ship was driven onto the flagpole by the wind and the rain and got stuck there, the way an elephant is tied to a post by its drivers. The flagpole began to sink into the sea taking the ship with it. The Brāhmins were overcome with fear and began to call out to their master Caṇḍasiṃha, to save them. Sattvaśīla heard their cries and, devoted to his master as he was, took his sword, girded his upper garment around his waist and jumped into the water after the flagpole without a care for his own life and safety. But that courageous man had underestimated the power of the storm and tried to battle the waves. As soon as he jumped into the sea, the ship was carried away by the wind and the waves and the people in it fell into the mouths of sea monsters.

'Sattvaśīla looked around himself underwater and saw a beautiful city. The water seemed to have disappeared and the city shone with palaces made of gold and jewelled pillars. It was adorned with gardens whose tanks had steps made of gems. There was a temple dedicated to the goddess in the city that was as tall as Mount Meru, with walls made of different kinds of jewels and a flag studded with precious stones. Sattvaśīla bowed to the goddess and sang a hymn of praise to her and then he sat down, wondering if all this was an illusion. Suddenly, a young celestial woman entered through a door from a shining chamber and stood in front of the goddess. Her eyes were like blue lotuses, her face like a flower in bloom, her smile like a bud, her body slim and pliant like a lotus stalk. She moved like a lake of lotuses swaying in a breeze. She entered the house of the goddess with one thousand attendants and entered Sattvaśīla's heart at the same time. After she had worshipped, she left the temple but she did not leave Sattvaśīla's heart. When she re-entered the shining chamber Sattvaśīla followed her into it.

'Inside the chamber was another city, as beautiful as a garden in which all the pleasures seemed to come together. Sattvaśīla saw the young woman sitting on a couch that was studded with gems and he went over and sat down next to her. He gazed at her face unmoving, like a man in a painting, while his limbs trembled and his hair stood on end. When she saw that he was smitten by her, she looked at her attendants and they, understanding her meaning, said to him, "You are a guest here and so avail yourself of all the things provided by our mistress. Get up, bathe and then eat something." When he heard that, Sattvaśīla was shaken out of his reverie and managed to stand up. He went to a tank in the garden that the maids pointed out to him. The moment he immersed himself in the tank, he found himself, to his utter confusion, back in Tāmraliptī, in the tank of King Caṇḍasiṃha.

'When he realized where he was, he cried out, "What is this? What am I doing in this garden when a moment ago, I was in that magical city? The nectar of the sight of that beautiful girl has changed into the poison of separation! I know it was not a dream because I was wide awake the whole time. Those cunning women from the underworld have made a fool of me!" He wandered around the garden like a madman, wailing for his lost love. The gardeners saw him burning in the fires of separation, covered with pollen that the wind had stolen from the flowers and they went and reported this to the king. The king was intrigued and came to see the sight for himself. He calmed Sattvaśīla and asked, "What is all this, my friend? You set out for one destination and have reached another! Your arrows have missed their mark." Sattvaśīla told the king all that had happened to him. The king thought to himself, "This man has fallen in love because of the acts that I committed in my former life. This is a good opportunity for me to discharge the debt of gratitude that I owe him." He said aloud, "Control your grief. I will obtain that girl for you. I will take you by the same path, back to that young woman," and so saying the king comforted Sattvaśīla with a restorative bath.

'The next day, the king placed the kingdom in charge of his ministers and boarded a ship along with Sattvaśīla who pointed out the way. When they reached the half-way point, as before, the wonderful banner rose out of the sea. Sattvaśīla said to the king, "This is the magical banner arising from the ocean. It is here that I must plunge into the sea and you must come after me." As they drew near the flagpole, it began to sink and Sattvaśīla threw himself into the water after it. The king followed and once they were underwater, they reached that wondrous city. The king was astounded and worshipped the goddess Pārvatī. He then sat down next to Sattvaśīla in the temple.

'Soon after they had arrived, the young woman entered the temple from the shining chamber like brightness embodied, surrounded by her attendants. Sattvaśīla said, "This is the girl I told you about!" and when the king saw her, he felt that Sattvaśīla's attachment to her was justified. Meanwhile, the young woman noticed the king with all his auspicious marks and thought to herself, "Who can this incomparable man be?" As before, she went to pray to the goddess and the king went into the garden with Sattvaśīla. Soon, the young woman came out of the temple where she had prayed for a suitable husband. She called one of her attendants and said, "Friend, go to the distinguished man that I saw and ask him to be our guest. He deserves great honour because he appears to be someone special." The attendant approached the king and bowing low delivered her mistress' message. The king replied casually, "This is enough for me. I don't need anything more." When the attendant told the young woman what the king had said, she decided that he was definitely a man who deserved honour and respect. She went to see the king herself, drawn towards him by his indifference to her hospitality, for she felt that he had been sent to her by the goddess as a reward for her devotion.

'The trees seemed to honour the young woman with bird song and showers of blossoms as she passed, their creepers waving in the wind like arms. She bowed to the king and begged him to be her guest. Pointing to Sattvaśīla, the king said, "I came here to worship the goddess that this man told me about. I came to her temple guided by the wondrous banner. I have seen her and now I have seen you. What more hospitality can I require?" The young woman invited the king to see her second city which was the wonder of the three worlds and the king laughed in reply. "Sattvaśīla told me about this place which has a bathing tank in its garden." "Don't speak to me like this," she said. "I am not deceitful. Besides, who would dare to deceive someone like yourself, who is worthy of respect? I have become a slave to your excellent qualities. You should not dismiss my invitation like this." The king consented to be her guest and with Sattvaśīla, he followed the young woman into the shining chamber. The door was opened and she led him in. There, he saw that wondrous city where all the seasons came together so that the trees always bore fruit and flowers.

'The city was made of gold and jewels, like the peaks of Mount Meru. The young woman made the king sit on a jewelled seat and honoured him appropriately. Then she said, "I am the daughter of Kālanemi, the king of the *asuras*. My father was killed by Viṣṇu and these cities that I inherited from him were constructed by Viśvakarmā, the divine architect. They provide all that you desire and old age and death cannot enter here. I consider you my father and place myself and all that these cities contain at your disposal.""If that is so," said the king, "then dear daughter, I give you to another man, this hero Sattvaśīla. He is my friend and relative." When the king, who seemed to embody the goddess' favour, said this, the young woman quietly agreed, for she recognized virtue when she saw it. Sattvaśīla married her and had the wealth and glory of those two cities bestowed upon him. The king said to him, "Now I have repaid you for one of the *āmalaka* fruits that you gave me but I am still indebted to you for the second one." He turned to the young woman and asked her to show him the way back to his own city. She gave him a sword named Parājita and a fruit that kept old age and death at bay. She pointed out the tank and the king plunged into it with the sword and the fruit. Immediately, he was back in his own land with all his desires fulfilled. Sattvaśīla ruled over those two cities as king for a long time.

'Now tell me, which one of the two showed more courage by jumping into the water?' asked the *vetāla*. The king was afraid of the curse and replied, 'I think Sattvaśīla was braver because he jumped into the water without knowing what would happen. The king knew what was at the other end when he jumped in.'

"The *vetāla* left the king's shoulder and returned to the *aśoka* tree. The king went to bring him back, for the wise do not give up until the task is completed.

"King Vikrama placed him on his back and began to walk. Soon, the *vetāla*, sitting on the king's shoulder, said, 'Listen to this story. It will take your mind off this labour.

The Three Fastidious Brāhmins

'Once, in the country of Aṅga, a Brāhmin named Viṣṇusvāmī lived in a village called Vṛkṣaghaṭa. He had become rich by performing many sacrifices and lived contentedly with his family. His wife was also a Brāhmin and they had three sons. The three young men were all of discerning taste and were well-versed in sacred knowledge. One day, when Viṣṇusvāmī had already begun one of his sacrifices, he asked his sons to fetch him a turtle. The three young men went to the seashore where, without much trouble, they found the animal that their father had asked for. The oldest brother said, "One of you will have to pick up this beast and take it back to our father. It is slimy and it smells of raw meat so I refuse to touch it." His younger brothers replied that they, too, did not want to touch the slimy turtle. The older brother began to berate his younger brothers, saying, "If you do not take the turtle home, our father's sacrifice will be disrupted. Both of you will go to hell and take our father with you!" The younger brothers laughed and pointed out how odd it was that the older brother could tell them what their duties were while being blind to his own obligations. "Don't you know how fastidious I am?" exclaimed the oldest brother. "I am so fussy about food that I don't touch anything slimy even when I'm eating!" "I am more fastidious than you are because I am very fussy about women," said the middle brother. Not to be left out, the younger one frowned and said, "Fools! I am the most fastidious of all because I am extremely fussy about the beds that I sleep in."

'And so, the brothers fell to quarrelling amongst themselves. Finally, they decided to go to the court of King Prasenajit to have their dispute resolved. When they got there, they presented themselves to the king and told him about their argument. "Why don't you stay here for a while and I will test each of you in turn," said the king. The three young men readily agreed.

'That evening, at dinner, the king led the visitors to a seat of honour and placed before them a most sumptuous banquet that included all the six flavours: sweet and sour, salty and bitter, astringent and pungent. The royal company began to eat with great enjoyment, all except the young man who was particular about his food. He just sat there with a disgusted look on his face. "Brāhmin, why are you not eating this delicious and fragrant food?" asked the king. Softly, the young man replied, "I cannot eat because the rice smells of burnt corpses." The king was taken aback by this response and said, "But this special rice is so fragrant and it's really quite perfect!" But the young man just sat there holding his nose. The king assembled his cooks to find out more about the rice that the Brāhmin refused to eat. When he pursued the matter, he learned that the rice had been grown in a field close to the village cremation ground. Amazed, the king complimented the Brāhmin on his sensitivity. "Truly, you are very particular about your food. Leave this rice alone but do eat something else!" said the king.

'When the three young men had retired to their rooms for the night, the king arranged for his most beautiful and irresistible courtesan to be sent to the room of the second brother, the one who was so fussy about women. The lovely young girl was escorted to the Brāhmin's room dressed in all her finery, her face radiant like the full moon at midnight. She was beautiful enough to excite even the god of love. But when she entered the young man's room, he swooned and covered his nose. He begged her retainers, "Please take her away or I'll die! She smells like a goat!" The retainers took the agitated courtesan away and ran to tell the king what had happened. The king summoned the second brother and said, "This young woman is my personal courtesan. She has been anointed with the best musks and sandal oils. Her perfume spreads in all directions. How can you possibly say that she smells like a goat?" But the young man insisted that she did. The king decided to investigate the matter. By asking a number of discreet questions, he discovered that as an infant, the girl had been separated from her mother and her nurse and had been reared on goat's milk. Once again, the king was amazed at the second brother's sensitivity.

'The youngest brother had announced that he was most particular about the bed that he slept in and so the king had arranged for seven of the finest cotton mattresses, covered with the softest, finest bed linen, to be laid out for him. The third brother settled down to sleep on the mattresses piled one on top of the other. But even before the first watch of the night was over, the young man leapt out of bed, clutched his back and screamed in pain. The bewildered courtiers noticed a deep weal on his back, shaped like a strand of hair. When they reported what had happened to the king, he commanded them to search under all the mattresses for the object that had caused his guest such discomfort. Under the very last mattress, the courtiers found a tiny hair. When the king saw the hair and examined the mark on the third brother's back, he was astonished. "How on earth did he feel this hair that was under seven mattresses?" wondered the monarch and actually spent a sleepless night himself, thinking about it.

'In the morning, the king rewarded the brothers with much gold in appreciation of their sensitivity and powers of discernment. The brothers stayed on in King Prasenajit's kingdom, forgetting all about their father, his incomplete sacrifice and the bad karma that would accrue to them for disrupting it.

"When the story was over, the *vetāla* asked King Vikrama, 'Remember the curse and tell me, which was the most fastidious of the three brothers?' 'I think the youngest brother, the one so fussy about the bed that he slept in, was the most fastidious. He is the only one who could not have cheated. The mark of the hair was clearly visible on his body. Besides, the other two could have got their information from someone else.'

"When he heard the right answer, the *vetāla* left the king's shoulder as before and the king, resigned to his fate, went looking for him again.

"King Vikrama braved that terrible night in the cremation ground. The night was dark like a *rākṣasī,* the flames from its funeral pyres like her fiery eyes. He went back to the *aśoka* tree and picked up the *vetāla* again and placed him on his shoulder. As he was walking back like before, the *vetāla* said to the king, 'I am tired of going backwards and forwards even if you are not. Listen and I will ask you a difficult question.

The Delicate Feet

'King Dharma ruled a small district in the south. He was the best among the virtuous but there were many who wanted to overthrow him. His wife was Candravatī, the princess of Mālava. She came from a good family and was extremely virtuous. They had a daughter, Lāvaṇyavatī, who was correctly named because of her beauty. When Lāvaṇyavatī reached marriageable age, the king was overthrown by his relatives who then divided his kingdom among themselves. The king fled for Mālava at night with his wife and daughter, taking many valuable jewels with him.

'The king and his family reached the forests of the Vindhyas and the night, which had accompanied the king all this way, took leave of him with tears that formed dewdrops. The sun rose over the eastern mountains, stretching its rays like a hand that warned the king against entering that forest which was infested with bandits. But the king travelled through the forest with his wife and daughter, their feet pricked by sharp *kuśa* grass, until they came to a Bhīl village. The village was inhabited by men who robbed and killed their neighbours and was avoided by good people as though it were the stronghold of Death.

'When they saw the king approaching from a distance with all his jewels, a number of Śavaras ran towards him with their various weapons raised, to rob him. The king said to his wife and daughter, "Those men will attack you first, so go into the jungle." Terrified, the queen and her daughter ran into the forest. The brave king, armed with his sword and shield, managed to kill several of the Śavaras who attacked him with arrows. However, the chief of the tribe fell upon the king and killed him while the whole village watched. The Śavaras then ran away with the king's jewels. The queen saw her husband being killed from her hiding place and took her daughter and fled into another forest that was far away. In the middle of the day, even shadows place themselves near the cool roots of trees, just like travellers. The queen sat down under an *aśoka* tree near a lotus lake, exhausted and weeping with sorrow.

'Meanwhile, a local chieftain who lived nearby came into the forest with his son to hunt. His name was Caṇḍasiṃha and his son was called Siṃhaparākrama. When they saw the two sets of footprints, the chieftain said, "Let us follow these beautiful and delicate footprints. If we find the ladies to whom they belong, you can take whichever one of them pleases you." His son replied, "I would like to have the one with the small feet. She must be the younger one and will suit me in age. The one with the larger feet must be older and will suit you." Caṇḍasiṃha admonished his son, saying, "What are you suggesting! Your mother has died only recently and after a virtuous woman like that, how can I desire another?" The son persisted, "Father, the home of a householder is empty without a wife. Haven't you heard the verse by Mūladeva? 'Only a fool would enter a house where there is no beautiful woman awaiting his return. It only seems like a house but is, in fact, a prison without chains.' If you do not take the woman that I have chosen for you as a wife, you will be responsible for my death." Caṇḍasiṃha finally agreed and they followed the footprints slowly.

'When they reached the lake, they saw the beautiful queen Candravatī, the pearls around her neck shining, resting under a tree. She was as dark as midnight in the middle of the day, and her lovely daughter Lāvaṇyavatī was like the pure moonlight that illuminated her. The two men approached them eagerly and the queen rose, agitated, thinking that they were thieves. But Lāvaṇyavatī said to her mother, "Don't be alarmed. These men do not seem like thieves. They are good-looking and well-bred so they must be noblemen who have come out hunting." But the queen was not convinced. Caṇḍasiṃha dismounted from his horse and addressed the two women. "Don't be afraid. We have come here out of love for you. You can confide in us. You seem like Rati and Prīti who are hiding in this forest in sorrow at Śiva having burned Kāma with his fiery glance[3]. Why did you come into this forest that has no human habitation? Your bodies suggest that you are used to dwelling in jewelled mansions. It causes us great sorrow that your feet, which should rest in the laps of serving women, have had to tread these thorny paths. The swirling dust that covers your faces dims their lustre and the harsh rays of the sun as they fall on your petal-soft skin, hurts us. Tell us your story. The sight of you suffering in this forest full of wild animals makes us sad."

'The queen sighed and, with sadness and shame, told Caṇḍasiṃha all that had happened to them. When he learned that the two women were unprotected by any man, Caṇḍasiṃha gently persuaded them to become a part of his family. He and his son placed the queen and her daughter on their horses and took them to the city of Viṭṭpāpuri where they lived. The queen helplessly gave in to Caṇḍasiṃha's wishes as though she had been born into a new life. For what else can a woman do who has fallen upon hard times, unprotected and in a strange land? Siṃhaparākrama made Candravatī, the queen, his wife because of her small feet and Caṇḍasiṃha took her daughter Lāvaṇyavatī as his wife since her feet were larger, for they had made this agreement earlier when they saw the footprints and who would go back on his word? So, from the mix-up over the feet, the daughter became the wife of the father and the mother became the wife of the son. Further, the daughter became the mother-in-law of her own mother and the mother the daughter-in-law of her own daughter. In time, they both had sons and daughters by their husbands and those children, too, had sons and daughters. Caṇḍasiṃha and Siṃhaparākrama lived in the city of Viṭṭpāpuri happily with their wives Lāvaṇyavatī and Candravatī.

"When the *vetāla* had finished the story, he asked the king as they walked along the path at night, 'The children who were born to the mother and the daughter through the father and the son, how were they related to each other? If you do not give me the right answer, the curse will befall you.' The king considered the question again and again but he could not come up with the answer. He walked on in silence and the *vetāla*, inhabiting the dead body on the king's shoulder, laughed and thought, 'The king does not know the answer to this question! Still, he is unperturbed and walks ahead with steady steps. I can no longer deceive this virtuous man and the mendicant continues to toy with me. I will play a trick on that wicked fellow and bestow all the success that he has earned on this king who has a glorious future.

"The *vetāla* said aloud, 'King, you seem to be unaffected

by these many journeys to and fro on this terrible night in the cremation ground. You seem quite unruffled and show great determination. I am pleased with your fortitude. I am now leaving this body. Listen to the advice I am going to give you as it is for your own good. Carry this body to the mendicant. He will immediately call me into it and honour me. But he intends to offer you as the victim of the sacrifice. He will tell you to lie on the ground in such a way that all your eight limbs are in contact with the earth. That is when you must tell him to show you how it is done. When he throws himself upon the ground to demonstrate, you must cut off his head with a sword. And you will obtain what he seeks—mastery over the *vidyādharas!* Enjoy the pleasures of the earth by sacrificing him, otherwise he will make you the victim. It was to prevent this that I placed so many obstacles in your way. Go now, may you prosper!' and he left the corpse.

King Vikrama Outwits The Mendicant

"The king realized, from what the *vetāla* had said that the mendicant Kṣāntiśīla was his enemy. But he went happily to where the mendicant sat under the banyan tree, carrying the corpse with him. The cremation ground was made more terrible by the blackness of the dark lunar fortnight. The mendicant sat in a *maṇḍala* drawn from the yellow powder of bones. The ground was streaked with blood and pitchers of blood were placed in the four cardinal directions. It was lit with candles made of human fat and nearby was a fire fed with oblations. The circle had all the material necessary for a sacrifice and the mendicant sat in it, worshipping his personal deity.

"When the mendicant saw that the king had arrived with the corpse, he was delighted. He stood up and praised the king. 'You have accomplished a difficult task for me. And to think that someone like you did this in such a terrible place and at such an inauspicious time! Indeed, it is true that you are the best of kings and that you are courageous. You place the interests of others before your own. Wise men say that the virtue of great men lies in the fact that they accomplish what they set out to do, even at great danger to their own lives.

"The mendicant felt that he had accomplished his desires and took the corpse from the king's shoulder. He bathed and anointed it, placed a garland around it and set it within the *maṇḍala*. He covered his own limbs with ash and put on a sacred thread made of human hair. He dressed in the clothes he had taken from a corpse and sat a while in meditation. He then called the powerful *vetāla* with *mantras* and made him enter the corpse and began to worship him. The mendicant offered him an oblation of fresh human blood in a skull as a vessel, flowers and sweet ointments, the smoke from burning human eyes and gave him human flesh. When he had finished his ritual, he said to the king who stood beside him, 'King, lie on the ground in such a way that all your eight limbs touch the earth. Perform an obeisance to the Master of Spells so that he grants all your desires!' The king remembered the words of the *vetāla* and replied, 'I don't know how to do this. You will have to show me how and I will do exactly as you do.' The mendicant lay on the ground and the king cut off his head with a sword. He wrenched out the mendicant's heart and offered that along with his head to the *vetāla*.

"All the creatures in the cremation ground broke into cries of joy and applauded from all sides. The *vetāla* then spoke to the king from inside the corpse. 'Mastery over the *vidyādharas,* which the mendicant was striving for, will be yours once you have finished enjoying the pleasures of the earth. And since I have tormented you so much, ask for a boon!' The king said, 'If you are pleased with me then all my desires are already fulfilled. But since your words cannot be uttered in vain, I will ask for this boon: may these twenty-four questions and answers along with their delightful stories, as well as this twenty-fifth concluding tale, become famous on earth.' The *vetāla* agreed and spoke further. 'These tales will have a special virtue. They will be known as 'The

Twenty Five Tales of the *Vetāla*' and will confer prosperity. Those who read even a single verse with respect, even those who only hear the tale, will be freed from their curses. *Yakṣas, vetālas, kuṣmāṇḍas* and *rākṣasas* will have no power where these tales are told!' and so saying the *vetāla* disappeared.

"Śiva was very pleased and appeared before King Vikrama with all the gods and after bowing to him said, 'Son, you have killed this deceitful mendicant who was so desperate to gain power over the *vidyādharas*. I created you out of a portion of myself, first as Vikramāditya, so that you could kill the *asuras* who had born as Mlecchas. This time you were created as King Vikrama so that you could defeat this evil man. You shall rule over the earth and all the realms below and then you shall soon be the lord of the *vidyādharas*. When you have grown weary of heavenly pleasures, you will become sad and will reject them on your own. Then you will be united with me. I give you the sword Parājita by which you will accomplish all this.' Śiva gave the king the sword and he disappeared after Vikrama had honoured him with flowers and devout words.

"Vikrama saw that the matter was over and that the night had ended and so he returned to his city, Pāṭaliputra. His subjects had heard all that had happened the night before and they honoured him joyfully. They spent the day celebrating and worshipping Śiva. Soon, Vikrama conquered the earth and the lower regions with the power of that mighty sword, ridding it of its enemies. Then Śiva appointed him king of the *vidyādharas* and after enjoying the pleasures for a long time, Vikrama was reunited with Śiva. Thus, he attained all his desires."

Mṛgāṅkadatta Wins His Bride

'When Mṛgāṅkadatta had been reunited with all his ministers, they sat down under a tree to rest. Tired, hungry and thirsty, the ministers ate the fruit that grew on the tree. This angered Gaṇeśa for without bathing they had eaten from a tree that he lived in and as a result, he cursed them. Mṛgāṅkadatta had to propitiate Gaṇeśa to release them from their curse and in a dream, Gaṇeśa, who was now pleased, told him that he would succeed in marrying Śaśāṅkavatī and that he would eventually rule the entire earth. Mṛgāṅkadatta and his ministers went onwards to Ujjayini and reached there to find that it was a truly well-fortified city. The only course of action open to them was to attack the city with the help of Mṛgāṅkadatta's forest allies. A huge battle ensued between the soldiers of the city and the forest people who had rallied around Mṛgāṅkadatta. Many heroes lost their lives and Mṛgāṅkadatta felt that the only way to end the destruction was to kidnap Śaśāṅkavatī and marry her. He did exactly that and soon she and Mṛgāṅkadatta fell in love with each other. Her father consented to the match and the wedding was celebrated in Ayodhyā in the presence of Mṛgāṅkadatta's family. Soon after that, Mṛgāṅkadatta was anointed king by his father and ruled his kingdom wisely and well.'

Piśaṅgajaṭa finished his story and Naravāhanadatta went to meet Lalitalocanā and took her back to Kauśāmbī. One day, Madanamañcukā disappeared and no one could find her anywhere. Naravāhanadatta was beside himself with grief and could barely function. A vidyādharī *named Vegavatī took the form of Madanamañcukā and tricked Naravāhanadatta into marrying her. Then she revealed herself and told him that Madanamañcukā had been carried away by the* vidyādhara *Manasavega who had been in love with her even before she married Naravāhanadatta. Vegavatī was Manasavega's sister and was prepared to help Naravāhanadatta get Madanamañcukā back.*

Vegavatī carried Naravāhanadatta to the realm of the vidyādharas. *There, she fought a terrible aerial battle with her brother and hid Naravāhanadatta in a cave for his safety. While he was in hiding, Naravāhanadatta married three women, Gandharvadattā, Bhagīrathayaśas and Prabhāvatī. Prabhāvatī took him to where Madanamañcukā had been confined. Naravāhanadatta took on the form of Prabhāvatī with the help of her magic powers and lived with Madanamañcukā. They had a tearful reunion and were overjoyed to be together again. But soon, Naravāhanadatta's disguise was discovered and Śiva himself had to intervene to prevent Manasavega from killing the future emperor of the* vidyādharas.

Śiva took Naravāhanadatta to live on Ṛṣyamūka mountain for some time before he returned to Kauśāmbī. When Naravāhanadatta returned to his earthly city, many vidyādhara *princes came and allied themselves with him and encouraged him to conquer the southern territories from Gaurīmuṇḍa and Manasavega. In order to fight the mighty* vidyādharas *on equal terms, Naravāhanadatta had to propitiate Śiva to get magic powers and suitable weapons. Śiva bestowed the necessary powers on the human prince and Naravāhanadatta went into battle. However, Gaurīmuṇḍa and Manasavega attacked and managed to scatter Naravāhanadatta's army and his ministers. Naravāhanadatta himself was carried to safety and went to live with his* vidyādhara *ally Amitagati in Vakrapura. Soon, his ministers returned and he was crowned emperor. Naravāhanadatta defeated Gaurīmuṇḍa in another battle but the powerful Mandāradeva, lord of the northern regions, remained unconquered.*

Even as the battles were being fought, Naravāhanadatta was marrying several vidyādhara *princesses so that his alliances would be strengthened. For the final battle against Mandāradeva, Naravāhanadatta had to pass through the cave of Triśīrṣa and collect the weapons and powers that resided there. The cave was guarded by Devamaya whom Naravāhanadatttta killed in single combat. Equipped to launch the final assault on the sovereignty of the* vidyādharas, *Naravāhandatta defeated Mandāradeva and became the undisputed ruler of the northern side of Kailāsa. Śiva then bestowed the magic powers and sciences on Naravāhanadatta permanently making him into a* vidyādhara *and encouraged him to give up his earthly home and live on Mount Ṛṣabha. In a spectacular coronation, Naravāhanadatta was made emperor of the* vidyādharas *and lived in splendour with his many wives.*

On earth, in the meantime, Udayana had retired from his kingdom and had sacrificed his body since all his aims had been fulfilled. Naravāhanadatta went to spend the rainy season with his maternal uncle in Kaśyapa's āśrama *to mourn his father's death. While he was there, he told his uncles and his minsters the story of the great king Vikramāditya. The gods pleaded with Śiva to rid the earth of the* asuras *who had been reborn as Mlecchas. So Śiva sent his most excellent* gaṇa, *Mālyavān, to be born as prince Vikramāditya in Ujjayini and defeat the Mlecchas. The young prince grew up heroic and virtuous and set out on a conquest of all the directions. He married many wives, defeated the Mlecchas and eventually ruled the entire earth.*

Padmāvatī

Hail to Śiva who appears in many forms and even though his beloved wife occupies half his body he remains celibate! He is beyond all qualities and is worthy of the world's adoration!

Hail to Gaṇeśa who waves away the bees that rise from his trunk and flaps his ears as if to fan away all obstacles!

Naravāhanadatta had won sovereignty over the vidyādharas *and after his father's death, he spent the rainy season in the* āśrama *of Kaśyapa with his uncle. One day, the* ṛṣis *and their wives asked him to tell them about the loneliness that he experienced when his beloved Madanamañcukā had been abducted by Manasavega. Naravāhanadatta said that he would never have been able to get through that terrible time had it not been for the stories that Gomukha told him. Gomukha told him a number of stories about lovers who had been separated and how they managed to survive. Naravāhanadatta repeated one of Gomukha's stories for the* ṛṣis *and their wives.*

King Brahmadatta And The Golden Swans

'There is a famous city on earth called Vārāṇasī. Like Śiva, it is adorned by the Gaṅgā which flows around it bestowing liberation on its peoples. The wind makes its temples' flags flutter as if they were calling all people, "Come here and attain liberation!" The roofs of its mansions are white like the peaks of Mount Kailāsa and here, too, Śiva's devotees wait to serve him as the *gaṇas* do in heaven. In the old days, the city was ruled by King Brahmadatta. The king was brave, generous and compassionate. He only worshipped Śiva and took good care of Brāhmins. His orders shook the earth, they passed over hills and rocks, they penetrated the seas and reached all the continents. His queen was named Somaprabhā and she was as dear to him as moonlight is to the *cakora* bird. He was happy to gaze at her face all the time. King Brahmadatta had a minister named Śivabhūti who was very learned and was equal to Bṛhaspati, the advisor to the gods.

'One night, when the king was sleeping in the moonlight on the terrace of his palace, he saw two swans flying through the sky. Their bodies gleamed like golden lotuses that bloom at the touch of the waters from the celestial Gaṅgā and they were surrounded by geese. When the swans disappeared from sight, the king was upset that he could no longer enjoy the vision that they created. He slept no more that night and in the morning, he told his minister Śivabhūti what he had seen and said, "My life and my kingdom are of no use to me if I cannot ever see those golden swans again!"

'Śivabhūti replied, "There is a solution to this. Listen and I will tell you. Prajāpati has created many different kinds of beings for this world, depending on the deeds of their previous lives. The essence of the world is sorrow, but many creatures get trapped in the delusion that happiness can be found in pleasures like a home, food and drink. They get attached to these things. Fate has decreed a different kind of home, food and drink for different kinds of beings, depending on the class and caste into which they are born. Construct a huge lake for these swans, covered with lotuses of all kinds, a place where guards will protect them from harm. Scatter the food that birds enjoy on its shores every day and water-birds will definitely begin to arrive from all over. Before long, those two swans will also be among the birds that come here and you will see them again. Do not be depressed about this!"

'King Brahmadatta had a lake made according to Śivabhūti's directions and it was ready in a short while. Soon, swans and cranes and ducks came to the lake and one day, the same pair of golden swans arrived and settled among the lotuses. The men guarding the lake went to report the event to the king and the king rushed to the lake, delighted, for he thought that his goal had been accomplished. He saw the golden swans and admired them from a distance. Then he reassured them by offering them grains of rice dipped in milk. The swans had bodies of pure gold, eyes of pearls, beaks of coral and their wings were tipped with emerald. The king took a great interest in the birds and spent hours at the lake watching the swans who had come there so fearlessly.

'One day, as the king was wandering along the lakeshore, he came across an offering to the gods that consisted of flowers that had not withered. He asked the lake guards who had made the offering and they said, "Three times a day, the two golden swans bathe in the lake, make this offering and then meditate. We do not know what this miracle means!" The king thought to himself, "Swans do not normally behave like this! There must be some reason for their actions. I will perform austerities until I find out who the swans really are." Thereafter, the king, his wife and his minister stopped eating and sat on the lakeshore meditating on Śiva.

'After the king had fasted for twelve days, the two celestial swans appeared to him in a dream and spoke to him in human voices. "Stand up, king! When you and your wife and your minister have broken your fast tomorrow, we will explain everything to you in private!" The swans disappeared and when the king and his wife and his minister woke up the next morning, they immediately broke their fasts. When they had finished eating and were sitting in one of the pavilions near the lake, the swans came up to them. The king welcomed them with respect and said, "Now tell me who you are!" The swans began to tell their story.

How The Ganas Were Cursed

"Mount Mandara is known in the world as the king of all mountains. The gods wander in its jewelled forests and its plateaus are watered with ambrosia from the sea of milk. Wondrous waters, trees, fruits and roots that counteract old age and death can be found there. Śiva roams its highest jewelled peaks and he loves them even more than he does

Kailāsa. One day, Śiva had to perform some activity for the gods and so he took Pārvatī to Mount Mandara and left her there after he had enjoyed himself with her. Grieving at their separation, Pārvatī wandered through those groves, haunting the places that Śiva loved while the other gods tried to console her.

"One day, Pārvatī was deeply disturbed by the coming of spring and sat under a tree surrounded by her *gaṇas*, while her mind fixed on her beloved. She noticed that one of her *gaṇas*, Maṇipuṣpeśvara, was looking lovingly at Candralekhā, Jayā's daughter, who was waving a *chowrie* plume over the goddess' head. He was her equal in youth and beauty and Candralekhā returned his loving looks as he stood by her side. The *gaṇas*, Piṅgeśvara and Guheśvara also noticed these loving glances being exchanged and they smiled to each other. Pārvatī saw them smiling and when she looked around in anger to see what was amusing them, she caught Candralekhā and Maṇipuṣpeśvara gazing at each other.

"Pārvatī, suffering from the separation from her own beloved, was enraged and said, 'Even though the god of love is absent, these two young people have managed to throw each other loving glances and these other two have been laughing at them! Let the lovers who are blinded by their desire become mortals. This indiscreet pair shall be man and wife in their next life. And the two that laughed, they will suffer a great many troubles on earth! First they shall become pathetic Brāhmins, then *brahmarākṣasas*, then *piśācas, caṇḍālas*, thieves, then dogs with their tails cut off, then various kinds of birds! These two were disrespectful when they laughed, even though their minds were pure!' A *gaṇa* named Dhūrjaṭa spoke up and said, 'This is not appropriate! Such excellent *gaṇas* do not deserve such a terrible curse for such a minor offence!' Pārvatī blazed with anger and turned to him, 'You shall fall into a mortal womb for not knowing who you are!"

"After the goddess had pronounced these terrible curses, Jayā the door-keeper, who was Candralekhā's mother, fell at her feet and pleaded, 'Have mercy, goddess! Place an end to the curse on my daughter and on these servants of yours who unknowingly offended you!' Pārvatī softened and said, 'When these people have gradually acquired true knowledge and when they all meet together and go to the place where Brahmā and the other gods performed austerities, then they shall return to us, free from their curse. Candralekhā and her lover and Dhūrjaṭa shall be happy as mortals but these other two shall be miserable!'

"The goddess fell silent and at that very moment, the *asura* Andhaka arrived there, having learned of Śiva's absence. He wanted to woo Pārvatī but he left after he had been ridiculed by her retainers. Śiva found out why the *asura* had come there and chased him and killed him. After that, he returned home. Pārvatī was overjoyed and she told him about Andhaka's visit. Then Śiva said to her, 'Today I have killed Andhaka who was one of my sons conceived by his mother who merely desired me. He shall now remain here as a black bee, for all that is left of him is skin and bones!' Śiva stayed with the goddess while Maṇipuṣpeśvara and the others descended to earth.

The Trials Of Piṅgeśvara And Guheśvara

"Now listen, king, to the strange story of Piṅgeśvara and Guheśvara. On earth, there was a Brāhmin settlement known as Yagñasthala. A rich and virtuous Brāhmin named Yagñasoma lived there. In his middle age, two sons were born to him. The elder was named Harisoma and the younger Devasoma. While they were young boys, they were invested with the sacred thread and then Yagñasoma lost all his wealth. Soon after that, he and his wife both died. The two boys were bereft without their father. They had no money and all their land was taken away from them by their relatives. They said to each other, 'Now we have to live on alms and no one here will give us anything. Let us go to our maternal grandfather's house which is far away from here. We have nothing and no one will welcome us if we come unannounced. But let us go there in any case, for we have no other choice.' Having decided that, they went slowly, begging along the way, to the settlement where their grandfather lived. When they reached there, they learned that their grandfather and his wife had both died.

"Covered with dust and full of despair, the boys went to the house of their maternal uncles, Yagñadeva and Kratudeva. The virtuous Brāhmins welcomed them with kindness and gave them food and clothes. The two boys stayed there, completing their studies. Slowly, their uncles' wealth also decreased and to start with, the servants were dismissed. One day the uncles came to the two boys and with deep affection, they said, 'We have become poor and can no longer afford to keep a man to look after our cattle. Can you do this job for us?' The two young boys were close to tears when they heard this, but they did as their uncles asked. They took the cattle to graze in the forest every morning and when they brought the animals home every evening, they were completely exhausted.

"As they watched over the cattle, they would fall asleep and, as a result, some of the cattle were stolen and others eaten by tigers. That upset the uncles very much. One day, a cow and a goat that had been earmarked for the sacrifice disappeared. The boys were terrified. They took the other animals home before the appointed time and went off in search of the missing animals. Soon, they entered a forest that was far away and they saw their goat, half-eaten by a tiger. They were very downcast and lamenting loudly, they said to each other, 'This is the goat that our uncles had reared for the sacrifice. Now that it has been destroyed they will be very angry. Let us cook and eat a part of what is left of the goat to appease our hunger. We can take the rest of it and go away from here and make our living by begging.'

"As they were roasting the goat over the fire, their uncles, who had been pursuing them, arrived and saw them cooking the goat. The boys saw their uncles from a distance and ran away from there in fear. The uncles were so angry that they cursed the boys. 'Since your desire to eat meat has made you act like *rākṣasas* you shall become flesh-eating *brahmarākṣasas*!' Even as the uncles were speaking, the two boys turned into *brahmarākṣasas*, with flaming hair, fangs coming out of their mouths and an insatiable desire to eat. They wandered through the forest catching and eating animals. One day, they attacked an ascetic to kill and eat him. The ascetic defended himself by using his magic powers and turned the boys into *piśācas*. As *piśācas*, they stole a Brāhmin's cow so that they could kill and eat it, but they were overcome by the Brāhmin's *mantras* and his curse turned them into *caṇḍālas*.

"As *caṇḍālas*, they roamed around with bows in their hands, terribly hungry. Next, they arrived at a village of thieves in their search for food. The village guards thought they were thieves and so they caught them and cut off their ears and noses. They beat them with sticks, bound them and dragged them before the chief of the village. When the chief questioned them, the boys were so frightened and so hungry that they told him their whole story. The chief felt sorry for them and had them freed. He said to them, 'Stay here and eat something. Do not be afraid! You have come here on the eighth day, the day on which we worship Kārtikeya, so you are our guests and must share in our feast!' The thieves then worshipped the goddess and made the two boys eat in her presence. The thieves liked the boys so much that they made them stay. The boys remained with the thieves, robbing and stealing with them and eventually, because of their heroism, they became leaders.

"One night, the two new leaders went with their band of thieves to rob a city that their spies had earmarked. The city was a favourite of Śiva's. Even though they saw a bad omen along the way, they went forward and ransacked the entire city, including the temple. The townspeople cried out to the deity for protection and in anger, Śiva befuddled the thieves and made them blind. The townspeople saw this as a sign of Śiva's favour and they fell upon the thieves with sticks and stones. Invisible *gaṇas* ran about among the thieves, throwing some of them off cliffs and smashing others against the ground. The townspeople identified the two leaders and wanted to kill them but at that very moment, the leaders turned into dogs with their tails cut off.

"All of a sudden, the dogs remembered their past lives and danced in front of Śiva, seeking his protection. When the common people and the Brāhmins and the merchants saw this, they were amazed. No longer fearing thieves, they were very happy and went laughing to their homes. The two dogs were released from their delusion when they woke to reality. They fasted and performed austerities that would please Śiva so that their curse would come to an end. The next morning, when the townspeople came to the temple to celebrate, they saw the two dogs sitting there, deep in meditation. They turned their faces away when they were offered food. The dogs stayed like that for many days and were noticed by every one. Then the *gaṇas* appealed to Śiva, 'These two are Piṅgeśvara and Guheśvara who were cursed by the goddess. These *gaṇas* have suffered for a long time, have mercy on them!'

"Śiva said in reply to their pleas, 'Let these *gaṇas* give up their being as dogs and become crows!" The dogs became crows and ate from the rice offering. They lived happily, remembering their previous births, with their minds fixed on Śiva. In time, Śiva was pleased with their devotion and he commanded them to first become vultures and then peacocks. In the course of time, those two excellent *gaṇas* became swans and they continued to propitiate Śiva. They pleased him by bathing in the sacred places and by fasting and meditating until they became composed entirely of gold and jewels and gained true knowledge.

The Curses End

"We are Piṅgeśvara and Guheśvara who were cursed by Pārvatī and endured many troubles until we became swans. The *gaṇa* Maṇipuṣpeśvara who was in love with Jayā's daughter and who was cursed by the goddess has been born a king on earth. That king is you, Brahmadattā! Jayā's daughter has been born as your wife Somaprabhā and Dhūrjaṭa has been born as your minister Śivabhūti. When we gained true knowledge and remembered the end of our curse as pronounced by Pārvatī, we came here that night so that you could see us. That plan has united us all and we shall bestow true knowledge on you! Let us go together to Mount Tridesa, sacred to Śiva, where the gods practised austerities so that they could kill the *asura* Vidyuddhvaja!"

Viṣamaśīla

Glory to Śiva, half of whose body is occupied by the moon-faced Pārvatī, whose body is smeared with ash as white as moonbeams, whose eyes shine like the sun and the moon and who wears a crescent moon on his head!

May Gaṇeśa protect you, who, with his bent trunk raised in the air, seems to be showering success!

While Naravāhanadatta stayed at the āśrama *of Kaśyapa, he heard many stories, the longest of which was the story of King Vikramāditya. That story contained many other tales within it and Naravāhanadatta listened to those as well. One day, the gambler Dāgineya came to the court of Vikramāditya and told the king the story of another gambler named Ṭhiṇṭhākarāla.*

The Gambler And The Gods

'There lived in the city of Ujjayini a terrible gambler called Ṭhiṇṭhākarāla, rightly named because he really was the terror of the gambling dens. He lost consistently and every day, the other gamblers gave him one hundred *cowrie* shells. He would go to the market and exchange them for flour. Then he would find a pot of water from somewhere, knead the flour into flat cakes and roast them over the fires in the cremation ground. He would eat them in front of Śiva, smearing the cakes with oil that he would take from the lamps that burned before the god. Every night he slept in the temple courtyard, using his arm as a pillow for his head. One night, he saw the idols of the Mothers[1] and the *yakṣas* inside the temple moving under the power of *mantras*. He wondered, "Why don't I make a plan by which I can acquire great wealth from this place? It would be wonderful if the plan worked and if it didn't, I will have lost nothing!"

'He then challenged the gods to gamble with him. "Come and I will play with you. But I shall roll the dice and you will have to pay me what you lose!" The gods were silent so Ṭhiṇṭhākarāla rolled the dice and staked some of his *cowrie* shells. For it is understood everywhere dice is played that if a player does not object to the dice being rolled, he has agreed to play the game. When he had won a lot of gold, Ṭhiṇṭhākarāla said to the gods, "I have won! Pay me what you have lost as you had agreed!" Though he said this many times, the gods still remained silent. The gambler grew angry and said, "If you stand there silently then I will do to you what is done to gamblers who do not pay and stand as if they were made of stone. I will cut off your limbs with a saw that has teeth as sharp as Yama's, for I do not care for anything!" He went up to the deities with a saw in his hand and at once, they gave him the gold. The next day, he lost all the gold that he had won in his gambling games. He forced the Mothers to play with him again and extracted money from them in the same way.

'Ṭhiṇṭhākarāla would do this every day until one day, the Mothers got very depressed about the situation. Cāmuṇḍī told them that among gamblers everywhere, the rule was that anyone who stated "I am out of the game" cannot be forced to play. Therefore, the goddess advised the Mothers to say, "I am out of the game!" when the gambler to play with him. The Mothers took this advice seriously and when night came and the gambler asked them to play with him, the goddesses replied together, "I am out of this game!" When the Mothers had refused him, the gambler invited Śiva, their master, to play. But the god, seeing that the gambler had seized the opportunity to play dice with him, said, "I am not in this game!" Even the gods have a fear of people who are immoral, irresolute and ruled by their senses.

'Ṭhiṇṭhākarāla was thoroughly peeved at being outsmarted by a gambler's rule and he thought to himself, "These gods have learned the rules of gambling and they have foiled my plan. I have no recourse now except to take refuge in their master!" Ṭhiṇṭhākarāla threw himself at the feet of Śiva and praised him, saying, "I bow to you who sit naked with your head on your knee since the goddess won your elephant skin in a gambling game[2]. When the gods give up everything at your whim and when you have no desires, your only possessions being your matted hair, your ashes and the skull that you carry, why is it that you are so greedy in my case when I ask for so little! The *kalpavṛkṣa* is no longer of any help to the needy and you no longer support me though you hold up the world! I am so disturbed that I have come to you for refuge. Please forgive my audaciousness, but you have three eyes and my dice has three eyes also, you have ashes on your body and so have I, you eat out of a skull and so do I. Be kind to me! Now that I have spoken to all of you, how can I talk to mere gamblers again? Help me get out of this terrible situation!"

'The gambler flattered Śiva with words like these and the god was pleased. He appeared before him and said, "Ṭhiṇṭhākarāla, I am pleased! Control your anxiety! Stay with me and I will give you all that you need to enjoy yourself!" The gambler obeyed the god's orders and stayed there enjoying all the pleasures that Śiva's grace bestowed upon him. One night, Śiva noticed that some *apsarases* had come to the temple tank to bathe and he told Ṭhiṇṭhākarāla that while the *apsarases* were bathing he should steal their clothes which they had left on the banks. "Do not return their garments until they give you the beautiful *apsaras* named Kalāvatī," said Śiva. The gambler did as he was told and the *apsarases* begged him, "Please give us back our clothes! You cannot leave us naked!" But the gambler was filled with Śiva's power and he replied, "I will return your clothes if you give me the young girl named Kalāvatī!"

'When they heard that, the *apsarases* realized that this was a stubborn man and when they remembered that Indra had cursed Kalāvatī to that effect, they consented. When he returned their clothes, they gave him Kalāvatī who was the daughter of Alambuṣā. They left that place and Ṭhiṇṭhākarāla stayed with Kalāvatī in a house that Śiva created with his powers. Kalāvatī would attend to Indra during the day but at night, she always returned to her husband. One day, she said to him with great affection, "Indra's curse that gave you to me as a husband has really turned out to be a blessing!" The gambler asked her why she had been cursed and she said, "One day, I saw the gods enjoying themselves in the garden and I praised the pleasures of mortals and criticized those of the gods as being superficial. Indra heard that and said, 'Be born a mortal, marry a man and enjoy those human pleasures!' It was because of this that we were united and this relationship has turned out to be very pleasant. Tomorrow I will return late from heaven for Rambhā has a new performance for Viṣṇu. I have to stay there until her performance is over. Do not be sad about my absence."

The Gambler Goes To Heaven

'Ṭhiṇṭhākarāla had become stubborn and demanding because of Kalāvatī's love and he said, "I want to see Rambhā's new dance! Take me there in secret." "How can I do this? It is not appropriate! If Indra finds out, he will be very angry," cried Kalāvatī. But the gambler insisted and finally, Kalāvatī agreed to take him with her, for she loved him dearly. The next morning, Kalāvatī used her powers to hide Ṭhiṇṭhākarāla in a lotus which she placed above her ear and in that fashion, she took him to Indra's palace. When Ṭhiṇṭhākarāla saw the beautiful Nandana which had a gateway adorned with Airāvata, he was thrilled and thought that he, too, had become a celestial. There, in Indra's heaven where the gods gather, Ṭhiṇṭhākarāla watched Rambhā's wonderful dance which was accompanied by the singing of the other *apsarases*. He also listened to the musical instruments played by Nārada and the other musicians, for nothing is impossible for those who have Śiva's favour.

'At the end of the dance, a court jester stood up and began to dance in the form of a goat. Ṭhiṇṭhākarāla recognized the goat and thought to himself, "I have seen this goat in Ujjayini where he is a senseless beast. Now here he is in Indra's court as a dancing jester! This must be some heavenly illusion!" The goat-dance ended and Indra went home. Kalāvatī put Ṭhiṇṭhākarāla back in the lotus above her ear and took him to his house. The next day, Ṭhiṇṭhākarāla went to Ujjayini where he saw the goat-jester who had come back there. He said to him arrogantly, "Hey! Come and dance for me as you did for Indra! Jester, show me your dancing talents or I shall be very angry!" The jester was stunned into silence and thought to himself, "Where could this mortal have learned so much about me?" When the goat refused to dance even after many requests, Ṭhiṇṭhākarāla hit him on the head with a stick. With his head bleeding, the goat went to Indra and told him what had happened. Through his prescience, Indra understood how this had come about, how Kalāvatī had brought the gambler to Rambhā's performance and how that deceitful fellow had seen the goat dance.

'Indra called for Kalāvatī and cursed her. "You brought your human husband here secretly out of love and this man has forced my goat to dance. For that, you shall enter an image on a pillar in the temple that King Narasiṃha has built in the city of Nāgapura!" Kalāvatī's mother Alambuṣā pleaded with Indra and at last, Indra pronounced an end to the curse. "Your curse will end when this temple, which has taken a long time to build, is destroyed and razed to the ground." Weeping, Kalāvatī came and told Ṭhiṇṭhākarāla about the curse, when it would end and how it was all his fault. Then she gave him all her ornaments and disappeared to enter the image on the front pillar in the temple at Nāgapura.

The False Ascetic

'Ṭhiṇṭhākarāla was consumed by the poison of being separated from Kalāvatī. He could neither see nor hear, and he rolled on the ground in a faint. When he returned to his senses, he thought, "Even though I knew better, I revealed the secret through my foolishness! How can people like me, who are fickle by nature, ever show self-control? Now I have to endure this terrible separation!" A moment later he stopped wailing and thought, "Why should I be so weak? I shall be resolute and think of a way to end her curse." The clever fellow put on the disguise of a mendicant, complete with deer-skin, beads and matted hair, and went to Nāgapura. In a forest outside the city, he buried four pots containing his wife's jewellery. He buried them in the four directions and within the city under the cover of night in the market in front of Śiva's temple, he buried a pot filled with gold, diamonds, sapphires, rubies and emeralds. Then the gambler built a hut on the banks of the river and pretended to be an ascetic, muttering prayers and meditating. He would bathe three times a day and eat only the food he got as alms after he had purified it. Soon, he became known as a holy man.

'Eventually, the king heard about him and invited him to the palace. The gambler refused to go there and so the king came to visit him and talked to him for a long time. When the king was ready to leave in the evening, the call of a jackal was heard in the distance. The gambler disguised as an ascetic laughed when he heard that and the king wanted to know what was going on. "It is nothing," said the gambler but the king insisted on an answer. "In the eastern forest outside the city, there is a pot of jewels buried in the earth. Go and take it. The jackal told me this since I can understand the language of animals," explained the gambler. Full of curiosity, the king went with the ascetic to the forest. The ascetic dug up the ground, pulled out the pot of jewels and gave it to the king. The king took the jewels and because he felt that the ascetic was truly a great and honest man, he began to respect him. He took him back to his hut and fell at his feet again and again. The king returned to the palace that night with his ministers, singing the ascetic's praises.

'In this way, the gambler would pretend to understand what animals said and gradually he gave the king all the pots that he had buried with his wife's jewels. As a result, the king, his wives, his ministers and all the townspeople became devotees of the ascetic and honoured him. One day, the king took the wicked ascetic to the temple and in the marketplace, the ascetic heard a crow cawing. At once, he said to the king, "Did you hear what the crow said? Right here in the marketplace, in front of the temple, another pot of jewels is buried. Why don't you dig it up? This is what the crow said, so come and take the jewels." He led the king to a spot and they dug up the earth and the ascetic gave the jewels to the king.

'The king was very happy and took the deceitful ascetic by the hand and entered the temple. Once inside, the gambler brushed against the image on the pillar which Kalāvatī had entered. Kalāvatī began to weep when she saw her husband, overcome with sorrow at the sight of him. The king and his retinue saw this happening and they were amazed. Gravely, they asked the ascetic, "What does this mean?" The clever fellow pretended to be full of grief and said quietly, "Let us go to your palace. I will tell you there for this is an unspeakable thing." When they reached the palace, the ascetic said, "This temple is built in an inauspicious place and it was started at an inauspicious time. As a result, something terrible will happen to you in three days. That is why the image wept when she saw you. So if you care for your physical welfare, smash this temple to the ground today. You can build another temple in an auspicious place at an auspicious time. Control this misfortune and establish your welfare and that of your kingdom."

'The king was terrified and immediately ordered his subjects to tear down the temple in a single day and started building another temple in another place. Thus, clever rascals can gain the confidence of princes and make them submit to their will! Now that Ṭhiṇṭhākarāla had accomplished his aim, he threw off his disguise and quickly went to Ujjayini. Kalāvatī learned of this and now that she was free of her curse, she met him on the road. She was delighted to see him and after reassuring him that she would return, she went to see Indra. Indra was surprised to see her but when he heard how her husband had rescued her, he laughed and was very pleased.'

Naravāhanadatta declared that the hermit's tales of love and separation had helped him get through the time without Madanamañcukā. Naravāhanadatta delighted the company in Kaśyapa's āśrama *by recounting the story of his life. When the rainy season was over, he returned to Mount Ṛṣabha with his wives, his ministers and his retinue. He remained the emperor of the* vidyādharas *for as long as he lived and his reign lasted an entire* kalpa.

This is the *Bṛhatkathā* that was first told on Mount Kailāsa by the tireless Śiva when Pārvatī asked him for a tale. It was spread throughout the world by Puṣpadanta and his companions who came to earth as Kātyāyana and others because of their curses. At the time, Śiva added this blessing to the story. 'Whoever reads the story that I have told and whoever listens to it carefully and whoever owns it shall be freed from the consequences of misconduct and shall become a wondrous *vidyādhara* and live in my eternal world.'

Glossary

Agni:god of fire; often depicted as a Brāhmin.

āmalaka:the fruit of *emblic myrobalan; āvla* or *āmla* in Hindi.

apsaras:celestial women of Indra's court; known for their beauty and their propensity to enter into relationships with humans.

Aṣāḍha:the month of June-July according to the Hindu almanac.

āśrama:hermitage in the forest where ascetics, sages and holy men live; those involved in worldly pursuits often retire to one of these retreats later in life.

asura:enemy of the gods.

bodhisattva:individual on his/her way to becoming a Buddha; usually characterized by postponing his/her personal enlightenment for the good of others.

Brahmā:part of the triumvirate of Hindu gods; functions as the Creator and the progenitor of all beings.

brahmarākṣasa:ghost of a Brāhmin who was guilty of misconduct in his lifetime; flesh-eating.

Brāhmin:priestly class at the top of the four-fold division of Hindu society.

Bṛhaspati:advisor to the gods.

Cāmuṇḍī:another name for Durgā.

caṇḍāla:lowest and most despised of all mixed castes, born of a Śūdra father and a Brāhmin mother.

dīnār:unit of currency, usually a gold coin.

Durgā:virgin goddess created from the combined energy of the male gods to overcome the demon Mahīṣa.

gaṇa:inferior deities in the service of Śiva; sometimes depicted as ugly, deformed or frightening.

Gaṇeśa:elephant-headed son of Śiva and Pārvatī; benevolent

deity worshipped as the remover of obstacles.

gandharva:male attendant at the celestial court of Indra; extremely good-looking and known for their skills in music and dancing.

gandharva:form of marriage in which only the spirits of the air are witness; usually due to an intense sexual attraction between the partners.

Garuḍa:bird who is Viṣṇu's vehicle.

ghee:clarified butter used in cooking as well as ritually in sacrifices and worship.

guhyaka:inferior magical being; Kubera's attendants and the guardians of his treasure.

Indra:divine king of heaven.

Kāma:god of love; often described as bodiless because he was burnt to ashes by Śiva's fiery glance.

Kālī:destructive manifestation of the goddess.

kalpa:a day and night in the life of the god Brahmā, four thousand three hundred and twenty million years.

kalpavṛkṣa:wishing tree of heaven.

Kārtikeya:son of Śiva and Pārvatī; patron of learning.

kheer:rice pudding.

kinnara:semi-divine being with the form of a man and the head of a horse.

Kubera:god of wealth.

Kṣatriya:martial and ruling class, second only to Brāhmins in the four-fold division of Hindu society.

kuṣmānda:evil beings that spread disease.

Lakṣmī:goddess of prosperity; wife of Viṣṇu.

lokapālas:guardians of the cardinal directions.

mantra:spell or incantation.

Mātali:Indra's charioteer.

mokṣa:final liberation in union with the Absolute; ultimate goal of Hindu life.

muni:holy and learned sage; has attained a divine nature through penance and the performance of austerities.

nāga:semi-divine being with a human face and the hood and tail of a cobra; dwellers in the under-world.

Nandana:Indra's paradise.

Niṣāda:tribe of the Vindhya mountains.

Pārvatī:wife of Śiva.

pāśupata:ascetic followers of Śiva in one of his more destructive manifestations.

piśāca:vilest of all malevolent beings; lower on the scale than *rākṣasas*.

Prajāpati:progenitor; one of the creators.

prajñapti:wisdom, prescience, knowledge; sometimes personified.

pratiśākhya:vedic verses.

Rāma:human incarnation of Viṣṇu whose mission it was to defeat the *rākṣasa* Rāvaṇa; hero of the *Rāmāyaṇa*.

rākśasa:malevolent magical being; live in cremation grounds, eat human flesh and harass humans.

Rāvaṇa:*rākṣasa* king of Laṅkā; enemy of Rāma.

ṛṣi:divinely inspired poet or sage; Vedas were revealed to the seven ṛṣis.

Sarasvatī:goddess of learning.

śāstras:various treatises on knowledge; law books; books of recognized or divine authority.

siddha:semi-divine being who is a 'perfected' individual; pure and virtuous; lives in the sky.

Sītā:wife of Rāma; abducted by Rāvaṇa.

Śiva:part of the triumvirate of Hindu gods; responsible for the destruction of the world; husband of Pārvatī.

Śrī:another name for Lakṣmī.

Śūdra:servitor class at the bottom of the four-fold division of Hindu society.

Vaiśya:cultivator and merchant class; third in the four-fold division of Hindu society.

vālakhilyas:thumb-sized sages who are very pious.

vāsu:Indra's attendant deities.

Vedas:holy books that are the foundation of Hinduism; divine knowledge that was 'revealed' to ancient seers.

vetāla:spirit that haunts cremation grounds and animates dead bodies.

vidyādhara:'holders of knowledge'; sky-dweller with magical powers like flying, changing shape and form; known for their interaction with humans.

Viṣṇu:part of the triumvirate of Hindu gods; responsible for the preservation of the world; husband of Lakṣmī.

Viśvakarmā:celestial architect.

Yama:god of death.

yoginī:witch or sorceress; attendant upon Durgā.

yojana:unit of distance.

Notes

Introduction

1 This quote appears on the backcover of the current Sanskrit edition of the *Kathāsaritsāgara*, Delhi: Motilal Banarasidass, 1970, as a blurb for the C.H. Tawney's English translation that was published in England in 1924.

2 The four *puruśārthas* are the four "goals" of Hindu life, i.e., *artha* (wealth), *kāma* (desire), *dharma* (righteous duty) and *mokṣa* (liberation from the cycle of birth and death).

3 Guṇāḍhya learns the *Paiśācī* language from the *piśācas*, a group of beings not unlike *rākṣasas*. Since *piśācas* are decidedly ungodly, *Paiśācī* was considered a crude and unsophisticated language, unworthy of preserving anything.

4 As mythical beings, *piśācas* are most often described as evil spirits that the Vedas place lower than *rakṣāsas*. However, E. Washburn Hopkins, in *Epic Mythology*, Strassbourg: Karl J. Trubner, 1915, p.46 cites Grierson who suggests that the *piśācas* inhabited the northwestern (sic) region of the subcontinent and 'were a tribe of omophagoi closely connected with the Khasas, Nagas and Yaksas.'

5 J.A.B. van Buitenen, "Story Literatures", in *The Literatures of India*, edited by Dimock et. al., Chicago: University of Chicago Press, 1974.

6 Romila Thapar, *A History of India*, Vol.1, Harmondsworth: Penguin Books, 1964.

7 F. W. Thomas, "Foreword", *The Ocean of Story*, Vol. 4, translated by N. M. Penzer, Delhi: Motilal Banarasidass, 1968 [reprinted].

8 F. W. Thomas, "Foreword", *The Ocean of Story*, Vol. 4.

9 Cited by N. M. Penzer, "Introduction," *The Ocean of Story*, Vol. 1.
10 *ibid.*
11 J.A.B. van Buitenen, *Tales of Ancient India*, Chicago: University of Chicago Press, 1959.
12 N.M. Penzer, "Terminal Essay", *The Ocean of Story*, Vol. 9.
13 F.W. Thomas, "Foreword", *The Ocean of Story*, Vol. 4.
14 van Buitenen, "Introduction", *Tales of Ancient India.*
15 F. W. Thomas, "Foreword", *The Ocean of Story*, Vol. 4.
16 R. C. Temple, "Introduction", *The Ocean of Story*, Vol. 1.
17 van Buitenen, "Introduction", *Tales of Ancient India.*
18 N. M. Penzer, "Terminal Essay", *The Ocean of Story*, Vol. 9.
19 van Buitenen, "Introduction", *Tales of Ancient India.*
20 N. M. Penzer, "Terminal Essay", *The Ocean of Story*, Vol. 9.
21 Romila Thapar, *A History of India*, Vol.1.
22 F. W. Thomas, "Foreword", *The Ocean of Story*, Vol. 4.
23 A. B. Keith, *A History of Sanskrit Literature*, Oxford: OUP, 1920.
24 From "Partial Magic in the *Quixote*", p. 230 in *Labyrinths* by Jorge Luis Borges, eds. Donald A. Yates & James E. Irby, Harmondsworth: Penguin Books, 1970. Significantly, no English edition of *The Arabian Nights* bears out Borges' account of the six hundred and second night. Like other literary chimera in Borges' work, this 'curious danger' may exist only in his universe of speculative idealism! Chimerical or otherwise, Borges has put his finger on *the* crucial aspect of the frame, its ultimate reflexivity.
25 Naravāhanadatta's adventures resemble those of Arjuna's in the *Mahābhārata* in that they are basically a preparation for a final war. Both Arjuna and Naravāhanadatta collect allies through a series of marriage alliances and collect magical weapons to strengthen their position as they move towards their rightful destiny. But Naravāhanadatta is nowhere near as charismatic a character as Arjuna and our interest in him remains limited.

26 See 'Translator's Note' for the treatment of non-human beings in this book.

27 John Dowson, *A Classical Dictionary of Hindu Mythology and Religion*, Calcutta: Rupa & Co., 1982 [reprinted].

28 E. Washburn Hopkins, *Epic Mythology*, Strassbourg: Karl J. Trubner, 1915.

29 *ibid*.

Kathāpīṭha

1 Mandara was the mountain used by the gods and demons as the churning pole when the ocean was churned. Even the spray from the churning could not turn Mandara white.

2 When Śiva fought the demon Andhaka, he pierced the demon's breast with a spear. Another spear used in the same battle had pierced the earth. Śiva pulled out the second spear but left the first one buried in the demon's breast.

3 Tāraka the demon was so powerful that the gods decided that only a son born of Śiva could destroy him. Śiva was away meditating and performing severe penances in the Himalayas. The god of love, Kāma, was sent there to pierce Śiva with one of his arrows so that Śiva could be distracted from his austerities by the pangs of love and then be inclined to produce a son.

4 The Sanskrit word used here is *sāma* which means 'to persuade' as well as being the name of a Veda. Therefore, while the libertine was suggesting that the Brāhmin persuade the courtesan to teach him, the unworldly Brāhmin took the sentence to mean that he should chant the Veda for her.

5 The libertines are suggesting that the Brāhmin be caught by the scruff of his neck and thrown out, a hold that is known as the 'half moon'. But the 'half moon' is also the name of a particular arrowhead that decapitates the enemy. The poor Brāhmin obviously got the two half-moons confused.

6 The queen said, *'modakair paritāḍaya'* which in Sanskrit means 'do not splash me with water'. The word *modakair* breaks into *'ma'* and *'udakair'*, i.e., 'do not' and 'with water'. The king, who was unfamiliar with the Sanskrit rules of vowel combination, thought the queen had said *'modakair'* i.e., 'with sweets' and therefore assumed that his queen had asked him to throw sweets at her.

Kathāmukha

1 Garuḍa was the son of Vinata and Kaśyapa. His father had another wife called Kadru who was the mother of snakes. One day, Vinata and Kadru had a bet about the colour of a horse's tail and they decided that the loser would become the winner's slave for life. Kadru cheated and won while Vinata lost and became the former's slave. She was so incensed that she passed on her hatred to her son, Garuda who became a sworn enemy of all snakes thereafter.

Lāvāṇaka

1 *Majjao* in Prākrit means 'cat' as well as 'my lover'.

Madanamañcukā

1 Triśaṅku was a pious king who wished to go to heaven after his death. Sage Viśvāmitra promised to help him in his endeavour even though it was prohibited by the gods.

Alaṅkāravatī

1 Niśumbha was one of the two demon brothers who were eventually killed by the goddess Durgā. They had attained great powers by performing penances and austerities in the mountains. In fact, the mountains trembled and bowed with the sheer might of the brothers' ascetic practices.

2 Viṣṇu is the only god of the Hindu pantheon who is supposed to come down to earth in various forms to free the world of mortals from the evil doers. Rāma was, amongst nine others, an incarnation of Viṣṇu and is often referred to as 'incarnating a part of Viṣṇu'. In this case, Rāma's brothers too incarnate other parts of Viṣṇu. However, it is rarely ever made clear which part of Viṣṇu is incarnated in whom and why.

3 There was a time when all mountains had wings and could fly around wherever and whenever they so desired. But after a while they became a menace to gods and humans alike as a result of which Indra cut off their wings with his thunderbolt. They then fell to the ground and have been stationary ever since.

Śaktiyaśas

1 The demon Maya build a city that was impregnable to the gods. But as the demons grew more powerful and threatened the world, Śiva was called in to destroy the city. However, the demons' city was protected by a boon from Brahma, so Śiva could only use a single flaming arrow to penetrate the city. As he prepared to shoot the arrow, his third eye blazed forth.

2 Soma is the juice offered to the gods during a sacrifice and is also drunk by the officiating priests. It is often associated with the moon which is thought to be the heavenly receptacle of the juice.

Śaśāṅkavatī

1 An ear-ring called, in Sanskrit, *dantapattva* or 'tooth leaf'.

2 *Karna* in Sanskrit means ear and *utpala* means lotus. Thus the young woman, by putting the lotus in her ear, indicated that she lived in the kingdom of King Lotusears or Karnotpala.

3 Rati and Prīti were the two wives of Kāma, the god of

love. At one time, Kāma was sent to disrupt Śiva's meditation so that the latter could produce a son to fight the demon Taraka. Śiva was so enraged with Kāma that he turned his third eye towards him and burnt him to ashes. Ever since then, Kama became bodiless and that was the reason for his wives' sorrow.

Viṣamaśīla

1 The Mothers were probably originally the female energies of the male gods and were eight in number. In time, they became minor female deities, who worshipped Śiva, most often associated with Tantra.

2 The elephant skin originally belonged to a demon called Gaya who tormented the gods and sages. Ultimately, Śiva killed the demon and took the skin which he then threw over his shoulders. Śiva and Pārvatī often gambled with dice to amuse themselves. In one such game, Pārvatī was able to win the elephant skin from Śiva, leaving his shoulders bare.

READ MORE IN PENGUIN

In every corner of the world, on every subject under the sun, Penguin represents quality and variety – the very best in publishing today.

For complete information about books available from Penguin – including Puffins, Penguin Classics and Arkana – and how to order them, write to us at the appropriate address below. Please note that for copyright reasons the selection of books varies from country to country.

In India: Please write to *Penguin Books India Pvt Ltd, 706 Eros Apartments, 56 Nehru Place, New Delhi, 110019*

In the United Kingdom: Please write to *Dept. JC, Penguin Books Ltd, FREEPOST, West Drayton, Middlesex, UB7 OBR.*

If you have any difficulty in obtaining a title, please send your order with the correct money, plus ten per cent for postage and packaging, to *PO Box No. 11, West Drayton, Middlesex UB7 OBR*

In the United States: Please write to *Penguin USA Inc., 375 Hudson Street, New York, NY 10014*

In Canada: Please write to *Penguin Books Canada Ltd, 10 Alcorn Avenue, Suite 300, Toronto, Ontario M4V 3B2*

In Australia: Please write to *Penguin Books Australia Ltd, 487 Maroondah Highway, Ringwood, Victoria 3134*

In New Zealand: Please write to *Penguin Books (NZ) Ltd, 182–190 Wairau Road, Private Bag, Takapuna, Auckland 9*

In the Netherlands: Please write to *Penguin Books Netherlands B.V., Keizersgracht 231 NL–1016 DV Amsterdam*

In Germany : Please write to *Penguin Books Deutschland GmbH, Friedrichstrasse 10–12, W–6000 Frankfurt/Main 1*

In Spain: Please write to *Penguin Books S. A.,C. San Bernardo, 117–6° E–28015 Madrid*

In Italy: Please write to *Penguin Italia s.r.l., Via Felice Casati 20, I–20124 Milano*

In France: Please write to *Penguin France S. A., 17 rue Lejeune, F–31000 Toulouse*

In Japan: Please write to *Penguin Books Japan, Ishikiribashi Building, 2-5-4, Suido, Tokyo 112*

In Greece: Please write to *Penguin Hellas Ltd, Dimocritou 3, GR–106 71 Athens*

In South Africa: Please write to *Longman Penguin Southern Africa (Pty) Ltd, Private Bag X08, Bertsham 2013*